Dear

Thanks for the reminder!

I hope you enjoy the book & I expect we will bump into each other again here or there.

Cheers
Norm
12/6/19.

SEARCHING
for **SATU**

ALAN BRUNSTROM

Love and Death in the Land
of the Midnight Sun

The Harwell Press
Harwell, Oxfordshire, UK

Searching for Satu

ISBN: 978-0-9933873-0-2

Published by The Harwell Press
Harwell, Oxfordshire, UK

First published by Citron Press 1999
This revised edition published by Harwell 2018

Copyright © Alan Brunstrom, 2015
All rights reserved

This book is a work of fiction. Names, characters and incidents are either products of the author's imagination or are used fictitiously. Any resemblance to actual persons is entirely coincidental.

Cover design by Jessica Bell
Interior design by Amie McCracken

CHAPTER 1
November, 1958

For her the cold had colours. First there was the grey cold, then the white cold and finally the blue cold. The blue of bodies, trawled from the freezing lake.

Now it was just the white cold but the wind mocked her stolen rags and she hugged the little boy close, sheltering him from the raw edge of it as best she could.

God, would he never come? Her ears had gone numb and her feet were like ice: but inside of her there was a rage that burned out the last vestiges of drug-induced submission. They had taken her daughter but they would never get the boy! There would be no meek surrender this time, no matter how many they sent.

Ricky whimpered in her arms and with a shock of guilt Satu realised she was gripping him too tightly. She smiled, ruffling his hair beneath the oversized woollen cap and grinning a reassurance that she didn't feel. Then a sound and a flicker of headlights, only half glimpsed through the blizzard, made her draw back into the blackness of the shed.

Please God, don't let it be the police. Not so soon.

The vehicle growled slowly down the street, bumping in low gear over the deep, frozen ruts. She nearly panicked as it got closer but then the wipers cleared the windscreen just enough for her to recognise the muffled figure of the driver. It was Marko. The one man she could still trust. The only man in this God-forsaken country who had stood by her through everything.

He pulled up right outside the entrance to the communal privy. She hadn't been able to risk seeking refuge in any of the houses, even in this ramshackle outlaw settlement: but now that wonderful smile of Marko's was bursting through the cold, the snow and the utter hopelessness of her case. With a surge of gratitude she ran up and hugged him, like a long lost brother. They were going to make it. They'd be out of the country before that Swedish bitch could do anything to stop them.

As soon as they were clear of the city she sank back against the worn leather seat - and finally it overcame her. For the first time since they took her baby from her, she started to cry.

She had lost so much. Her hopes. Her Lover. Her daughter. She pulled the little boy close and held him as if he was the last thing she had left in the world, as he almost was. And then she drew a veil across it. A veil she would lift only once, on the last day of her life.

CHAPTER 2
Friday, 15th May, 1981

As they burst out of the clouds, Ricky laughed for the first time in six months. The sky was so impossibly blue and the cumulus so absurdly like cotton wool that he couldn't help himself, although the woman beside him clearly thought he should have tried. For the next hour he did nothing but stare out the window, entranced by the wakes of the ships far below as they cut across the blue-grey waters of the North Sea. They had passed Sweden and were heading out over the Baltic before an announcement from the captain interrupted his reverie.

'... the temperature in Helsinki is 25 degrees Celsius, that's 77 degrees Fahrenheit. Welcome to the frozen north.'

It seemed so unlikely that he commented on it to his neighbour, whose chilly response sent him back to his porthole just in time to see a great archipelago begin to fill the horizon.

From twenty thousand feet, Ricky's first impression of his homeland was that a heavenly jeweller had strewn diamonds over a cloth of blue velvet. Across his whole field of vision the sea flashed and sizzled with light, reflected upwards from a thousand wave-lapped islands. He had no idea there were so many islands in all the world, or so many boats. They were a fleet beyond numbering and yet he had hardly begun to take it all in when the crew announced preparations for landing and soon they were flying over a patchwork of pinewoods and fields. It was like a dull pause after the wonder of the coast and as they touched down and taxied to the terminal his elation began to fade, oppressed on all sides by a brooding monotony of pine trees.

Saying goodbye to the cabin crew, Ricky stepped down onto the soil of another country. *His country*. He waited for a leap of recognition but none came. It was the land of his birth, the country that had given him his very name – Ricky *Suomalainen* - yet to him it was as mysterious as a forbidden room to a lonely child.

Once inside the terminal his mood lightened. The easy efficiency of the place was a relief from the crowds he had left behind in London and by the time he gave his passport to the immigration officer he was feeling almost relaxed. But to his surprise she asked, 'Oletko sinä Suomalainen?' (*Are you Finnish?*)

It took Ricky a moment to work out what she'd said - and when he did it flustered him. 'No. Yes. I mean, I was born here. I've not been back since I was two.'

The officer gave him an appraising look, then changed tack. 'You are the first person I have seen who looks worse in real life than in their passport.'

Her features remained stern and correct but he realised he was being tested by a dry, Nordic humour and that he was expected to respond in kind. Unfortunately it had been so long, it was beyond him. 'I know, I've not been well. Perhaps the change will do me good.'

'We must hope so. How long are you staying?'

'Just ten days.'

'And where do you go in your ten days?'

'I'm hoping to find some relatives in Tampere.'

Apparently satisfied, she stamped the passport and handed it back, still straight-faced. It was only when he made to go that she finally smiled. 'Welcome home, Mr Finn. I wish you good luck.'

He felt a sudden lump in his throat and could only grunt a reply. Yet when he lugged his suitcase onto the concourse and saw Tim basking there in the sunlight, he felt a rush of joy.

For his part, Tim gave the merest hint of a nod. 'Nice flight?'

'Yup.'

They regarded each other in silence for a moment, gauging the things that couldn't be spoken. Then Tim's normally laconic expression lifted and became almost animated. 'This weather is unbelievable. Two days ago there was snow on the ground.'

'Really?'

'Yeah, it's been one of the worst winters in living memory. You're dressed with typical English pessimism, I see.'

Ricky fingered his heavy wool jacket regretfully. He had bought it at Oxfam, for the funeral. 'I thought it was supposed to be cold in Scandinavia?'

'For a Finn your ignorance is amazing. Finland isn't part of Scandinavia - and in summer it's hotter here than England. We get this bus.'

'How do I pay? I haven't any small change.'

Tim snorted and handed him a ticket. 'Overdressed, overwrought and over here.'

'Thanks. How far is it into town?'

'Twenty minutes. You look ill. And you'll have to ditch that jacket: I'm not taking you out on the town looking like a consumptive Irish navvy.'

Ricky grinned. It was as if the intervening year with all its horror had never occurred. Tim was as religiously insulting to his friends as he was meticulously polite to strangers. You knew you had passed the test the moment he started abusing you.

'Where are we going?'

'I'm taking you on a whistle-stop tour of Helsinki before we get the train to Tampere. After that we're going dancing.'

'Dancing?'

'You'll manage.'

Ricky doubted it but knew better than to argue, so he sat back and looked out the window as the bus sped into the city. Tim put his nose in a book, in a characteristic display of tact dressed up as indifference. Yet when they arrived at the central station, he led off at such a pace that Ricky had to protest.

'Thanks for giving me a hand. This thing weighs a ton.'

'Got my hands full,' said Tim, nonchalantly waving his slim holdall. 'Why do the English abroad always pack as if they're going on an expedition up the Amazon? I bet you've even got bog paper in there.'

Ricky's stepfather had worn his Scottishness like a badge of injured pride: but it wasn't the accusation of being English that got Ricky's goat. Having dropped off his suitcase at left luggage, he decided enough was enough.

'Tim!'

'What now?'

'If you don't decelerate some, I'm going to shackle you, you lanky git. I'm here for ten days, you know? I don't need to see the whole effing town in the first ten minutes.'

They were stony faced for the merest instant - then both grinned at once. Tim pointed to a church opposite. 'Seen anything like that before?'

'Yes but not in Europe. That's an onion dome: it has to be Russian, right?'

'Eastern Orthodox. East meets West, Ricky: that's what Finland's all about. Now quit bellyaching and don't lag.'

'This whole place is weird: it's kind of strange and familiar at the same time.'

'I do hope you're not about to tell me it's awakening subconscious memories.'

'No: but that pizzeria over there is definitely awakening something.'

He led the way inside, barely noticing the waitress who showed them to their table. But as she leant forward to arrange the settings, the light from the windows haloed her. In that instant his heart stopped still.

He had only ever seen one photograph of his mother as a girl in Finland. She was standing by a tree in a garden with a picket fence behind her and the sun shining through her hair. She had been about nineteen.

He stumbled over a chair leg and had to grab for the table to save himself, his skin clammy with sudden sweat. The girl politely ignored his confusion and asked if they wanted anything to drink. Tim answered for both of them and by the time Ricky looked up again, the image was gone. But it had been there. Just for a moment it had been her face, her eyes, her smile. The way her hair brushed her cheeks, the colour of it…

When she returned for their order, Ricky kept his eyes fixed on the menu. Mistaking his reaction, Tim snorted derisorily. 'Christ you're repressed! It's pathetic, ogling in secret. If you must stare, at least do it openly.'

Ricky started to say something, then thought better of it. He saw now that the resemblance was only superficial, a trick of the light more than a true similarity of feature. Yet he still couldn't do as Tim said. Perhaps it was because he hadn't been with a girl for so long but he couldn't meet her eye and it took all his willpower to feign normality.

'So, where are we going on this guided tour?'

'Harbour, open-air market, Russian coffee house: the standard itinerary.'

'And we're really going dancing tonight?'

'Yeah, at a disco in Tampere. It's Friday night, Ricky: it's what good-looking single guys do. You can come, too.'

'Oh, thanks! How long does it take to get there?'

'Couple of hours.'

'I'll be completely knackered.'

'You'll surprise yourself. Come on, let's go.'

Ricky fumbled with the unfamiliar currency and then hung back to thank the waitress. He did it partly out of politeness and partly out of admiration: but most of all he did it to reassure himself that she was not a reincarnation of the mother he had left dead in Scotland six months before. The frankness of her smile made him blush all the way to his ears; and his thanks were lost in an incoherent mumble as he fled for the door.

CHAPTER 3
June, 1955

There are moments that stay with us all our lives, their clarity preserved as if in crystal while everything around them fades. As soon as Satu came up on deck, she knew that the passage through the Helsinki approaches was such a moment. There is nothing in the world like entering a new port through narrow, rock-bound reaches where the smell of the sea is pungent with the promise of fresh starts.

She looked up and saw Captain Fitzpatrick lean over the wing of the bridge to gauge the distance at the narrowest point, calling out to the pilot in the wheelhouse as he did so. The awesome mass of rock slid past so close that she could smell the grass at the foot of the fortress walls. Then they burst out of the narrow channel and there before her was the whole vista of the harbour. Where he would be waiting. She was coming to him on one of their own family's ships. The Scottish branch and the Finnish branch back together again. It was perfect. Just too perfect.

CHAPTER 4
May, 1981

'I thought everything was going to be stern and grey. I wasn't prepared for all this light and colour.'

The market stalls ran right up to the edge of the harbour, where a line of boats selling fresh vegetables formed a picture more akin to the Mediterranean than the Baltic. Tim grunted, indicating a pair of giant ferries passing each other in the distance. 'They run between here and Sweden. People joke that it's called the Viking Line because of all the drunken rampaging onboard.'

That brought back too many bad memories. Second-hand and distorted by his mother's hate but all he had to go on. The words were out of his mouth before he knew it. 'My father was a sailor. Did I ever tell you that?'

'Occasionally, in your cups.'

'A sailor and a drunk. That's all she'd ever say. For all I know, he could be on one of those ships right now.'

'Would you know him if you saw him?'

'No.'

'Would you want to?'

Ricky stayed mute. There weren't the words. He gazed at the mirage-like quality of the view: the soaring sky; the calmly rippling waters of the bay; the thin ribbon of buildings between; and under his breath he muttered, 'Where only man is vile.' Then he turned and followed Tim back across the cobbled square, where 26 years earlier a red-haired girl had walked hand-in-hand with the man she loved.

If there was any memory in the stones, Ricky didn't feel it. He was too busy swallowing a burning wreck of emotions.

'The coffee house: my favourite building in Helsinki.' Tim's words brought him back to the present, to the base of a broad, tree-lined boulevard.

'It looks like something out of Doctor Zhivago.'

'It should. It's turn of the century Russian.'

Ricky took in the intricate fretwork of wood and glass, with its pointed roofs and exquisite corner turrets. He thought it one of the most extraordinary buildings he had ever seen - but not so extraordinary as his ability to notice such things within minutes of being visited first by a vision of his mother and then by the ghost of his father. It was what he had come for but not what he expected.

They wandered on through the government quarter, Ricky gawping up at edifices that seemed to have been built for a race of men twelve feet tall. When they reached the Lutheran Cathedral, standing stark against a cloudless sky, it struck him as having all the vivid, two-dimensional unreality of a dream. And then a flash of colour snapped him out of it.

'Wow, look at that!'

'Yeah,' agreed Tim, 'I like the pastel colours. The Russians built the whole place exactly like Leningrad.'

'Not the buildings, stupid,' said Ricky, gazing after a couple of girls in summer dresses. 'You said they're not Scandinavians, right?'

Tim looked at him askance. 'You really don't know anything about it, do you?'

'I've had twenty years of pointedly not discussing it. If the Finns came from darkest Asia, I'm sure mum would have taken good care not to tell me.'

'Actually they did.'

'Really? So they're a bunch of Asians with fair complexions and a funny language?'

'Yeah. You can see it in their faces, especially the women. They have those broad faces and high cheekbones: I think it makes them incredibly beautiful.'

'You'll hear no argument from me on that score.'

His mother was only half Finnish and her red hair probably came from the Scottish side: but suddenly it struck him as bizarre that he'd gazed at her face a million times without realising that her beauty was not European but Asian. That, more than anything else, finally changed the way he thought of her. It made her no longer Sandy Carr but Satu Suomalainen. The name she had refused to use. The name that had driven him here, in search of both their pasts.

'How could she not have liked this?' Ricky asked later, as they lazed in the Russian coffee house, stuffing themselves with pastries and watching the world go by.

'Maybe she was here in wintertime. Maybe she didn't have a generous friend to buy her coffee and cakes. Maybe we'd better run or we'll miss the train to Tampere.'

They reached the station with barely two minutes to spare but Ricky stopped dead at the sight of the carriages on the platform next to their own.

'Tim, that train's going to Leningrad.'

'Yeah, so what? Come *on*.'

'You mean they can just hop on a train and go to Russia?'

'Yeah, they don't even need a visa.'

'But what about the Iron Curtain?'

'They don't have that here.'

'They must have.'

'No, they don't. Their Presidents go fishing together instead. We get on this train together. If it leaves without us we're stuck here all night.'

'Alright, I hear you. But how come? This is the Red Army we're talking about, not the Red Cross. Why aren't they stomping all over the place?'

'I dunno, politics bores me. We're about to miss it, Ricky.'

'Don't play dumb. Almost the only thing my mother ever said about the split in our family was that it had to do with the war against Russia.'

'OK, OK! I've got a friend at the university who knows all about that shit. I'll introduce you.'

'Thank you.' Ricky heaved his case aboard, then grinned in sudden good humour. 'You see? Plenty of time.'

The carriage was stifling from standing in the sun, so they threw open the windows and as they did so the train moved off.

'I can't believe this country: 80 degrees in May and the trains run on time. It's like Switzerland without the Swiss.'

'Truer than you know. There are only ten rich families in the whole country: nine are Swedish and the tenth's Swiss. They make the chocolate.'

Ricky looked at him so deprecatingly that for once Tim actually seemed embarrassed. 'It's the language classes. I have to swot up on this stuff to provide topics to discuss with my students.'

'Well swot on, old bean. Nothing like a well-informed guide.'

It only took a few minutes for the train to clear the city and a few more to pass through the suburbs and reach open countryside. The scenery was restful rather than inspiring, so Ricky decided to put his guide to the test. 'What's that?'

'Cow.'

'And that?'

'Fir tree.'

'My, you do know your stuff. This country would be a real dodo for playing "I Spy", mind.'

'Wait till you see the lakes.'

'Enumerate them.'

'Nobody knows. They get a different number every time they count. The last time anyone tried they reckoned it was about 60,000.'

'That's a lot of lakes. They had a lot of islands when I flew over, too. What else have they got?'

'Space. Education. Freedom. Alcoholism. Beautiful women. Trees.'

Ricky stretched languorously, half-closing his eyes so that the countryside outside sped by in a somnolent blur. 'That's an abundance of riches. Wake me when something interesting comes along.'

He must have dozed off, for presently Tim was kicking him under the table.

'Uh? What's up? Are we there already?' He opened his eyes to see a massive castle, squatting beside a lake.

'Hämeenlinna,' said Tim.

'Very nice, too.'

'Häme is the name of the province. Linna means a castle. There's another one at Savonlinna, where they hold the opera festival.'

'Savonlinna. Would that be linna as in castle and Savo as in the local province, perchance?'

'Yeah. Savo people are famous for being talkative and extrovert. People from Häme aren't.'

'And which province are we staying in?'

'Häme.'

'Oh-oh.'

'Don't worry: at this time of year everyone's so extrovert you'd think the whole country was on uppers.'

'Right: no upper like a good dose of sunshine. So it'll be rocking in Tampere tonight?'

'Yeah. You won't be able to keep up.'

Ricky rather confirmed this by dozing off again, until an attendant came down the carriage with the refreshment trolley. Something happened during the intervening minutes to change his mood completely. He bought a coffee and sat nursing it in silence, then put it aside and pulled an envelope from his pocket, extracting a hand written sheet that he carefully smoothed out on the table. When he spoke, his tone had an edgy, almost pleading tone. 'I want to go to this address in Tampere and I really need you to act as interpreter. When I rang up, the guy at the other end didn't speak any English.'

'That's the address your mother left you?'

'Yes, Kirkkokatu 221. Do you know it?'

'Yeah, I think so. We can stop off there tomorrow morning.'

Ricky nodded absently, wondering what they'd find. It had taken years to persuade his mother to give him an address for their relatives in Finland. In the end he'd had to wait until she was actually dying before she relented. And what she had revealed was shockingly different from anything he had anticipated. All those years to get one page of hand written scrawl - but no amount of time could have prepared him for what it contained.

After all the waiting and wondering, his first attempt at making contact had proved such an anticlimax. It hadn't occurred to him that they wouldn't speak English. He supposed he shouldn't have been surprised, given that his mother and grandmother had concealed their very existence for quarter of a century.

He looked vacantly out the window and found his eyes misting with tears. Mum had been so very consistent. She had always refused to admit the existence of any living Finnish relatives; and she had refused even to discuss his father, except to tell him that he was a Finn and a drunk and a bastard. Ricky didn't even know if he was alive or dead. Hell, he didn't even know his *name*.

So he had retaliated in kind. He had held it against her all through those last months: an unspoken question that in the end had worn her down, just as he secretly hoped it would. The guilt of what he had done, combined with the shock of what she had finally told him, was too much even now. Presently he had no choice but to surrender to the memories, letting them take him back there, to the room in which he had spent the most terrible day of his life.

CHAPTER 5
November, 1980

She had planned to tell him about Satu as soon as the morphine could no longer control the pain. The first time it happened he came all the way from London for nothing. She had known the remission would only be temporary but she never anticipated this sudden collapse.

And Ricky had so little money. He pretended it wasn't a problem but she knew he couldn't afford another trip so soon. He might call her the world's most protective mother but there really had been no need for him to go all the way to London to get out from under her wing. Why couldn't he just have gone to Newcastle as she suggested?

She was rambling again. She had to pull herself together but it was so hard. As soon as the morphine mist cleared, the pain would get to be more than she could bear. There were only a few short periods in each day when she could keep her mind clear. She felt like a tightrope walker, with violent gusts of wind blowing first from one side and then the other. If she fell, she'd never get back up again.

The next time she opened her eyes, there he was. She must have fallen asleep and from the clock she saw that nearly three hours had passed. Ricky smiled as soon as he saw she was awake.

'Hi, mum. You look like death.'

She was appalled at how difficult it was to summon up the energy to speak. 'Cheeky sod. You took your time.'

'I know, I'm sorry. Can you believe the bloody bus broke down? I had to wait two hours for the relief coach. I'm freezing. Can I eat your grapes?'

She smiled, though God knew what kind of grimace it must look like to him. All the time he was speaking, his eyes never left hers. There were always the two conversations going on between them: the spoken one and the one that mattered. She watched him sit down by her bedside, picking off the grapes one by one and munching them like an exotic delicacy. Heaven only knew when he'd last eaten any fresh fruit. He looked so pale and thin.

Dear God, *he* looked pale and thin! Couldn't she stop being a mother for just five minutes? For just long enough to die in. It certainly hurt enough to die: and the mist was still there. With a silent groan of despair she realised that she'd fallen off the tightrope. Then the pain came in a great surge and she couldn't hold back the cry of agony. She was aware of him going white as a sheet and reaching out to clasp her hand.

'Mum?'

She could hardly focus. Now she'd have to fight the drugs and the pain together. She could feel herself slipping away and there was nothing she could do. It hurt too much, the effort was like swimming through tar and she couldn't do it anymore.

Then, suddenly, TK was there. TK, of all people! She felt the anger coursing through her and heard someone shouting and then she realised it was her own voice. 'Leave him alone, you bastard! I'll kill you, I swear it! Get away from him!' She saw the shock on his face, saw him back away just as he had the last time, on the island. Coward. He was always such a bloody coward. He shouldn't have come. He shouldn't ever have come back. He had no right.

'Mum?'

'Ricky?'

'Yes Mum!'

Thank God, he was still there. Perhaps there was still time. 'Find Satu, Ricky.'

'What did you say, mum?'

He seemed to be coming and going, moving in and out of view. What had his father been doing there? She had to get a grip on herself. His eyes were full of sorrow but she could see the yearning behind them. It was only right that he should know, at the end.

'Find her, Ricky. Find Satu.'

'But I don't know anyone else called Satu, mum. Only you.'

'Not me. It's the family name: we called her by it, too.'

'She's a relative? In Finland?'

He had it. Thank God.

'Mum, is she related to my father?'

She shook her head, then nodded, biting her lip against all the different kinds of pain. There was so much that she had to tell him, why couldn't she find the words?

'What was that? Mum, I don't understand.'

What was wrong with the boy? Didn't he know how hard it was? She fell back on the pillow, then tried again, forming every word carefully to make sure it was clear. Every breath was like a dagger inside her.

'Oh God, Mum: you're speaking Finnish.'

What?

'Finnish, mum. You were speaking Finnish. You never do that.'

No! How could she have been? Oh God, it hurt so much - and all to do again. Then suddenly the pain seemed to fade back, as if it was waiting in the wings and she knew she could take one last breath and it wouldn't hurt so much. It would be enough - and then it would be over.

'We called your sister Satu, too.'

'My *sister*?'

'Born first. Oh God!'

'Mum? I have a *sister*? A sister in Finland? Mum, don't, *please*...'

Everything was fading away. Please God don't let them hurt him. Oh God, I couldn't save Satu, please look after my boy.

I love you, Ricky.

CHAPTER 6
May, 1981

Nobody had told Ricky that she was dying. He'd thought she was in remission and that it was just another false alarm and he'd come in and cracked jokes about how she looked and then she died right there in front of him.

It had been necessary for the hospital staff to summon help to move him from her room. He had been sitting huddled in the chair by the bed, rocking back and forth, oblivious to anything going on around him. Or so they told him, for he remembered little of the next few days. The police had found him wandering down by Leith Docks, frozen half to death and apparently mute. They had taken him for a drug addict and he'd spent the night in the cells, which at least saved him from hypothermia.

It had been nearly six months before he was well enough to act on what she had told him. He lost his job after the first two and if it hadn't been for Niamh, the Irish nurse he'd been living with, he might have lost his mind, too. In the end it had been too much even for her. The only thing he remembered clearly about that period was the way his mother's words had been burning holes in his brain every day.

He looked down at the crumpled sheet of paper. Her hand had closed around it as she died and he had kissed each finger as he gently prised them away, kneeling beside the bed with tears streaming down his cheeks. The letter contained nothing but a name and an address and from the shaking scrawl he had realised what an effort it must have been for her to write even that much. Yet she must have known nothing more was needed. His path was set from that instant.

So he had come here, to search for the girl his mother had been and for the daughter she had borne in that other life of which he had been completely ignorant. His one point of contact with his missing past. His sister.

He looked up just as Tim was cautiously poking his head over his book.

'OK?'

'Yes. Sorry.'

Although capable of sensitivity, Tim preferred ruthlessness whenever he thought the patient was up to it. The moment they arrived in Tampere he bundled him out onto the platform with a brusque, 'Come on, we can dump the bags here. The disco's only a block away.'

Ricky started to protest, then recognised the tactic for what it was and embraced it gratefully. Tim was right of course: at the prospect of something as simple as a dance, the adrenaline started to pump and all trace of the tiredness that had dogged him for months was gone.

'Are you ready yet?' demanded Tim.

'Yes, all fired up and raring to go. So what's this disco like?'

'It's a big building with a bar and women. You drink at the bar and dance with the women.'

'Oh, you're in one of your helpful moods again.'

Tim snorted - and they went dancing.

CHAPTER 7

———

Like discos the world over it had a style council hanging around outside but Tim ploughed straight through, leaving Ricky to catch up as usual. They headed for the bar and set themselves up with drinks in their hands before turning to survey the scene. It was early but half the tables around the dance floor were already taken, mostly by women or mixed groups. The average age was about 22.

'So how does this work?'

'You have to learn some Finnish.'

'Oh great.'

'Nah, it's easy. Here the men have to formally ask the women to dance. You just walk up and say, "Haluatko tanssia?" That's "Would you like to dance?".'

'What's Finnish for "Get Lost"?'

'Yes is "kyllä" and no is "ei" but they probably won't say either.'

'How do they say no, then?'

'They don't. It's considered impolite to refuse. So even you have a chance.'

'Bit of a bummer for the girls, though.'

'They have a let-out clause. You get to have two dances, then you escort her back to her table. She doesn't have to dance with you again, so she knows she won't get stuck with someone she doesn't like.'

'Positively Jane Austen. Can you have more than two dances?'

'Only if she offers. She won't do that unless she really likes you, so it's not likely to happen in your case.'

'How do you dance here?'

'Arms and legs.'

'Give me a break.'

'You can dance like in England, you don't have to know ballroom stuff. Hold her for slow ones, dance separately for fast ones. But you're not allowed to dance in a group or with the same sex.'

'That's a bit quaint.'

'It's the convention. British conventions probably seem pretty strange to them, too.'

'What, closing the pubs all afternoon and sleeping with hot water bottles? Surely not. And they really have to say yes?'

'Not if they think you're completely repulsive.'

'So I might be in with a chance, then?'

'Not likely.'

'Love you too. What is it you say again?'

'Haluatko tanssia.'

'Right. That doesn't mean "I think you have a face like a warthog" by any chance? OK. And you just ask anyone?'

'Yeah.'

Ricky sipped nervously at his drink as he surveyed the scene.

'Go and ask someone,' Tim commanded.

'Right, in a moment. When I've finished this beer.'

'God, you're pathetic. Look, I'll show you.'

Tim sauntered around the semicircle of tables, made his selection, asked his question and got his girl. It all seemed very straightforward: which did nothing to calm the butterflies in Ricky's stomach. But what the hell, nothing ventured, nothing gained...

There were at least a hundred available women, so with the instinctive judgement of the male on the make he halved it by those who were in tight conference, quartered it by those who were dogs and then began fine-tuning. Some of them were so stunning that Ricky knew he wasn't even in their league and he had to act or lose his nerve, so he zeroed in on a pretty brunette who was sipping at her drink while her eyes roamed the room.

'Haluatko tanssia?'

She nodded and got up almost without looking, following him to the dance floor because he couldn't bring himself to lead her by the hand like everyone else. When they arrived it was halfway through a mid-tempo number, so he turned and started to dance. She smiled and followed his lead and after a couple of seconds he broke the good news. 'Do you speak English?'

Her face showed surprise but not dismay and then she laughed. 'But you spoke Finnish before!'

'Yes. About the only words I know.'

'But how did you know what to say?'

'My friend told me. He's an English teacher here.'

'Ah.' She looked at him wryly. 'Cunning, eh?'

Ricky grinned back uncertainly. He wasn't sure about cunning. 'You speak really good English. How do you know a word like cunning?'

'As cunning as a fox,' she mused, then laughed again. 'Because no-one speaks Finnish of course, so we have to learn other languages. I learned "As cunning as a fox" in the first year at school.'

'How many languages do you speak?'

'English, Finnish, Swedish and a little German.'

'Wow! What do you do? I mean, what is your job?'

'Oh, I'm a secretary.'

'Right. A secretary with four languages. I can't manage more than one, let alone Finnish. You know it's the most difficult language to learn, next to Chinese and Japanese?'

'But not for me!'

They both smiled at that and the next dance was a slow one, so he held her close and then asked if she wanted to dance again and she said yes. After the next two he took her hand and led her back to her seat. It all seemed quite easy: and back at the bar Tim came dangerously close to paying him a compliment.

'Cute girl.'

'Very. She also speaks four languages.'

'Par for the course. They all learn Swedish and most of them speak some Russian or German as well. Four's pretty typical.'

'Grief. What's yours like?'

'She's a naval architect from the shipyards.'

'Oh, yeah, right. I had one of those, was it last week or the week before?'

Tim shook his head. 'It's not so unusual. Sixty per cent of university graduates here are women.'

'Smart as well as beautiful, huh? You know, I think... Jesus, look at that!'

The two girls who had just walked in would have turned heads anywhere: but the lesser blonde was mere wallpaper against her friend.

'Horrorshow!' agreed Tim.

'I thought people that beautiful only existed on celluloid.'

'You could dance with her.'

'Me? You must be joking. I'm not even in her class.'

'Class? You're hardly the same species. But this isn't England. She'd probably find you quite interesting. We're the only foreigners here.'

'Whaddya mean, the only ones? The place is bloody full of 'em! Do you really think so?'

'Yeah, I do.'

Ricky gulped – and yet for all their superficial banter, the quaint formality of this mode of dancing appealed to him. He certainly found it easier than trying to appear natural and relaxed.

She was leaning up against the wall at one end of the bar and as Ricky watched she turned her face towards him and all his senses woke up together. She smiled slightly when their eyes met, holding his gaze with the good-natured openness of her race, then moving on with neither dismissal nor invitation, to take in other fields of vision. It was as if a soft breeze had brushed his cheek amid the hot and smoky atmosphere of the club.

'God, she's absolutely gorgeous. Why don't you go and chat her up?'

'You're the one she's showing an interest in.'

'Really? You think so? But she might not even speak English.'

'Then you won't feel insulted when she tells you to piss off in Finnish.'

'Why don't you introduce us? You're good at that sort of thing. Your height always breaks the ice.'

'Hello, this is my mate Ricky. He wants you to give him oral sex but he's too much of a wimp to ask you himself. Just go and talk to her, for fuck's sake.'

But it was too late. Even as they were speaking, a big Finnish guy moved in on her and proceeded to make a right arse of himself. Yet her composure under siege impressed Ricky mightily.

For some reason he found himself thinking of the photo of his mother in the garden. There was something familiar about her face: something about the way the strength of those features was softened by the fullness of her cheeks. They dimpled slightly when she cast an apparently stray glance in his direction and it nearly made him choke on his beer.

Tim eyed him ironically. 'Fancy her a bit, do you?'

Fancy her? He was awe-struck. And he was still considering how to raise the siege when her girlfriend did it for him, forcing the big oaf to move back a pace. Something the friend said made her laugh and the sound of it came to Ricky across the crowded room, natural and melodious. He gave thanks to God, for few attractions survive a silly laugh.

She was altogether such a bombshell that Ricky acted totally out of character. He walked over to the bar with his now empty glass in hand, aiming to lean against the counter and catch her eye as he waited to be served. But to his alarm she turned her gaze on him as he approached. He hadn't anticipated being given the once over himself, still less this slow, cool appraisal. Her eyes had such a calm, amused intensity that he almost forgot his lines: and yet somehow he managed to clobber the competition with just a few words of Finnish.

'Hei. Puhuteko Englantia?'

She looked at him blankly for a moment, then burst out laughing. 'But your accent is terrible.'

'Oh no, did I say it wrong?'

'Not really but it sounded funny. We are not used to hearing foreigners speak Finnish. You are English, yes?'

'Yes, well, Scottish. How did you know?'

'You look English. Those are terrible shoes. They say the English always dress well except for their shoes.'

He laughed nervously and she smiled and tapped him on the chest. 'So, do you know any more words of Finnish?'

'I'm afraid so.'

'Say something to me.'

Before he could oblige, the big Finn said something that Ricky couldn't follow except in tone. But he could swear her answer was, 'Yes but now I'm talking to this English guy.' And then Ricky got it. The oaf didn't speak English and she was quite happy to use it to freeze him out. So he put half the words he knew into a sentence that he wouldn't have believed himself capable of uttering.

'Minä luulen sinä olet oikein kaunis tyttö.' ('I think you are a very beautiful girl.')

The Finn snorted, then shrugged and moved off in disgust as both girls burst out laughing.

'OK, for that I forgive the bad accent.'

'Oh God. I never said anything like that before in my life.'

'Oh, the cool type, huh? But that is a shame.'

'Not really, I'm just British, we don't express our feelings very much.'

'Just like the Finns! But at least you have learned the right words to say.'

'I don't know much else except "thank you" and "can I have a beer?".'

'But that is almost all you need!' She winked at him and added, 'Except for one thing, of course. Do you know how to ask a girl to dance?'

'Haluatko tanssia?'

'Kyllä.' She held out her hand in mock formality and he reciprocated with a bow, knowing that her palm would be cool and dry, her grip easy yet firm. He led her out onto the floor and she draped her hands on his shoulders as she picked up the conversation. 'So, what is your name?'

'Ricky.'

'Hello Ricky, I'm Satu.'

He froze, staring at her like a dummy. The words for a reply wouldn't come and he struggled to blurt out a response. 'I'm sorry...Satu...?'

She looked at him curiously. 'Yes. Does that sound so strange in English?'

'Not Satu Suomalainen, by any chance?'

Now it was her turn to look wooden. 'No,' she said rather stiffly, 'Satu Savolainen.'

'Oh. Oh, right.' He laughed nervously. 'For a moment I thought you might be my long lost sister.'

'You have a sister in Finland who is lost?'

'Yes, her name's Satu Suomalainen.'

She frowned for a moment, then her face cleared and she laughed. 'But what a coincidence!'

'Yes, isn't it? You don't know her, by any chance?'

'No, I don't know any other Satus. So, are we going to dance?'

'Oh, yes. Absolutely.'

Get a hold of yourself, you idiot. And relax. You're dancing like a puppet with half its strings missing. He groaned inwardly. Oh dear Christ she was beautiful.

'And is your surname also Suomalainen?' she asked, as his feet finally began to find the beat.

'Yes, that's right. Well, kind of. My mother changed her name to Carr when she got married but I never liked it. I prefer to use Suomalainen. It reminds me of who we really are.'

For some reason that seemed to confuse her. At any rate a strange mix of emotions flitted across her face and she sounded almost curt as she prompted, 'So you are from a Finnish family?'

He began to reply but she put a finger to his lips, then tilted her head to one side in a mime of consideration. Finally she put on a serious expression and nodded. 'Yes, you could be a Finn.'

He nodded back, blessing the DJ for playing a song that let them dance slow and close.

'And you have come here to find your sister?'

'Yes, well, my whole family, really. My mother left Finland when I was only two years old. We lost contact with all our Finnish relatives.'

'So that is when you lost her? How strange! And who is your tall friend?'

'That's Tim. He's an English teacher here in Tampere.'

'Ah. He is the one who teaches you how to pick up the girls in Finnish?'

'Yes. Unfortunately we haven't got beyond Lesson One yet.'

'But he has done well so far, I think.' She teased him with eyes so blue, they were all the lure he needed. The next song was a fast one and she reeled him in further with every move she made. When he asked if she wanted to dance again she said, 'No, let's get a drink and talk.'

Once they were leaning up against the bar she began a relaxed but quite systematic interrogation.

'So, how long have you been in Finland, Ricky?'

'Um, about ten hours.'

'Ah, you have just arrived. And how long are you staying?'

'Only ten days, I'm afraid.'

He could see her take mental note of this information, storing it away as if it might be of relevance later.

'Is this the first time you have been here since you were a little boy?'

'Yes it is.'

'And how do you like it, your country of birth?'

'It's amazing. I love everything about it.'

'Hmmm.' Her brows furrowed in the sexiest of frowns and he hurried to justify himself.

'I thought Finland was supposed to be cold and dark and miserable. But it isn't. It's warm and friendly and full of light and colour and the girls are, well...' He trailed off in a salacious grin. 'Let's just say I love Finland.'

She laughed. 'Yes, you must be a real Finn.'

'Is that good or bad?'

She looked at him quizzically. 'It's too early to tell.' Then she changed her expression to one of mock gravity. 'So, you like Finnish girls?'

'Absolutely.'

'And what do you like so much about them?'

'Oh, there are so many things.'

She fixed him with a surprisingly hard look. 'Tell me five.'

'Well, um, OK. I love the Asian faces of the women, so broad and open and proud. And your hair is wonderful, I've never seen such an absolute blonde.'

'So, you like blondes. This is not original. There is more to Finland than blonde girls who are easy to get.'

'I didn't mean that! And besides, those are just the first two…'

She looked at him critically and he gauged he had about five seconds to dig himself out of the hole. 'Right. OK: tell me, how many languages do you speak?'

'Only two. Well, I know Swedish of course but I don't like to speak it.'

'And?' he prompted, praying he was right.

'So, yes, I know some German and some Danish but that's not so hard when you know Swedish. I only speak it with my friend from Copenhagen.'

'Right. So really you speak five languages.' He grinned, sure of himself now. 'And how old are you?'

'I am twenty-four.'

'The same age as me. Are you a university graduate?'

'I am a student at the university but I am not yet a graduate.'

'Right. So you're a blonde, Asian beauty and a highly educated person who speaks five languages. There you are: five things I love about you!'

She wriggled her nose in concentration, going through his words in her mind and then turning on him playfully. 'But that was only four! You have to tell me five!'

'That's easy. You said your name was Savolainen, right?'

'Yes, of course.'

'Then you must be outgoing and sociable.'

'How do you know that?'

'I've been doing my homework. You must be from Savo and Savo people are famous for being sociable and talkative.'

'But yes, it's true!'

'Well there you are then: beautiful Asian face, amazing blonde hair, really smart, skilled linguist, outgoing and sociable. Five.'

He watched the light dance in her hair as she laughed and could think of no words to describe it. To come close, platinum would have to be warm and possess the texture of satin. The dimple was back in her cheeks and he saw now it was a signal, telling him when her cool look masked a smile.

'So, are you staying here in Tampere?'

'Yes but I'm not sure where. Tim takes care of that sort of thing: I just do what he tells me. How about you: do you live here in the city?'

'No, just outside. It is not so far.' She paused, then spoke almost as if thinking aloud. 'So, you have ten days in Tampere? That's not long - but maybe it's enough.' The hint of an expression animated her sphinx-like features but he couldn't read it and was distrustful of projecting his fantasies, so he enjoyed them in silence.

'Where do you live in England?' she asked suddenly.

'London. My family is from Scotland but I moved down south after university.'

'Do you have a girlfriend in London, Ricky?'

'No. Well, um, I split up with someone a little while ago.'

'Aha.'

More information storage: and it seemed to help her decide something.

'So, I should go back and join my girlfriend. She will be getting angry if I am ignoring her all evening.'

'Yes, of course. Maybe I'll see you later?'

She didn't answer directly but put her empty glass down on the bar, tapped him twice on the arm and walked away. He went back to his own drink - still half full - and presently Tim came off the floor and joined him.

'You've done really well. She's got an incredible arse.'

'She's got an incredible everything. She's even a nice person. How can anyone be that beautiful and not conceited?'

'You know she's refused every other man who's asked her since?'

'No, really?' Ricky looked over to where she was sitting and he could have sworn she flashed him a glance. They were too far off to be sure but she seemed to be talking only disinterestedly to her friend.

'Is it OK to ask her for another dance?'

'Well, you won't get to shag her standing here. Not unless you've got the world's longest dick.'

'You have such a way with words. Her name's Satu by the way: the same as my sister.'

'Kinky.'

'Don't go there. Anyway, how are you doing?'

'Swopped the naval architect for a waitress in a pizza restaurant.'

'Why?'

'Cos she's not so smart and only half as pretty.'

'You mean she'll shag you?'

'Yeah.'

'What's her name?'

'Who fucking cares?'

They both laughed at the old lads' joke and knocked back more beer.

'Well, I don't suppose I've got a chance except in my dreams,' Ricky said after draining his glass, 'but I think I'll go and ask anyway.' So he did. He went over and said, 'Excuse me, would you like to dance again?' and the results were something of a surprise. Satu's girlfriend tossed her head in annoyance and Ricky guessed she was pissed off with constantly being the one who wasn't asked - but he could hardly dance with them both.

'You are not dancing with anyone else?' Satu asked, as if his behaviour required an explanation.

'No, I just want to dance with you again.'

'But now you have the chance to meet many different Finnish girls.'

'Yes but I still only want to dance with you.'

'Ah.' She paused, then locked eyes with him and said, 'Me too'.

Oh, thank you God.

They had already exchanged all key verbal information while standing at the bar and after two slow dances they had exchanged a lot of subliminal information as well. Her scent was subtly intoxicating: strawberries packed in straw, fresh and yet deliciously musty. She was obviously completely aware of the effect she was having on him but he didn't try to kiss her because he couldn't believe she'd let him. It was all so cumulatively erotic that when he led her off the floor he had to hold one hand in front of himself to hide the extent of his interest.

When they got to the table she said, 'You can stay and talk if you like.' He practically jumped into the nearest seat and her girlfriend simultaneously jumped out of hers. Some sharp words passed between them and the girlfriend stomped off. Ricky looked up apologetically from the small stain on the table that he had been studying while they argued.

'I'm sorry about your friend.'

'It's OK.' With scarcely a shrug she turned all her attention back to him. They talked, had another drink and then danced some more. Tim was on the floor with a diminutive, mousey-haired girl, who was clinging to his waist and laughing at the imbalance in their respective heights. His friend never showed intimacy in public but Ricky could see at once that he was going to score.

He smiled to himself and stole another glance at Satu. They were dancing so close that the curves of her face appeared impossibly soft, as if he was seeing her through the hazy focus of an art movie camera. Then before he knew it the last song ended and the lights went up. He found himself saying, 'The last dance, how romantic.' He even bowed self-mockingly from the waist, thinking *what the hell am I doing* but saying, 'Thank you very much.'

They both paused, uncertain. He looked around and the place was breaking up, glasses being cleared, people milling about and heading to the doors, the coupled and the luckless. Well, it had been a nice fantasy while it lasted but it was over. Time to go. He turned back to her. 'Thank you for a really nice evening. I really enjoyed myself.'

'Aha. Yes, it was nice.'

A shadow of disappointment flitted across her face and he kicked himself. They had been getting on so well but in the circumstances there was nothing to be done. He had a wild urge to ask if he could go home with her but he suppressed it at once. She'd never go with him, not just like that, they'd hardly met. The fatal word escaped his lips from someone else, some Scots Presbyterian git who was cohabiting his brain. 'Goodnight.' The moment he said it he knew it was a mistake, a final error.

'So, yes, goodnight.' She turned and made for the door and suddenly he was sure but even as he started after her she was lost in the throng and gone.

Ricky headed back towards the bar with a sick feeling in the pit of his stomach. He could see Tim's head above the crush and closer to ground level he found the pizza girl still attached.

'What happened?'

'Nothing. She went home.'

'What did you do wrong this time?'

'Nothing. I didn't do anything. I mean, what could I do? We only just met: she was hardly going to invite me back to her place and bonk my brains out, was she?'

'Did you ask her?'

'Of course not.'

'Why not?'

'Well, I mean...'

Tim sighed, looked at the pizza maid and cast his eyes heavenwards. Then he explained it to him. 'It's a lot different here than in England, Ricky. It's not nice girls and slags here: it takes generations of uptightness and repression to perfect that. In Finland if a girl goes out with a guy and has a nice time, she'll probably round off the evening by sleeping with him. They don't associate sex with sin the way we do. Their morality is much more logical and straightforward.'

'I don't think I want to hear this right now.'

'Did she like you?'

'I think so. Oh hell, I know she did.'

'Did she say thank-you-and-goodnight?'

'No. She sort of hung around...waiting on me, I guess. Oh shit. I was the one who said goodbye.'

'Yeah, you blew it.'

The magnitude of it floored him. 'I just let the most beautiful girl I've ever met walk away because I couldn't believe she might want to go with me.'

'Don't be too hard on yourself, Ricky, it is almost impossible to credit.'

'Why didn't you tell me this earlier?'

He was pissed as hell and could have done without Tim's jibes: and yet once they got outside his disappointment began to fade until he even started to see a bright side. He might have blown his chances but at least she'd been interested enough for it to have been a possibility. It had been ages since anyone had looked at him that way. Not surprising, really: he knew what the last few months had done to him. And here he was on his first night in Finland, coming within a whisker of making it with a dream girl.

A lovely girl, a beautiful night and a new country: suddenly it seemed as if anything was possible.

They had a long walk to reach Tim's place but Ricky didn't mind. The air was coolly refreshing and he loved to walk cities by night, especially in the soft, continuous dusk of a night such as this.

The road they followed out of town rose up the wooded flank of a ridge, before branching off into a dirt street lined with old wooden houses. By the time they reached Tim's front door Ricky was so tired he was ready to drop.

'I'm shattered. What time is it?'

'Two o'clock.'

'God. It's still light out there. Where do we sleep?'

'You're in here, on that mattress.'

'Where's the bathroom?'

'It's communal. You have to go out into the street and then through the first door on your right. Watch your step going down the stairs.'

'Jesus, a bit primitive, isn't it?'

'It's better than some characterless modern flat in town.'

'Yes, I can see how plumbing would bore you. Well, if you don't mind, I'm for a visit to the bowels of the earth and then bed.'

Twenty minutes later Ricky was crashed out on his mattress, staring at the ceiling as he alternately lulled and tormented himself with thoughts of Satu. At first it was more of the latter, not least because of the sounds coming from the other room, where Tim was energetically bedding his pizza waitress. But before long even the rhythms of their lovemaking had a soporific effect upon him.

Not a bad homecoming, he thought sleepily to himself, as he

imagined Satu in bed beside him. And tomorrow he would start his search in earnest, not only for his sister and his mother but now perhaps also for the girl he had just let slip through his fingers. As he fell asleep they were all so equal in his thoughts that the three of them mingled deliciously into his dreams.

And are not dreams sometimes premonitions?

CHAPTER 8
June, 1955

God, how she loved to dance! In Scotland it was almost the only release, except for the drink of course and that had been out of the question with parents like hers.

But no more of that! No more dour, grey streets and dingy halls and drunken men who wore string vests and stank and groped your bum as they danced with you. No more hand-me-downs and home at 10 o'clock. Now it was time to have some fun.

She knew he was a good dancer. More than once he'd cut a dash at the ceilidh and he hadn't even known the steps. God, what a laugh he'd been! And now here they were together, on his own turf!

Through the fug of smoke she saw him flash that amazing, boyish smile and hold out his hand to her. She went to him as if through a magic mist and it went up her nose so that she sneezed on it and then they were both laughing, tears in her eyes from the smoke and the sneezing and the pure joy of it all.

He smelt of beer and tobacco and the salty smell of the sea that never quite left him and she loved him so much that her legs were like treacle.

Oh God, how she loved this country.

CHAPTER 9
Saturday, 16th May, 1981

The light woke him early and for awhile he watched the dust floating in the sunbeams as they streamed through dingy lace curtains. Then thirst drove him to get up. He was looking about for something to drink when the door to Tim's room opened and the pizza waitress came through, put a finger to her lips and went out the front door without a word.

Ricky stuck his head into the bedroom and saw that Tim was doing a good impression of a semi-submerged log. There was also a balcony, so he tiptoed outside and found a rickety chair propped against the railings.

The view was stupendous. The house was perched on the face of a steep ridge, with colourful wooden houses tumbling down the hill towards a lake that stretched far into the distance. The sky was palest blue and it was obvious the day was set to be a scorcher. For a few minutes Ricky soaked up the peacefulness of the sleeping village, then he decided enough was enough and went inside to hustle up some sustenance.

'Get up you lazy bastard,' he said cheerfully, pulling back the drapes and slamming the door. 'I need entertainment and breakfast.' The log groaned and shifted. Encouraged, Ricky started to sing 'Early One Morning'. This was more than sufficient for his purpose and he soon judged the log to be capable of conversation. 'You've run out of breakfast, I demand satisfaction.'

'Uh, what time is it?'

'Ages past seven. Nearly eight.'

'God, what's got into you this morning?'

'Must be something in the air, I feel all perked up and ready to go.'

'Well I won't stop you.'

'I need breakfast: coffee, croissant; that sort of thing. I can't eat scenery.'

'There's a shop up the road but it doesn't open till eight-thirty.'

'Then I'll go for a stroll until it does. Would it be asking too much to have the kettle on by the time I get back?'

Ricky was barely ten paces out the door when he came to a parting of the ways, where an unmetalled track fell away precipitously towards the lake. To his right it continued up the scarp via a tremendous flight of wooden steps, while ahead of him the main road angled gently up the face of the ridge.

The dirt streets and wooden houses made the place so like the Wild West that he half expected to see Wyatt Earp come walking down the street. Some of the houses were little more than shacks but others were substantial affairs of two or three stories, surrounded by gardens and outbuildings. Their colours were as varied as their designs and the architecture was clearly European but beyond that he was in new territory.

The other thing that struck him was the smell. In later years all that would be required to transport him back to Finland was a hint of that pungent aroma. It was a trigger to total recall, as precise as a dog's memory of its master's scent. It seemed to emanate from the road, its saline qualities merging with the musty odour of yellow-red earth, the cleaner aroma of sun-baked wood and the tang of rising sap. It was no gentle fragrance but a wellspring of strong vapours, not unpleasant but like a powerful inhalation that routs out the last remnants of a winter cold.

Whatever its source, it was great for clearing away the cobwebs. After the first hundred yards he was swinging along like a grenadier, savouring the smell of Pispala as something so tangible he could practically taste it.

Here and there, breaks between the houses gave him clear views to the lake. At first it seemed ethereal, with mist wisping through the trees that lined the shore. But the sun was already well up and the mist was dissipating fast. Even as he walked from one viewpoint to another the sky brightened to a bolder blue and the waters of the lake changed with it. He smiled and picked up his pace. It was a great day to be alive.

At the crest he encountered an ugly modern school and decided to double back along the ridgetop. Having tested his Finnish with the shop keeper, he got back laden with food and questions.

'Yeah,' said Tim, through a mouthful of bread and chocolate, 'this place is famous as a centre of workers and students. Pispala used to be outside the city limits, so they built their houses however they pleased. They're still a pretty rebellious bunch: they even have a communist MP.'

'I thought the Finns hated the Commies?'

'They do and they don't. The Reds and Whites fought a civil war just like in Russia. Actually the Reds made their last stand right here in Pispala.'

'I never heard of this war.'

'Hardly anybody outside Finland has.'

'Well, they built themselves a beautiful place, anyway.'

'Yeah, I'm really looking forward to being here through the summer. Going to that toilet when it's minus 20 is no joke, I can tell you. Most of the older houses still have dry toilets in sheds out the back.'

'You mean wooden seats over a big hole? Jesus, it really is like the Wild West.'

Tim gestured up the road. 'We're having a carnival here tomorrow. There's a procession along the main street and then a concert in the sports field.'

Ricky nodded absently. 'Sounds interesting. But before we do anything else, I need to go and see if we can find my relatives.'

'Sure, we'll stop by there after we've been to sauna.'

'Been to where?'

'To *sowna*. What people in England wrongly refer to as "having a sawna". The only Finnish word in the English language and we mispronounce it. Also it's wrong to say, "I'm going to have a sauna." It's "I'm going to sauna".'

'How about, "I'm not going to sauna, 'cos I got a bad feeling about it"?'

'Nah, that's completely wrong. It's, "I'm going to sauna with my mate Tim because when I'm in Finland I do as the Finns do".'

'Is this absolutely necessary? Oh bugger. What's it like?'

'Bracing. But don't worry, the ice melted last week. Started to, anyway.'

'Jesus Christ, you don't mean we're going into a *lake*?'

'Quit your whinging,' said Tim, as they left the changing rooms and headed down through the trees towards the shore. 'This is going to be one of the best experiences of your life.'

'The last experience of my life, more like. So what do we do now?'

'Jump in the lake.'

'You're joking.'

'No, you always start and finish with a cold plunge.'

'If I survive this, I swear to God...'

'Just don't let the side down by screaming. Remember you're British.'

Ricky gingerly followed his friend across the smooth rocks to the water's edge, where two burly Finns were climbing out by way of some iron railings. They were as impassive as statues but Ricky noted with a shudder that the ice came to within a few feet of the steps.

'You really mean we climb down that?'

'No, you'd wimp out before you were half way in.'

'So what do we do?'

'Jump!'

'Oh shit!' yelped Ricky as he was showered in icy spray.

'Come on in, the water's lovely!'

'You look like a fucking polar bear in there. There's no way...'

But of course there was; and he did. When he hit the water there was a split second's delay before the shock registered and then every nerve in his body screamed at once.

'Exhilarating, yeah?' cried Tim, with a kind of deranged earnestness.

'Mother of God! It's annihilating. How long do we have to stay in here?'

'I don't know about you but I'm getting out now, before my balls drop off.'

Spluttering an obscenity, Ricky rocketed out of the water, only to discover that the gentle breeze had developed a knife-like edge. They sprinted for the sauna and were inside before he had time to ponder the next part of his ordeal. Half-blinded by the gloom, he sat down on a vacant bench, vaguely aware of beefy bodies all around.

As his eyes adjusted to the gloom, Ricky took in the windowless wooden interior with its tiers of L-shaped seats, most of them occupied by burly, middle aged Finns. In the centre a bucket of water and a long-handled ladle stood beside an iron brazier in which stones glowed dull red.

There is a sixth sense and it is temperature. It took Ricky about ten seconds to become aware that it was massively hot. The heat seemed to grow exponentially, first reaching and then passing searing point, until it entered a new realm for which he had no words. Seeing the look on his face, Tim advised, 'You shouldn't stay in here more than twenty minutes at a time.'

'Twenty? I don't think I can last two. My God, it's like a blast furnace.'

'The thermometer says it's 120 Celsius.'

'That's impossible! We'd be dead!'

'Nah: when you came in you were insulated by the cold water. But as it evaporates you start to sweat. It opens up the pores in your skin and sweats out all the grease and toxins. When you go back into the lake it washes them away and the heat insulates you from the cold.'

'It would take six frogman suits and a heated codpiece to insulate me from that! Shit, this is getting to be more than I can bear already.'

Ricky made to get up but his friend restrained him. 'Not now. Wait until the *loulou's* passed.'

'The what?'

Tim pointed to a man who had just lumbered to his feet and dipped the ladle into the water bucket. 'When he throws that on the stones, it'll create a wave of humid air that feels twenty degrees hotter than hell. If you're moving for the door when it hits, you'll think you're on fire.'

Even as he spoke, the water exploded on the hot stones with a whoosh and Ricky braced himself for...he knew not what. And nothing happened. He was starting to relax again when Tim whispered, 'When it hits, don't fight it. Try to open yourself to it.'

Too late. Out of nowhere his whole body was enveloped in the most incredible, invasive heat. His very eyelids burned and but for Tim's warning he'd have run for the door in panic.

'Breathe through your mouth, not your nose,' Tim advised as the wave slowly subsided. And then, 'Ready to go back to the lake?'

'Yes! Let's get out of here!'

Once outside, Tim mentioned as if in passing, 'You did pretty well, considering that this place only attracts the real hard core. Most of them have been going in through the ice all winter.'

'You mean you brought me here to hang out with a bunch of strength-through-joy fanatics? Jesus, friends like you! And now I suppose you're going to tell me that jumping into this lake is a lot easier the second time?'

'No, the second time is the worst. You know what to expect.'

He was right about that: and yet once actually in the water it no longer felt so paralysingly cold; and once back in the sauna he was able to sit contentedly on the bottom tier, watching with interest as the droplets vanished from his body.

Then Tim shattered his reverie by asking, 'Just how much do you know about these relatives of yours?'

Ricky looked at him in surprise, then shrugged. 'Nothing, really. I don't even know who else lives there, besides my sister.'

'You haven't contacted them at all, apart from that one phone call?'

'I wrote as well but I never got a reply.'

'So you don't know for sure that she's actually there.'

'She must be! Her name and address were the last thing my mum gave me. She didn't have much else to leave but I can tell you, discovering you have a sister beats all.'

'She never spoke about her before?'

'Never. And God knows I asked about our family often enough.'

'You don't have any idea why she never told you?'

'No. I don't know what happened back then but it must have been pretty bad to make her refuse to talk about it, even after all those years.'

'Your father deserted her. I'd call that pretty bad, wouldn't you?'

'Right: but it doesn't explain why she never told me about my sister.'

'Maybe your father got custody.'

'Maybe. All I know for sure is that mum hid her existence from me all my life. And she wasn't the only one. When I was a kid I used to ask my gran about our family history and I got the impression she'd hoped to be safely in her grave before I was old enough to raise the subject.'

They fell silent for a while, stumped for anything further to say. Then an old Finnish guy walked over to the bucket and filled the ladle to the brim.

'This is going to be a big one.'

Ricky closed his eyes to the all-encompassing fire bath and this time it felt as if he was being cooked alive. Somehow he managed to hold on until it abated and then he ran for the lake, which extinguished him like a hot coal.

As he emerged, Tim decided it was time to show mercy. 'In future we'll go to the sauna in town. They never heat it above 100 degrees.'

'No frozen lake?'

'Heated swimming pool.'

'Wimp heaven.'

By the time they were towelling down, there was a warm, tingling sensation seeping through Ricky's body: and when they emerged into the sunshine he was conscious of feeling tangibly clean. Secretly he thought he might even get into it, given time: but then a chill gust off the lake took his mind straight back to his mother's graveside in Edinburgh.

The wind off the North Sea had been so bitter that even the grave diggers had retreated to their bothy. Ricky had been so ill he barely made it to the church and the cold had brought on such a coughing fit that he feared his lungs might haemorrhage. They had to halt the service to let him recover. Well, what passed for the service, anyway: the only other mourners had been the minister and a couple of his mother's old work colleagues. Apart from Ricky there was not a single family member left to see her off.

'Do you know the most consistent characteristic of my family, Tim? They're all dead. They're always bloody dead. But not this time. This time they're alive - and they're here, in this city. I can feel it.' He stared at his friend almost belligerently, as if challenging him to doubt it. There didn't seem to be anything else to say, so they went to find his sister.

The two of them stopped across the road from number 221 and stood for some time observing it. It was an ordinary house in an ordinary street. Presently Ricky went over and rang the doorbell. Tim joined him and after awhile he rang again.

'When did you phone them?'

'A couple of days ago. Perhaps they're out.'

'Looks like it.'

'I should have got you to ring first. Maybe we should leave a note.'

'Let's ask the neighbours.'

Ricky was suddenly unsure of himself. He could feel the depression lapping around the edges of his mind and he began to think this had been a mistake. Tim went next door, leaving Ricky shuffling his feet as he listened to the doorstep conversation in this impenetrable language that was supposed to be his own. But the shaking head was clear in any tongue.

'He says there's never been anyone of that name living there.'

'What? Is he sure?'

'Yes. He's been here fifteen years and the people who used to live next door were here when he arrived. They were called Karlsholm and they moved out two years ago.'

'Shit.'

'Yeah. He doesn't have a forwarding address but he says they moved to Turku after their elderly mother got sick.'

'Who answered the phone, then?'

'There's a new family living there now. They don't speak English.'

'But they might have a forwarding address, right?'

'Yes but they're away on holiday for two weeks.'

'Oh great.' Ricky slumped his shoulders in defeat. 'I guess that's it then.'

Tim watched him resignedly, knowing it was useless to try and pep him up when he was like this. But as they were leaving the neighbour called them back - and this time Tim returned with a glimmer of hope.

'His wife just reminded him that the daughter of the family who lived here before *was* called Satu - and he reckons she's still in town. He doesn't know where she's living but he's seen her around a couple of times.'

'Satu? The daughter's name is Satu?'

'Yes. But Satu Karlsholm, not Suomalianen. Katerina Satu Karlsholm. He said something strange about it. Apparently her grandmother always called her Katerina but she only ever answered to Satu.'

'That can't be a coincidence, surely?'

But what did it mean? He'd never heard of any relatives called Karlsholm: and if she was the one he was looking for, why would his mother have called her Satu Suomalainen? Unless she'd married, of course. He sent Tim back one more time but although the neighbour was wonderfully patient, in the end he shook his head. Ricky was left not knowing whether to feel downcast or hopeful.

The only possible explanations seemed to be: 1) that his mother had got the address wrong; 2) that his sister had married into the Karlsholm family; or 3) that Satu Karlsholm had married someone who *was* a Suomalainen.

If he had the wrong address then he could probably find the right one from a few simple enquiries. The second option didn't fit: the girl who had lived there was the daughter of the house, not their daughter-in-law. And if Satu Karlsholm had married a Suomalainen, why would his mother send him to her, instead of directly to his sister? Maybe she was some kind of go-between? But that wasn't what her note said. It was more than he could fathom.

Yet he had to find her. Somewhere out there was a girl of his own blood. A girl who could make him feel no longer so terribly alone. A girl who could help him to understand what had driven his mother away from this country with such a legacy of bitterness that twenty years had not formed so much as a scab across the wound.

Despite the confusion over the address, he was starting to feel a strange certainty that he would find her. None of the difficulties amounted to anything by comparison with the one enormous fact: he had a sister. The thought lifted him so much that he presently realised he must be grinning like an idiot, judging by Tim's ironic smile.

'Happy now?'

'Yes, thank you.'

'Can we go on?'

Ricky nodded and Tim indicated the road ahead. 'There's something I want to show you on the way back.'

'Don't tell me: we jump in buckets of ice and then dance over hot coals.'

'No - but if you ever have grandchildren, this is something you'll want to tell them about.'

'My chances of having grandchildren just got baked and frozen to the point of negligibility: but what the hell, in for a penny, in for a pound.'

Tim led off along a pathway that angled down towards the lake. Ricky brought up the rear, so engrossed in his thoughts that he didn't notice where they were going until his feet started to sink into soft, white sand. Looking up, he gaped in surprise. Curving off to the right was a perfect crescent beach, while to the left a peninsula of glacially smoothed rocks reached out like a jetty. The cove was fringed by a grassy glade, with a backdrop of pine trees rising up to a wooded ridge. Tim went a few yards down the beach, then turned and stretched out his arms. 'Welcome to Finland.'

'You said that already. But this *is* different.'

Carefully folding his jacket, Ricky flopped down right where he was. After a while he took off his shoes and socks and ran his toes through the sand. It was so fine and dry it ran off his skin like water. As soon as he lay back, the warmth of the sun and the lapping of the lake began lulling him to sleep. Then a series of sharp cracks stirred him to look up again. 'What was that?'

'The ice. It's breaking up in the sun.'

'I can't get over that. It must be nearly thirty degrees and there's still ice on the lake.'

'Go and look in the trees behind you.'

Ricky got up and mounted the grassy bank but he couldn't believe what his eyes were telling him. He had to plunge his hands into it and bring it back down to the beach until it fell from his fingers and still it didn't seem real.

'Snow. It's snow!'

'You're sharp today.'

'Am I dreaming here?'

'Just lie back, close your eyes and think of England.'

He did and a minute later they were both laughing out loud.

'Tim, this is wonderful.'

'A fortnight ago the snow was a foot deep on this beach. It doesn't normally last so long: you'll probably never see this again.'

'I don't believe I'm seeing it now.' He lay back once more and let the sun pour its life-giving warmth into him, feeling the glow of the sauna course through his body as the lake sent its cooling breezes to caress him. He imagined the snow melting beneath the trees, while above him the sky was purest blue. He was adrift in a universe of sensations. He had no idea how long he lay there, fifteen minutes or fifty. Only the fleeting shadow of a passing bird brought him back to wakefulness. 'Will it be gone by tomorrow?'

'Probably. The weather forecast says this hot spell is set for days.'

'Yesterday I felt so sick and tired I was walking around like a zombie. Now I feel like a million dollars. Did we somehow sneak into paradise?'

'Close enough. We're in Finland in May.'

'So where do we go from here? What other treats have you in store?'

'We should get back to Pispala and see my friends about the Carnival.'

'All this and Carnival too.' Ricky took a last look around, marvelling. Then they went on up the hill.

CHAPTER 10

One of the traits Ricky most deplored in himself was the way he became uptight on first meeting people. He could be in a perfectly relaxed mood, at one with all creation; but introduce him to someone and he'd suddenly start saying inane things in a loud voice and laughing like a hyena. It was as if he had a demented doppelganger, whose mission was to jump out at parties and ensure that his alter ego came across as a complete prat.

But on this day Mr Doppel-Ganger must have been asleep. They got to the big house where Tim's friends lived. They pushed open the wicket in the paling fence, calling out 'Hei' as they entered. They crossed the lawn to the bench where two guys and a girl were sitting in the shade of a tree. They went and stood in front of them and Tim started the introductions and Ricky was thinking, 'Here it comes', just waiting for the familiar tightening of muscles that would announce the onset of prattling nerd syndrome.

One of the symptoms was that Ricky didn't take in peoples' names when they were introduced. It didn't matter if there was one person or ten, he'd forget them instantly. The names didn't even go in one ear and out the other: they never made it past the audio filters that were a key part of the condition.

Yet this time he not only heard their names but a minute later he could still remember them. He was so stunned that he sat down beside the girl without waiting to be invited and when she said, 'Would you like a beer?' he just nodded and took it from her as naturally as if she was an old mate.

Naturally? An old mate? This girl? He'd been separated from girls at the age of eleven and not reintroduced to them until adulthood: for most of his teens, girls like her had been present only on the inside of locker room doors.

Now, with a detachment that felt as if someone else was doing it, he noticed how her hair looked blonde in the sun but light brown in the dappled shade of the tree. She had soft, blue-green eyes that were slightly lined around the edges, in a way he would normally have associated with an older woman who smiled a lot. Anna. Her name was Anna. It was amazing. He was looking her straight in the eye and he could actually remember her name.

'Thanks, Anna.'

Good grief, was that it? No gawky stupidity, no crass compliment? Just, 'Thanks, Anna'? She could have been his *sister*. But then he found out there was more. The doppel-ganger wasn't asleep, he was alive and well and a totally reformed character who could engage a pretty girl in conversation only two minutes after meeting her. 'This is such a nice garden. Do you all live here?'

'Yes, except for Harri and he's always here anyway. Is this your first visit to Finland?'

'Yes it is.'

'Well, you are very welcome.'

She moved over to give him more room and he got himself comfortably settled, beer in hand and feeling that life could be a lot worse. Sitting in the shade on a hot, sunny day, with a friendly girl beside him and no pressure to perform: if this was a typical Finnish Saturday, then he might just relocate.

The two guys exchanged some words in Finnish and Anna, mindful of their guest, turned to explain. 'We're planning a carnival here tomorrow, you must come!'

'Yes, Tim told me about it, it sounds fun. But I'm afraid I don't have anything to wear.'

'Oh, we can easily find you something, can't we, Harri?'

'Sure, no problemo,' drawled the Finn, who must have honed his English on a thousand Hollywood movies.

Ricky had taken one look at Harri and thought, 'Greek God'. Besides the standard blue eyes and blonde hair, he was built like one of those sculptures the ancient Greeks created to demonstrate the perfect male form. He even smiled like a hero. It was all Ricky could do not to take an instant dislike to him.

'Hey, Pekka,' Harri continued, 'what about that English hat you found?'

As if set off by a trigger, the other guy gave a barking laugh and smacked the table with his palm, saying something that provoked general mirth.

'Excuse me,' he said once he'd calmed down, 'I'm being very rude.'

'That's OK.'

'No, I shouldn't laugh at you without sharing the joke, it's not nice.'

Pekka was a slightly built guy with long mousy hair and a rather aquiline nose. His John Lennon shades made him look like a hangover from the Hippy era and there was something alluringly dirty about him. Ricky suspected he'd be very successful with pretty, well brought up girls who were attracted to dissolution. He could imagine them swearing they'd rather die than sleep with him, all the way to the bedroom door.

To his surprise, Ricky discovered that he had to acknowledge the apology before Pekka could be induced to continue. But once he did, the guy quickly became effusive.

'I have been going through the attic looking for outfits for the carnival and I found an old hat, like the English wear to work. We were discussing how none of us looked right in it, when you arrived.'

'What is it, a bowler?'

'That's it!' Pekka hit the table again. 'A bowler hat, I couldn't remember the name, it was driving me crazy.'

'I'd need an umbrella, too: and a copy of The Times.'

Evidently the Finns didn't get irony. In fact for some reason his suggestion caused the whole assembly to fall about in hysterics.

'I can lend you an umbrella,' Anna said, 'but what about the paper?'

'I've got a copy of *The Times*,' announced Tim, blithely. 'I get a copy sent over once a week, for my English classes.'

'You closet Tory.' Looking around at their faces, Ricky realised there was no escaping it, so he sighed acceptance. 'Ah well, it's good to know I'll be giving so much amusement.'

'You'll be perfect!' concluded Pekka, beating out a tattoo of delight on the tabletop. 'Pispala's very own Englishman!'

'Shall I stick a Union Jack in my hat as well?'

'Oh, don't worry,' said Anna, finally picking up on his tone, 'you don't have to if you don't want.'

'I'm going as a big vegetable,' added Harri.

Ricky said nothing to this. He couldn't recall it ever having come up in conversation before and he was at a loss for a suitable reply.

'And I will be a Turkish belly dancer,' said Anna, fluttering her hands above her head. 'So you see, everyone will be dressed up.'

'What about Tim?'

'I thought I'd go as a tree.'

Ricky regarded them all with a false but convincing gravitas, then flashed a smile and raised his beer. 'Of course, I'd be delighted.' Then he did his best to change the subject. 'Tell me, Harri, what do you do?'

'I'm a builder.'

'Harri built his own house,' said Anna, with a certain pride.

'Really? That must be very satisfying.'

'It's not so unusual here,' Harri observed. 'I built my house in four months with some friends and my cousin.'

'Do you have your own company?'

Harri laughed. 'No, I work for a big company who are building all over southern Finland.'

Harri's statement quite smashed Ricky's preconceptions. To his English mind, the house, the garden and the obvious education of the three Finns placed them squarely in the middle class. 'You don't live here with the others?'

'No, I live in town but Anna is my cousin so I am here quite often.'

'Oh, I see!' Ricky looked at Anna with new eyes. 'So you helped build the house?'

'Yes, I have been making the windows.'

'Anna is quite a good carpenter.'

'Wow. You're not a builder, too?'

'No, I am a nurse.'

'Right. A nurse who builds houses in her spare time. And what do you do, Pekka? Rocket science?'

'Pekka's the one I told you about who's studying Finnish-Russian politics at the university.'

'Oh, right. That's great: maybe you can answer some questions for me about the war?'

It was as if a dark cloud had passed across the sun.

'What a terrible subject!' exclaimed Anna. 'Why would anyone want to know about that?'

Ricky could only stutter, 'Um, I'm just interested in Finnish history, that's all. I was hoping you could tell me about some of the things that happened back then.'

'Sure, if you want,' said Pekka coolly.

Fortunately Tim was ever alert to the need for diplomatic intervention. 'Ricky's trying to trace his family here in Finland and he thinks some of them may have been killed in the war.'

'Your family is Finnish?' asked Pekka, one eyebrow arching into sight above his shades.

'Yes, partly. Actually I was born here.'

'Oh, but why didn't you say?' cried Anna. 'Maybe we can help you find some of your relatives!'

There was a brief silence while the Finns exchanged glances. Ricky sensed that they were forming a judgement on whether or not this outweighed the offence he had given to some unspoken credo.

'Welcome home,' said Harri at last.

That was the moment when Ricky realised that the most important thing of all had just happened: he had been accepted.

'Thank you.'

'Is your mother Finnish or your father?' asked Pekka.

'Both. My mother was half Finnish and half Scottish.'

'Oh, but then you are really a Finn!' said Anna, beaming at him.

'Not really, I'm afraid. We left when I was just a toddler. I don't remember anything about it.'

'You don't speak any Finnish?' queried Pekka.

'Only a very little. My grandmother used to speak it when I was young.'

Anna gave him a smile of encouragement, 'And have you planned to meet with some of your relatives?'

'I hope so. This morning we went to what I thought was my sister's address but there was some kind of confusion. It seemed to be the wrong place. I'm not sure what to do next.'

'You have a sister here in Finland?'

'Yes - but I've never met her.'

'But that is wonderful!' Anna directed an excited babble of Finnish at the others, who were now looking at Ricky with obvious interest.

'We will help you.' The announcement, from Harri, was delivered as a statement of fact, undemonstrative and unequivocal. Ricky saw the same acceptance on all their faces and it brought a lump to his throat.

'Thank you.'

'You are very welcome. But now, we have a carnival to organise...'

As the day wore on the visitors grew more numerous and the discussions more animated, until presently Ricky leant back against the tree and closed his eyes, listening to the babble of Finnish as if it was the buzzing of bees. A little later he got up and went for a walk, wandering down the garden to a point where he could get a view of the lake.

Presently Pekka came over and handed him the bowler.

'Oh, right, thanks.' Ricky put it on, secretly pleased that it perched rather than sat on his head, lending him a nicely ludicrous air. They shared a laugh about it, then stood in silence, surveying the view. Finally Ricky asked, 'What's that big island over there?'

'Viikonsaari. There's a restaurant where they sometimes hold concerts: it's quite a good place to visit.'

'There's a ferry?'

'Yes, it goes from the centre of town.'

'OK, I might do that later in the week. Thanks.'

Pekka grunted and turned to go but Ricky stopped him. 'Excuse me but Anna said you could help me find my sister and I was wondering how, exactly. I thought perhaps there might be some kind of public record office?'

'That's right, it's called the Pastor's Office. It started through the Swedish Church but it has become the record system for the whole country.'

'Do you think I'll be able to find her there?'

'I should think so. The records are very comprehensive and it's quite easy to use, everything's computerised.'

'Do I have to make an appointment?'

He shook his head. 'On Monday I'll take you down there and introduce you to the guy who runs it. We were at college together.'

'That's fantastic! Thanks!'

Pekka nodded as if this was very routine and Ricky, more than satisfied, walked back with him to rejoin the others.

'Now we have a real Englishman!' declared Harri, seeing him approach.

'Yes,' said Anna, 'It's perfect. But now we must decide where to eat. Why don't we go to the fish restaurant?'

'I don't know,' said Tim, looking at Ricky. 'It's pretty rough.'

'So? I can take care of myself.'

To his irritation, everyone laughed.

'Ricky,' said Pekka, 'that restaurant is run by three middle-aged women because no man could control the kind of customers they get.'

'Why should that bother me any more than you?'

'Well,' said Tim, 'I'm not the one wearing a bowler hat.'

CHAPTER 11

Their way took them down steep scrambles between the houses, to an outcrop where an old factory perched high above the lake. It struck a chord in Ricky from some half-forgotten holiday with his mother. He remembered holding her hand as they peered down into a deep gorge, while the setting sun cast long shadows over the derelict mills below.

'It's a textile mill,' replied Pekka to his unspoken question. 'It's our main industry here.'

'It looks English.'

'Actually,' said Tim, 'it was built by a Scot called Farquarson.'

Ricky got up onto a rock and scanned the far shore, where half a dozen similar red-brick chimneys punctuated the skyline. As he did so, the nearby mill started to turn a glorious reddish-gold in the evening sun.

'Is it still working?'

'Oh yes,' said Anna. 'I have two girlfriends working here. They made this scarf. They make clothes of all kinds. They are quite chic.'

'So it's a big employer?'

'Yeah,' said Tim. 'Speak to any girl in Tampere and if she's not a student, it's a safe bet she works in one of the mills.'

Ricky nodded absently, then jumped back down beside them. They descended the ridge to the point where it met the town and made their way to an unpretentious building in a side street. Inside there was a single large room with an open counter at the back that gave access to the kitchen, where the women who owned the place dispensed beer, food and menus with no-nonsense cheerfulness.

Ricky looked at the menu and couldn't understand a single word. Harri saw his expression and grinned. 'We have 300 types of fresh water fish that live nowhere else.'

'Right. Why don't you order for me?'

'Good idea,' agreed Harri. 'Beers for everyone?' He spoke to one of the women at the counter, who presently slopped an overflowing glass in front of each of them, including Anna. Ricky's surprise was unguarded enough to make her laugh with her lips to the glass, so that she blew beer all over the table.

'What is wrong with your face?' she said, wiping the froth from her mouth.

'I'm sorry?'

'You have such a face. You look as if you have seen something terrible.'

'I'm sorry, it's just that I'm not used to girls drinking pints.'

'What is a pints?'

'A beer. A big beer, a half-litre.'

'Oh.' She gazed into his eyes with a very serious expression and he knew with horrible certainty what was coming. 'What sort of beer should we drink?'

He shifted uncomfortably. 'Um, any sort you like, I suppose.'

'Well, thank you, that is very kind.'

'It's just that in England we have a sort of convention that girls only drink half pints - small beers - if they drink beer at all.'

'Oh, so pints are for men.'

'Well, yes.'

She suddenly raised her voice, in case there was anyone on the table who hadn't heard them. 'So, I shall be a man for tonight. When I want to be a woman again I can buy a small beer. That is very convenient. But don't you have any other way of telling the difference between a man and a woman?'

'I think I'd like to die now, please.'

'Oh no, don't do that. You must live so you can tell me if I do anything else that is not like a woman.'

'Oh shit.'

'Anna Fifteen, Ricky Love,' intoned Tim. 'Kippis!'

'Kippis!' Everyone raised their glasses and took on beer.

'Kippis is Cheers, right?' said Ricky, for something to say.

'Yes but sometimes we say Skol,' said Anna, nudging him in a friendly fashion. It's Swedish but we use both.'

The meal arrived in time to grant him a reprieve from further embarrassment. It was hearty fare and he hid his face in it until he felt safe enough to try again. 'You're a nurse, then?' he opened as they were about to order another round.

'Yes, a lady nurse, so this time I will just have a small, woman beer.'

'I surrender. Don't shoot me any more.'

'OK, I accept.'

'Just a small one, Anna?' asked her cousin in English.

'Yes, thank you, Harri.'

'Ricky?'

'I'll be a woman, too.'

'OK. Two women and three men? That's good.'

'Yes, now whenever we go drinking we will always think of Ricky and your man beers and woman beers.'

'Right but now tell me about your job, *please*.'

'Oh, you want to change the subject?'

'More than life itself.'

She looked at him with her mock-serious gaze, then grinned and relented, chinking glasses with him to seal it. 'OK. I am working with women who are having babies, I am not sure how you are saying this in English.'

'You work in a hospital maternity ward?'

'No, not in a hospital. I am working mostly in the community.'

'Oh, so you're a midwife?'

'Is it so?'

'Yes. Delivering babies with mothers at home? We call it midwifery.'

Anna giggled at the unfamiliar term. 'Well, it is the first time anyone has been calling me this. Midwifery. That is quite a funny word. Hello, my name is Anna, I am a midwifery.'

Ricky grinned. 'No, not quite, you are a midwife. Midwifery is the specialism.'

'Is it so? Perhaps you would like to come round to my house sometime and teach me more of these funny English phrases?' And with that she gave him a comic-raunchy look that he found impossible to distinguish from the real thing.

'I'd love to. When would be convenient?'

'Tuesday. Four o'clock on Tuesday would be convenient.'

It was the easiest date he'd ever made but it never occurred to Ricky that she was being anything more than friendly. The idea that women might find him attractive was such an unfamiliar concept that he didn't recognise the evidence of it, even when she was sitting next to him, knocking back a pint and inviting him round for tea. Ricky hadn't had too many girlfriends.

A couple of minutes later Anna glanced at her watch and got up to go, pleading final preparations for the carnival. Ricky stood up as she did, provoking wry smiles from the others.

'Fancy her, do you?' smirked Tim the moment she was out the door.

Ricky looked him in the eye and killed all further jibes stone cold dead. 'No,' he said, 'she reminds me too much of me mum.'

CHAPTER 12
July, 1955

She must have read her father's letter a dozen times, searching in vain for some faint glimmer of hope, some tiny crack in the merciless terminology of condemnation. It made her so sick with fright that she had nearly gone back home to try and make peace. In the end, though, TK had persuaded her that time would heal and she had to believe that he was right. She had to believe that both her parents and his would eventually forgive and accept.

It was ironic, really. She had come to Finland imagining that she could reunite the two halves of the family: and the moment their respective parents found out about it, they had united in disowning them.

But she felt in her heart that it would come right in the end. TK always said that he could make anything work out right. And she believed him.

CHAPTER 13
Saturday 16th May, 1981

When they got to the pub they found a line of Finns queuing up outside, like a herd of milch-cows waiting for their turn at the dairy.

'It must be packed solid.'

'Don't worry,' said Tim. 'They limit the numbers, so you have to wait for someone to leave before you can go in.'

As if in confirmation, a couple emerged from the pub and the queue shuffled forward as the doorman waved the next two in.

'How long is this likely to take?'

'Maybe half an hour,' said Pekka. 'If you want to get in without queuing you have to come early.'

'What happens in winter?'

'You get cold.'

'You mean you still have to queue like this?'

'Oh yes. A few months ago I came here when it was minus twenty. The fillings in my teeth froze up and it hurt so much I had to run back home.'

'Jesus, I hope the beer's good.'

'We don't have so many pubs,' added Harri. 'It's not like in England. Here there are only a few and always there are queues.'

'I bet the doorman has a lot of friends.'

They laughed rather bitterly at this and a few minutes later, as if to illustrate the point, a flashily dressed couple got out of a Mercedes and called to the doorman. He looked over and waved them across, there was some hail-fellow-well-met and in they went.

'I hate that, snarled Pekka. 'Some of these doormen are real bastards.'

'I don't get it: I thought Finland was all socialism and equality. What do you have to do, pay him?'

'Lick his arse.'

'No thanks.'

They all laughed, yet once they got inside Ricky began to appreciate the system despite its irritations, for the place was at that perfect point of being crowded but not packed. It was just as well - because he promptly got further lessons in Finnish drinking etiquette. Within two minutes he'd been pushed, jostled and generally treated like a piece of furniture by about a dozen guys, all of them built like brick shit houses. He didn't know whether to fight, shove or scream: but fortunately Tim came to his rescue before he lost it.

'They don't go in much for saying 'excuse me'. You just push past. It's not considered rude.'

'Well it bloody is by me! The next one comes along, I've a good mind to nut him.'

'They'd swat you like a fly. Really, Ricky, there's no side to it. You just have to learn to be very tactful.'

'Well how about ever so tactfully getting me a drink to calm me down?'

'Yeah, alright. You want a big one?'

'Oh yes. You obviously gotta be a man around here.'

'It's called an iso tuoppi. Iso means big.'

'So tuoppi is beer?'

'No. It means a tankard, I think. Beer is olut. If you want a small one you ask for keski olut.'

'And there's no word for please, right?'

Tim chuckled at his annoyance. 'They're very forthright. You can just say "Iso tuoppi" without saying "Please" or "Thank you".'

'Right. Well, gimme an iso tuoppi and make it snappy.'

He obliged and they joined Pekka and Harri standing by a table in the corner. Ricky took one sip and exclaimed, 'This is really tasty!'

'It's also really strong.'

'You'll get completely pissed after three of those,' predicted Tim.

'What were we drinking in the restaurant?'

'Keski olut.'

'Number Three Beer,' enlarged Pekka. 'This is Number Four Beer, it's the strongest.'

'What about Number Two Beer?'

'It does not exist.'

'That's logical. How about Number One, is that an existential joke?'

'Yes, really it is,' laughed Pekka. 'Number One Beer is the most heavily advertised beer in the world, compared to how much of it is drunk.'

'How come?'

'Because it has hardly any alcohol but it is illegal to advertise the strong beers, so the breweries spend a lot of money advertising Number One Beer, which nobody drinks.'

'This country is almost as strange in its drinking laws as England.'

'Yes, it is really stupid,' asserted Pekka.

If Ricky was fooled by this into thinking that Pekka had a worldly-wise view of his country's peculiarities, he was soon corrected. Seeing that they were all close to finishing their glasses, he made to get in the next round, whereupon there was a shocked exchange of glances.

'You don't do that here,' said Tim rather hurriedly.

'Sorry?'

'You don't buy rounds here. It isn't done.'

'How do you mean?'

'It's considered quite insulting to try and buy drinks for other people. You can buy one for a friend but that's the limit.'

From their expressions Ricky surmised he'd done something about as tactful as ordering sherries for a group of Yorkshire miners. 'Oh God. Sorry guys, I didn't realise. In England we always take it in turns to buy drinks for everyone. No offence intended.'

Pekka paused for a moment, then shrugged it aside. 'That's OK. We're not so used to English drinking habits, either.'

Ricky escaped into the crowd by the bar and managed to order another beer without causing any further international misunderstandings. He'd just taken his first swig when the crowd parted and there she was. She looked round almost at once, as if she'd felt his eyes burrowing into the back of her head.

'Hei, Ricky!'

'Satu! It's nice to see you again.'

'You remember my friend Tiina, from the disco? I'm afraid she doesn't speak much English.' She turned to the girl beside her and said something briefly in Finnish. The previous night's row was evidently forgotten, for the other girl giggled and gave him a sly grin. He nodded back and exchanged pleasantries as best he could.

'Look, I'm sorry about leaving like that. It was rude of me.'

'In what way?'

'Well, um, it was a bit sudden.'

'But you had to go with your friend. I hope you have found out where you are staying now?'

'Yes, we're up on the ridge, in a place called Pispala?'

'But that is where I am living!'

'You're joking! Really? If I'd known, we could have gone home together.' He realised the implication even as the words left his mouth, which made him blush, completing his discomfiture. Satu laughed gaily and tapped him on the arm in mock remonstrance.

'So that is what you were thinking after all! And I was imagining you didn't like me! But now we are neighbours, so you must tell me, in what street is Timi living?'

'Pispankatu.'

'But of course, I know this street well! I have many friends there.'

'You do? Brilliant! So whereabouts in Pispala do you live, exactly?'

'At the other end of the village, past the school, beyond the old tower.'

'Right, I think I know where you mean. Are you going to be at the Carnival tomorrow?'

'Yes of course. So, we shall see each other there?'

'Yes, absolutely. But tell me, what are you going as?'

'I'm sorry, I don't understand you.'

'What are you dressing up as?'

'So, I see. Just as myself. But in some colourful clothes.'

'Right. This is all such a coincidence, I mean you living in the same place as Tim and having the same name as my sister.'

'Did you find her yet?'

'No, not yet. It's very strange: I went to this house today, to the address my mother gave me but she wasn't there.'

'Yes? Perhaps it was the wrong address.'

'I guess so. But the strange thing was, there had been a girl called Satu living there a while ago, only she had a different surname.'

She looked at him with sudden intensity. 'What house is this?'

'It's near the railway station: Kirkkokatu 221. The people who used to live there were called Karlsholm: you don't know them, by any chance?'

Something changed in her as he said it. From being all gaiety her face froze like marble. He raised his eyebrows in enquiry but she looked away as if from something unpleasant. When she turned back, her eyes flitted around the room distractedly. With no idea of the cause, Ricky just kept talking.

'The girl who used to live there was called Katerina Satu Karlsholm. But I guess you don't know her?'

'No. I told you, I don't know any other Satus.'

'Right. Sorry. It just struck me as an odd coincidence. I thought it wasn't such a common name.'

'It is not so uncommon, either.'

It was as if a frost had come between them. They fell into an uncomfortable silence and both looked round to see how their companions were faring. He knew he shouldn't let it drag on; but before he'd decided what to say, she turned back to him as if nothing had happened.

'It must be so great to have a brother or sister! My parents have no other children. There is only me.'

'Right. That's what I thought, too.'

'I am not understanding you, Ricky.'

'I mean that like you, I thought I was an only child. My mother only told me I had a sister a few months ago, just before she died.'

Satu's eyes widened into a sea of brilliant blue. 'That is, how do you say this, bizarre?'

'That's how you say it alright. She told me that my sister's name was Satu, like yours, and she gave me the address of the house in Kirkkokatu. But that's all. The rest is a mystery.'

He saw the startled look come back into Satu's eyes and the way her body stiffened; but before he could ponder what it might mean she recoverd herself and the moment passed. Concluding that it was probably safe to continue, Ricky added, 'Maybe she got it wrong, or maybe these Karlsholm people are connected to my sister.'

'Could be. Are you going to try and find them?'

'Yes, of course. I'm going to the record office on Monday, so with any luck the mystery will be solved in a couple of days.'

'On Monday. Yes, I see.'

Ricky thought she seemed distracted: and then it hit him that he'd probably bored her catatonic with all this stuff about his family. He cast around for something else to talk about but once again she pre-empted him.

'Tell me something, Ricky.'

'Yes, of course. What is it?'

Before she could reply a huge Finn barged past them on his way to the bar, shoving Ricky right up against her. He managed not to spill his beer but he had to grasp her by the waist to steady himself and the instant he touched her it felt as if a light turned on inside him. Even the sensation of her hair against his face would have been enough to send a thrill right through him - but a moment later that familiar fragrance of strawberries and fresh straw wafted into his nostrils and he was lost.

Satu glanced at his hand on her waist, then looked up at him from a range of about three inches. As he apologetically stepped back she smiled and said, 'We are not so polite as you.'

'No, well, it's pretty crowded in here. But I'm sorry, you were about to ask me something?'

'So, yes.' She seemed to collect herself, as if needing to prepare for what she was about to ask. 'Ricky, why did your mother only tell you about your sister just before she died? Is it OK that I ask this? Last night you said you had lost your sister but I have not been imagining that it was so strange. I thought perhaps she just left home and so you have lost touch.'

She was interested after all! He did his best to hide his excitement with a shrug. 'I honestly don't know. She hated Finland because my father was a Finn and he deserted her. But other than that, I just don't know.'

He was on the point of explaining further when Tiina returned and the two girls exchanged some rapid-fire Finnish. Satu turned back to him with an expression of regret. 'I'm afraid I have to go now, my friends are leaving. I cannot be ignoring them every night or they will not be my friends much longer!'

He knew he let his disappointment show. 'Oh, yes, of course. But we'll meet tomorrow, right?'

'Yes, at the Carnival.' She regarded him in silence for a second, looking quite grave. Then she laughed and said, 'Until tomorrow, Ricky Finn,' before turning and slipping away through the crowd.

He drifted back to the others on cloud nine.

'You look ridiculously pleased with yourself,' said Tim.

'You could say that. Get us another beer, mate.'

Tim obliged and Ricky suddenly realised he'd been drinking almost continuously since lunchtime. Without the stimulus of Satu's presence there was nothing to counteract the beer's effect and he fell off the edge of his own adrenaline as if off a cliff.

He nearly lost it right there but they got him outside in the nick of time. The way back was a blur, his racing brain unable to process half the images that were whirling through it. Yet even as he nose-dived into sleep, one thing was clear to him: after Satu, nothing could be the same again. And tomorrow his search would start afresh, with not just one Satu to pursue but two. Or was it three? It was weird: the place seemed to be full of Satus.

CHAPTER 14
Sunday 17th May, 1981

After an hour in the town baths Ricky felt better than he had in ages. He couldn't imagine a greater contrast to the cramped seediness of the municipal baths back home, where the fear of swimming had been drilled into him. By the time he returned to Pispala, all trace of his hangover was gone and he was totally up for Carnival.

Any worry he might have had about looking ridiculous was dispelled by the sight of a giant carrot walking up the street just ahead of him. And that wasn't the only unusual sight: the whole of Pispankatu was alive with people in fancy dress, all moving with leisurely purpose in the direction of the school.

By the time he got there quite a crowd had assembled and a band was playing acoustic electric music, half-way between folk and rock. The musicians appeared to have been transported from the Summer of Love, bedecked in an eclectic mix of denim, corduroy and cotton that was reprised throughout the audience. Only a minority wore true fancy dress but everyone had made some concession to the spirit of Carnival.

Ricky soon spotted Anna through the crowd, his eyes drawn by the striking colours of her costume. She wore baggy Turkish pantaloons in vivid purple, a tiny embroidered waistcoat in gold and scarlet - and very little else. Mauve and crimson veils were braided into her hair, cascading about her in a manner at once inveigling and demure. It was a nice belly, he noticed with a thrill of pleasure as she turned and waved in response to her name.

'Hei! I see you are wearing it!'

'Right. Today I march for England.'

'You look very fine.'

'Thank you. I *feel* bloody ridiculous. But you look fantastic. Great waistcoat!'

'Well, thank you. There are many colourful girls here today.'

It was true. All through the crowd, young women had turned out in a fantastic array of costumes. Kaftans, scarves, shawls and ribbons of every hue were moving and flowing with their owners in a riot of colour, made even livelier by a joyful hubbub of laughter and greetings.

Everywhere there were banners and placards. Most were knocked up on old bits of wood or card and Ricky had no idea what any of them said until Pekka turned up bearing the universal sign of nuclear disarmament. He was wearing a tropical suit (minus tie) and a small black fez. With his Trotsky shades he was the caricature of a middle-eastern secret agent.

'Hei, Ricky, Anna.'

'Hei. Have you seen Tim?'

'He's over there, trying to blend in with that group of trees.'

They all looked over and laughed. Tim was standing next to one of the local man-mountains, his lanky frame a perfect foil to the massive bulk of the Finn. His hair, stuck through with a handful of twigs, was just touching the lower branches. It looked as if a bird had started to build a nest on top of his head but then abandoned it after a storm.

'Hei, Tim, mitä kuuluu?' called out Pekka.

'Kiitos hyvää,' the tree replied, waving a branch in their general direction.

'You were being formal to be funny, right?'

Pekka looked at him in surprise. 'You understand that? Of course. Normally we'd just say "Hei".'

'Right. But tell me, is it true there really isn't a word for please?'

'That's right.'

'But there must be, surely?'

'No, not really. We say "Ole hyvä" when we're giving and receiving things but it's not quite the same.'

'That's weird. I never heard of a country before where you couldn't say please.'

'If you think that's odd, did you know the Koreans have no word for "No"?'

'No, really?'

'Really. They have ten ways of saying "Yes" instead. If something is impossible, they say "Yes" very faintly but there is no way of saying an absolute "No" in Korean.'

'Wow! I must get to meet some Korean girls. So tell me, what do all these signs mean?'

'We are making Pispala a nuclear free zone. And some of them say "Independence for Pispala".'

Ricky nodded solemnly and was saved from the need to comment by a general stirring of the crowd, heralding the start of the procession. Pekka and Anna joined the head of the parade, just behind the band and some placard bearers. A beefy musician in blue denims and a woollen cap kicked it off with a leisurely, rolling pace beaten out on a snare drum. As they started off down the street the rest fell in behind, so that the crowd issued forth from itself into a column that soon stretched 200 yards down Pispankatu.

In normal circumstances Ricky's costume would have made him feel a right idiot but compared to those on either side he felt like a thin slice of normality in a sandwich of the bizarre. On his right was the giant carrot and on his left was a fine pantomime dragon, carrying a placard which read 'Kauan Elakoon Pispala ja Rock'. It meant absolutely nothing to Ricky and he was afraid to ask.

'Great day,' said the carrot in English.

'Harri?'

'Yes, it's me,' conceded the carrot. 'Nice suit.'

'Thanks. I like your leaves.'

'Thanks. Anna made them.'

'I thought she liked you?'

The carrot laughed. Ricky had never marched beside a laughing carrot before and it made him feel positively surreal. It was clear that the whole community had turned out, all either marching or lining the route to watch and all with uniform good humour. Ricky couldn't imagine the residents of his neighbourhood in London acting like this: there would have been posturing and petty theft and then a nasty little riot.

It was a long street and the procession ambled along as people called out to friends and generally took their time. It was probably two o'clock when they reached the end of the street but by then Ricky was no longer with them. Half-way there he saw Satu standing by the side of the road and he lost interest in everything else.

She stood out in this crowd as she would in any other. Where brilliance was commonplace, she had a neatly sophisticated style that put her in a class of her own. Beneath a loose knit scarlet shawl she wore a sleeveless white top and scarlet slacks, with simple white shoes. Her hair needed no adornment and she wore almost no jewellery. Ricky thought she looked quintessentially Finnish and in that moment he didn't care if he never found the Satu he had come to search for. He made his way to the edge of the procession, breaking ranks to stop before her at the side of the road.

'Hei, Ricky! You look very English. And you are getting noticed!' She nodded toward the nearby TV crew who were busy snapping up this picturesque cameo of 'typical Englishman greets local beauty in Pispala procession'.

'Fame at last! Do you think we'll make the evening news?'

'Perhaps. Are you coming to the concert?'

'Yes, I thought so. Are you going there now?'

'In a minute. I was hoping to meet some friends but I haven't seen them.'

'Oh, you're by yourself?'

'Yes.'

'Great! I mean, we can go together. If you'd like.'

'That would be nice. Now I have an escort in a funny hat.'

'Ah. Right. Perhaps I should lose the costume?'

'No, it's OK.' She laughed. 'But you can change if you like.'

'It *is* a bit silly, isn't it? Look, Tim's house is right there, why don't I get changed and then we can walk down together?'

She nodded and so they waited until the tail of the procession had passed and then walked over. The door was unlocked and Ricky went to the refrigerator and looked inside. 'Voila! Two beers.'

They clinked bottles and she grinned and said, 'I thought you were going to change your "attire"?'

'Oh yes, I forgot. Won't be a minute.'

He went into Tim's room and closed the door while he got rid of his hat and his funeral jacket. As an afterthought he threaded the tie around his waist in place of a belt, in a style they had often affected at school. Then he went back into the front room, twirling the loose end in his hand and declaring, 'There is never a time when a tie is not appropriate.'

'You are quite difficult to understand. So many double negatives. Is that how English people are normally talking?'

'No. Most of us use much more complex, old fashioned forms of speech.'

'But you are making fun of me, I think.'

'Just a little.'

'OK, we will go to the concert now.' She put her beer down on the table with an empty thud. Ricky looked at it in surprise. Either this girl could drink or she was really thirsty. He took a last swig, left his own beer half finished and opened the door for her.

As Satu went by, her hand brushed his hip and she took hold of the end of his tie, pulling him after her as if on a lead. She didn't say anything, just put her hands in her pockets and led him along. It was incredibly erotic. He did his best to match her insouciant air but the pace was too slow for his gait and he couldn't affect nonchalance with his heart pounding fit to burst.

The procession was out of sight now and the street almost clear of people. Satu began pointing out the houses of her friends as they strolled by.

'Do you live in an old house like these?' he asked.

'No, it is quite new. It is not so pretty but it has everything modern.'

'Hot and cold running water, an inside toilet, that sort of thing?'

'Of course. I even have central heating.'

'Luxury of luxuries! But not so necessary now.'

'No, today it is nice to live in one of these old houses. But in winter it is not so much fun.'

'I bet. How cold does it get?'

'It was minus thirty for a few days this year.'

'Minus thirty! Jesus, I don't know how you cope. In England everything stops if there's even a whisper of snow.'

'But for you it is not usual. We are used to it - but we don't like it so much.'

'It must be wonderful, though, to come through such a long, dark winter and emerge into this.' He gestured at the evidence of spring all around and she turned her head to look at him.

'Yes, it is quite wonderful. We all go a little crazy at this time of year, when you can stay up all night and it is light twenty-four hours a day. Everyone feels full of life. We call it the Summer Madness.'

'And are you mad, too?'

'Oh yes. Quite mad.'

Before he could enquire what form this madness might take, they arrived at a point where the ground fell away to their right through the woods. A coloured tape had been wound between the trees to form a perimeter, guarded at intervals of about twenty yards by people wearing day-glow armbands. Satu gestured towards the woods beyond. 'The concert is down there.'

'At the bottom of this hill?'

'Yes, the sports field is at the bottom, through the trees.' She surveyed the perimeter like someone studying the form at a race meeting. When she had completed her review she gave a little nod to herself and her nose twitched discernibly. 'I don't feel like paying, it's too expensive. I think I will go in the back door.'

'You mean through the trees?'

'Yes. I can run quite fast, I don't think they will catch us.' She looked once more at the stewards, then at him and said simply, 'Come.'

Before he realised what was happening she had released his tie and was gone, ducking under the tape and taking off with sudden, astonishing speed. Even as Ricky negotiated the ribbon and started to follow, he was conscious of her flitting through the trees like a deer. A couple of stewards shouted after her and took off in pursuit. Their reactions were so much faster than his that before he could get properly underway they were already converging to cut him off.

Ricky put on a spurt of speed and leapt over a patch of briars, striving to keep the darting scarlet figure in view as he dodged through the trees. Just as he thought he was going to make it, one of the stewards intercepted him, her arms outstretched to prevent him shouldering past. She was a girl of about twenty, so he could hardly make an issue of it. Slamming on the brakes, he put up his hands in defeat and retreated back up the slope, cursing himself for his slowness. He looked back just in time to see a flash of blonde hair disappearing into the distance and it made him head-butt the nearest tree in frustration. He'd let her slip through his fingers *again*!

And then quite spontaneously he started to laugh, replaying that mental image of Satu running through the forest, fleet as a deer. She must have had twenty yards on her nearest pursuer. That girl could *move*.

It was obvious he should go to the official entrance as quickly as possible and meet up with her inside: but when he got there it was to find that things were not going well. A large crowd had gathered outside the gate, with only a thin trickle of people paying to go in. He found Tim and the others at the front, arguing with the stewards.

'Hei, what's up?'

Tim turned and shrugged. 'It's too expensive. It's supposed to be Pispala's carnival but the concert organisers have made it so expensive that hardly anyone from Pispala is going in.'

'What are you going to do?'

Anna shook her head, looking and sounding very angry. 'It is not right. Everyone is here to have a carnival, to celebrate with really a good spirit and here are some people who just want to make money out of them.'

'Yeah,' agreed Tim, 'It's ridiculous.' Aside to Ricky he said, 'They're really pissed off. Apparently the concert organisers never agreed the price with the carnival committee and now they're having a real set-to about it.'

'Capitalist entrepreneurs not welcome, huh?'

'Yeah.'

'Satu's in there. She gatecrashed. I got caught.'

'Careless of you.'

'Very. And now I suppose I have to sacrifice love and lust for friendship and principle?'

'Yeah.'

He did his best to put a brave face on it, turning with a smile to the huddle of glums beside him. 'Well, at least we can still see the band from here. They can't make us pay for that, eh?'

He regretted his words immediately. So many of the crowd had been craning over the heads of the stewards to see the stage that a large panel van was brought up and parked across the entrance, completely blocking the view. Rising to the occasion, Ricky gave the van driver two good English fingers and turned back to his friends. 'So, stuff their concert, what else is there to do in this town? More to the point, what is there to eat? I'm starving.'

Pekka slapped his thigh and laughed, his anger dissipating as if it had never been. 'He's right! Let's make a picnic and get the band from Pispala and have a concert of our own.'

'OK,' said Harri, 'We can get some beers and eat in the garden.'

'This is really a good idea,' beamed Anna. 'We can all go back to our houses and bring some food.'

'Yes and everyone must bring something to drink!' cried another.

'This is turning into a fucking Enid Blyton story,' muttered Tim under his breath.

'Shut up and smile, Noddy,' breathed Ricky through clenched teeth. 'I'm the one with something to moan about. And do you see me moaning? Not me. I've got my happy face on.'

They went back to the house and cleared out the fridge, meeting up again in the garden of Anna's house, where Harri was busy sorting out a mobile barbecue. Ricky handed over his two bottles of duty-free white Rioja to Pekka, who was managing the bar. It provided only half a glassful for each of them, which seemed embarrassingly short measure, but actually the chilled Rioja made a very fair aperitif. Moreover his offering seemed to set off a chain reaction, almost akin to the feeding of the 5,000. Everyone brought out their own secret stash and all of a sudden the place was knee-deep in nosh and grog.

The Finns only seemed to have one sort of item to put on the barbecue: strings of evil looking sausage that Ricky eyed with overt suspicion. Seeing his expression, Harri held one up on a fork for inspection. 'This is Grilli Makkara,' he announced, as if that explained everything.

'We usually eat them at Midsummer,' added Pekka. 'They're a Finnish delicacy.'

In Ricky's experience national delicacies were the culinary expression of the dark side of the national psyche but he nodded politely and watched the steady stream of people coming in off the street, each bringing at least half a crate of beer.

'They stock it away for a rainy day,' Tim commented. 'The Finns just love drinking.'

Pekka nodded his agreement. 'In England, if you want to get a laugh all you have to do is mention sex: any comedian can reduce an English audience to hysterics with even the most childish sexual innuendo. Here in Finland you can do the same thing with drinking. If a Finnish comedian gets up on stage and staggers about pretending to be drunk, the audience will fall out of their chairs.'

'It's whatever you can't get,' asserted Tim.

'Yes,' agreed Anna, 'the English are quite inhibited about sex I think: but we in Finland are very mixed up about alcohol because it is so difficult to buy.'

'Really?' said Ricky, raising the bottle up to his lips and drawing a cheer of laughter that confirmed Pekka's thesis with a single swig.

'That's right,' said Harri. 'Most towns in Finland have just one state-run alko where you can buy alcohol and it shuts before every public holiday.'

'In country places,' added Anna, 'people have to drive fifty kilometres to buy their supply, so of course they buy huge amounts and then drink for two or three days until it's all gone.'

'I'll drink to that!' shouted someone, to widespread mirth.

'But why is it so restricted, if everyone loves to drink?'

'They don't,' said Anna. 'Many people in Finland are not drinking at all. But they are making the laws for the rest of us.'

'It's like this,' Tim said quietly, 'half the population drink nothing and the rest drink like madmen.'

'It used to be just the same in Scotland!' exclaimed Ricky. 'Then they changed the law to let the pubs stay open all day and alcohol related crime fell by half. The way to deal with drinking is to let people behave like adults, instead of treating them like children.'

'That's right!' Pekka almost shouted his agreement. 'If you treat people like children they act like children. It's so fucking patronising.'

This led to such a chorus of assent that the conversation extinguished itself, leaving Ricky free to try the infamous Grilli Makkara. Anna came and stood beside him and they bit off bits of sausage and munched away in companionable silence. To Ricky's relief it was unexceptionable, really nothing more than an oversized Frankfurter.

'I'm sorry that you were not able to find your sister yesterday. Would you like to tell me something more about your family?'

'There's not much to tell.'

'Well, that is usually the beginning of a long story. You said yesterday that you are half Finnish and half Scottish but I think really you are three quarters Finnish?'

'Right. My mother was half-Scottish and my father was all Finn.'

'You hated him.'

'I still do. Funny, really, hating someone you've never met. He left us when I was still only a baby. That's when my mother took me to Scotland.'

'You have been brought up there?'

'I went to school there but I left as soon as I could. My mother married a Scot and he tried to make me Scottish, too. We never really got on, so of course I resisted that absolutely. Anything Finnish was treated as if it was dirty, so being English was the only way to go.'

'Your mother never talked to you about your family here in Finland?'

'No. The little I know I learned from my grandmother.'

'Timi has told me that your mother died recently. I am very sorry, Ricky.'

'It's OK. It was a while ago now.' He gave an ironic laugh. 'I'm through the 'shock phase' and the 'immobilising grief phase' and the 'anger phase'. I'm told that I'm entering the 'coming-to-terms-with-it phase' and can look forward to the 'fond remembrance phase'.

The problem is that mostly what I remember is the last few months and those remembrances aren't fond. She died of cancer, Anna: it's not a pretty death.'

'No, it is not.'

He saw the nurse's knowledge in her face and gave her a grim smile in recognition of shared experience. 'Something happened here that made her leave and never have any further contact with the place. Even after twenty years she hadn't forgiven - and even dying she wouldn't tell me what it was. Most of all I think I want to know what caused that pain.'

Anna was motionless, not mewing sympathy, just quietly absorbing what she heard. 'You have no other family in England?'

'No. My family have a remarkable capacity for dying off. In a hundred years I don't think there's been a male among us who made it past sixty.'

'And the female ones?'

'My grandmother made it to seventy-two. It's only because of her that I even know my real name: otherwise I think my mother would have pretended we had no Finnish connection at all. I had to call myself Carr until my stepfather died. This probably sounds awful but it was a relief when he died and I could take my real name back.'

'You have quite a lot of bitterness, I think.'

'Yes. Maybe. I don't know. Sometimes it's difficult not to feel pathetically sorry for myself. Sometimes I feel angry at people for dying on me all the time. Even my mother. I loved her so much and then she died like all the rest and I discovered that I'd never really known her at all; that she had a whole secret life I knew nothing about.' He smiled thinly, for it had been a lie to say he was past the anger phase.

'I think I feel the same way people did after the Titanic went down. Everything they felt certain about suddenly sank beneath them and afterwards they couldn't feel certain about anything ever again.'

'Have you tried to find your real father?'

'No. Sometimes I get curious but I've spent a lifetime hating him and it would be awkward to find out he's not really that bad. I prefer the familiar ogre.'

'Then we will have to help you find your sister, I think.'

'Thank you again for offering. Do you think there's anything else we can do, besides going to the Pastor's Office?'

'I think so. There are not so many Suomalainens: maybe we can find the right ones - and Satu is not such a common name.'

'I was wondering about that. I've encountered two of them already - and my mother told me it was the family name. I was beginning to think it must be as common as Catherine or Jane.'

'Well, it is not a rare name but there cannot be so many people called Satu Suomalainen. We will ask around. Finland is not so big like England and even Tampere is not such a big town. We will find your family, Ricky.'

Having the thing he most wanted offered so freely made him feel self-conscious but Anna seemed to read his mind, distracting him by suggesting they get another beer. She took his arm as they walked over to the house and the easy familiarity of it caught him by surprise - although he did his best to hide it.

'There is quite an English invasion here just now,' she observed. There has been an English football team here the last few weeks and now there is a Shakespeare play at the summer theatre.'

'Really? Which one?'

'A Midsummer Night's Dream. It is meant to be very good - there are some quite fine Finnish actors taking part.'

'It's in Finnish?'

'Yes but the Director is from Czechoslovakia. He is quite famous, he made a film about trains. Hmm, I'm not sure what it is called in English but in Finnish it is something like Watching Trains Carefully.'

'Closely Observed Trains!'

'Is it so?'

'Yes, I can't remember his name, though.'

'Vaclav Neckar.'

'That's it! So he's here in Tampere directing this play?'

'Yes. Would you like to see it?'

'Absolutely. Well, I suppose so. It's in Finnish, though?'

'Well, yes but you will still know the story of course and it is in the open air theatre; you cannot leave Tampere without seeing this place!'

'OK, done! I'd love to go. Is it easy to get tickets?'

'Yes, I can get them. I have been thinking of going on Wednesday.'

'Great. Is anyone else coming?'

'No, I was going alone but it will be more fun to go with an Englishman.'

At that point they bumped into Tim, who instantly demanded, 'You bin chatting up this bird then?'

'Yeah mate. Got me a date.'

'You're always getting dates with her. Why don't you ask someone else for a change, like that Satu you've got the hots for? Oops, did I queer your pitch?'

Anna giggled. 'When are you going to ask me out, Timi?'

'I've told you before, I don't go out with midgets.'

'Well, that is really a shame. I will just have to keep making dates with Ricky.'

They clinked bottles and chatted away happily. Looking around the garden, serene in the dusk, it was beyond him how his mother could have failed to love this country. He was feeling more confident now that he would find his sister but he was having doubts about the other part of his quest. Perhaps it might be wiser not to find out too much about the cause of his mother's torment. Some things were better left alone and he wanted to make up his own mind about his native land, without any interference from her unforgiving spirit.

If there was any hint of smugness about this train of thought, an instant later it vaporised. He was listening to Anna and Tim sharing a joke when he caught a glimpse of something that caused the blood to freeze in his veins. A figure was passing by in the shadowed half-light of the street. He started to cry out her name but it choked in his throat and a chill swept over him, as if the cool night air had turned to icy fog.

The others seemed unaware of what was happening. Behind them, the figure walked through a beam of light from the house. As it did so the hair turned from blonde to red and the face seemed to take on an air of terrible sadness. In that moment it was no longer the woman he had lost in the woods but the one he had lost in the cancer ward.

He tried to tell himself that it must be just a trick of the light. He didn't believe in ghosts and he could only suppose that an unholy mix of grief and alcohol must be causing him to hallucinate. But that didn't stop his skin from crawling.

He went up the garden filled with a mix of longing and terror. By the time he reached the fence and looked out after her, the street was empty. Anguish and relief rose so strongly in his gorge that he threw up a stomach-full of beer.

He had to steady himself on the fence and take in great gulps of air before the palpitations calmed. By the time he had recovered enough to rejoin the others Ricky knew for sure that it could never have been enough to search only for his sister. If he was ever to have any peace, he had to keep faith with his mother, too. He had to lay her troubled soul to rest before he could rid himself of the anger and uncertainty that he felt every time he thought of her.

Tomorrow, he told himself. Tomorrow the Pastor's Office would be open. Tomorrow he would discover the truth.

CHAPTER 15
September, 1955

―――

She couldn't believe how soon autumn was upon them. One look at the colours on Pynikki ridge brought to mind the fable of the cricket and the ant. She and TK had been chirping away merrily all summer as if the money would never run out; as if people whose parents had disowned them didn't have to get jobs to support themselves. But now summer was over and it was time to be an ant.

The leaves had started to turn even before the end of August. Every day the crispness in the air was a little bolder and snapped out a little more briskly as the sun's rays departed. She had noticed it the first time she came to Pispala, looking for work.

She had gone to the textile mill below Pynikki ridge as her last hope. There wasn't a job to be had in the whole of Tampere, least of all for someone like her. She hadn't set foot in the country since 1939 and despite her father's best efforts her Finnish was rusty and overlaid by a strong Scottish brogue. Yet oddly enough, that was what had saved her. That – and Eva.

Eva had been in the foreman's office when Satu arrived and on hearing the strange accent she piped up that her cousin in Scotland spoke just the same way. Then it turned out that a woman on Eva's shift was expecting within the next few days and almost before Satu or the foreman knew it, the thing was settled.

Satu went away feeling like a million dollars. It was her first real job. And TK would be pleased, she knew he was getting irritated with her never having any money of her own. At least now she wouldn't have to rely on him sending her part of his wages when he went back to sea.

If only he would let her speak to his parents. But he had flown into a rage when she suggested it and made her promise never to go near them. She had never seen him so angry - but it passed as quickly as it had come and afterwards he explained that his mother was a woman of strong passions and that he was the only one who knew how to handle her. It was essential they keep a low profile until she had got used to the idea. Satu smiled as she thought of it. He was right of course. TK always knew best.

CHAPTER 16
Monday 18th May, 1981

Ricky arrived in a state of semi-somnambulism, the dark images of the previous night no more than a hazy memory. As soon as he hit the water he started to revive, his muscles loosening as he swam, until even his brain cells gradually came back on line.

He was about halfway down the pool when he saw a familiar figure waving to him from the far end. The sight filled him with such confusion that he missed his stroke and got a noseful of water. She was standing in hip-deep water, wearing a one-piece swimsuit and a bathing cap and the moment he saw her, Ricky realised he didn't know which one she was. Choked and appalled, he slowed down to buy time while he tried desperately to work out if it was Anna or Satu.

He was pretty sure it *was* either Anna or Satu, since there were only so many blonde Finnish girls of his acquaintance - but he could no more tell them apart than Tweedledum and Tweedledee. With their fair complexions, broad faces and neat figures they were terrifyingly alike - and the damned bathing cap did nothing to help. All the women in the pool seemed to be wearing them, so he figured it was either a regulation or a conspiracy. The water slapped at his face, blurring his vision and by the time he was ten feet away he was in such a tizz that he wouldn't have known his own mother.

He rose out of the water with a smile of greeting but his eyes must have given him away because her first words were, 'Hei, Ricky. Don't you recognise me?'

Actually no, not without your clothes on. 'Hei, yes, of course.' Then she grinned and he knew her. The colour of her eyes, the dimple in her cheeks and something else that communicated itself across a whole range of senses all struck him at once. He felt like a man reprieved from hanging. 'I didn't know you came here too, Satu. How long have you been here?'

'Oh, about ten minutes. You swam right past me just now and I made a face at you but you didn't notice. You looked very serious.'

She did such a good imitation of his long, serious look that he had to laugh in acknowledgement. 'Yup, that's me alright. I'm sorry, I was miles away: I need to be here at least half an hour before I wake up.'

'Me too! I always come here in the morning before I do any studying.'

Ricky realised she was looking him over and nodding to herself as she spoke, so he returned the compliment but with far more reason to appreciate what he saw. She had the easy poise of a dancer, with curves that proved there was a God. A message passed between them and she grinned and threw down the gauntlet. 'Race you to the end.'

He ran his gaze over her body once more and knew she was built for speed. Refusal was impossible, so he just nodded. Satu smiled in anticipation of triumph and they took up positions in adjacent lanes. When they launched off she sliced through the water like a tuna, leaving him in her wake from the first second. She beat him easily but he enjoyed the contest and the surge of power in his muscles as he forged through the water after her. It was coming back to him. The day before he had barely managed two lengths without a rest.

She laughed when he reached her, the same light, pleasant laugh that had attracted him in the disco. There was no crowing in it and no mockery: just the sheer pleasure of the race.

'You're as graceful in the water as a dolphin. It's lovely to watch you.'

She liked that and he saw her accept the compliment, taking it as something that was no less enjoyed for being her due. They matched routines for half an hour and then joined each other for coffee and pastries in the cafe overlooking the pool.

'So, you are going to the Pastor's Office today?'

'Yes, Pekka's taking me there a bit later. I really hope I can find them.'

'Of course, I think it is quite certain. Everyone is in there, even me.'

He wasn't sure what she meant by that and she didn't give him time to enquire. 'Would you like to go to the theatre on Wednesday night, Ricky? I am thinking of going to see a play by Shakespeare.'

Oh, BUGGER. Of all the nights and all the plays...

'Ah, I'd love to but I'm afraid I've already been invited by a friend of Tim's. It's really unfortunate, I'd love to go with you.'

The cheeks dimpled again and her eyes sparkled at him. 'But I expect she is pretty, this friend of Timi's.'

Actually, he thought to himself, some people could hardly tell you apart. 'Well, yes, I suppose she is, quite. Oh damn. Perhaps we could go out together another night?'

She put on a frown and mocked him with her eyes. 'Choices, choices. Only three days in town and already he's in such demand.'

'But what about tonight? We could go to the pub?'

She looked thoughtful for a moment but then shook her head. 'No, I am going dancing tonight. I will have to take a girlfriend to the theatre after all. She is not so cute as you but it will be easier to concentrate on the Shakespeare.'

This floored him and he blundered around for something to say. 'What are you doing today, studying?'

She glanced at her watch. 'Yes. Oh, and I have to hurry, I have a lecture in five minutes.'

'Is it far?'

'No, quite near and I have a bicycle.'

He stood up as she did, unable to hide his disappointment and nearly knocking over the milk jug in his awkwardness. 'Oh, right. Ah, then I'll see you again later, I hope.'

'Yes, perhaps.'

Perhaps. The prospect of only *perhaps* was devastating, impossible to bear. He *had* to see her again. 'But really, when shall we meet?'

She paused in getting her things together and then spoke in mock-Shakespearean manner. 'When shall we three meet again?'

He did his best to smile but she picked up her bag and made to leave. 'It's a small town. We'll bump into each other.'

'Oh, right. Then I guess I'll see you...'

She was off toward the doors even as he was speaking, once more leaving him floundering in her wake. And then something awoke in him and he astonished himself by calling out to her as she pushed open the doors, his voice cutting across the babble of the cafeteria with a mixture of entreaty and command. 'Satu!'

She turned in the doorway, holding the swing doors open while she waited, one eyebrow ever so slightly raised.

'I want to go to this play with you.'

There was silence for a moment, every head in the cafe turning to catch her reply.

'OK.' Without another word she gave a backward wave and skipped down the steps to the exit as the doors crashed to behind her. He stood with his hands on the table as the doors swung back and forth and then were still.

'Damn.' He sat down as he said it, shaken by the strength of the emotions she aroused in him. As he did so he knew that catching her was like trying to catch Pegasus: once seen, there was no choice; the thing had to be attempted.

CHAPTER 17

He met Pekka outside the pool and walked with him the few blocks to the Pastor's Office, where generations of clerics had recorded each official event in the life of every person in the country.

Or so they thought. At first it seemed likely to prove so, for the system had a relentless Nordic efficiency. They turned up just after ten o'clock and by half past, with the aid of Pekka's introduction, he had the full attention of a guy who appeared to have been put on this earth for the express purpose of helping Ricky Suomalainen run his elusive family to ground.

'You understand how our records are kept?'

'Ah, no, not at all.'

The record keeper obviously found this answer highly satisfactory. He gave a contented little sigh at the prospect of having to begin from the beginning. 'The records were originally collected by the Lutheran church and collated by parish. There are separate registers for the larger Swedish parishes, which overlap with the Finnish ones. I myself, Bengt Larsson, belong to a family that is listed in the records of the Swedish parishes since 1593. In the big towns like Tampere they have been brought together into a central register, so any family in the area can be found here.'

'Do they record just births, deaths and marriages?'

'No, here we are also recording many other things, for instance from the census. We have a file for every person in the area.'

At that, Ricky's heart skipped a beat, certain that he was home and dry. 'How far back do they go?'

'In some special cases, like my own, they date from the Sixteenth

Searching for Satu 93

Century. They are quite complete from the Eighteenth Century to the present.'

Bengt was deliberately vague about how some of this information was obtained but it all seemed open to public scrutiny, even by a foreigner. There was a fee to pay but that was nothing against the value of what it bought.

'We can begin now, if you are ready? You are wanting to find some members of your family here in this area?'

'Yes but I'm afraid I don't know much about them. Do I have to begin at a particular point?'

'No, you can give me any name and date. The entire system is computerised, so we can make an on-line search in real time.'

It struck Ricky as characteristic of the Finns to be five years behind in popular culture and five years ahead in computer technology. Up to that moment he had never actually used a computer, whilst Bengt had obviously never been told that long hair and flares died with the Seventies. Ricky suppressed a smile and reeled off the names Sandy and Satu Suomalainen, confident that he was now just a printout away from the answer to all his questions.

It took rather longer than Bengt had expected. There appeared to be some difficulty in running down a cross-reference and when he tried to access it, the computer flashed back something that he didn't seem to like very much. After a bit of haruumphing he finally came up with one rather scant file. From his expression, he was embarrassed by the paucity of what he had found.

'These are your mother's details, yes?'

'Yes but I thought there might be more? I was expecting details of my sister Satu, too.'

'I am sorry. According to the records there has been no other person named Satu Suomalainen living in the Tampere area for the last 50 years.'

'That's strange! And look, there doesn't even seem to be a record of my birth.'

'You were born here in Finland?'

'Yes. Right here in Tampere.'

'On what date?'

'29 September 1956.'

Bengt quickly banged in his name and date of birth and Ricky watched as his expression turned to a frown. 'I have no record of you here.'

'But you must have! I've even got a copy of my birth certificate with me – look, it's right here.' He pulled out his envelope of papers and handed it to Bengt, who was now looking distinctly perturbed. After a quick perusal, the record officer's frown grew grim.

'Where did you get this document, please?'

'From my mother. Why, is something wrong?'

'Yes. This is not a real Finnish birth certificate.'

Ricky started to laugh but the look on Bengt Larsson's face caused him to bite it off half-formed. 'How can that be? Are you sure?'

'Yes, I am quite sure. It is a forgery.'

'But how can you tell?'

Larsson said something in Finnish to Pekka, who thought for a moment and then did his best to translate. 'The insignia at the top of the page are wrong and also the way that the details of the child have been filled out is not consistent with the practice of the doctor whose signature is there. He thinks the signature itself is a forgery.'

Ricky looked from one to the other, quite stumped. It was Bengt who eventually broke the silence. 'How long have you had this document?'

'I don't know. As long as I can remember.'

'It is quite interesting. Only twice before have I seen false papers like this.'

Ricky had to swallow an instinctive protest. The guy was dismissing the only evidence he had of his own origins. It choked him but in the end he gave Bengt the prompt he was obviously waiting for. 'Really, when?'

'They were all from the same period. I am thinking that at around this time someone in Pispala was dealing in false documents. A black market, you understand?'

'Yes. What makes you think it was based in Pispala?'

From the look on the guy's face, that was self-evident.

'But surely you can find *some* record of my sister or myself? Of me, at least? Even if we can't find her, we know that I'm real.'

'I am sorry. There is no record here of anyone by the name of Ricky Suomalainen. It is quite an unusual name, this mix of British and Finnish.'

'There must be something else we can do.'

'Of course. Perhaps there is a simple explanation. We should continue to look at other records, yes?'

'Yes! Right, absolutely.'

As Ricky had expected, there was no indication of who his father might be. Nor did his mother's file tell him much, except that she had been born in Viipuri in the east of Finland, rather than in Edinburgh as she had always implied (and as she had falsely declared on his forged birth certificate). The only other thing he learned from the file was that although she had lived in Tampere, there was no record of her from six months before his birth until about six months after, when she was listed as working at a textile mill near Pispala. With a leap of his heart he realised it must be the same one he had stood beside just a couple of days ago.

'There seems to be something missing here,' Ricky observed, pointing to what he presumed was a cross-reference to another record.

Bengt nodded and then broke the bad news. 'Unfortunately the files from Viipuri have been spread around the country and many have been lost.'

'Oh. Why's that?'

'This town is now in the USSR. It was taken by the Russians after the war. Some of the files will probably be in the office in Helsinki and some of the others appear to have been transferred to Turku.'

'Can we access them from here?'

'I am afraid not. However, if you will be going there I will contact the Helsinki and Turku Pastor's Offices and have them prepare the files.'

'That's really kind of you but I'm afraid there isn't time. I have to go back to England on Sunday.'

'Well, you could make an application in writing and they will send you copies of the records.'

'Good, thank you. But listen, are you absolutely certain there's no record of my sister here? No other Satu Suomalainens at all?'

'The system is quite foolproof in this respect - but only if someone was born here or lived here under that name. Perhaps you and your sister were born in England and your mother wished to conceal the fact. That may explain the false birth certificate.'

'No, that's not likely. My mother hated Finland: she would never have admitted that I was born here unless it was true.'

'Would you like to trace back through her parents, to see if that tells us anything?'

'I can do that?'

'Of course. Their names and their date and place of birth are on your mother's birth certificate. You see, they're right here.'

Ricky looked but there seemed to be some mistake. 'But that's not my grandfather.'

'Your grandfather's name was not Eero?'

'No. It was Ernie.'

Larsson looked at him strangely and pointed to the electronic version of the certificate on the screen before them. 'Your grandmother was Janet Graham, a Scot?'

'Good grief. Then it is my grandfather.'

'You did not know who your grandfather was?'

'Yes. No. I didn't know his name was Eero. We always called him Ernie.'

'That is not uncommon. As you know yourself, people have often been changing their names, especially in the earlier times. Sometimes they did it to avoid taxes and debts, or to escape from a scandal. In fact it is less usual to change the Christian name, except in cases like this where someone goes to live in a country where their name is not easy for foreigners to use.'

'But then anybody could be anybody.'

'I'm sorry?'

'Anybody in these records could give one name and actually be somebody else.'

'Well, it is not so easy to deceive the system. Usually people only lied about such things as whether or not they were married, or how many people lived with them. It would be almost impossible to disguise their whole history.'

Despite Bengt's conviction, Ricky's few remaining certainties evaporated. If she existed at all, his sister could be going under any name she chose and he had no way of finding out. The whole system was based on good Finnish honesty. Except, as Bengt said, that it would be hard for anyone to erase themselves totally from the records.

What was it Satu had said? They have everybody in there, even me? She probably meant that even the rebels of Pispala were in the records, if you only knew where to look. He didn't, so he followed the Suomalainen trail back in time to see if it gave any clues.

Grandfather Ernie proved strangely elusive. Bengt seemed rather frustrated with his disinclination to lead a regular, well documented life.

'His is an odd case. He is recorded as having been born in Scotland. He comes and goes from the records from about 1910 to 1940. There is no record of his death.'

'He died in Scotland in the 1950s.'

'Yes? That is logical. If he had died here it would certainly be recorded.'

Ernie's parents were easier to follow but there were still gaps in the records. Mauno Suomalainen and his wife had produced three sons and two daughters, Grandfather Ernie being the middle child. They seemed to have migrated between Viipuri and Scotland, where Mauno appeared on the record of a house sale in 1912. The address was in Leith, where one end of the family shipping line was based. It seemed to be of only peripheral interest until they came to Mauno's mother, Ricky's great-great-grandmother. Whose name was Satu Suomalainen. *Another one.*

She had been born in Viipuri in 1852 and was clearly recorded as having died in Leith in 1951. That was only five years before Ricky was born, yet until that moment he had never heard of her. Besides Ricky's great-grandfather Mauno, she had also given birth to a daughter who had married a Swede called Eric Vaasa and emigrated to the USA some time in the early 1900s. Various documents indicated that this original Satu had married one Juri Hämäläinen but there was no marriage certificate and she had kept her maiden name, as had her son Mauno. There was no further trace of Juri Hämäläinen after the mid-1880s. It was a dead end.

Ricky wasn't very good with family trees, never having had much more than stumps to climb around in before. It was left to Bengt to remind him that his Grandfather Ernie had brothers and sisters and that he, Ricky, therefore had great uncles and aunts. Which meant that he probably also had cousins. Not sisters but real live relatives nonetheless.

This was more like it. Within a couple of minutes branches were sprouting out all over his family tree, right there on the screen in front of him. For an hour they poured over records that showed a host of relatives he'd never heard of: Grandfather Ernie's brothers Rudi and Kari; Kari's wife Elvira; and his two sisters, one of whom had died young and the other in childbirth.

Great Uncle Rudi had died in 1919. Bengt muttered to himself, cross-referenced another file and presently turned to Ricky and told him something quite shocking. 'I cannot be sure but I think that Rudi Suomalainen was killed here in Tampere during the civil war. He was apparently a communist and he has been recorded among those executed after the fighting in Pispala. You understand about this?'

'The Reds and the Whites? Yes, I think so. He was my grandfather's brother, right? Was he older or younger?'

'He was the eldest. He was born in 1902 and died at the age of 17.'

'Jesus! Excuse me. They shot him at 17?'

'It would seem so. It was a brutal time. I'm sorry.'

'No, it's all right, you're being really helpful. Please go on.'

But in fact there was only one more important piece of information. All of these aunts and uncles were long dead and appeared to have died childless. They had left behind only two tangible connections to present day Tampere. Great Uncle Kari had been killed in 1942 and was recorded as being buried in the military cemetery in the centre of town. And his wife Elvira was still alive. Bengt handed Ricky a printout of her address.

He had found a living relative. She was old, distant and only by marriage. Yet it was not so much a straw to a drowning man as a big, fat life raft complete with survival rations.

Ricky thanked him profusely and collected up a bundle of papers with all the details they had discovered. He was just about to leave when a thought struck him. It was so blindingly obvious that he couldn't imagine why he hadn't thought of it before. 'Excuse me, but could you look up an address and tell me who lived there a couple of years ago?'

'Is this the address of another Suomalainen?'

'I'm not sure. I had this address for Satu Suomalainen from my mother but when I went there no-one knew her. It seems the family who used to live there had moved several months ago and I don't know where they've gone. They're called Karlsholm. According to the neighbours there was a daughter called Katerina Satu Karlsholm living there and I'm wondering if she might be related to Satu Suomalainen in some way.'

As soon as he introduced the Karlsholms to the equation, Bengt's whole attitude stiffened. His response was clipped, even defensive. 'I'm sorry, this is not regular.'

'Look, I don't want to do anything improper: I just want to know if there was ever a Satu Suomalainen living there, or anyone else who might be related to me and if so, where they are now.'

Bengt pondered this for five long seconds, shaking his head slowly all the while. It was obvious that he was going to refuse, until Pekka spoke quickly to him in Swedish. The record officer listened - and finally nodded.

'I can look up the address and see if any Suomalainens have lived there. That is as much as I can do.'

'Thank you, I really appreciate it.'

It only took a couple of minutes and the answers were unequivocal. The previous residents were the Karlsholms, just as the neighbours had indicated; and no Suomalainens had ever lived at that address. Ricky knew he was pushing both his luck and Pekka's influence but there was one thing more he had to ask. 'The Karlsholm family do have a daughter called Satu though, right?'

Bengt looked distinctly uneasy. 'This is not your family, I think?'

'I don't know. I was just wondering if you could check on any possible connection. The neighbours thought that she was still living here in Tampere.'

Bengt shrugged and turned back to the console, apparently accepting this as fair enough. But it led nowhere. After ten minutes of searching he shook his head with an unmistakable air of finality. 'I am sorry, but there is no record of such a person living in Tampere. Katerina Satu Karlsholm and her family moved to Turku, as you have said. There is no evident connection between this family and yours. In fact they are an old family from Sweden who have married into some Finnish families from the north and east of Finland.'

'None of them still live here?'

Bengt shifted in his seat, obviously knowing more than he was saying.

'Please, if there is someone still here, perhaps they could help me?'

'I'm sorry. This information is private. Without a known family connection, I cannot tell you anything more.'

'How can we know that unless I ask them? What harm could it do?'

'I am sorry. I cannot help you further.'

Catch 22. Ricky looked at Pekka but they had reached the end of his influence. He could hardly complain: it was a lot further than he would have got in England.

So that was that. He thanked the punctilious Mr Larsson again and took his leave. Once outside he took his leave of Pekka also, shaking him by the hand for the trouble he had taken. Then he walked off by himself, to think through what he had learned.

It boiled down to the fact that the family had been big once but that all the other branches had either died out or disappeared. Perhaps the survivors had emigrated in the hard times around the turn of the century, as Larsson suggested. Maybe his real family connections were now all in America, rather than here in the old country.

Yet that didn't explain his mother's note, or why she had put false information on a forged birth certificate. And it didn't begin to explain what had happened to his sister. Obviously he should now follow his one solid lead: great aunt Elvira. But first he had to get some lunch because he suddenly realised that he was starving.

He walked into the centre of town and had a pizza and a glass of beer in a restaurant overlooking the weir between the upper and lower lakes. The beer made him feel sleepy and he whiled away the first part of the afternoon on a park bench beside the river, his brain too muddled to disentangle the complexities of his family tree. It was nearly three before he decided to resume his quest, whereupon he got out his map, located the street and started walking.

The address was quite close by, in a block of 1950s flats. His aunt's name, Elvira Suomalainen, was written by the bell in elegant but faded lettering. He rang but there was no answer and leaving a note didn't seem practical. Making up his mind to return next day, he wandered off in the general direction of Pispala, with no particular object in mind. He had gone perhaps two blocks when the heat of the sun drew him into an invitingly shady gateway, in search of a place to sit and rest. Once inside he took one look at the rows of identical white headstones and realised that he had wandered into the war cemetery. The hush of the place and the precise parade of the dead were unmistakable.

He found himself walking the silent lines as if it was what he had come here to do. He walked slowly, reading the bare details of each short life and violent death. Often there was not even a name, just the date of death. The rise and fall of the fighting, mirrored in the numbers of the dead. The average age was about 22. The same as in the disco, he suddenly thought.

He had seen such places twice before. The first time had been as a kid, in some corner of Flanders that he would never be able to find again. He and his mother had stopped *en route* to the Channel ferry and passed through a small gate set into a thick green hedge. Inside was the most beautiful garden Ricky had ever seen. Even at the age of ten it had awed him. The fact that mass death could evoke such a place made a greater impression upon him than any book or film about war would ever do.

A Scottish uncle's name had been on one of the headstones and his mother wept when she found it, although neither she nor Ricky had ever known him. It was not the one death that moved them but the many.

The second time had been high up on a mountain in Italy, overlooking the Liri Valley from the monastery of Monte Casino. A great semi-circle of headstones straddled the mountainside in an amphitheatre of death. The radiating spokes of the graveside paths, the stony ground in which they were set and the bare headstones all contributed to a starkness that was terrible in its simplicity.

And now here, in this corner of a Finnish park a thousand miles to the north. He sat down gratefully on a wooden bench, surrounded by dead men who were almost all younger than he was. Men who had fought on what his history books called the wrong side. Fought and lost and laid to rest in this little plot, smaller and more intimate than the others he had seen, yet at one with them.

After what seemed a long time he sighed and got up. It might have been only a few minutes; time moves at a different rate in places of peace and contemplation. But he felt refreshed and ready to move on, like a man dying of thirst who stumbles upon a canteen and is revived by two gulped mouthfuls.

He walked back towards the gateway, looking at the names as he went. About halfway along he stopped before one of them, not really surprised at all by what was written on it.

Kari Suomalainen
1915 - 1942

There were flowers at the foot of the stone, almost but not quite dead. Most likely they were his wife's: Aunt Elvira's. But she was out and the flowers were wilting to dusty death and who could say when they would next be renewed? He made up his mind and walked purposefully out of the cemetery to a flower shop that he had noticed earlier in the day. It was further than he remembered and probably half an hour had passed by the time he returned.

He was clutching a small bunch of red carnations, purchased from a florist on whom he had been able to use one of his few stock phrases. 'Anteeksi. Kuinka monta kukkat maksavat?' (Excuse me.

How much do the flowers cost?) He had used the formal form of a phrase that most people would have reduced to just 'Montako?' (How much?) and it had earned him a smile from the florist. He was still feeling quite pleased with himself for this little success, made sweeter by the fact that he had understood the price quoted and had no difficulty with the change. As a result he strode confidently up to the grave, pulled out the dying flowers and replaced them with his own. He was turning round to look for somewhere to dispose of the old ones before he saw her.

She was looking at him with an intense, short-sighted stare, a bent old woman in black standing ten yards away along the path. It didn't occur to him at first, he just nodded to her and walked over to a nearby bin and tossed in the flowers. He might never have known but for the fact that he paused to stand before the grave as he left. He had almost reached the exit when she called out in Finnish. It was a faltering cry in a voice croaking with age but he knew at once what it was she had said.

'Who are you?'

It hit him then. The fresh bunch of flowers in her hand, the fact that she had stopped halfway down the path leading to that same grave, the intensity of her stare. The way he had unceremoniously tossed away someone else's tribute.

Hers.

The necessary words came to him as he retraced the few steps towards her. She was standing directly in front of the headstone now, looking first at his flowers, then at him. She was peering, so he came close before deploying such words of introduction as he could. 'Anteeksi. Minä olen Ricky Suomalainen. Mitä kuuluu?'

She gave a small, soundless gasp that never touched her eyes, as if she too was somehow prepared for this meeting across the years. Then she peered with a concentration that strove to make up for the ravages time had wrought on her sight. Finally she nodded. 'Sinä olet Satuun poika.' (You are Satu's boy.)

It came as a statement, clear and convinced. He had met his Great Aunt Elvira.

CHAPTER 18

The old lady appeared to speak no English and was partially deaf, whilst Ricky's Finnish was woefully inadequate for the task. Yet two human beings can always communicate when they both really want to.

It was apparently unnecessary for him to produce any proof of his identity. However poor her sight might be now, it was good enough to recognise family features that must have been imprinted indelibly in her inner eye.

He gave a gesture of apology for the flowers and took the replacements from her hand, arranging them beside his own before standing back to admire them. It didn't require a degree in Finnish to grasp the muttered comment this provoked. After she had stooped down to repair the damage, he had to concede that the result was more like a floral tribute and less akin to an exploding fragmentation bomb.

She gestured for him to take her arm and he walked slowly beside her as they left the cemetery and headed back to her flat. She said nothing *en route*, evidently concluding that it would be wasted breath. Nor did she need to, for her apartment spoke volumes: illustrated, chronological and astounding.

To a person whose home had never contained more than three family snapshots, his aunt's tiny flat seemed like the National Portrait Gallery. She made coffee while he poured over the pictures, handling the silver and brass frames as if they were fragile treasures of incalculable value.

A young man expressing an interest in family portraits is a guaranteed object of satisfaction to an elderly female relative. Before long they were clucking and tutting over them like a couple of hens counting chickens, although the amount of definite information communicated was minimal. None of the photos had names on the back and although he knew the words for uncle, cousin and suchlike, he was so ignorant of the connections between these people and himself that few of them held any meaning for him.

There was a heart-stopping moment when he recognised a photo of his mother as a child, his look of wonder presided over with smiling assent by the old lady. There was another photo, old and browning, of a woman who looked very like her, in the dress of the Victorian middle class. And finally there was a clear though to his eyes slight resemblance between himself and several of the men in the pictures. They shared the same rather formal way of standing with their hands behind their back (what his mother called his "Prince Charles"); the same slim but broad-shouldered figure; and the same small ears and almost feminine nose that contrasted against the determined set of the jaw. He wasn't good with faces (Satu could attest to that!) and he might not know exactly who all these people were - but there was no doubting they were family.

After an exciting and yet rather frustrating hour he had established only that nearly all of them were dead. Elvira herself seemed to be the only exception. She was his grandmother's sister-in-law: so why the hell had his gran never mentioned her? By their silence, she and his mother had all but denied Elvira's existence. It seemed to be mutual, too: mention of his grandmother's name drew only a studied silence from the old woman.

He tried drawing a family tree but the old lady wouldn't play ball. She pointed from the crude diagram to people in the photos a couple of times and said 'cousin'; but nothing specific enough to make any real progress.

So he tried his sister, the living Satu Suomalainen. He expected it to resolve everything but incredibly it solved nothing. Surely the old woman must be aware of the existence of so close a relative? Yet after several minutes of saying and writing the name, pointing to the family tree and imploring her to concede at least the fact of the connection, he was none the wiser. Initially he thought she was hiding something but eventually he concluded that she wouldn't admit to his sister's existence because she was unaware of it. If anything, the visit brought him several stages closer to a sneaking suspicion that had been forming in his mind ever since the failure at Kirkkokatu.

What if there was no sister called Satu Suomalainen? What if his mother had misled him in the confusion of her final delirium? After an hour with his aunt, he was almost ready to conclude that this great pictorial array of ancestors was as close as he was ever going to get to his family in Finland. Elvira apart, the Finnish side appeared to share a single, absolute characteristic with the British side: they were all dead.

He decided he had achieved all he could for one day and that the sensible thing was to come back later with an interpreter. He got across the idea that he had to go but would return and he made, so far as he could tell, a definite appointment for Thursday lunchtime. No other day or time seemed to be acceptable, so he nodded his agreement, repeated the details in the best Finnish he could muster and made his farewells.

As he left the flat he was once more unsure whether to feel elated or downcast. Every discovery seemed to make his family's past even murkier, while bringing him no nearer to finding the Satu he was searching for. But as he walked out into the evening sunlight another thought struck him. Perhaps all the pieces of the puzzle were already before him - and he had only to recognise the pattern.

CHAPTER 19

The Student House was old and dingy, scarcely modified from its origins as a dance hall in the last century. Its walls and ceiling had been stained brown as an Amsterdam bar by generations of guiltless smokers, while its atmosphere was an exuberant mix of intellectual intensity and ingenuous fun. Above all it was crowded, noisy and hot: in fact altogether it was one of the best places Ricky had ever seen. It was also, Pekka assured him, the place everyone went on Monday nights.

The venue had so much character that Ricky supposed some faceless authority would eventually get around to demolishing it in favour of something modern and anodyne. That suggestion got Pekka going for about ten minutes without even pausing to draw breath. Finally he burnt himself out and went off to the bar to cool down, returning with two half litres of beer and a chess set. Ricky challenged him at once.

He loved chess and might easily have passed the whole evening totally engrossed: but half an hour into the game he glanced across the room in time to see a large, woolly bear of a man take Satu out on the dance floor and spin her around like a top. It so distracted him that he lost a rook and two pawns in quick succession and had to summon up all his guile to stabilise the situation. To the growing crowd of onlookers it looked like a great comeback - but the fire that drove him was jealousy, not the will to win. So *this* was what she meant when she said she was going dancing!

The big guy was a truly hateful specimen. He was built like a barn, he smiled like an idiot and he could dance like a dream. How come these continentals always knew how to dance properly? Taking a girl in your arms and moving her around to your lead - it was an unfair advantage. That guy should have been out on the streets demonstrating for world peace and throwing rocks at policemen and instead he was making deft little moves all over the dance floor with Ricky's girl.

Ricky looked down at the chessboard and realised he had made another mistake. Then inspiration struck and a minute later he was able to catch Satu's eye and wave her over with a captured bishop. To his great satisfaction she came as soon as the next dance ended.

'Hei, Ricky.' She looked down at the game. 'So, you're a chess player. But I think Pekka is quite good, how are you doing against him?'

'I'm letting him win so cleverly that he'll never realise.'

Pekka laughed and took another pawn. Satu joined the onlookers, who were engaged in swilling beer and debating the strengths and weaknesses of each position. They were quite dedicated and Ricky found their enthusiasm so catching that he even managed to put thoughts of Satu temporarily to one side, so they only occupied about 40 per cent of his brain. He played one of his best games ever. He was always at his best when the situation was desperate and Pekka had him cornered and was pushing hard.

They had been playing for about an hour when a noisome drunk came over to join the party. He began by leering over the board to check out the positions; and then in broken English he began telling Ricky what to do.

At first Ricky ignored him politely enough, nodding a couple of times as if in agreement and then making his next moves unaltered. The first time this happened the drunk muttered loudly to himself. The second time he spat on the floor. The third time that his advice was disregarded, he said something clearly offensive and then swept the board clean with one swipe of his arm.

There was an awestruck silence. Everybody was looking at Ricky, for some reason seeing him rather than Pekka as the epicentre of the coming blast. Ricky could see Satu out the corner of his eye, holding her breath. Looking up at the drunk's leery face, he smiled sweetly and said, 'Thank you *so* much for your assistance. Without your intervention, I believe I would have lost the game.' Then he winked at Pekka and released his king, who alone was still standing, flipping him over in the universal gesture of defeat.

The whole crowd let out their breath in unison, like a collective sigh. Then everyone laughed, except for the bewildered drunk, who ended up grinning inanely at a joke he couldn't quite fathom. Ricky felt a light hand on his shoulder and the thrill of it went right through him.

'So, you are a good loser. I have been hearing that this is something the English do well.' Her eyes danced at him, taking the barb out of her words.

'If we concede defeat gracefully, it's because we're too polite to let people know how easily we can win.'

'Oh, is that right?'

'Absolutely. I could, for instance, dance much better than that large, hairy man you were with just now, except that I wouldn't like to make him look bad. It might upset him.'

'Yes, and he is much bigger than you.'

'He's enormous. Is he your boyfriend?'

'But you are jealous!'

'Not at all. Green is my usual colour.'

'It suits you. May I sit down?'

'Oh, of course, excuse me.'

She sat on Pekka's vacant chair and flashed him a grin. 'Matti is not my boyfriend but he would like to be.'

'Hmm. He really *is* a good dancer. Like a bear on skates.'

'If he gave you a bear hug there would be nothing left.'

'Don't tell me: I expect he's also a really nice guy. Gentle and funny and a speaker of seven languages.'

She laughed. 'But why are you so worried about him? You should be telling me about you.'

'Right! With my fascinating life, how can you fail to be captivated?'

'Is that right? And what have you been doing today in your fascinating life? Have you found your sister?'

'No but I've just met my aunt, who I never met before. In fact I didn't even know she existed.'

'But that is very strange.'

'Yes, isn't it? I was walking around town after leaving the Pastor's Office and I ended up in a war cemetery, near the city centre...?'

She nodded, encouraging him to continue, so he related what he had learned, winding up with the way his father had deserted his mother, leaving her with a young child and no means of support.

'But what a rat! So tell me, what is his name?'

'I don't know. The only thing I know about him is that he was a Finnish sailor.'

Something flitted across Satu's face but she shook her head, as if clearing her mind of something fanciful.

'Did I say something wrong?'

'No, I was thinking it is so like a sailor to do that. But did your mother never tell you his name?'

'No, never. I think I saw him a few times when I was a small child, so she couldn't pretend not to know who he was: but she always refused to tell me.'

'But surely you can find out from the birth certificate?'

'No. It says 'father unknown'. And anyway, it's a fake.'

'But why would someone want to forge a birth certificate?'

'Beats me. But someone did and it seems pretty obvious it was my mother. You know, when I was a teenager she always used to get really upset when I asked her about my father. In the end she showed me the birth certificate and then she burst into tears and made me promise not to look for him any further. Now I find that she forged the certificate; that she was born right here in Finland; and that according to the records she never even had a son, let alone a daughter. I really don't know what to think any more.'

Satu reached out her hand and touched him on the arm but the gaze he turned upon her was sharply enquiring. 'You remember when we first met in the disco and you told me your name?'

'Yes, you looked as if you had seen a ghost.'

'Not a ghost. But maybe a long-lost sister.'

'But I am not her. I have told you, I have no brothers.' She gave him a rueful grin. 'And if I did, I am sure I would take care not to lose them.'

'What star sign are you?'

'Virgo. Why? Oh, you are still thinking that maybe it's me?'

'I'm a Virgo, too. When is your birthday?'

'So, why don't you tell me yours first?'

'September 29th.'

'What a coincidence!' She burst out laughing and patted him on the arm. 'Such a face! No, don't worry. My birthday is September 27th.'

'But what year?'

'Oh, you are asking a lady her age now?'

'Please.'

'OK. 1956.'

'That's the same as me.'

'Is that right? Well, then we cannot be brother and sister. Are you pleased or disappointed?' She winked and gave him a provocative leer.

'A bit of both, I guess.'

'But now you have found some of your family, you will soon find the others and then everything will become clear.'

'I wish I was so sure.'

'You will go back to see your aunt again?'

'Yes, I'm taking Tim along to act as interpreter.'

'Then I think it is quite certain you will find your sister.'

Actually he was thinking that his chances of finding that Satu were as dim as his chances of catching this one: and she picked up on it at once.

'What are you thinking?'

'Oh, nothing, really. It's just a shame I can't stay longer than ten days.'

'So, you will have to make the most of them!'

The way she looked at him made him feel like the centre of the known universe: yet he knew that at any moment she might turn the same frank gaze towards some other object, with equal apparent exclusivity. Between the bright glow of her attention and the darkness of total eclipse there was just the turn of her head. Ever since they'd met she had been as elusive as a genie, materialising in front of him and then vanishing again. And hey presto, she proceeded to do it again. He was about to take the conversation further when the bear called to her from the dance floor. She gestured that she'd be with him in a moment, then turned back to Ricky with a smile and proceeded to give him a swift and totally unexpected kiss on the cheek.

'I have to go now or Matti will be getting angry. Come and rescue me later.'

Ricky watched her return to the arms of the yeti, who obviously gave her a few harsh words about leaving him at a loose end. He saw her shrug and go back onto the dance floor as if nothing had happened. Tim came by and distracted his attention with some talk about their plans for the morrow; and the next time Ricky looked up there was a full-scale altercation going on.

The Yeti had Satu by the arm and was pulling her towards the door, talking angrily to her as he dragged her along. She was struggling to break free and talking back but it was too noisy for Ricky to hear what she was saying. Then it all went suddenly and horribly wrong. The Yeti let go of her arm and shouted right in her face, his features red with anger. Satu shook him off furiously, stood back a pace and slapped him, spitting out some words that made Ricky glad about his lack of vocabulary. And then, incredibly, Matti hit her. It was a full-on strike across the mouth and it sent her reeling into the nearest table.

Ricky was on his feet like a spring released, tunnelling through the crowd before Pekka or Tim could stop him, his earlier restraint obliterated in an all-consuming fury. His outrage was so great that he never even considered how hopelessly outmatched he was. Fortunately he was still six feet away when two bouncers grabbed the giant Finn and propelled him out the door at warp speed. Ricky was left standing beside Satu, who turned away from him, shielding her face with her hand as she lowered herself into a vacant chair. He wasn't sure whether to join her or let her be, so he waited close by until she looked up from where she was sitting. She had her compact out by then, examining the damage to her mouth. Finally she raised her eyes and to his surprise gave a rueful smile.

'The face that launched a thousand shits.'

Her propensity for unexpected English axioms seemed fathomless and he sank into the chair opposite with no idea how to reply. Satu was silent for a few seconds, then put the compact away and sighed. She was obviously trying hard to keep it together but Ricky could see that her hands were shaking.

'I'm so sorry, Satu. You asked me to come and rescue you and I was too late. I didn't realise how serious it was.'

'Neither did I.' She paused, then levelled her gaze at him with a disquieting intensity. 'Ricky, tell me something.'

'Anything.'

'Where can you find a man who isn't married or queer and who wants to talk to you and not just screw you?'

He was silent, floundering in it. She gave a grim smile and nodded to herself before continuing. 'I thought so.'

Her words hit hard below the belt and he couldn't bear to sit there and meekly accept being tarred with the same brush. 'There's nothing wrong with mixed motives, Satu.'

'Oh, is that right?'

'Yes, it is.' He hesitated for a moment, then decided he owed it to himself to answer the question she had posed. 'If two people love each other, is their love lessened by desire? Of course not: love and desire reinforce each other. That's how it's meant to be. That guy was an animal, not a real man. Don't write us all off just because some of us fancy you as well as liking you.'

His eyes held hers the whole time he was speaking and he could feel himself flushing but he refused to look away. Finally, after what seemed like a very long time, she reached across and ran the tips of her fingers gently across the back of his hand. 'That's a great line, Ricky.' Before he could protest she rose quickly to her feet, gathering her bag to go. 'So, perhaps you're right. Perhaps there's still hope.'

'Where are you going? I'm sorry, I mean, when will I see you again?'

'On Wednesday, at the play.'

'Right, yes, of course. But where shall we meet up?'

'In the square by the old clock tower.'

'What time?'

She looked back in the act of moving towards the exit. 'About six.' And with that she was gone.

Ricky looked round to find Tim and Pekka standing a few feet away. They raised their glasses to him in silent unison, with wry smiles on their faces.

'What?'

They just exchanged knowing looks and drank their beer.

'*What?*'

They burst out laughing and when he demanded to know what was so funny, they wouldn't tell him. The more he asked the more they laughed and in the end they just bought him another drink and told him not to worry about it. The bastards.

CHAPTER 20
November, 1955

She should have left him the first time he hit her. He had come back from a six-week voyage, dropped off his kit and gone straight to his parents, full of promises that this time all would be resolved. She waited up half the night and when he finally returned it was nearly three in the morning and he was roaring drunk. She knew at once where he'd been: the gypsies who graced every Finnish town with their traditional costumes also cursed them with their trade in illicit spirits.

When she asked how it had gone TK ignored her at first. Foolishly she had pressed him and he grew more and more angry until finally, incredibly, he hit her.

After that he stormed out into the night, leaving her huddled and sobbing on the bed. Next morning she had gone to work with a huge bruise on her face and Eva had taken one look and told her to move in with her and Marko for a few days. She would have done so, too - but for the fact that she found TK waiting for her when she got home. She had never seen him so contrite, so full of remorse. He promised over and over that it would never happen again, that it was just the effect of the raw alcohol, that he couldn't live without her.

In the end she stayed, telling herself that it was an aberration brought on by her provoking him when he was drunk and still smarting from another rejection by his mother. But no matter how she tried, nothing could suppress the realisation that it could never be the same between them again.

CHAPTER 21
Tuesday 19th May, 1981

Ricky had not anticipated taking his morning coffee with a man who had spent five years on the Eastern Front, fighting the Russians. He had been brought up to think of such people as baby-killing fascists: but he couldn't imagine anyone less like baby killers than the old doctor and his wife.

Tim had invited Ricky to tag along on one of his private lessons and while the others were exploring some obscure areas of English grammar, he picked up a book from the coffee table, his attention caught by the cover photo. It showed a procession of monks and priests in front of a huge church.

'Valaamo,' stated the Doctor, who had seen his interest and announced the name as if it was of special significance. 'It was the centre of Finnish Orthodoxy.'

'Where is it?' Ricky had asked, innocently.

'It is on Lake Ladoga,' replied the doctor's wife, with an edge to her voice, 'in what is now Russia.'

'Oh, I see. What happened to all the monks?'

'They had to move out, as we all did.' The doctor spoke as if he was merely stating an historical fact, rather than recalling a personal tragedy.

'You lived on the island as well?'

'Not quite. We lived in Karelia, on the shores of the lake.'

'Really? I just found out that my mother was born in Karelia: in Viipuri, wherever that is.'

The doctor exchanged glances with his wife. 'It was the main city of Karelia and an important port. The Saimaa Canal enters the sea there, linking the Baltic to the Finnish lakes. Today it is called Vyborg.'

'My family ran a shipping line,' Ricky said, almost to himself. 'I wonder if that's where they got started? Later on they moved to Turku.'

'That is typical of what happened. The people of Karelia, like the Orthodox monks, were spread throughout Finland after the war.'

The doctor's wife sighed at her husband's words, then brightened visibly. 'But now we have another house, on another lake and it is time we went there.'

The old couple had planned a grand tour when they learned that Tim had a guest staying with him; and fifteen minutes later they were all heading east out of the city in the doctor's new Saab. Their route took them at first along a modern expressway, then south on smaller roads that soon began to show the effects of the winter. Frost-heave had splintered the tarmac and trucks had chewed great potholes out of the surface, so that before long the doctor was manoeuvring the car around huge craters.

'Does it get this bad every year?'

'More or less. They usually repair the roads by the end of May but this year the snow stayed late and there was a lot of damage.'

By means of intermittent gaps in the trees Ricky figured they were about half-way down the lake's eastern shore by the time they turned off onto an unmarked sandy track that led to the house. The building stood on a promontory jutting out into the lake. On either side there were tiny beaches of white sand, with a rocky knoll at the far end overlooking a wooded islet that lay temptingly close to shore.

They parked beneath the trees and went inside, to find not so much a house as a palace in wood. At ground level there was a single huge room, open plan except for two massive wooden posts that supported the pitched roof beams. The dining table was ten feet long and three feet wide, with benches on both sides and carved-back chairs at each end. The whole thing was an essay in the strength and beauty of simplicity.

A small hall gave access to a veritable museum of stone sinks and wooden washboards, with stairs leading up from the kitchen to two large bedrooms that provided privacy and stunning views to the far shore. Outside there were rocking chairs on a verandah facing the lake, where the sound of lapping water provided a constant soporific.

'It's absolutely beautiful!' Ricky enthused. 'Do you really own all this?'

'We inherited it from the family of the local Bishop many years ago. In the old days, when the children were younger, we had many wonderful times here. Often all the family and their friends spent the summer holidays here and the house would be full of noise and laughter. I miss those times. Now it is just two old people and too much peace and quiet. It makes a nice change to have visitors.'

'Well, I'm very glad to be here. But excuse me, where is your bathroom?'

The doctor's wife laughed. 'It is out the back. It is not like you are used to, I'm afraid.'

'I'll show you,' said Tim, betraying previous experience.

'One of these famous dry toilets you were telling me about? If it's anything like the house, it must be a palace among bogs.'

'No, actually it's really basic.'

Ricky followed him to the shed outside and sucked air through his teeth at the sight that greeted them when they opened the door. 'Jesus, they don't even have anywhere to wash their hands.'

'They have a whole lake.'

'Hmm. Not exactly my idea of cleanliness: it freaks me out not having running water in a toilet. I'm with the Indians on that.'

Tim snorted. 'With the Americans, more like. You confuse sanitation with civilisation. This is as clean a lifestyle as you can have: the open air, a sauna and a lake full of fresh water.'

When they got back the doctor gave them a guided tour, winding up at a short flight of steps leading down to a sunken doorway, where a low turf roof rose just above ground level. Despite crouching, Tim managed to crack his skull on the lintel.

'The sauna is the first thing a Finn builds when he starts a new house,' stated the doctor, as soon as he had satisfied himself that his guest had not become a patient. 'In the old days the family would live in the sauna until the house was completed. Mothers would give birth in the sauna, sick people would be taken there to recover or to die. In a land of cold and dark, it is a place of warmth and comfort, a womb.'

'It's certainly womb-like,' agreed Ricky, surveying the cosy shelf-seats set close around the brazier.

They emerged back out into the sunlight, blinking at the strength of the reflection off the water as they strolled out onto the rocky knoll. The water between it and the island was so clear and shallow that he could see the smoothly sculpted rock of the bottom all the way across.

'Can you drink the water?'

'Certainly. It is quite pure here.'

On an impulse Ricky stooped down, cupped his hands and drank, then splashed his face. It was cold, delicious and instantly invigorating.

'Wonderful! I think I could get used to this. Do you come here every year, for the summer?'

'Yes, more or less. All of Finland goes to its summerhouse in July and August. The country almost stops.'

'What's the weather like then?'

'Usually the weather will be beautiful, like this, right up until the time you take your family to the summer house. Then the thunderstorms begin.'

'It sounds horribly like seaside holidays in England.'

They walked back to the porch and sat on the rocking chairs, drinking beers and eating sandwiches while they talked. From somewhere far off came the occasional sounds of children at play, floating to them across the water.

The doctor, becoming more relaxed with the sun and the beer, began regaling them with old stories from the sauna. At first his tales all skirted the comic fringes of the war but later, as the day wore on, they expanded into a wide range of subjects that all shared a theme of rustic Finnishness.

'There was a magazine here in Finland until recently which was devoted purely to soldiers' tales from the war. You can imagine what they were like: they all began with 'When I was in Karelia....' The strange thing about this magazine was that a readership survey showed 60 per cent of the readers were women.'

'Yes, yes!' chimed in his wife. 'All my friends used to read this magazine. My favourite stories were about the baseball players.'

Seeing their blank expressions, her husband elucidated. 'In Finland we have a game like the American baseball. In Karelia it was always said that the best grenade throwers were the baseball players. Whenever you wanted to knock out a particularly troublesome trench or bunker, you sent for a baseball player.'

'The Russians,' added his wife, 'Didn't play baseball, so they were outclassed.'

'It's a good job,' said Ricky. 'If they'd had baseball bats they'd have knocked you all to hell.'

They laughed and drank more beer.

'When I was younger,' the doctor went on, 'I used to go hunting. Moose. In the north east, up by the border. The moose hunters in Finland all wear red caps and drink a lot of beer. Consequently they shoot a great many things, including each other. I sometimes think I have treated more bullet wounds since the war than I did during it. Each year there is a column in the newspaper that records all the things that have been shot during the hunting season. It is a kind of competition. The biggest thing they ever shot was the Helsinki-Rovaniemi express train. They must have thought that was one big moose.'

When he had finished his current beer the doctor prescribed himself an afternoon nap. His wife pottered about the house, tweaking this and dusting that. Tim and Ricky sat on their rockers and communed with nature.

'I think I could stay here forever,' Ricky announced at length.

'You always say that just before you get up and leave.'

'It's a fair cop,' Ricky conceded, getting to his feet with a yawning stretch. 'I think I'll go for a walk along the lake.'

Tim picked up a newspaper and placed it over his face against the sun and the first of the summer's flies. Ricky wandered off along the shoreline, glad of the dappled shade of the trees. When he got back an hour later he had not seen another soul.

By the time the doctor woke up again, Ricky was ready with a question. He had been uncertain about asking before but the jollity of the old man in his wartime reminiscences had been reassuring.

'Where could I find out more about the war with Russia?'

The doctor eyed him seriously, then nodded. 'What is it that you wish to know?'

'I lost some of my family in the war. I'd like to learn something about it.'

The old man pondered this awhile before recommending a course of action. 'There is a war museum at Parola, near Hämeenlinna. It is quite easy to reach from Tampere. If you like, I will drive you there later in the week. It will be easier to find out what you wish to know there than by other ways.'

There was much of what Ricky had suspected in that final sentence: more than just the difficulty of translating books that would be available only in Finnish. He made a silent resolve to go there as soon as possible. Something told him that his family had an even closer connection with that dark period in the country's history than his uncle's death. Then they both fell silent, each lost in his own thoughts. Finally the Doctor sighed and got slowly to his feet.

'Too many bad memories. Too many good friends that one could not save. Not much good has come out of that time but I hope you find what you are looking for.' He sighed again. 'And now, we should pack up these things. It is a long drive back to town.'

CHAPTER 22

They drove back right around the lake, getting home just in time for Ricky to keep his appointment with Anna. He found her beneath the same tree in the garden, reading a book. When he asked her what it was, she responded by reading him a short passage out loud. It was French poetry. He couldn't imagine anyone else he knew managing to do that without seeming like a poseur but coming from her it seemed quite natural.

They sat together for a while drinking Earl Grey tea while they talked about their day. Then she asked him about his main purpose.

'Well, have you been finding out anything more about your family?'

'Yes but not the things I most want to know. There's no trace of my sister and my mother's ancestors all seem to be dead, except for one old lady. Oh, and there's also a mysterious family called Karlsholm but the guy in the record office refused to tell me anything about them.'

'Well, if you have some names it will help when we are making telephone calls for you. We have been thinking of ringing up all the other Suomalainens in town. If you like we could ask about Karlsholms, too.'

'Thanks, it would help a lot. I'm really grateful for this, Anna.'

'You are quite welcome.'

'I've got some details here from the Pastors' Office; they're quite easy to follow. Perhaps you can show them to the others and I'll pick them up later?'

'Yes, you can collect them when we go to the theatre.'

'Oh.'

She looked at him enquiringly.

'Ah, I meant to tell you...um, I'm afraid I can't make it.'

'Well, that is a shame. You are doing something else?'

'Yes. Well, no, not exactly. Oh shit. I'm going with someone else.'

'I see. Is her name Satu?'

Ricky hardly dared look at her, his face a confusion of surprise and embarrassment. 'Yes,' he blurted out.

'Good.'

'I, ah...pardon?'

'It is better that you are going with her.'

'It is?'

'Of course. I think you are liking this girl quite a lot, yes?'

Ricky blushed and she laughed. 'You are worse than a Finn! It is nothing to be embarrassed about.'

'I'm not. I was just afraid that you'd be offended. Have you bought the tickets already? I'll pay for mine, obviously.'

'No, I have not bought them yet. I will go another evening, I think.'

'Oh, but there's no need. You could join us...'

She rolled her eyes at him, making him regret his stupid suggestion at once. 'Enjoy your evening with Satu, Ricky. I think that you will need to keep all your attention just for her. She is a very popular girl.'

'Yes, well, she would be. I mean, you know, someone as beautiful as she is... ' He stammered to a stop, tongue-tied by his own clumsiness.

'You should not be worried by anything you hear about Satu, Ricky.'

'What sort of thing?'

Anna hesitated, then evidently decided she had gone too far not to continue. 'She is quite a wild one.'

'Oh.' Ricky looked at her rather blankly. 'How do you mean, exactly?'

'She is enjoying herself quite a lot. She loves her freedom, I think.'

'You mean she has a lot of boyfriends?'

'I think she is having quite a lot of everything in life. This is what makes her fun to be with, yes?'

'Well, yes, I guess so. She's very vivacious. Yes.' Ricky looked at her with painful uncertainty. 'You think I don't have much of a chance with her?'

'Oh no, I think you are having a very good chance. And so is she.'

'I don't know. I'm not exactly Macho Man.'

'This is not something we are short of in Finland.'

'I'm not really noted for my sparkling wit, either.'

'Ricky.'

'Yes?'

'Don't try too hard with this girl. If she likes you it is because of what you are, not because of what you think you should be.'

'Right. Yes of course, I see.'

Anna laughed. 'I think that you don't really know what I am talking about.'

'No. I do. Well, sort of. You think she really likes me?'

'You are the one she is going to the play with.'

He didn't know how to answer that but Anna took pity on him. 'Just be you. I think I know what she feels. You are nice when you are being funny but most of all you are nice when you are serious and sad. I think perhaps that you are something good for her. Now, what else have you planned for tomorrow?'

'I don't really know. All suggestions gratefully received.'

'Well, why don't you go to the Workers' Museum?'

'The Workers' Museum?'

'Yes. It is a block of old Tampere houses that have been made to look as they were in past times. You can learn a lot there about how Finnish people used to live.'

It sounded dull as ditchwater to Ricky but he was developing a keen respect for this girl's opinion, so he mentally pencilled it in for next morning. With luck he thought it might even teach him something about the Finland that his mother had known. 'OK, thanks, I'll do that.'

'And what are you doing tonight?'

'Ah, I'm not really sure. Nothing much, as far as I know.'

It may have been true as far as he knew but in a sense he could not have been more wrong. For just as buildings crash and burn long after an earthquake has subsided, so the effects of his arrival were shaking houses of cards all over Finland, even as he spoke.

CHAPTER 23

Bengt Larsson was by nature both curious and meticulous. He was also from one of the best Swedish families and therefore anticipated no problem in resolving the questions raised by the records he had investigated for the Englishman. He made a few discreet enquiries first, among his family and a number of his Swedish-Finnish friends. All agreed with his initial thoughts. If someone was investigating the Karlsholm family, then the head of that family should be told. In the process she would doubtless be pleased to help him clear up the issues that were of concern to him. Specifically, the missing signatures and the fact that certain documents which rightly belonged in the central archive were being held privately.

Obtaining the co-operation of the switchboard operator at the clinic proved no more difficult than he anticipated. It was actually rather pleasing that this person was so correct in establishing his credentials, which of course were impeccable. In no more than two minutes he was put through to her private apartment.

The voice that answered the telephone belonged to someone who was obviously Finnish and stupid. Finally, however, this intellectually challenged individual was ordered to pass the receiver to the person whose business this was: Katerina Karlsholm, one of the wealthiest women in Finland.

Five minutes later Bengt Larsson sat in a state of shock, the telephone still in his hand. Even after he hung up he sat motionless for a while, considering what to do. The issue was highly sensitive. On the one hand were the inconsistencies in the records, the significance of which was starkly reinforced by Katerina Karlsholm's extraordinary response. On the other hand, she was highly influential. Conceivably influential enough to reach even into the records of the past.

Perhaps he had been over-hasty in concluding that he should inform only one party. It was always wise to be even handed. He picked up the telephone again and dialled a number in Pispala. It rang a long time but he expected that. When it was answered, he grinned in a way that made his face look suddenly younger and more human. 'Pekka? Stoned again? Yes, working late as usual. Is that English friend of yours still here? Yes? Good. There's something I think he should know…'

In Turku, Olli Savolainen put down the telephone after talking to his daughter. It made a dull clunk, missing the cradle. He had to try twice more before it sank home. His wife looked from the phone to his face and knew that it was worse than bad.

'Olli?'

'That was Satu.'

'What is it? What's happened?'

'She wanted to ask me about someone. Someone she'd just met.'

'Another boyfriend?'

'She said not. Pray God that it's not.'

'Why? What's wrong? For God's sake, Olli, you're frightening me. Who is it?'

Her husband looked at her with a face the colour of ash. Hilda had a terrible premonition even before he nodded, half closing his eyes. 'It's Ricky Suomalainen. He's come back.'

She gave a cry like a bird strangled by a pouncing cat. Then fear found the words. 'No! It must be stopped!'

Ricky Suomalainen, the cause of all their concerns, was comatose under a table in Pispala. Harri had come round shortly after he got back from Anna's and they played cards and drank whisky for a couple of hours, during which time Ricky lost most of his spare change. He was so tired that presently he fell asleep in the middle of a hand. The last thing he remembered was Tim remarking that their old school friend Terrence O'Neal was coming to see them at the weekend.

Pekka arrived sometime later and he and the others carried on until two in the morning but Ricky knew nothing about it. They just laid him out beneath the table, covered him with a blanket and continued playing. He woke up next morning to find himself lying on the floor with a small pile of Marks beside him. He remembered then that he had been holding a straight flush. It was the first hand he'd won since the game began and he hadn't even been there to play it.

CHAPTER 24
Wednesday 20th May, 1981

The Workers' Museum comprised the sole remaining block of old Tampere houses. They were wood-built onto stone foundations, with the surrounding roads still cobbled just as they had been when the whole town was set out this way. All the others were long gone, swept away in fires or redevelopment but here the clock had been deliberately turned back.

Oddly, the street outside had a particularly good view of the space age Tampere Tower. It made the transformation all the more striking when he went through the narrow entrance passage and found himself taken back from the late Twentieth Century to the mid Nineteenth.

The block was formed of eight single-storey buildings set around linked courtyards. The rooms of every house were arranged as they had been at a different date, ranging from the 1870s to the 1950s. The details were so vital and exact that they looked as if the residents had just stepped out a moment ago.

Ricky learned a lot walking through those Finnish rooms. He had thought he and Tim were slumming it by sharing two rooms without a bathroom for a week but it was a revelation to see how five young men had managed in one room, folding and stowing away their narrow cots each morning. It was incredible that a family of seven had lived for twenty years in two cubby-holes each smaller than Tim's bedroom. And the tiny flat shared by two maiden ladies from the textile mills oozed a feeling of modest respectability that would have sat comfortably in a scene from Jane Austen.

He saw his family in almost every room. His great, great grandmother

Satu must have lived in just such accommodations as that family of seven, when she had been bringing up her children here in the 1870s. It wasn't difficult to see the attractions of emigration. The room that really spoke to him, though, was the last. It was from the 1950s: the time when his mother had been here.

It had been a time of terrible deprivation, right after the war, when everything was in short supply. At first sight the room didn't look so different from an English working class interior of the period, although that was hardly a standard of affluence. On closer inspection, however, he discovered that almost everything was made out of paper. The suitcase under the table, the women's handbags, their hats and even their shoes were all paper. It was the only thing they had in abundance.

With a shock he realised just how his mother must have lived over here. She must have been dirt poor, unable to provide properly for herself because she had a baby to care for and so presumably couldn't hold down a job. And nothing but blighted hopes from that son of a bitch who deserted her as soon as their son was born. As his eyes halted on a baby's feeding bottle by the stove, his mother's words came back to him like a bolt from the blue.

'We could have starved. He knew I was pregnant and he left me with nothing.'

With sudden clarity, Ricky realised that his father had abandoned them even *before* he was born. He let his eyes wander over the pitiful contents of the room and more memories came, snatched pieces from discussions between his mother and gran as he played in the pool of warmth before the range in the house in Leith. Now they came to life as vividly as the exhibits in front of him.

'How could anyone not have wanted him? His own son! But he couldn't get back to sea soon enough.'

Even at the age of three or four Ricky had known she was talking about his father and with the intuitive understanding of a child he had quietly absorbed it because if he showed his interest he knew she would shut up at once.

Yet she wasn't the only one who had been reticent. All his life there were things about his father that Ricky himself had shied away from. As he grew older he had sometimes even been secretly relieved by his mother's refusal to tell him anything about her lover. He had accepted her silence as much out of fear as from consideration for her feelings. Even now the memories were like hooded phantoms. He would catch a fleeting glimpse but fear would cause him to freeze even as he reached to pull back the hood and reveal the face beneath. It had been the same with his vision of Satu in the garden. Every time he reached for a memory, some part of his mind would ensure that it escaped him. But it was deeper and darker than that.

'Who am I?'

The thought came as if out of nowhere, startling him with its double-edged simplicity. The crux of the matter was not, *'Who is my father?'* but an even more intimate question.

Sometimes he could actually see his father but the face was never clear. He supposed that the memories were from when he was a toddler, shortly before they left Finland. Always he was in a big room with light streaming in through tall windows and his father was moving restlessly around him as he sat on the floor. But whenever he tried to see his father's face, the image was blurred.

Ricky was certain this was not just a childhood fantasy. He knew that his father must have visited them when they were still in Finland because he could recall other early memories, not of the man himself but of his mother's evasive explanations later on. He supposed that at the beginning, when she still had hope, she must have referred to him as his father. By the time he was old enough to ask difficult questions, she must have begun laying the smokescreen that still obscured most of what he was looking for.

And it had all started here, in a room presumably much like this, with paper shoes and twenty degrees of frost and not enough money for food and fuel. He wondered who she would have turned to in such a predicament. She must have known who her relatives in Finland were. If pride or shame had prevented her from returning home, surely she would have turned to them?

Something so terrible had resulted from that plea for help that it had made her cut off all ties with Finland for the rest of her life. And Aunt Elvira must be one of those she had turned to. She was his mother's aunt, his grandmother's sister-in-law: and even back in those days, as a Finn she would probably have had a more liberal attitude to an illegitimate child than Satu's puritanical Scottish kin ever could.

So despite her apparent innocence, Aunt Elvira had to know.

Something else occurred to him as he looked around the last rooms from the 1940s and 50s. People who left even this low level of security to go and live in Pispala had to be at the last extremes of something. In her day Pispala hadn't been just a quaint suburb suffering creeping improvement: it had been the end of the line. According to the records she had stayed in Pispala before she went back to Scotland. Had she been driven there by desperation, or did she have friends who had taken her in? Had she been in some of the same ramshackle houses and even seen some of the same faces as he himself was doing now, a quarter of a century later?

He knew the answer at once, from his soul. His mother's enemies would have been the respectable, middle class people: well-off relatives with something to lose who spurned her in her most desperate need. Her friends would have been found among the ebullient anarchy of Pispala. For sure someone must have helped her, or she would scarcely have survived, let alone got passage back to England. He thought he could see it in these rooms. The quiet determination and the spirit of mutual assistance lived on in each and every one of them.

He retraced his steps through the museum, walking the halls of their past lives as if he was in a church. When he went out into the sunlight, he knew that he had found part of his answer. He had seen his mother's past and understood something of her pain.

CHAPTER 25

Ricky was always early: the bigger the date, the earlier he was. After 25 minutes he was beside himself at her tardiness, even though the town clock had only just struck six. Yet when she arrived his annoyance was forgotten in an instant and when she asked if he had been waiting long he lied cheerfully and with no sense of irony. They strolled off together towards the lower lake, taking their time as the sun mellowed and the shadows lengthened in the quiet streets.

At first it seemed that Satu was leading him intriguingly astray. After making their way along the beach where Tim and he had sunbathed, she skipped over the grassy bank and plunged into the woods behind, where the snow was now but a memory. As they advanced, the conifers thinned and became interspersed with deciduous trees, while the undergrowth grew lusher and more manicured. By the time they arrived the environs were so like his image of the Garden of Eden that he was almost purring with anticipation.

Presently they found themselves being funnelled through a gap in the trees by a coloured rope, to a point where attendants collected their tickets and indicated the way to the auditorium. Ricky was charmed the instant he saw it.

'What a fantastic place!'

'Yes,' agreed Satu with a gratified smile, 'it is something special.'

The stalls stood on a revolving circular platform, banked to let the audience step right onto the bottom level, while the rearmost seats almost touched the lower branches of the encircling trees. Yet it was the stage rather than the famous revolving structure that made the theatre so exceptional. The grassy clearing around the auditorium formed a natural stage about twenty feet deep, merging indefinitely into the surrounding woodland. It both encompassed the audience and placed them at the centre of the whole enchanted circle.

The image of a secret clearing in the woods was soon a living dream. Even as they were finding their seats, a strange, ethereal piping announced the beginning of the play. And then they were all laughing as a woodland fairy jumped out from the bushes and began to dance before them. From over to the left came another and then a third and soon the whole clearing was alive with music and dance. For a few minutes the people of Oberon and Titania were tumbling and frolicking all through the clearing, leaping over bushes with the aid of hidden trampolines as the music reached to a climax and then the seats began to revolve and the audience laughed and clapped in delight.

They came to rest facing towards the lake, the first scene bringing with it a cool breeze that caused Satu to draw the shawl around her shoulders. It was all in Finnish and Ricky had about as much idea of what was going on as if he'd been watching a Wagner opera. He hadn't liked to admit his ignorance but he had never seen or read "A Midsummer Night's Dream" and had only the vaguest notion of the plot. Yet it really didn't matter, for its charm transcended both time and language. The guy playing Puck was such a master of visual comedy that after the first act Ricky's ribs hurt from laughing.

He knew as if with the benefit of hindsight that there would never be another night quite like this. It was not just that he was sitting in an enchanted lakeside dell, laughing fit to die at Puck and Bottom playing Shakespeare in Finnish to the whim of a Czech director. That was just the background to his dream, rather as the sun staying in the sky all night was just lighting, bathing the whole fantasy in a ghostly twilight. The substance of the dream was Satu. He watched her in profile, the way she laughed, the way the light shimmered in her hair, the way she gave herself totally to the moment: and he wanted her so badly that he ached with it.

When the play was done, the two of them literally danced off into the woods together, captivated by the joyful magic. They chased each other through the trees, skipping up the steep slopes and bursting out from behind the trunks, Satu pirouetting and Ricky turning somersaults, something he had never done before in his life. By the time they got back to Pispala they were beyond laughter, their sides heaving as they gasped for breath.

They stopped at last in a part of the village he hadn't seen before and all at once he realised they were outside her house. She looked up at him with a serious, pensive expression: and then she said the words that he most wanted to hear. 'So, would you like to come in?'

'Oh, right - but it's quite late. Didn't you say you have to work early tomorrow?'

'Yes but tonight I don't feel so much like sleeping.'

'Oh, OK.'

He followed her up the stairs to the front door, his hopes rising with every step. She let them in and offered him coffee and he took it with shaking hands and was doubly glad of it because his mouth was suddenly dry. She'd brought him home and invited him in! He was still trying to accept that it was real when it got even better.

'So, this kitchen is not so great. Shall we go to my room?'

'Um, yes, alright.'

Taking his hand, she led him upstairs and down a long corridor. Her room was at the end, overlooking the lake. He was glad to see that she wasn't particularly tidy and his eyes moved several times to the slightly rumpled bed.

They went over to the window, looking out across the tree-tops to the midnight lake as they sipped their coffee. Part of him was infinitely relaxed while other parts burned with longing. He slipped an arm around her waist and she neither aided nor resisted but continued to sip silently at her coffee while she gazed out the window.

'I've had a great evening, Satu. Thank you.'

'Mmm, me too. I think this was a good Puck, yes?'

'He was a great Puck. I want to stay with you tonight.'

She looked at him now, her face grave but calm, still neither giving nor pulling away. 'So, you want to be my special friend?'

He grinned at the phrase but her face clouded ominously.

'A lot of men have wanted to be my special friend these last months but afterwards they were not my friends anymore. They made me feel so bad inside.'

The pain in her voice cut him and quite instinctively he reached out a hand to her, then pulled it back half-way as the inhibition awoke in him. 'I'm not like that.'

She stared into his eyes with a candour and vulnerability that wrenched his heart. Any half-decent actor could counterfeit what she was searching for – and he wondered if she could see the turmoil he was struggling to conceal. 'No,' she said at last, 'I don't think you are.'

He wished he could be so sure but he almost jumped for joy at the test passed. To confirm it he put his hand to her waist, exerting the lightest of pressure, to draw her in if she would come. And she did, putting her coffee down on the windowsill and holding him by the arms while she surveyed him with a steadiness that was almost a frown.

'Tell me, Ricky, what do you think of me?'

Apparently the tests were not yet over. But for all his longing, he did his best to let go of guile and speak from the heart. 'I think it's amazing how easily we get along together. We hardly know each other but I feel completely relaxed with you. I also want you so much that I'm trembling - and yet I'm so at ease it's almost as if we were brother and sister.'

'So, we feel the same. Sometimes it is a great freedom to be with a stranger from another country. They know nothing about you, about all the bad things you have done. You can start new with them.' Her eyes never left his, never wavered in their appraisal and after a few seconds she gave a sort of nod. 'So, I suppose you want to go to bed with me and be my friend, too?'

'Yes.'

She considered this for awhile and then evidently made up her mind because she slipped from him and went and sat on the bed, patting the space beside her. 'I'd like to talk for a while first. I want to know you better, even if we only find out some of the bad things.'

He nodded agreement and sat close enough to put his arm around her. It wasn't very comfortable, so presently he lay across the bed instead, pulling her down so they could lie face to face. He kissed her forehead lightly through the soft veil of her hair and it felt like heaven. Then he started to talk about what he had been doing since the last time he'd seen her, saying the first things that came into his mind. 'Yesterday I visited a marvellous house in the forest, far to the south, by the edge of the lake.'

'So, what house is that?'

'It's a palace made of wood, built by a great bishop who loved his flock so much that he went to live as far away from them as he could.'

She smiled and said, 'A palace, in our forest?'

'It's a summerhouse, really. An old retired couple took it when they had to leave Karelia after the war. It was so beautiful and peaceful, I could have stayed forever. And they are such nice people.'

Satu smiled broadly. 'We have a saying about people from Karelia. My mother taught this to me when I was very young and some new people moved in next to us. She said that when we lost Karelia, we lost good land but we gained good neighbours. I have always thought this is a nice saying.'

'Yes it is. And there's something more: I've just found out that my mother's family came from Karelia.'

'So, hello, neighbour.'

She grinned as she said it and he drew her in and kissed her and her mouth was soft as a dream. Her body felt so good beneath his hands that it made him want to take her right then and there but she held him back and wriggled her way out from under him. They were silent for some time before she spoke again.

'Penny for your thoughts.'

'Pardon?'

'Oh, I thought you were saying this in England. I meant to ask what are you thinking?'

'I'm sorry, you're right, that is how we say it. I was miles away.'

'Can I join you?'

'Yes, of course. It was the smell of your hair that set me dreaming.'

'Was it a nice dream?'

'Very. It smells of fresh straw.'

'What is straw?'

'It's like, um, wheat. After it's been harvested.'

'That's nice. But I suppose it means you want to harvest me.'

'God, I wasn't thinking that. Actually I was thinking about my mother.'

He saw at once that this was the wrong thing to say, though he wasn't sure exactly why. A shadow passed over her face and she drew away, only fractionally but enough for him to notice. Yet whatever it had been, it was quickly gone and a moment later she was smiling at him again.

'Do you always think about your mother when you are taking a girl to bed?'

'God no! I was thinking about when we first met in the disco and how for a moment, through all the smoke, I smelt a hint of fresh straw. I knew at once that it was one of those moments I'll always remember. And just now I looked at you and realised I'll always remember this moment, too. And it occurred to me that I have no idea how my mother and father met.'

She rolled over onto her back, her face both sad and happy. 'You know how to say very nice things to me. I think you must have got quite a lot of girls with this line.'

'It wasn't a line. It's the truth. Most people know how their parents met, don't they? What about yours?'

She laughed. 'Yes, it's true! They met on the railway station in Seinäjoki. My mother always laughs when she tells people about it and says it was the most unromantic place she could imagine!'

'There you are then. I even know how Tim's parents met. But not my own.'

The shadow passed over Satu's face again. It was as if the mention of his parents affected her personally in some way. 'You really don't know very much about your family here in Finland, do you?'

'No.'

'But you must know some things. Why don't you tell me about them?'

After the Workers' Museum he was conscious that he somehow knew more than he understood and he wondered if talking about it might help him to see through the hazy memories of his childhood.

'When my stepfather died, I was secretly glad. We'd never been close and I was just getting to the stage of being obsessively curious about my real father. Of course I used to ask my mother about him when I was little but she'd always made it perfectly clear that the question was unwelcome. She could be very final in the way she treated questions that she didn't want to answer.'

He fell silent again, thinking of that sudden, sharp glare and the toss of her head as she turned it away, the mane of red-gold hair giving the dismissal a regal finality, like a lion dismissing a challenge not worthy of its attention.

'When I was 14 I really gave her hell over it. And I changed my name back to Suomalainen within a month of my stepfather's death. It was the kind of calculated turning of the knife that adolescents are so mercilessly good at.'

Satu stiffened beside him and looked at him with sudden intensity. 'You have refused to use your stepfather's name?'

'Yes, it never seemed to fit. I always felt like a Suomalainen, if that makes any sense.'

She relaxed again but now, unseen by him, there was a new light in her eyes. 'So you always knew this name, Suomalainen?'

'Right. It was my mother's family name. My grandfather died before I was born but my grandmother was still alive, so it wasn't anything mum could have concealed. Though I think she would have done if she could.'

'You think she hated Finland so much?'

'Absolutely. She and my grandmother used to have terrible silent arguments about it. I'd take advantage of my gran's presence to plague mum with difficult questions and I could see the looks that passed between them. Sometimes gran would start to answer and my mother would stop her with a 'don't you dare' look that could have frozen a volcano. And like the little shit that I was, I played one off against the other to try and get a hint of the truth. And sometimes just for the sheer hell of it.'

'You should not blame yourself for this, Ricky. It is natural at that age. It is not something to be ashamed of.'

'The worst of it is that after I found out she had cancer, I spent more time worrying about not knowing who my father was than I did worrying about her.'

'I do not believe that is really true, Ricky. You are too hard on yourself. But did you ask her about your father again?'

'Not until the very end. I never spoke to her about it after I realised how ill she was, not until the last time I saw her. It was awful. She was trying so hard to be brave and to hold herself together and all I could think about was that she was going to die without telling me and then I'd never know.'

He trailed off, his face a picture of desolation. Satu reached out and touched his hand and presently he regained enough control to continue.

'It seemed as if she was getting better. She was out of hospital and looking the best I'd seen her in months. The crisis seemed to have past, so I went back down to London. Three days later she was dead. It took her so quickly it was terrifying. And all I could think about was that I didn't know the name of my bloody father. She was dying right in front of me and I barely even spoke to her because I couldn't ask her about the only things that were really on my mind. It was only after she was dead that I remembered all the other things I wanted to say. But too late. Too bloody late.'

'Ricky, it's alright. We never really expect that people are going to die. You shouldn't be hurting yourself like this: I think you should be proud.'

'Proud?'

'Of course. She must have known you wanted to ask about those things and she must have been so grateful that you didn't. Even if you didn't recognise it, she will have known how much you loved her. It's not always the things on our minds that are the most important.'

'Do you really think so?'

She smiled and ran her fingers through his hair. 'Well, yes, I think I know a good person when I meet one.'

He felt something inside of himself melt, but almost immediately he was struck by a thought that made him give a sudden, stark laugh. 'My God, I forgot why I was here. I was all set on seducing you and instead I've ended up telling you about my mother dying of cancer. Brilliant! That must rate as the biggest turn-off ever.'

Her response, when it came, was so softly spoken that it was little more than a whisper. 'Oh no: I have been hearing much worse things, and from men I like much less.'

She got to her feet then and walked to the door, closing it behind her and leaving him alone in the room. He supposed she must have gone to the bathroom so he went and stood by the window, looking out at the lake while he waited for her to return. When he heard the door open again he turned to see: and he could barely credit what his eyes were telling him. Satu was drifting across the room in a long, white nightdress that flowed over her body as she moved, diaphanous yet demur. Her fringe shadowed lowered eyes and her hands were at her sides as she approached, silent as a ghost. She stopped at the bed and before he could find any words she had pulled back the covers, taking them right off to expose the plain white sheet. Then she looked up at him and smiled sweetly, almost sadly. 'It's quite warm, we won't need these.'

He was at a loss: in that moment all he knew was a kind of awe. Yet his hands took her and drew her to him and his lips kissed her hungrily. She responded with a gentle giving, until finally she disengaged and held him back, pointing to the door across the room.

'The bathroom is out there.'

'Oh, right. I'll just be a minute.'

He washed as quickly and thoroughly as he could. He wanted her so much it actually hurt. It had been so long since he'd had a girl and she was so gorgeous he hardly dared to believe it. He kept expecting that something would happen to mess it up: but when he came out she was lying on the bed with the same sad smile on her face. He lay down beside her, his hand miraculously ceasing to tremble as he traced his fingers slowly over her body. Just before he kissed her again she said, 'You are the best thing that's happened to me in ages.'

He looked at her in genuine amazement. 'I'm not so special.'

'Oh yes, you are. Believe me, I know.'

He recognised the obvious implication about her recent past and knew a moment of uncertainty: yet only about himself, never about her. But then the confidence of lust overtook him and he got up and quickly stripped off the rest of his clothes. He was rock hard already and he clambered quickly back onto the bed, entwining his legs with hers and pressing kisses onto her as his hands roamed at will. She was pliant but too passive and presently he drew back and looked at her in silent enquiry. But she turned her head away and wouldn't meet his gaze.

He was too far-gone to hold back any longer, so he cupped one hand around her breast and bit gently through the material of her gown until the nipple rose beneath it. His other hand pushed the nightdress up her thigh, caressing as he went - and still she neither responded nor resisted. Finally the gown was trapped between her body and the bed, so he knelt between her legs, preparing to lift her and remove the last impediment all in one easy movement.

Satu opened her eyes and put her hands on his arms, gently restraining him as she met his gaze. The mix of feelings in her expression was strange to him and hard to read. There was fondness there and something that he thought was sorrow but as she spoke he realised they were on different planets.

'You know what I wish?'

He asked with his eyes.

'I wish that we didn't do it.'

It hit him like a hammer blow - and yet the response that came unbidden from his lips was, 'Oh… OK,' even as inside his head he was screaming, 'Oh shit, shit, Shit!'

Satu was watching him very closely but evidently saw nothing that belied his response. She pulled herself back up the bed a little and they were both silent as he flopped down beside her, burying his face in the pillow, his erection still hard against her side.

She put her arm around him and hugged him, her face close to his, her breath on his cheek as she spoke. 'I really need you to be my friend, Ricky.'

He couldn't take it any more, so he rolled over onto his back and stared at the ceiling, thinking unchristian thoughts. But after a little while he reached out his hand to gently stroke her hair. From the corner of his eye he could see her looking at him with such an expression of fragile hope that it melted the frustration in his head, even if it didn't touch other parts of his anatomy.

'Is it alright?' she asked, anxiety clear in her voice.

'Yes, it's OK. Really.'

She was loudly silent, not hearing the same reassurance in his tone. He knew it and made a gargantuan effort.

'Oh God. Look, I really do want to make love with you but if it's not what you want then that's OK. We can just sleep together. It's alright.'

She gave him a beautific smile and kissed him on the lips in such a sisterly fashion that he could have strangled her.

'If you had met me a few weeks ago, I would have gone with you without a thought. I went with so many men. Now I wish I hadn't but at least I've found out what it is to have my freedom and that's something, isn't it?'

He supposed it probably was and he would very much like to have been one of the men she'd had it with. Yet he considered it impolite to say so and tried to tell himself how important it was to show he really cared for her.

Their eyes met again, neither of them certain what the other intended.

'I know you must think bad things about me, to invite you here and then ask you just to be my friend.'

He shook his head but he knew she could see the truth. He watched her absorbing what he couldn't hide and as she did so her face crumbled and she bowed her head and said, 'I'm sorry, Ricky. If you really need to have a girl, of course I'll do it for you.'

This was too much for him and he rocked back in equal exasperation and bewilderment. 'I don't understand, Satu. What's going on?'

She responded with a tone and expression that he could only construe as desperation. 'I just need you to be my friend, Ricky. I've been hoping someone like you would happen but I never really expected it.' She lowered her gaze and her next words came very quietly. 'But you can have me if you want to.'

'I don't know what to say...'

'I know. It's quite simple but now I feel ashamed. When we first met, even when you came home with me just now, I thought it would be like all the other times. I expected to go to bed with you and that afterwards you would be like all the others. But I still hoped. And the more you talked, the more I found I liked you and I began to hope some more, but by then it was too late. I'm sorry for doing this, Ricky, I didn't mean it to turn out this way but just now I saw maybe there was a chance. Perhaps I don't have the right and I should just go with you and not ask you this. But I've been with too many men these last months and I want so much for you to be my friend.'

She said nothing more but simply looked at him until, finally, he got it. She meant exactly what she said. For months every other man had fetched her, fucked her and forgotten her and now she was praying that here at last was someone who would be what she needed him to be.

'I am your friend.'

He saw the relief and happiness flood into her face and even before she replied it felt as if a good spirit had touched his heart.

'You see, you really are the best thing that's happened to me in ages.' She bent forwards across the bed and gave him another sisterly kiss, which was not what he wanted but which he yet savoured as infinitely precious. He even managed to stroke her cheek in his best attempt at brotherly affection.

'Satu, I'd rather just be with you than do it with most other girls.'

It was at least half-true: and yet the discovery that she only wanted him for a friend was a knife in all his hopes. It was almost more than he could bear.

'So, you really are a special man.'

He could see her eyes watering as she said it and her face was such a double-edged sword that it was finally too much for him. He slumped back, closed his eyes and groaned. He liked her more than lust itself but he was rock hard and his balls ached so badly he could hardly move.

Ricky felt her get up and step away from the bed and he supposed that now he'd have to sleep on the floor, or lie beside her all night without touching her. He wasn't sure which would be worse. Then he heard her say, 'So, I don't think I need this' and he opened his eyes to see her reach behind herself to undo something. Before his astonished gaze she slid the gown off her shoulders and let it fall to the floor.

She was wearing a pair of tiny white briefs and nothing more. He stared at her in the half-light, the loveliness of her body numbing even his confusion over what was now being offered. As she came back onto the bed he shifted to give her more room but she just shook her head and knelt beside him, reaching forward to kiss him once more. And then, incredibly, her hand closed around his cock with a cool, firm grip and she gave a little laugh at the hardness of him and said, 'So, at least I can help you with this.'

He didn't reply: he couldn't speak. He almost came at once with the sheer electrifying shock of it but she took him in hand quite matter-of-factly, as if this was perfectly normal. It was so devastating that he nearly gagged but she just concentrated on taking care of his need, her features quite serious and her art unlike anything he had ever known.

Several times she brought him to the edge, only to hold him back, apparently intent on prolonguing his pleasure as long as possible. Then, as if to prove to him that he still had the capacity to be amazed, she smiled and said, 'You really have a nice one, Ricky' and without another word she kissed him once where it counted most and then went down on him.

Ricky had only been with three other girls and only one of them had ever done this for him. If he was honest, it had been something to be endured rather than enjoyed. But Satu was amazing. Her lips and mouth were so soft and her tongue so deft that after barely a minute she had him crying out in the most exquisite ecstasy he had ever known. When at last he could stand no more she suddenly intensified her tempo and brought him off with half a dozen deep, wonderful strokes. She kept working on him as he came, until he subsided with a bone-deep groan. Yet even then it was not over. She finished off diligently, before giving him an affectionate parting kiss and then rising up with a beautiful laugh of enjoyment at her own handywork. 'There. Now you can sleep.'

She was wrong about that. All he could do was lie there, staring up at the ceiling, poleaxed with pleasure. When he had regained the power of speech he reached across to stroke her hair as he exclaimed, 'Oh, Satu, you are the sweetest girl I've ever known.'

'But not so sweet as the ones who do it with you, eh?'

'That was better than anything anyone else has ever done for me.'

She squeezed him tight for that and when he put his arms around her she said, 'I feel safe with you.' She nuzzled close up against him and he touched her ear with the softest of kisses, forgiving himself the lie that had so disarmed her. However blissful it might be to feel her breathing slow into sleep beside him, what he felt most of all was a hard and raucous yearning: for the thing she had done was like a delicious appetiser to a man with a whole year's hunger to satisfy. But she was right of course: she was safe with him. She had invoked the magic talisman of friendship and to Ricky that was sacrosanct.

In the end he lay with her until her body's rhythm lulled his own into harmony and he dozed off into dreamland. He dreamed that he was his father and that Satu was his mother and she kept saying that she just wanted to be friends but he laughed as he rode her and then his mother was there as well, pointing at Satu and saying something that he couldn't understand. He awoke to find Satu mumbling and restless, so he stroked her hair until gradually all was calm again and he held her in his arms and slept.

CHAPTER 26
Christmas, 1955

He returned in time for Christmas, just as he had promised. She never really expected him to and the moment she saw him standing in the doorway, all the weeks of loneliness and doubt were forgotten.

It probably wouldn't have happened but for her getting half pissed at the work party before he arrived. He pulled her onto the dance floor at once and afterwards they demolished half a bottle of vodka together at the bar without ever taking their eyes off each other. She needed no encouragement to go out behind the mill with him.

It was freezing in the woodshed, with flurries of snow coming in under the door but they'd not felt it. He pushed her up against the woodpile and opened her coat and she loved the feel of his hands on her body and the taste of vodka mixing with the salt and tobacco on his lips. She wanted him so badly that they both laughed when he lifted her skirts and got his hands inside her knickers. Then he'd lifted her right off the ground, forcing her back against the wood so that the sawn ends were jabbing into her back.

'Have you got a thing?' she asked, trying to hold him off until he could reassure her. He just laughed and undid himself, then got one hand behind her right knee and hoisted her leg up into the crock of his arm. She suddenly realised he was about to put himself into her and her voice became frantic.

'No, not without... TK, don't, please!'

But it was too late. She felt the force of him driving into her, hefting her upwards as he fucked her. She tried to push him off but he was too strong, ramming himself into her again and again until she was gasping at the force of it and the logs were grinding into her kidneys. He kept one hand around her throat while he screwed her and when he came he bit her so hard on the neck that he drew blood. The mark lasted well into the New Year: the year in which her child would be born. There was never any doubt in her mind about when she had conceived.

'Happy Christmas', he said when he withdrew at last.

CHAPTER 27
Thursday 21st May, 1981

When he awoke she was giving her hair a final brush in the bedroom mirror. He watched, unseen and delighted, as she stood and smoothed down her dress. It was a simple print frock and she looked so lovely that he could have cried.

His first attempt at conversation was somewhat inhibited by the fact that he had a mouthful of bedclothes, besides which only half his brain seemed to be functioning. 'Uh, hello. What time is it?'

'Ah, I didn't want to wake you. It's seven o'clock.'

'Oh God.' He buried his face in the pillows.

'Well, you don't have to get up, sleepy-head. There is everything here for breakfast when you want it.'

'Uh, thanks. Why was it you had to get up so early?'

'I have to make a practical work in the country for my course.'

'A field trip?'

'So, yes, that is it.' She put down her hairbrush and looked at him. 'You are going to see your aunt later today?'

He had to think about this before it came back to him. 'Yes. I'm meeting Tim at noon.'

Her expression suggested some unspoken dissatisfaction but he couldn't see why and he wasn't feeling bright enough to worry about it.

'You will be there most of the afternoon, I expect.'

'Yes, I guess.'

'Did she know your mother well?'

'I'm not sure.' He became vaguely aware that she was hanging around, as if expecting something. He did his best to focus on her and he thought she was on the verge of saying something but instead she gave a little shrug and turned towards the door.

'Satu.'

'Yes?' She answered without looking back, her hand on the doorknob.

'I'm still your friend.'

The light caught her hair as she turned and the smile she gave him would have rewarded Atlas for a whole year's work. 'I'm glad.'

'I mean it. I meant everything I said last night. You were wonderful. I enjoyed sleeping with you even more than, ah...than that very fine Puck.'

She laughed and blew him a kiss.

'Can I see you tonight, when I get back?' He watched her thinking it over and when he saw the dimple in her cheeks he knew he was there. But it was not quite what he had bargained for.

'So, yes, I know where we can meet.'

'Yes?'

'At the women's choice disco.'

'Pardon?'

But without another word she opened the door and went straight out, a mischievous smile breaking over her face as she started to close it behind her.

'Satu! Wait! I don't know where that is...'

'Timi will know,' she called, her words cut off by the closing of the door.

He flopped back onto the bed with a groan. The little minx, what was she setting him up for? Pretty soon though he gave up wondering about it, as he smelt her hair on the pillows and the warm scent of her body in the sheets, so instead he lazed in the memory of her until he was sated and then showered and dressed and set out to rendezvous with his translator.

CHAPTER 28

Something curious happened when Elvira answered the door. Just before she greeted them, his aunt drew back her head and gave a stiff little nod. She was all smiles afterwards, so Ricky assumed the nod must have been in recognition of their promptness and he put it out of mind.

She led them through to the sitting room and for the first half hour serious conversation was impossible. Elvira was in constant motion to and from the kitchen, plying them with drinks and hors d'oeuvres and refusing to discuss anything other than their health, the weather, Tim's height and how glad she was to see them. Finally she commented on how much Ricky resembled the men of his family, giving him his entry.

At first all went well, with Tim having no trouble in keeping pace with Elvira's reminiscences. She seemed perfectly at ease with the subject, wandering extensively and somewhat erratically but without obviously avoiding anything. Yet after a while Ricky began to suspect that her apparently random forays down memory lane were in fact carefully structured.

When he asked about his mother, his aunt was all smiles but the reminiscences were all limited to a few specific periods in her niece's youth. Equally, there were no bounds to her pleasure in recalling her contacts with his grandfather Ernie down the years: her brother-in-law had evidently been a favourite. Yet Ricky's grandmother was notable by her absence. When he mentioned her, the reaction was similar to that first, stiff nod at the front door.

He suddenly knew where he'd seen this reaction before. He'd once had a girlfriend whose parents considered him to be below their social level. Actually he'd been quite chuffed to be cast in the role of undesirable boyfriend. One day she'd taken him round to their house and her mother had come into the room without realising he was present. Her face had been all animation, lit up just like Elvira's and then she had seen him. Her features had frozen and she had given that same stiff nod. It was an acknowledgement from a person brought up to believe that the civilities have to be observed but quite unable to disguise their dislike of the recipient. In Elvira's case, it was as if she was at once both pleased and appalled to see him.

If it had been only his grandmother who provoked this reaction, he could have dismissed it as simple dislike. But it gradually became clear that Elvira's frosty dismissal appeared not just when particular individuals were mentioned but even when particular *periods* were mentioned. The more he probed, the more apparent it became that her memory was highly selective, capable of freezing out anything that displeased her. And without exception the things she excluded were the very people, places and periods in which he was most interested.

Eventually he decided to broach the subject they had both been studiously avoiding. 'Aunt Elvira', he began, with an attempt at the stern determination of a man who knew the facts and now wanted to get at the reasons, 'I want to know about my father and why no-one would help my mother when he deserted her.'

He watched Elvira closely as Tim translated but he knew she had understood his gist from tone and manner alone. She shifted her gaze and fidgeted with the hem of her skirt as she listened. Then she looked at him and gave that damned nod.

At first he thought she might actually refuse to answer but after a short pause she muttered something that Tim obviously couldn't follow. Not for the first time Ricky noticed how Tim was incredibly diplomatic when it counted, adopting a tone of perfect politeness as he asked her to repeat herself. Elvira looked annoyed and said something sharp. Tim replied in a most courteous manner, as if seeking a small clarification for his own better understanding. Finally she nodded again and threw out a curt sentence, turning her head away as she finished in clear indication that she would say no more.

Ricky looked at him expectantly and Tim had to think before putting it into English. 'I couldn't follow all of it but she said, 'that *something* family' and I think, 'those *filthy* people'. The Finns have the best swear words in the world and I don't know all of them but something stronger than 'bastards' came up.'

'That was it?'

'She said she hasn't spoken to your father's family for over forty years, that she doesn't know where they are and that she doesn't want to.'

'Forty years? Are you sure?'

'Yes.'

This was unexpected. All his life he had known there was an unspeakable hurt between his mother and father, which extended to his grandparents. Yet if what Elvira said was true, then the rift between their families had formed long before his mother and father even met. It implied that his experience was but one episode in a dynastic feud stretching back to before the Second World War. He looked at her in blank bewilderment.

'But why? What did they *do*? Aunt, who *are* they?'

His ignorance seemed to touch her more than his confident demands. She cast a sideways glance at him, looked away, then cast another. But she wouldn't meet his eyes and a moment later she got quickly to her feet and walked out of the room, with a turn of speed surprising in one of her age. Ricky glanced at Tim, who could only shrug.

Only a moment later Elvira returned, carrying a photograph. It was not one Ricky had seen before and the grimy film of dirt on the glass suggested long storage. His aunt jabbed a crinkled finger at two men standing in the centre of the picture. They were on a quay and behind them was a large freighter. From their clothes, Ricky judged that it was probably taken sometime in the 1930s.

The man on the left he recognised from photographs in his grandmother's house as being his grandfather Ernie, who had died a few months before he was born. The one on the right he didn't know. He looked at Elvira for explanation and she said, jabbing her finger first at one, then at the other, 'Eero ja hänen liikekumppani Juri.'

Grandfather Eero (alias Ernie) and his business partner, Juri. Whom Ricky had never heard of.

After that the story unfolded so fast it was difficult to keep up. It rapidly became clear that there was another side of the Suomalainen family history of which Ricky had been completely unaware. It was based around the family shipping business, in which grandfather Ernie and his partner Juri were the key players. Yet it seemed that Juri wasn't a relative, or at least not a Suomalainen. When he asked his aunt if they were related, she gave a definitive 'No' that was so strong it did rather make him wonder. But when he pressed the point by asking Tim to check what Juri's family name had been, she sniffed and gave that look again. And then she said, with a note of scorn that translated without any assistance, 'Karlsholm.'

The same name as the family who had lived at the address his mother had given him. The family that Bengt Larsson in the record office had been so unwilling to discuss. Despite Elvira's protestations that they were not related, it was stretching credulity too far to believe that it could be a coincidence. Suddenly it seemed more than probable that the Satu he was looking for was Katerina Satu Karlsholm after all. But if so, Elvira was not about to admit it.

In fact his aunt displayed an almost pathological hatred for anything associated with the Karlsholms. She seemed to blame them for nearly everything bad that had happened over the past half century, not just to her own family but to the whole nation. Evidently when the war came, Juri and his wife (whose name Elvira refused even to utter), had somehow cheated Ernie into bankruptcy and sold out to Finland's enemies. Whether that meant the Russians or the Nazis wasn't clear; she seemed to imply both.

The story was rendered even murkier by the fact that Elvira's hatred went all the way back to the civil war between the Reds and Whites, for it seemed she blamed the Karlsholms for the death of her brother-in-law, Ricky's great uncle Rudi. Tim couldn't make much sense of the tale but she claimed to have been present during the battle of Pispala and to have actually seen Rudi shot by a firing squad under Juri's personal command. She was almost incoherent during this part of the story and by mental arithmetic it was obvious she couldn't have been more than eight at the time.

Ricky didn't know what to make of it, except that it had kicked off the feud and that Elvira regarded the Swedish Karlsholms as neo-fascist scum who'd sold out their country, swindled their business associates and murdered her own brother-in-law.

Then she told him that his father was a Karlsholm. Worse, he was the son of Juri Karlsholm and his unspeakable wife. In short, Ricky's mother had run away with the son of the family ogre.

Now, finally, Ricky felt that he understood his mother's plight. How could she ever have gone back home after that? She would have stayed in Finland and starved first.

But for him. She was, after all, a mother and so in the end she had gone home: not for herself but for her son. Ricky recognised immediately that only some terrible rejection by his father's family could have driven her to do so. That rejection had cast a shadow over his whole life.

Elvira spoke of the treatment her niece had received at the hands of the Karlsholms with such a mixture of vitriol and vagueness that Ricky felt sure she had only indirect knowledge of what had passed. Yet the bare outline was enough: Satu had gone to Juri Karlsholm and his wife and had been not merely rejected but humiliated and abused.

'What was her name, Elvira? Juri Karlsholm's wife?'

One glance at Elvira was enough for him to register the hatred that any mention of this person provoked. Her lips remained firmly sealed but he had to know. The name he was asking for was, after all, that of his own grandmother.

'Aunt Elvira, please... tell me her name?' Once again he thought she would refuse but in the end she spat it out, as if it were a bad piece of meat.

'Katerina!'

Ricky recognised it at once as the name of the girl who had lived in Kirkkokatu: the one she had apparently rejected in favour of her middle name, Satu. Now he felt sure that his mother had not made a mistake in her letter. Despite everything, she must have deliberately sent him to the Karlsholms, though he could only guess whether it was for reconciliation or retribution.

To Ricky's surprise, it felt as if a great load of anger had fallen away from him. His mother had carried this burden alone for more than twenty years but in the end she had recognised his right to face it for himself. And one part of what had to be faced was that the old lady sitting in front of him must herself have turned his mother away in her moment of greatest need.

Elvira had returned to the joys of denouncing his father's family when her diatribe slowed and trailed off, caught and held by Ricky's stare. He waited until she was silent before he put it to her. 'You knew I'd come back. You were waiting.' Even before he heard Tim's translation, he could tell from her expression that she not only understood but also accepted the guilt of it.

'I've waited all these years. I knew she would never forgive me but I always hoped her son might. I was afraid you would never come but I waited anyway.'

'Why wouldn't you help her?'

It was agonising having to wait for this to be translated, not least because of the pain in the old woman's face. But he was remorseless in his need.

'Those dreadful people...that family. Even now... I can't bear to think of them. What they did. If it had been anyone else, anyone at all. She could have gone with the devil and I wouldn't have cared. I wanted to help, truly I did. But it was him...'

'My father?'

She shook her head, evidently in the affirmative. 'I was right, in a way. You look so like him.'

'I look like my father?'

Ricky thought he saw it all now. Elvira had hated his father's family long before his mother came to her for help. Knowing this, Satu must indeed have treated it as a last resort. And it must have struck Elvira as the ultimate betrayal, to have gone with the enemy and borne his son; a son whose resemblance to his father was evidently so strong that the sight of him on the doorstep was enough to provoke that reflexive nod.

The sight of *him*, yes. But what about *her*?

'Aunt Elvira, you say that I look like my father. But what about my sister? You haven't told me anything about her.'

Elvira's reaction to the word 'sister' showed that she had been waiting for this. To Ricky's alarm, there were suddenly tears in the old lady's eyes. 'I never saw her. I never saw either of you. I turned her away before you were born, God help me.'

'Before I was born?'

'Yes, when Satu was pregnant. She came to me after your father tried to make her have an abortion.'

'Then what happened to her? Where did she go?'

'God forgive me, I would not help her, any more than her own parents. I told her she had shamed our good name, just like her mother. So she went back to those others. To her.'

'To my other grandmother? To Katerina Karlsholm?'

Elvira just shook her head but Ricky couldn't stop now. 'Aunt, I'm sorry, I don't mean to upset you but I have to know. I came back to find my sister, you understand? Until my mother died I never even knew she existed. If the Karlsholms know where she is, then I have to speak to them.'

Elvira nodded through her tears, holding a small lace handkerchief to her face. It was some time before she regained her composure and Ricky took the opportunity to complete the question. 'My sister was also called Satu, wasn't she?' Again, his aunt nodded. So it was true and she had known it all along. But why hadn't she told him before? Why the denial?

'What happened to her? Where is she?'

'They took her.'

'Took her? Who took her?'

'The Karlsholms.'

'The Karlsholms took my sister?'

Elvira looked up at him, mist still clouding her eyes. For the first time, Ricky began to sense there was something worse to come. 'Mum told me that Satu was born before me but I can't find any record of her.'

'There are no records. Katerina Karlsholm has seen to that.'

'I don't understand you. How can that be?'

'She has great influence.'

'But surely she couldn't get rid of....' he trailed off, appalled by the import of what he had been about to say. *Of the evidence.*

As he felt the blood draining from his face, Elvira seemed to gather strength. 'Your sister is not a Suomalainen any more: she never really was. No-one else knew about her birth. She was alone, your mother, with no-one to protect her. They took her baby and she could do nothing.'

Ricky looked aghast at Tim, who was visibly shaken by what he was translating.

'Why? Why on earth would they do that? When was this, Aunt Elvira? When was my sister born?'

The expression on Elvira's face mixed surprise and woe in equal proportions. 'But you are twins.'

He reeled, his hand going instinctively to his forehead to calm the rush of blood that was about to burst his temples. The word came out dully, not even as a question. 'Twins.'

'Yes. She has never told you?'

'Oh God, I don't think I can cope with this.'

The old lady sighed, touching her eyes once more with her handkerchief. 'Poor Satu. It must have been more than she could bear, even to think about it. This I can understand but it has made things harder for you, nephew.'

'What happened to her? Where did they take her?'

'Nobody knows. It was the scandal, of course. They wanted to keep it quiet. They made your mother sign papers and then as soon as the baby was born, they took her away. She must have been given to foster parents, or perhaps to a home.'

'Have you searched?'

The old lady shook her head. 'It would have been useless. The Karlsholms were even more powerful in those days than today. Even if they had been forced to admit what they had done, they had documents proving she had agreed to the adoption. It was all she could do to save you.'

Ricky sat bolt upright. 'But how could that happen? How could they take my sister and not me?'

'Because you were born later. They never knew about you.'

'I don't understand.'

'They did not know there were twins. When your sister was born, they took her away with them at once. You came after they had gone.'

To Ricky, this was verging on the incomprehensible. He knew next to nothing about childbirth but surely it would be obvious if a woman was having twins, or if she was still pregnant after giving birth? And yet...

'Your mother knew that if she caused trouble, she would lose you, too. So in the end she had no choice but to return to Scotland with you and to abandon her daughter.'

'Oh God.'

'She never tried to find her again?' asked Tim, too absorbed in the tale to remain a spectator.

'No, she never came back.'

'She couldn't,' said Ricky, with the beginnings of understanding. 'She had nowhere to turn. If it really was a legal adoption she wouldn't have had a leg to stand on. My God, what a nightmare.'

Now at last he thought he understood. Everything about his mother's attitude towards both Finland and his father fell into place. The bastard had not only got her pregnant and then deserted her, he'd also forced her to give up her child. How could she ever have told anyone about her lost daughter after that?

Even as he thought of that lost sister, a face came to him: the face of the one Satu he *had* found. And whole new layers of horror burst upon him.

They had been flirting together, comparing star signs. They had been so amused to discover they were both Virgos, born just a couple of days apart. September 27th and 29th, 1956. It had reassured him that she was not the one.

The nausea struck like a wave, his whole body flushed with sudden sweat. Then his skin turned icy cold and the colour drained from his face. He was conscious of them looking at him in alarm but he couldn't speak. For a moment he actually thought he was going to throw up on the carpet.

As quickly as it had come, the panic passed. After a couple of deep breaths he forced himself to start thinking rationally again. Neither Tim nor his aunt must be allowed to suspect. They didn't know about her birthday and they mustn't get an inkling of what he was imagining.

He collected himself and smiled his apologies. He was feeling a little off colour. No, of course it wasn't the cakes, he had just not been feeling very well lately. Probably it was delayed shock from his mother's death, coupled with the excitement of all these discoveries…

Eventually he even managed a smile: and that was when he finally remembered to ask Elvira about his father's Christian name. When she told him, he almost didn't believe her.

It was Thorvald.

The sudden release of tension was so great that Ricky burst out laughing. He'd always assumed that his father was at least worthy of hatred, rather than merely contempt. But he couldn't hate someone called Thorvald: it would be like hating a Wally. Elvira looked at him as if he was nuts but it would have been hopeless trying to explain it to her, so he could only grin inanely.

'Thank you for telling me all this. I'm afraid it's rather hard to take it in: I guess I'll have to go away and think about it for a while. But I really do appreciate your helping me; I know it can't have been easy.'

She looked at him with obvious relief. And then she asked him a question. 'You will not meet with him?'

When Tim translated Ricky looked at her in surprise, though on reflection it was a natural enough thing for her to have asked. 'I don't think so. I don't really want to find him. I just needed to know who he was.' It was at least partially a lie but he judged it to be the best thing for her to hear.

'Good,' she said, 'I thought you would search for him.'

'Is he here, in Tampere?'

'I don't know. Perhaps.'

'Well, anyway, I think I know all I need to know about him, don't you? I'm a Suomalainen, after all.'

She blinked, taken aback, then gave a small smile. 'Yes. You look like him but you are not like him. You are your mother's son.'

'Right. Always have been and always will be. I couldn't ask for any better.'

They both smiled - and the bond was sealed between them. What could not be forgotten was forgiven.

'You will search for her, though? For your sister?'

'Oh yes.'

She nodded, clearly uncertain of his chances. He was monumentally glad that no-one was privy to the nature of his uncertainties on *that* score.

None of them wanted to prolong it after that and they took their leave as soon as politeness allowed. As they headed back to Pispala, Ricky felt a new and grimmer determination. There was unfinished business to attend to. Now he knew part of the truth, he had to discover the rest, whatever the cost. His mother always said he had a slow fuse but God help you when it burnt to the end.

So God help Mr Bengt Larsson at the record office if he tried that punctilious crap again. And God help the Karlsholms when he finally tracked *them* down. But first he had to find out whether or not it was possible that Satu could be his sister and he had to find out at once. He had to find someone who would know about the birthing of twins, to set his mind at rest. Or else God help Ricky Suomalainen.

CHAPTER 29
8 March, 1956

It was too cold to sit but she was too nauseous to walk and the chill got right into her guts, making it even worse. Then the cramps came again and she doubled over gagging, crying out for help that wouldn't come.

Why hadn't he come? She raised her head to look out the window but the condensation had frozen on the inside and rendered it completely opaque.

Oh God, help me. She doubled up again and when the cramps subsided she was looking at the empty stove, where the last of the wood had gone last night. It was minus five inside the room and she had no way of getting warm. More than anything in the world, she just wanted him to hold her tight and make her feel safe and warm. If he'd only come back soon, everything could still be alright. He'd always said that he could make anything work out right.

But if he didn't come quickly, he'd find her frozen stiff. She could feel her face going numb, the breath forming a thin layer of frost on her skin. Deep-frozen Satu. Still, at least that would solve the problem

It had all gone bad so quickly. Yet she'd forgive him everything if only he'd stand by her now. Please God, make him stand by me. I'm so frightened...

She gazed through the frosted glass and tried to imagine the warmth of her mother's kitchen in Leith. It was useless. She could never go back now, they would never forgive her. Oh God, what had she done? Just a few months ago it had all seemed so perfect. If only she could go back to the summer. If only she had been more careful. If only.

She pulled herself upright and wiped a sleeve roughly across her face. Pull yourself together: you got yourself into this mess and you're the one who'll have to get yourself out of it. If he comes in here now he's going to take one look and run a mile. Stand up and walk. Make yourself do it, there's no-one else.

And then she heard something that made her heart fly to her mouth. Familiar steps crunched on the snow outside and a shadow passed the frosted window. There was a rough knock and then the door was flung open the way he always did it. The smell that she loved came in with him, along with a blast of freezing air.

He gave the room a sweeping glance that took in everything and then gave an exclamation of disbelief. 'The bloody fire's out. You'll freeze.'

She nodded, her eyes bright with the hope that had ignited the moment she saw him. Despite everything, she still believed. 'There's no more wood.'

'So why didn't you go and get some?'

'There's no money, either. And I couldn't, I was sick.'

'Why? What the hell's wrong with you now?'

She summoned up all her courage and told him. Her eyes never left his face all the while she was speaking and at the end, even before he said a word, she knew that she was lost. She saw in quick succession the shock, the disbelief, the flicker of guilt and then the unbelievable thing, the thing that she had never expected. His words, when they came, only served to confirm it. He was so unemotional, so logical, so in control.

He had done this before. She was not the first.

CHAPTER 30
Thursday 21st May, 1981

He found Pekka drinking coffee in the kitchen, his Trotsky glasses on the table in front of him. He looked surprisingly beaky without them and as Ricky came in he was rubbing his eyes with his fists.

'Ricky. Excuse me. Hei.'

'How's things? Is Anna here?'

'No but she should be back soon.'

'Good, there's something I really need to ask her. Oh, and I heard from Tim that you were trying to get hold of me. Something about a message from the guy at the record office?'

Pekka blinked and dragged his hand over his face, then fiddled with his glasses before putting them on, never raising his eyes. 'Yes, there was something.' He hesitated and glanced up briefly. 'Perhaps we should wait for Anna.'

'We might as well talk while we're waiting and I can discuss the other thing when she comes.'

Pekka took off his glasses again, studying and then replacing them. After a heavy pause he said, 'I think it is better if we wait for Anna.'

Just as Ricky finally realised that something was wrong, the door opened and Anna stuck her head round the frame with a merry, 'Hei!' The moment she saw him her face clouded in a way ominously reminiscent of his aunt's nod. Ricky looked from Pekka, sitting stonily at the table, to Anna, standing in the doorway with an expression of grievous concern on her face. Then he sat down.

'Shall I make some coffee?' she asked, coming into the room and closing the door quietly behind her.

'I get the feeling that might be a good idea.'

They sat around the table and waited for someone to start. Ricky broke first. 'Look, I'm really grateful that you're helping me to search for my family: but if you don't tell me what you've found out, I'll go nuts.'

Pekka let out a long breath. 'Bengt Larsson at the Pastors' Office called me on Tuesday night. I've been waiting for a chance to tell you about it.'

'Oh, right. What did he have to say?'

'It seems Bengt knows more than he told us when we went to see him. It seems there were other records, which he did not show you.'

'Really? About my family?'

'About your mother.'

'What sort of records? What do they say?'

'When he first made a search, there was a cross-reference to another file that he could not access. This file was not held in the Pastor's Office but in another location.'

'Is that usual?'

'No, I believe it is very unusual. Bengt was quite surprised by it.' Pekka gave the ghost of a grin. 'I think it really pissed him off.'

'That might explain why my mother's file was so thin. And now he's got it? He has these other records?'

'He has seen them. He has not been able to make a copy.'

'Why not? He's the records officer, isn't he?'

'They are private files, held by another institution. But he has read them and told me what they contain.'

Pekka hesitated again and Ricky looked from him to Anna, unable to fathom their reluctance. 'What is it? What's wrong?'

'Most of the records belong to a private hospital.'

'You mean she was ill? Oh, you mean a maternity hospital. Has he found out where we were born?'

Anna reached across the table and took his hand. He looked at her fingers, at the way they were touching him. Then he raised his eyes to hers and a feeling of dread started to spread over him. 'What sort of hospital?'

'Oh Ricky, I'm afraid she was ill. She had to spend some time in a psychiatric hospital.'

His eyes widened as if he had been struck. 'No!'

'It is nothing to be ashamed about. Very many people are experiencing problems like this.'

'No! It's not true. She was never like that!'

'Please don't get upset, Ricky. You must listen to what Pekka has been finding out. You have to understand what it was like for her: the reasons for what happened to her.'

He turned wild eyes on them, as if they were aliens who had suddenly revealed their true faces. *A mental hospital.*

Pekka cleared his throat, settling his glasses deeper onto his nose. He gave Anna a worried glance and she nodded for him to go on.

'According to the report, she was sent to the hospital to be treated for nervous exhaustion, hysteria and obsessive behaviour. According to Bengt the report is rather vague. In fact he says a number of things about it are rather strange...'

Ricky gave a bitter laugh. 'And I thought understatement was a British thing.' *They put her in a mental hospital. They stole her baby and then they locked her up.*

'Tell Ricky the rest, Pekka. He should hear everything.'

He flinched at the prospect of there being more and he didn't want to hear it but Pekka, once started, was all duty.

'Ricky, there were two reasons given for your mother's incarceration. The first was for her own protection, so that she could be treated.'

'And what was the other, having a baby without a permit?'

'In a way, yes.'

'What?'

'Ricky, she was found to be negligent in caring for her child.'

'What do you mean?'

'I am sorry but I am only telling you what is in the record.'

'Fuck the record! No, shit, I'm sorry... I mean, I understand that, Pekka. But what did it say? What *exactly* did it say?'

'Bengt saw several documents. The first was a psychiatrist's report and the second was the record of her committal to the hospital. The report said that from the evidence of neglect and because of her mental condition, she was not capable of carrying out her duties as a

Searching for Satu 167

mother. It recommended that she be placed under medical supervision and that the child be placed in a home.'

'Wait a minute. What was the date on these documents?'

'I took a note. Yes, here it is, they were dated the same: June 29, 1958.'

Ricky cursed softly. 'You're sure there was only mention of one child? Did they give a name? Was it a boy or a girl?'

'A boy. The records said very little about the child, only about the mother.'

'Oh Jesus.' *She lost me as well. I was less than two years old and they came back and took me as well. His poor mother. Where did she find the strength to survive it?*

Yet the revelation brought relief as well as pain, for it explained so much. That was why she had always been so over-protective: and that was why as a child he had always clung so tightly to her.

And then something else occurred to him. 'But hang on a minute, we didn't stay there: she brought me away. It's the one thing she was always perfectly clear about. The ship brought us into Leith on a bright, breezy day in November 1958. She always used precisely those same words to describe it.'

Pekka hesitated again and Ricky realised there was still more to come.

'Yes, that is right. The last record is from November 1958.'

'Bengt seems to have overlooked quite a lot, first time round. What was it? A release form from the hospital?'

'No. It was a rather strange document.'

'Another one.'

'You should not blame Bengt so much. These records were not in the Pastor's Office and he has gone to a lot of trouble to find them. Also, I agree with what he says about this last one.'

'Yes?'

'There should be a police report. That is the logical thing to expect but the only record is this one from the hospital.'

'Pekka, you're killing me. What are you trying to say?'

'Your mother left the psychiatric hospital before her treatment was complete. According to their files, this was reported to the police: but the police have no record of it. It is very strange.'

Ricky's brows drew in, then his eyes widened in sudden understanding. 'Of course, that's it! Don't you see? She must have escaped and rescued me and got us both out of the country before they could stop her!'

'It is not clear what happened. There is no record of any of this in the children's home.'

'But that is very strange,' interjected Anna. 'Surely they must have reported it?'

'You would think so - but in fact the children's home has no record of Ricky at all. There is only the admission proposal from the psychiatrist and then the hospital report that his mother had absented herself.'

'My God.'

They both raised quizzical eyebrows at him.

'They never reported it! I bet they never recorded me as being in the children's home in the first place, or else they put me in there under a false name. And I bet the committal documents were well dodgy.'

The other two looked uncertain at this, though maybe just confused by the unfamiliar language. He saw their doubt but the more he thought about it the more confident he became. It was all starting to make sense. 'My guess is that they couldn't risk telling the police.'

Pekka nodded slowly. 'I think you are right.'

'Pekka, you said Bengt found these records a bit weird, right?'

'Yes, he did.'

'Why? What was it about them?'

'Yes, I see what you are getting at. He didn't think about it much at first but later, after he made some enquiries, he became more suspicious. For instance, there was only one doctor's signature on the committal form.'

'And there should normally be two?'

'Yes, there is an attachment for the results of a second examination, which can be made either before or after admission. This attachment was present but the same signature was on both forms. That is sufficient only to send a patient for evaluation. Always there should be a second opinion before any formal committal is made.'

'You're saying that my mother spent a year in a psychiatric hospital on the say-so of one bloody doctor?'

'I am afraid it looks that way.'

'Bloody hell! I thought this sort of thing couldn't happen in a civilised country! So what *else* did Bengt find that struck him as strange?'

Pekka grimaced at the difficulty of finding the right words. 'They were all, how do you say this in English: 'in the family'?'

'I don't follow.'

'They all had something to do with the same family.'

'The Karlsholms.'

'Yes. I think that Bengt is worried about making trouble with them. He is from a Swedish speaking family and from what he has told me, the Karlsholms are quite influential in that community.'

'Don't tell me the doctor was a Karlsholm?'

'No, but the legal official who counter-signed the committal form was one of them.'

'Right, I get it. So there was just the signature of a doctor and a magistrate and he was a Karlsholm.'

'Yes. His name was Juri Karlsholm and at the time he was head of the Karlsholm family. And in fact the doctor had something to do with the Karlsholms, too. The clinic where your mother was treated is owned by a charitable foundation whose chief official is Katerina Karlsholm, who was Juri's wife. And the children's home...'

'Is another Karlsholm establishment?'

'Yes.'

'It was all a fix, from first to last!'

'Bengt is quite worried about this. He has not said so but I think he suspects that the documents are not correct.'

'Pekka, you don't have to be Einstein to work that out.'

'This could explain why there was no police report.'

'Of course! They couldn't afford to go to the police. The cops probably didn't know anything about it. My God, they shut her up in a madhouse and stole both her children and all the while she could have blown the whistle on the whole thing. She must have thought she was alone and helpless but actually *they* were probably terrified of *her*.'

'I think so. When she escaped, she will have thought that the police would pick her up if she didn't get out of the country immediately. Even if they weren't looking for her, I wonder how she did it? In those circumstances it could not have been easy.'

'She'd manage. There was an inner toughness to her that's hard to describe. She seldom even raised her voice because she didn't have to - just the tone of it was usually enough. And she would have gone through rivers of ice for me.' For a few seconds Ricky's face softened, only to be replaced by a grim smile of realisation. 'It was all bluff. It was all some kind of desperate bluff by that Swedish Bitch.'

'Who?'

'Katerina Karlsholm. It was her family's address that my mother gave me. She's the one behind all this.'

'Perhaps. But we don't know enough to be sure.'

'No but I can imagine plenty. Think about it. There was never a record of our birth in the registers. Somehow Katerina Karlsholm managed the whole thing. By putting me in that home she could make me disappear. I guess she must have done the same thing with my sister: but it could only work if she managed to keep my mother out of the picture. If mum had only known, she could have brought the whole house of cards tumbling down on top of them.'

'But Ricky, why would these people want to steal her children in the first place? What were they afraid of?'

'I don't know. I really have no idea, except that my sister and I were illegitimate and maybe an embarrassment to them. Could that really have been such a big deal?'

'It is hard to say. People were having different attitudes in those days.'

'Well I tell you this, Anna: I'm going to find out.'

'But what about Ricky's sister? The records have not been saying anything about her?'

Pekka shook his head in bemusement. 'No, there was nothing.'

'Are you sure? Was Bengt certain this time?'

'I think so. There was no mention of your sister.'

'But of course they took her much earlier. It all fits with what my aunt told me. They took her when she was born but they didn't know about me...' He stopped in mid-sentence, then looked at Anna and smacked himself on the forehead. 'Of course! I nearly forgot! That's what I wanted to ask you.'

'Is it so?'

'Yes: and it's a really weird question. Look, you're a midwife, right?'

'Yes, of course.'

'Right. Well here's the really strange thing. When we visited my aunt, she told me that my sister and I are actually twins.'

'No!'

'Yes. According to Aunt Elvira, Satu was born first and they took her away without realising my mother was pregnant with twins. So when I came along later, they knew nothing about it. It seems completely unlikely to me but I was wondering if you could confirm whether or not it's medically possible?'

'Oh, but that is fantastic! Is it really so?'

'That, Anna, is what I need to know. And believe me, a lot hangs on this, so please don't say anything unless you're 100 per cent certain. But now please, tell me: can twins be born two days apart?'

CHAPTER 31
Saturday 27th September, 1956

Satu had been prepared for the possibility that she might be alone when the contractions started. Tessa might be absent most of the time and taciturn to the point of sullenness when she did put in an appearance; but at least the midwife had been willing to talk about what to expect. So Satu had dutifully done her exercises and practised her breathing. God knew there were few enough other ways to fill the time.

Except thinking. For someone who had never considered herself much of an intellectual, Satu reckoned she had become one of the world's great thinkers. She half expected to wake up and find her brain had worn out. She thought about everything that had been done and said since she set out to Finland to be with him. She went over and over it, trying to see things from everyone else's point of view and to imagine what else she could have done. Most of all, she tried to find a way to forgive him.

It was very hard.

Not so hard, though, as forgiving herself. Perhaps she should have been a Roman Catholic instead of a Presbyterian. The Roman faith was more in keeping with what she was doing. It was like paying a penance: a nine-month penance followed by a spell in purgatory and then, just possibly, she might be able to redeem herself. Not that she had any real choice. There was nothing else she could do. She knew it but she also knew that nothing would ever heal this wound.

She wanted so much to keep the baby but it was impossible. It would have been irresponsible to reject Katerina's proposal even if she'd had the courage to do so. She could hardly even support herself in this bloody country, let alone a child. And there was nowhere else to turn. Her parents would never take her back: not now. She corrected herself with a stab of pain. Her mother would never take her back.

After her father replied to her first letter by saying that he never wanted to see her again, TK had persuaded her that all she needed to do was stay away and they would eventually forgive her. Believing him had been yet another in the long line of incredibly naive and stupid things that she had done because he was everything to her and she thought he was strong and clever and understood the way of the world. God, what a fool she'd been.

She had heard nothing more from her parents for nine months. She wrote letter after letter but all went unanswered until the last, when the telegram came.

At the time she had thought life couldn't get any worse. First she had been left alone for weeks on end in the middle of winter, never knowing when his ship would bring him back. Yet in retrospect that had been nothing compared to the moment when she discovered she was pregnant. That had been the most awful moment of her life, at least until she found out there had been others before her. Then she had wanted the earth to open up and swallow her.

She went first to Elvira, who wouldn't even let her in the house. TK's parents went one better: they never even came to the door but simply had the butler throw her out into the street. Little by little she had uncovered the truth about them. TK had lied about everything. When his parents found out about their involvement, they had threatened to disinherit him. Far from trying to win them round at every opportunity as he pretended, he had actually taken care to keep her out of sight while telling his mother that he had dumped her. It was a measure of how low she had sunk in self-regard that she still chose to believe he had kept her close with the aim of forcing his mother's hand, rather than just as a convenient soft berth whenever he happened to be in town.

Finally, in desperation, she had written home to tell her parents that she was pregnant and to beg their forgiveness. At that point she would actually have left TK and gone home, if only they had been willing to take her back. But it was too late. Into that desolation had come her mother's telegram.

Satu. Your father suffered fatal stroke yesterday. Mother.

All the congenital weaknesses of the Graham family were summed up in those eight words: grotesque economy; a tendency to burst arteries under stress; and a spirit of unforgiveness that would have awed an Old Testament prophet.

She had been physically sick for days with a mix of grief, pregnancy and guilt. It had not even been possible to attend the funeral. She was living with a sailor whose family owned a shipping line, yet nobody would help her get home to bury the father she had killed with her wantonness. Least of all TK.

That had been the moment when love started turning to hate, yet even then she found that she could not truly hate him. His offhand belittling of her feelings; his long absences; even the other women: she was prepared to forgive them all if he would just show her that he still loved her. Instead of which he had demanded that she have an abortion.

He had been so very practical about it, setting it out as if he were talking to a class of not very bright schoolchildren, or the board of a large company:

- there would be a scandal;
- her parents had already rejected her;
- his parents would cut him off as well;
- they had no money;
- she would lose her job; and
- she was much too young and had her whole life ahead of her.

He had been in all respects a thoroughgoing bastard, mercilessly twisting each argument like a knife in her womb.

The fury with which she had thrown him out had amazed them both. Afterwards, trembling and sobbing yet flushed with a kind of demented pride, she had stood for some time in a state of shock. Then she had walked all the way to Pispala through fifteen degrees of frost to ask Eva and Marko for help. Such was the extremity of her desperation. She, a Suomalainen and a Graham, with the stiff-necked pride of both, had gone to her only friends and admitted that she needed their help.

Which they had given without a moment's hesitation, just as she knew and feared they would. It was not merely the drummed-in prescription against exposing one's need to any but family that had kept her from asking them before. She felt like a millstone around their necks. They had so little and so many mouths of their own to feed: how could they even make room for her and her child, let alone feed them?

None of which mattered to Eva and Marko. They would cheerfully have found a way and doubtless that close-knit community of rebels and anarchists would have rallied round and shared in her support. But she could not have it. As soon as her initial panic was over, as soon as she had been hugged and loved and felt human warmth again, she had known that it could not be so. She had not come to Finland to be a burden others. Nor would she bring a child into the world with none but poor strangers to help care for it.

TK had been right. The remorseless practicality of his arguments could not be denied. She had returned to her room in Tampere while Eva, loving, reluctant Eva, made the necessary arrangements to terminate the pregnancy.

And there, one winter's afternoon, Katerina Karlsholm had come to her with a proposition that changed everything.

Her coming was a total surprise and yet like Genghis Khan she was preceded by the awesome impact of reputation. This was the woman who had reputedly made a fortune trading with Nazi Germany, using ships she had swindled away from Satu's family. Her name had been an obscenity in their house for as long as Satu could remember, uttered in the same tone and even in the same sentence as that of Hitler and the other great Bogeymen of the era.

Satu was taken so unawares that the peremptory knock on the door gave her no premonition and she opened it with innocent curiosity.

The woman who stood before her had the proud intensity of an eagle. Dark eyes glared out from a face too strong to be beautiful. Her jet hair was cut short in a fashion at once chic yet severe and although Satu stood five foot six and had the advantage of the doorstep, her visitor still towered over her. She was dressed from head to foot in dark grey, the only flashes of colour the surprisingly generous line of her mouth and the rubies set into a solitary silver brooch.

Seeing her, Satu was filled at once with childlike sensations of foreboding, as if she had been summoned for punishment without knowing her crime. Being a practical person she shook them off as quickly as they had arisen. But she knew the feelings had shown in her face and been noted. She recognised instinctively that this woman would see and understand every human frailty.

There had been the most perfunctory of introductions.

'You are Satu Suomalainen?'

'Yes. You must be...'

'I am who you suppose me to be.'

'Won't you come in...'

She had to step backwards before she could even finish the invitation. Katerina cast a single glance around the room and from her expression Satu knew that she missed nothing. The mere physical sparseness would not have detained anyone's attention but this woman understood implications and drew conclusions, all in one sweep of the eyes. Yet her words betrayed no trace of contempt. Everything she said in that first interview had been surprising.

'I see my son is not a complete fool, however much he tries. You are quite a beautiful girl. You deserve better.' The slightest toss of her head indicated that she was referring to the room, rather than to her son.

'I think I have what I deserve.'

That brought a sharp look and the first twist of contempt to the mouth. 'Self pity is unbecoming. A person in your position cannot afford to make themselves any less enticing than they already are.'

'And just what would you suggest?'

There was the trace of a smile around Katerina's mouth now, as one recognising an opponent worth crossing blades with. 'You have spirit. Good. A woman in a hopeless position should always either conceal it or use it. You could of course try the latter approach but you will find that I have no sympathy. You are not the first of my son's whores to get themselves into this condition and doubtless you will not be the last. Yes, you do better to keep that fire in your eyes. That I can respect.'

'If you've come here to insult me, you can leave now. Why should I care if I have your respect or not? Why are you here?'

To Satu's surprise, something softened in Katerina's face at this. It was as if the eagle had sensed that its intended prey was one of its own kind.

'I am here to make you a proposal.'

'A proposal.'

'You are faced with an unpleasant choice. Kill your baby now, or watch it starve later.'

Satu's outrage was so great that she could barely draw breath to attack before Katerina continued. 'I am prepared to give you a third option: one that will allow your baby to live and thrive and have all the opportunities that you cannot provide for it.'

It was impossible for Satu not to listen to such an offer and they both knew it. But it took a huge effort to master her anger and even then she could give no more than a breathless nod, mute indication that she would hear what the other had to say. Katerina took her acquiescence so much for granted as not even to wait for the confirmation.

'As you must be aware, I am a person of considerable wealth and influence. It is in my power to ensure that your child is adopted into a good family, where it will be well provided for.'

'I've thought about adoption of course. Why would I need your help?'

'To ensure your child's future well being. Do you want it to grow up an ignorant peasant? And there is also the question of your own well-being, over the months before and after the baby is born.'

Satu was silent, unsure of her ground and her temper. Katerina saw it and pressed home her advantage. 'You have no rights here. My son will not marry you and if you refuse to have an abortion he will abandon you altogether. Your own family has disowned you and you will soon have no source of income.'

Despite herself, Satu hung her head at the truth of it.

'I am prepared to pay for your upkeep during your pregnancy, together with medical care adequate to your needs. After the child is born you will be given money enough to keep you for a few months, or to pay your passage back to Scotland.'

It took every ounce of Satu's willpower not to break down. The effort to maintain an even voice was almost superhuman. 'Why are you doing this?'

The reply came in a voice of steel. 'Because I will not have scandal.' She paused and again there was the slightest softening in her face. 'And because the responsibility is my son's and therefore, in some part, mine.'

For several seconds Satu was silent, contemplating what was being offered. Logic told her that this woman's motives must go deeper than a desire to suppress scandal. That was just the tip of the iceberg. But she couldn't see what the rest of it might be, or how it could be dangerous, so in the end she looked up and met Katerina's eye. 'You know I have no choice.'

Satu tried to read the older woman but the attempt was futile. She couldn't hold her gaze and as her eyes fell they settled on the cutlery that lay on the rough wooden table. Her words came in a voice that was curiously detached. 'My grandmother used to say, when you dine with the Devil, be sure to use a long spoon.' She touched the metal implement before her. 'I feel my spoon isn't long enough but it's the only one I have.'

Katerina gave a tight smile of triumph. 'There are conditions.'

'Of course. I suppose there would have to be.'

'You will be required to sign certain papers.'

'About the adoption?'

'Yes. Related to the adoption.'

'Related to it. I see. No, in fact I don't see at all. Related how, exactly?'

'You will agree never to attempt to contact the child again. That is, of course, quite normal in cases of adoption. You will also relinquish all claims to any part of the Karlsholm businesses.'

So that was it. Now she understood what this was really all about. From everything that TK and her own parents had told her, Katerina's guiding motive was the desire for control: of her family and its fortune and above all of the family business. This woman had fought all her life to wrest it away from anyone else, starting with the Suomalainens. Most of all Katerina must fear a union between her own son and her rivals' daughter, for that was the one thing that could revitalise their languishing claim to the business.

'And what price discretion? You said you wanted to avoid a scandal but you haven't said anything about keeping it quiet.'

'I was coming to that.'

Satu had sensed even then that something was not right. Perhaps she should have probed harder, resisted longer: but her hand was so weak and Katerina could see all her cards.

'You will not speak to anyone about the child, about the identity of the father or even about the fact of your pregnancy. Except for the people I send to you, you will never discuss your condition, or this arrangement, with anyone.'

'For how long?'

'You will never discuss it with anyone for as long as you live.'

'That's ridiculous.'

'I do not find it even mildly amusing. I am surprised that you do.'

'You can't keep something like this hushed up forever. I can't possibly agree to that.'

'You can and you will. Make no mistake: my offer is dependent upon your complying with every clause. One slip will invalidate the whole. If you speak to so much as one person about any aspect of what we have discussed, I will cast you into the gutter without a penny.'

'How can you conceal it? It's going to be pretty obvious soon enough.'

'You will remain for the term of your pregnancy in a private house provided for the purpose. You will not venture out. Your meals, your clothes, everything that you require, will be brought to you.'

Satu looked at her more in disbelief than anger. 'You aim to lock me up?'

'I mean to keep you out of sight until the child is safely adopted and then I mean to ensure that no outsider ever knows what has been done. Yes, exactly that - and I will settle for nothing less.'

'But people already know.'

'Who? Who knows?'

'My mother. My friends.'

'Your mother has disowned you. She wants no part of this baby. Your friends? Who are they? You will give me their names and I shall see to it that they are silenced. They cannot be of any consequence.'

'More than you imagine.'

'You will not see them. You will not talk to them. You will not tell them where you are.'

'I shall!'

'You're a little fool if you think you can bargain with me! You will do exactly as I say or forfeit everything. You know what that would mean.'

Of course she did. And what else was there to do? Yet pure belligerance drove her to give it one more try. 'Alright! But even if I agree to stay in this house of yours and not tell anyone until the baby is born, how can you expect me to keep silent about it later? For the rest of my life? It *is* ridiculous.'

'If your own shame will not silence you, other things may.'

'You mean money?'

'I anticipated that you might seek to extort money from us in future. I have made appropriate provision for that eventuality.'

'I don't want your money!'

'That is easy to say now, yet even now it is not true. If it were, we would not be having this conversation.'

'That's different. It's for the baby.'

'Yes. Today it is for the baby and next year, what then? And the year after that, and five years on? Don't take me for a fool.'

'Then what are you proposing?'

'Something to ensure your compliance. A link between your good faith and the continued well-being of your child.'

Satu looked at Katerina as if she was a creature from another planet. It was monstrous. And when the creature outlined what she had in mind, it was also merciless. Only then did Satu begin to understand the true depths of Katerina's motivation. Only then did she begin to see how wide the gulf really was between TK and his mother.

Yet there was also humanity of a sort in what she proposed. More, there was recognition of the family responsibility which Katerina had alluded to at the start. However cruel such an agreement might be for Satu, at least it secured the greatest material security for her baby. In fact, it secured the child's birthright. On that they had discussed at length.

And on that one point Satu had been unmoveable. She would sign away her own rights to the Karlsholm family fortune but she would not sign away those of her child. She saw at once that her enemy was incensed by this refusal but given the nature of their covenant, Katerina had no choice but to give way in the end. In accepting, she even descended briefly into her version of humour.

'It is agreed, then. I shall send my solicitor early tomorrow to arrange the details. You will find him unprepossessing but efficient. He reminds one of an undertaker, which is not a bad quality in a lawyer.'

'What about medical care?'

'There is a woman, Tessa, I have used before. A midwife. She will take care of it.'

Satu had just nodded.

'There is one thing more,' Katerina added, turning for the door.

'Yes?'

'You will not see my son again.'

'But that's not...'

'I do not mean that you may not, I merely state it as a fact. He will not return. Unreliable though he is, of this you may be sure.'

'Why? What have you said to him?'

'He has gone away. A particularly long voyage. It is better that way.' And with that parting shot she left, as abruptly as she had arrived.

Next morning the lawyer had come and the terms had been signed and witnessed. Satu was not surprised to discover that the documents had been drawn up even before Katerina made her proposal. She had bent to Katerina's will exactly as that overpowering woman knew she must.

And so she had come here, to the prison that had held her these last six months. Not that it was bad, as prisons went. Above all it was warm. It had been so long since she had been warm that for the first couple of days she was content just to feel it soak into her bones. There had been plenty to eat, too. What with the pregnancy and having so little to do, she had actually grown quite plump. She must have put on well over two stone.

The most difficult thing had been the loneliness. She had been allowed to send a letter to Eva and Marko, thanking them for their help, requesting their continued discretion and telling them that her mother had relented and sent for her. It was the least hurtful lie she could think of. Once cut off from them she saw no-one but Tessa, who was hardly the most convivial of companions.

But God she needed her now!

Satu had thought she was prepared. She had thought she knew enough to cope even if Tessa wasn't there when it started. In fact she did manage to fight off the first rush of panic when the contractions began. She went through to the bathroom, practised different positions to reduce the pain and cursed Katerina to every corner of hell for denying her the means to summon help when it was most needed.

After awhile she began to think she was on top of it, that she could hold out until Tessa's regular noontime call. Then her waters broke and she lost it. She was alone, she was frightened and she didn't know what to do. What if it went wrong? For fifteen terrible minutes she sat on the bathroom chair weeping uncontrollably, lost to all reason. Then another contraction came and she screamed at the pain and the fear and the awfulness of it all.

The contraction lasted perhaps a minute. When it had passed, so too had her panic. She would not be defeated! She would not lose control. Above all, she would bring her baby into this world, even if she had to deliver it herself. She had to fight to regain her breathing pattern and to stem the rising hysteria but she had achieved both before the next contraction came.

It was not yet serious. Everything had been going normally and there was no reason to panic. Tessa would be there soon, she almost always came about noon. Grumpy, sullen and wooden tongued, but there. She had only to hold on until then.

It was 11:05 when the contractions began. By the time Tessa finally appeared it was quarter past two and they had already become noticeably more frequent and painful. Tessa took one look from the doorway and the shock on her face was comic. She looked as if she had been slapped. Then she came over and from her first breath Satu knew where she had been.

With a sudden, horrible certainty she understood her attendant's long absences and dull-faced moroseness. The midwife was an alcoholic. Perversely, the effect was to banish the last of Satu's panic and make her even more determined. When Tessa disappeared out the door, calling out that she would be back soon, Satu took it stoically. As usual, she could count only on herself.

Within a few hours, however, any such self-confidence had evaporated. Even when Tessa returned it needed all of her undoubted experience to pull Satu through the endurance test of her labour. There were no complications but it still left her close to exhaustion and broken on a rack of pain by the time the second stage began. By the clock on the wall she began to bear down at 11:15pm. At eight minutes to midnight the baby was born.

It was a little girl. Satu saw her only once, for a few seconds. She never even knew how much she weighed. For at quarter to midnight, with the timing of the devil, Karerina Karlsholm came into the room and at ten minutes past, having satisfied herself in the most cursory manner that the mother was not in any immediate danger, she bore the child away.

The conversation between them was the briefest imaginable and it would stay in Satu's memory forever. Katerina had leaned over her with a look of surprising humanity. 'As I thought, you are a natural mother. You will have other children.'

'I want to see her.'

'It is not wise. Better that you do not.'

'Please. Let me see my baby.'

There was a frown of displeasure, as if such weakness was a disappointment. 'Very well. Just for a moment. But remember our agreement. Tessa, show her the child.'

The midwife had brought her across, for such a terribly short time. Satu could not even hold her, had scarcely enough time to take in the miniature contours of her face.

'Oh God, she's beautiful.'

'Enough. Tessa, give her to me now.'

'Katerina!'

'Yes?'

'What will they call her?'

For some reason Katerina would not meet her eyes. She seemed irritated, impatient to get away. 'It has not been decided. What does it matter, anyway? It is folly to wonder about such things.'

Satu had fallen back, utterly dejected. The last she had seen of her baby was a tiny shrouded figure in the arms of the woman who carried her away. She had thought then that it was all over. Tessa had busied around her, cleaning her up and telling her she was lucky because there was no tearing. In fact she was so well that she would likely be able to go next day, if she wished. She was still very big but that was normal enough, it would take several days before she got back to anything like her normal shape. Anyhow, Tessa had other things to attend to and could not stop. She would return in the morning. As an afterthought, she pointed to the envelope that Katerina had left behind. Satu didn't have to look inside to know that it contained her forty pieces of silver.

All that night she alternately slept and wept. Tessa returned at mid-morning but she was so drunk that Satu sent her away after less than an hour. At 12:30, the contractions began again.

Satu didn't know what was happening to her. She thought at first that something was terribly wrong, that it was some ghastly post-natal problem. Only when the contractions intensified did she suspect the truth.

Many times down the years, looking at her son, she would feel once more the exact mix of emotions that welled up in her at that moment. Joy and desolation, triumph and fear, love and wonder had all burst upon her in that first instant when she realised she was giving birth to a second child. A child that nobody would steal from her!

It was the greatest triumph of her life, born not just from the natural triumph of any mother but also from the realisation that her compact with Katerina did not cover this. She had snatched a last minute victory from the jaws of defeat.

But if her triumph was great, it could never be pure. She had lost her daughter: the little girl who she would always think of as Satu. Yet at least her little Satu was alive and well! She would grow up wanting for nothing. She would never know what she had lost. Neither of them must ever know. Not at least until they were old enough to look out for themselves: Katerina was too dangerous to cross. But at least she would keep this child! For some reason Satu felt sure it would be a boy. He would be hers and he would be safe.

Everything that had seemed so overwhelming before now seemed simple and obvious. New life reset all the perspectives. She would stay with Eva and Marko until the baby was old enough. Then she would go back to Scotland and present him to his grandmother. And despite everything Janet Graham would take them in, for they were family. The ones you had to help, no matter what. The idea of an illegitimate child was one thing but the reality was quite another.

The next contraction almost made her laugh at the truthfulness of that. He was real, alright. And now, somehow, she had to do this alone. And why not? There were women in Africa who went off into the bush by themselves to give birth. She'd read about it in an old copy of National Geographic. But what proportion of them and their babies died? And what proportion of them had twins? She was too tired, she hurt too much, it had been almost more than she could bear the first time. And now without even Tessa to help...

She was losing it again when there was a knock on the front door. She was too surprised to react and could only lie there uncertainly as she heard it open. Then a familiar voice called out, filling her with joyful astonishment. A moment later there were footsteps in the hall and there, standing in the doorway, was Eva. Behind her, Marko's vast bulk filled the whole frame.

As Satu rested between contractions, Eva explained how they had found her. 'It was that drunk told us.'

'Tessa?'

'Yes. She was down the pub as usual and she asked me when my next was due. Always looking for an opportunity, that one. Anyway, I didn't tell her to piss off, 'cos you never know when you might need her, do you? Even drunk, she knows what's what. Delivered half of Pispala, she has. So, anyway, she's usually good for a story so I buys her one to oil the wheels.'

'Tessa good for a story? But I can hardly get a word out of her.'

'Oh but you haven't seen her when she's drinking, have you? Different animal altogether, ain't that right, Marko?'

'She can talk.'

'She can. So I asked her the latest scandal and bugger me, she says she's looking after this girl who's locked up in a house in town. Then she goes sly, like she's said what she shouldn't have. But I know how to deal with that. So out it comes. She's doing it for some rich Swedish bitch and I'd never guess who. Like hell I wouldn't! Talk about penny's dropping!'

'But Katerina will go mad if she finds out! It will ruin everything! No, really Eva, if I break my agreement with her, it will be the baby that suffers.'

'Don't you worry about that, love. Tessa won't be saying another word to anyone. Marko fixed it. He can be very persuasive, can't you, Marko?'

'She will be quiet about this now.'

'But why? She wasn't before.'

'We reminded her what Katerina would likely do to her if she blabbed and then we told her what Marko would definitely do to her right after. From the look on her face, she got the message. Anyway, she won't know anything about this surprise package you're about to deliver. So where's the worry?'

'I suppose you're right. Yes, you are. Katerina's already got what she wanted: there's no reason for her to harm us even if she finds out.'

'That's right. So you just concentrate on getting through this. Later Marko will put you in the van and drive you home while I clean up. If that Swedish Bitch ever comes back, it'll look like you've cleared out.'

'Yes, you're right. She'll assume I've gone back to Scotland. Even if she realises what's happened, as long as I don't threaten her, our agreement will still stand. My poor Satu will be looked after and I will have my son.'

'A son you think? Well, and why not? I've known others who could tell. And unless I'm very much mistaken,' Eva added, glancing at the clock on the wall, 'he'll not keep you waiting much beyond midnight.'

CHAPTER 32
Thursday 21st May, 1981

'But wouldn't it be obvious? If a woman were carrying twins, surely after the birth of the first child it would be obvious that she was still pregnant?'

Anna shook her head. 'No, it does not always happen that way. A woman does not get back her shape for some time afterwards. If she was thin then it might be seen; but if she was a normal size it could easily not be recognised.'

'Surely the doctors would examine her?'

'Of course, if she was having proper medical care then it would be noticed. But perhaps your mother was not well looked after?'

'Actually I don't really know.'

'Well, if there was no trained person to examine her, or if they did not pay much attention, then it is quite possible it would not be noticed.'

'But wouldn't she realise herself?'

'Not necessarily, not from how she felt. You should remember there was no ultrasound back then, no scanning, so it had to be done by feeling the mother's stomach with the hands. If this was done by a doctor then it would probably be detected quite some weeks before birth because often with twins it is difficult to identify for instance the head.'

'And if nobody cared enough to examine her properly?'

'Then it could be a surprise to her, too. Yes, that is very possible.'

'And you say the twins could be born as much as a day apart?'

'Yes, certainly I have known of cases at least twenty-four hours apart. They cannot be identical twins of course, as those come from the same placenta.'

'No, they wouldn't have been. It would have been a boy and a girl, born with at least a full day between them.'

'Then yes, it is perfectly possible. In those days, particularly in rural areas where there was little or no medical supervision, it would not be the first time this has happened.'

'My God.'

'You are sure now that you have not just a sister but a twin?'

'Yes.'

'But Ricky, that is wonderful!'

'It rather depends on the identity of the twin.'

'Again, please?'

'Nothing. A private joke.'

'Ricky, what is the matter?'

'Really Anna, I can't tell you right now. I'm sorry, I'll explain everything as soon as I can but I have to get some things sorted first.'

Jesus, just a few little things! And before he could even begin, Anna was reminding him of the problem's awful immediacy.

'Is Timi working still?'

'Yes, he's got another lesson until six. Oh God, that's right, we have to go to some disco. Jesus, what time is it?'

'It is nearly six already. What disco is this on a Thursday night?'

The thought of it nearly gave him a heart attack.

'Ricky?'

'Yes? Oh, right. It's called the Women's Choice Disco, whatever that means.'

Anna laughed loudly and wagged her finger at him. 'Well, then I think you will be taken care of tonight. But why are you not going out with Satu?'

'I am. That's where she arranged to meet me.'

Anna nodded her approval and grinned at him. 'I think she has a sense of humour, this girl.'

Oh God, no. Don't let it be Satu. Please God, just don't let it be her...

'Are you alright, Ricky? You look pale. Is something wrong?'

'No. Nothing at all.' He flashed his most brilliant smile, wondering that they didn't notice its ghastliness. 'So tell me what to expect at this Women's Choice thing.'

'No, I think I will leave you to find that out for yourself.'

If you only knew. 'Gee, thanks. What are friends for?'

Anna laughed. 'You will not have such a bad time, I think. Now, here is Harri. You should all go together.'

Tim arrived around half-past six to complete the triumvirate. They agreed there might be safety in numbers but Pekka could not by any means be persuaded to join them. The Women's Choice Disco required a jacket and tie, items that he swore he wouldn't wear even to his own funeral. For several minutes Ricky had been unable to pay much attention to the discussion going on around him but when Pekka announced his position on ties, Harri declared that he didn't even own one and for some reason this struck Ricky as sacrilegious. When Tim offered to lend him one, they discovered he had no idea of how to do it up. Ricky was flabbergasted that an educated European could be innocent of such a thing. With a perfect transfer of anxiety, he allowed himself to be so scandalised as to exclude everything else from his mind.

Half an hour later, suitably bedecked, they set out. Ricky's anxiety could be displaced no longer and he was literally trembling at the prospect of seeing Satu. If his friends noticed anything, they just put it down to nerves at the prospect of what a Women's Choice disco might involve.

It didn't take him long to find out. There was no queue and the doorman let them in with a guttural joke that Ricky was glad he didn't understand. Once inside, the first thing he noticed was that there were only a handful of other men present. When he asked what the deal was, the others just laughed. Finally Tim said, 'The clue's in the name, Ricky.' And so it was.

They sat together in a tight knot, doing their best to look cool while they sussed out the situation. At first they held their ranks, like a beleaguered band of foot soldiers huddled back to back against a swirl of cavalry. But the swirl was impossibly seductive and within a few minutes they began to lose cohesion. Once they broke ranks they were easy pickings.

Harri was the first to go. His new-found chic, combined with his godlike looks, made him simply irresistible.

Tim, always a consummate actor, put on his cool, arrogant persona and attracted women like moths to the flame. In the land of the gorgeous blonde, the tall dark stranger is king.

Ricky remained as chaste as an unasked maid.

At first it was a relief. He was having stomach cramps just thinking about Satu and he didn't want to be entangled with anyone else when she arrived. But there was also the fear of getting asked to dance by someone ugly: a basic piece of ego education that girls learn early and men seldom if ever.

After half an hour he realised that the danger of his being asked was a lot less than his conceit had suggested, so he tried to tell himself it was funny.

After a further hour, during which the others had girls queuing up while he hadn't been onto the dance floor once, he realised that being asked by anyone is a lot better than not being asked at all.

After two hours he swore to himself that he would never again leave the short, fat, spotty ones sitting alone at the side of the room.

After nearly three hours, with the place scarcely an hour from closing, Satu finally put in an appearance. She came towards him across the dance floor in a short satin dress that flowed over her body like water and the first sight of her vaporised all his anger and humiliation. She stopped at their table with just enough of a flounce to send the material of her dress rippling over her like wavelets. Ricky didn't get up to greet her because his legs had turned to jelly and he wasn't even sure that he could speak.

'Hei, Ricky. Have you been here long? I just got here. I went for a drink first with some girlfriends.'

'Not long, no. Um, well, actually yes. About three hours. You look amazing.'

She flashed him a smile and looked about the room. 'Are you alone?'

'No, Tim and Harri are here. They're both dancing.'

'I don't think I know Harri, which one is he?'

'He's a friend of Tim's. He's that blond guy over there.'

'But he is very good looking.'

'Yes, he's a big hit with the girls tonight.'

'So, I bet you have been a big hit, too.'

'Ah, no, not exactly. I, well, I was waiting for you. I thought you were going to be here much earlier.'

'Oh, I am sorry if you have been waiting. But you should have been dancing! You must have made all the girls quite sorry if you were refusing to dance with them.'

'That wasn't really a problem. Would you like to dance?'

She looked at him in surprise and then gave her nice laugh. 'But no, you cannot ask me that here! It is the women's choice tonight.'

'Oh, right, of course. Sorry. Stupid of me.'

'But may I join you?'

'Oh God, yes: of course. I'm sorry, I don't know where my manners are tonight.' He leapt to his feet and pulled out a chair for her, scrabbling to cover his flustered state. 'I'm a bit put off balance by all this.' He indicated the room at large and she grinned as she sat down.

'So, you don't like being the one to be asked, eh?'

'It's alright if you *are* asked, I suppose.'

'But this is how it is for us women most of the time. Tonight it is our turn. You men should know what it feels like.'

'I guess you're right. May I at least get you a drink?'

'Yes, that would be nice.'

'Is it alright to do that here? I mean, men can buy drinks for women?'

'But yes, of course.'

'Right. Silly of me. What would you like?'

'Vodka and lime.'

It took an age getting served at the bar. The place was packed and it was not in his nature to barge in front of a woman, which was a problem as they made up seventy per cent of the clientele. When he got back, Tim was sitting at the table with a couple of Bulgarian girls and Satu was dancing with Harri.

When Ricky saw it, the feeling that hit him was instant and awful. He did his best to put a brave face on it but he was no good at small talk, the Bulgarian girls didn't speak much English and anyway there was only one thing he could think about. To his shame, it wasn't even the terrible thing he had to tell her that was skewering his guts:

it was the fact that after refusing to dance with him she had stood up with Harri without even waiting for him to bring her drink.

His eyes kept going over to the two of them. Even as he watched, Harri slid his hands down to her arse and Ricky had to drive his fingernails into his palms because there was nothing else he could do. Harri knew how to hold a girl close and yet move with an easy grace that made them glide across the floor as if they were one. The sight of it made Ricky feel physically sick.

The second dance ended and Harri led her back to the table. Only the fact that Ricky knew it was the convention to lead the girl by the hand kept him sane. He couldn't believe the feelings welling up inside of him. Until that moment he'd never known what jealousy was. Shit, he could hardly bear to look at them.

'Ricky, your friend Harri is really a good dancer! Oh, thank you, you got my drink. But why aren't you dancing?'

'I haven't been asked.'

'Oh, but I'm sure there are lots of girls here who want to dance with you.'

'Evidently not.'

She was miraculously impervious to his tone. He was giving off vibes akin to a sulking volcano, even Tim was getting them from ten feet away with a voluptuous Bulgarian to shield him. And then, just when he had finally plucked up the courage to say something, Satu turned away altogether and started chatting to Harri. At that point Ricky just wanted to die. It felt the same as when he was seventeen and the first girl he'd ever asked out had put him down before a crowd of their friends.

'So, what have you been doing since I last saw you?'

The sudden question caught him off-guard, so that he answered without remembering to sulk. 'I went to see my aunt. I found out something surprising.'

'But that is good news! What have you discovered?'

The enormity of the answer overwhelmed him, leaving him dumbfounded. When he finally managed to respond, he was so lost that he told her the truth. 'I discovered it's not a sister I've been looking for. It's a twin.'

'But that is incredible! How can you be having a twin and not be knowing this?'

He paused and her eyes stayed with him, free of any hint of artifice. His spirits dared to raise themselves a few inches above the parapet and he plunged on, eager to get to it while he still had her attention. 'Satu, you know how I asked about your birthday?'

'Yes, of course, we have been born only two days apart.'

'Right. Doesn't that strike you as a strange coincidence?'

'No, why should it? It is just a little coincidence, I think.'

Ricky saw the light-hearted tone reflected in her face and he knew at once that if this thing was true, then she had absolutely no idea of it.

'It's funny how everywhere I look I find Satus but never the one I came to search for.'

'Yes, that is quite funny. You still have not been able to find her in the record office?'

'No. They said there was no such person living here.'

'Perhaps she has changed her name, like you did.'

'Yes, I think she must have done. You see, I think she was adopted.'

'Oh, so that's why you have never known each other?'

'Yes. I think she doesn't know I even exist, just like I didn't know anything about her.'

'But that will be a very big surprise for her.' She gave him a sly smile over the rim of her glass. 'A very nice surprise.'

'Satu.'

'Yes?'

But he couldn't do it. He would rather not know than risk having his worst fears confirmed. So instead he said what he really wanted to say. 'Will you come out to dinner with me? Tomorrow?'

She looked surprised that he should ask such a thing. And then he saw a frown pass across her brow. 'Oh, but I cannot. I have to go to my parents tomorrow.'

'You're leaving?'

'Yes, just for a couple of days.'

'A couple of days?'

'Just until Sunday.'

'But I'm leaving on Sunday.' The tone of finality in his voice was like that of a man announcing his own death. Satu was quite struck by it, in fact she seemed to see him properly for the first time since she'd arrived.

'Ricky, what's wrong?'

'I was really hoping to see you again.'

She gave him a cursory smile, then creased her brow in another frown. 'At what time are you leaving?'

'Um, I don't know exactly. About 11 o'clock I think, or maybe noon. Look, I don't want to push, but I really do need to see you. There are... there are things we have to discuss.'

She thought about it, then turned away and talked rapidly in Finnish to Harri, who looked at his watch. For a dreadful moment Ricky thought they were discussing when to leave together: but a second later she looked back at him with a smile - and everything changed.

'So, I can come back on Saturday evening. There is a train from Turku at about six o'clock.'

'You'll come back early?'

'Of course. I had not understood you were leaving so soon, or I would have made a different arrangement. I thought you were here until Monday.'

'Thank you! Really, I mean it. But look, I hope I'm not spoiling your plans?'

'No, it is what I am wanting to do. I'm sorry I can't come any earlier but my parents have been insisting very much that I come home. There is something they want to talk about and they are being quite strange about it.' She gave a little laugh. 'Everyone wants to talk to me all of a sudden!'

'Do you think we can still go out to dinner together?'

'I don't think so. It may be difficult to get away even on Saturday but I can always make up some excuse. I am good at excuses. They never believe them of course but it's the thought that counts. Anyway, I will not be back until maybe after eight o'clock. It is better if we meet in the pub.'

'Right. In the pub, about eight o'clock. Yes.'

'But it will be a little later before I can get there. Don't be upset if I am not there at eight. You should not be waiting three hours for me again!'

'I'll wait all night if I have to.'

She snorted at that but he could tell she liked it. He was still wondering whether or not to resume the discussion he'd flunked out of when the DJ made an announcement and Satu touched him on the knee. 'So, shall we dance?'

He jumped up like a jack-in-the-box. Satu held out her hand and he led her to the floor and when they got there he turned and put his hands on her waist but to his bewilderment she laughed. 'You look so serious!'

'I can't help it. I have a naturally serious face.'

She laughed again and gave him a peck on the cheek before bursting apart to dance. If emotions were truly physical Ricky would have been torn asunder, stretched first one way and then another until bone and sinew could take no more. Yet instead his body remained bizarrely intact and even capable of dancing, while his eyes took in the fabulous creature before him.

Satu in motion was like a cat captured on film at the height of the chase: movement so graceful that it appeared effortless, like a breeze blowing over a wheatfield, or a porpoise playing in the wake of a passing boat.

The next song, inevitably, was a slow one. The DJ crooned something over the opening bars and the floor was suddenly filled with guys being dragged out for the final smooch.

'The last dance, how romantic.'

Ricky looked at her in surprise. That was his line, turned in her lips into a mischievous come-on. And then they were in each other's arms and moving together but each in a separate universe of thoughts and emotions. Ricky was reeling, too taken up with his own feelings even to begin to understand hers. He had put off the dread hour because he didn't want to know the truth. He wanted her, God knew he wanted her above all things: but not for his sister.

When the lights went up he kept hold of her, determined not to make the same mistake as before. And as usual he didn't have to make the running.

'So, what shall we do now?'

'I want to walk you home.'

Satu gave him a quizzical look, as if surprised at his insistence. 'OK.'

It was a long way but he would have been glad to walk all night, just to put off the final moment. He knew it was stupid and that he would have to face it all in a couple of days anyway: but then again, hope springs eternal. He didn't know anything yet for sure. His star had been rising and falling ever since he arrived and anything was possible...

They walked arm in arm, Satu chatting away merrily, Ricky grunting monosyllabic replies and cursing himself for being tongue-tied just when they most needed to talk. When they got to the foot of the ridge he took her hand and she accepted it, Ricky marvelling that she didn't seem to notice the tension in him. He had to let go again as they climbed the scarp but by the time they got to the top he was starting to relax, calmed by the beauty of the dark woods and the clouds skidding across the half-lit sky.

As they crested the ridge Satu suddenly darted off into the shadows, reappearing in a patch of light a moment later, running towards a children's playground. He caught up just as she settled herself onto one of the swings, so he took the next and she swung gently back and forth, letting her feet drag across the ground. He pulled a bit harder, keeping his feet clear but holding back enough to be able to talk.

This was what she seemed to want, to sit there in the cool night air, swinging lazily and chatting to him as easily as if she were a child talking to herself. He wasn't sure whether this put him on the level of her brother, her secret companion, or her teddy bear: and he didn't really care. It was enough to be there with her, enjoying the sensation of the pine scented air on his face and the familiar, childhood rhythms of the swing.

'This is where I always used to come when I was growing up, when I wanted to be alone. I feel free here.'

'I know what you mean. I've felt it ever since I came here.'

'Really?' She began to swing then, going higher and higher until she suddenly let go of the ropes on the upswing and flew through the air with a little shriek of pleasure. He followed and presently the two of them were meandering their way down between the trees, sometimes close, sometimes a little apart.

The clouds were obscuring the midnight sun for the first time since he'd arrived and it was black in the shadows of the trees and the old houses. She stopped at last in the shadow cast by the block of flats where she lived and rooted in her bag for something, before cursing softly and moving back into the light to aid her search. Finally she pulled out a bunch of keys and Ricky knew they had arrived at the moment of truth. Satu held up the keys in confirmation. 'So, I will see you on Saturday, at the pub.'

For awhile they just stood there, until Satu broke the silence just as it was becoming awkward. 'I would ask you in for a coffee but I have to get up early tomorrow to go to Turku.'

'Oh, right.'

'Thank you for walking me home. It was very gallant.'

As always he was taken aback by her propensity to come up with unexpected English phrases - but then he pulled himself together and finally managed to say what he had been trying to deny all evening. 'I really want to come in with you.' Her face was half in the shadows, so he could see only the sheen of reflected light from her hair and a hint of blue from her eyes. 'I really want to be with you tonight. I've been wanting to say it all evening but I couldn't find the right moment.'

She reached out her hand and touched him lightly on the forearm. 'Oh Ricky, I'm sorry, I didn't mean you to think this. But I have been stupid, I should have realised.'

She was apologising to him. He could hardly believe it. He'd made her think she had led him on: and her embarrassment brought home the monstrous potential of what he had been contemplating. 'No, look, really, I didn't think that...I was just hoping. You know, a guy will hope. I didn't expect anything.'

Her hand stayed where it was and she came further out of the shadows. She was looking right into his eyes, trying to gauge his feelings. 'I really have to get up early tomorrow. But I am afraid that you mind?'

He could see she was torn. She didn't want to reject him but she didn't want to sleep with him either. In the circumstances he seized upon that as a profound relief: a perfect excuse not to press the issue.

'No, it's OK, really. I just wanted you to know how I feel.' She looked straight at him, her face unreadable. He had started, so he had to finish. 'I don't want to be just your friend, Satu. Not even just your special friend.'

Her eyes scanned him with what he could have sworn was affection tinged with regret. Then she took her hand from his arm, her mind made up. 'We will see each other on Saturday. I will try to be early. But now I have to sleep. You know your way back?'

'Yes, no problem. Thank you for a lovely evening.'

'Good night, Ricky.'

'Good night.'

She reached up out of the darkness and kissed him, quickly and on the cheek to avoid any risk of capture and complications, then stepped to the door. Her key was scraping in the lock when she turned back for a moment. 'There is something about you, Ricky Suomalainen. Like meeting someone for the first time and feeling that you have met him before.'

He tried to answer but the words gagged in his throat. She didn't say anything more. For a few seconds she waited for his reply but none came. Then the door closed behind her and the moment was gone. He was left alone on a darkened street, drowning in a sea of troubles.

CHAPTER 33
Friday 22nd May, 1981

Katerina Karlsholm sat in an electric wheelchair, contemplating the two pictures on her desk. The first was of Adolf Hitler, Albert Speer and herself taken during a meeting at Oranienburg in 1943. She kept it for amusement's sake, as a reminder of the vanity and stupidity of men. And they had thought *they* were screwing *her*.

But that had been a long time ago and the issue now at hand was far more important than memories of old triumphs. Her granddaughter smiled out at her from the other frame and Katerina sighed. It was a brief sigh, expressing the exasperation of the old for the young but it was not entirely lacking in affection.

All the men in their family were such weak fools. Only the women had ever amounted to anything. Now, after more than fifty years of unstinting effort she had encountered a problem all too common among empire builders: a shortage of worthy successors. Out of the whole array of linked and divided families, it had come down to this: one slip of a girl who refused even to acknowledge her own name.

That in itself was irksome but the spirit it showed was far more important. Her granddaughter was the only one capable of taking over the running of the business and Katerina was determined that nothing should compromise that inheritance.

She had not built up this empire to see it destroyed by the weakness and folly of her sons, still less by the Suomalainens. It didn't surprise Katerina in the slightest that the girl was wild and occasionally reckless. Let her screw around for a while and get it out of her system. Let her hide out in that slum and imagine herself to be free and independent. Let her even call herself by whatever name she chose, if it helped exorcise her demons. In the end she would come around. They both knew it.

But it could all be destroyed if that little swine Ricky Suomalainen was allowed to muscle in. God blast him! Katerina looked down at the table, to where her clenched hand had struck with such force as to bounce the china cup out of its saucer. It was typical that Sandy Carr – or Satu Suomalainen as she had been then - had found a way to meddle even from beyond the grave. Just as it was typical that she should have saved up her final shot all this time, only to fire it off blindly, trusting to luck that it would find its mark. But then she had always been a surprise, one of the few real surprises of Katerina's life. So lacking in judgement and yet in the end so... redoubtable. Did the boy have her qualities?

It was second nature for Katerina to consider her opponents' strengths but the sensation of dread that Ricky Suomalainen brought was uncharacteristic. He was all that she most despised: an illegitimate male Suomalainen. Yet if he managed to seduce her granddaughter away from her, he could wreck everything!

It was infuriating that she could not simply have him expelled or arrested but the discomforting fact was that she had nothing on him. By staying out of sight so long he had remained untainted. While she had grown old and weak.

Where was the army of arse-lickers who would have jumped to her bidding even five years ago? All gone except for a handful of morons like that big oaf Lars, who kept out her useless son and the rest of the parasites. Her ability to enforce her will upon others was declining with every passing month. Take that pompous little shit from the record office. Two or three years ago she'd have had him out of a job in no time, instead of which he was tramping all over the burial ground, tripping on old bones. He might be too stupid to understand their significance or too spineless to do anything about it if he did - but she could only hope that the same went for Ricky Suomalainen.

And if not, what then? Katerina moved the electric wheelchair across the room, a reflex from the days when she would have paced the floor to vent her frustration or to work out a stratagem. For the first time in her life she had no plan. Besides influencing her granddaughter remotely, through her parents, she could see no concrete course of action that would eliminate the threat he posed. All she could do was to trust that the years they had spent preparing the girl would cause her to feel a natural revulsion towards this meddlesome bastard.

God knows it ought to. Katerina Satu might be headstrong but she wasn't stupid. And surely even she could not be that perverse?

CHAPTER 34

Ricky found it hard to escape the conclusion that he had become ensnared in a giant honey trap. All he had achieved since arriving in Finland was to fall in love with someone who might be his twin sister. Now his whole future depended on what happened during a few short hours on Saturday night and the time in between loomed like a trip across the wasteland, to be endured for no other reason than to reach the far side.

Into this slough of despond came a telephone call from the old doctor at his lakeside house. When the old man reminded him about their plan to visit the war museum at Parola, Ricky embraced it largely as a way of taking his mind off problems that he couldn't fix. He never seriously expected it to fill in any of the missing pieces in the puzzle of his family history.

After skirting Hämeenlinna they drove for miles through a vast pine forest, before turning off onto a narrow road that wound its way down to the museum. There on a remote terraced hillside dedicated to an obscure war, Ricky found the first solid evidence to support the story told by his Aunt Elvira.

One of the museum's terraces contained a line of British-built tanks from the 1930s; little marvels of period engineering that were now almost impossible to imagine as serious instruments of war.

'English, like you,' said the doctor, patting the wafer thin armour of the nearest machine.

Ricky nodded and took a couple of photographs. 'Yes. Sorry we didn't send something more substantial.'

The doctor smiled, at the comment and the knowledge it revealed. 'It was better than nothing. At least you tried to help us.'

'If I remember my history right, we nearly sent an army as well.'

The old man nodded. 'How differently the world might have turned out if you had sent your men here to fight the Russians, instead of sending them to Norway to fight the Germans.'

'It's hard to imagine. Like finding yourself on the wrong side by mistake.'

They both smiled at this, for it was uncomfortably close to the bone. Yet there were things Ricky needed to know and he suspected that he would get a better response here, from the good doctor, than he had received from Pekka and the others in the garden of the house in Pispala.

'It's funny. I know you wiped out the first Russian invasion in 1939 but I have no idea what happened afterwards.'

'Oh yes, the start of the Winter War is the part people always like to remember. We won the admiration of the world then - but not much else. You can see here what assistance we received: British tanks, German guns. Neither were enough. The Russians wore us down by sheer numbers.'

'Is that when you lost Karelia?'

'For the first time, yes. Stalin wanted to push the border back beyond striking range of Leningrad.'

'And later, when the Germans invaded Russia, you fought alongside them against the Russians?'

The old man gave him a long, measuring look. 'Of course. We fought to regain what we had lost, while the rest of the world turned itself upside down around us. We called it the Continuation War.'

'How did it go?'

His guide gave an ironic laugh at this turn of phrase. 'We regained our old borders and there we stopped.'

'You could have advanced further?'

'Oh yes. We were positioned across the northern approaches to Leningrad. When the Germans came up from the south, the only way in and out of the city was across Lake Ladoga. We could have pinched it off but Mannerheim, our commander, took the decision not to invade Russia. He remembered what we were fighting for - and it was not Nazism.'

'I think I understand. If you'd won, Finland would have become a

Nazi puppet state and if you'd lost, Russia would have annexed the whole country in revenge.'

'Exactly. We held onto our borders until the summer of 1944. Then the Russians launched an offensive that knocked us out of the war.'

They continued the tour together, tracing the snowballing scale of the fighting from the exhibits on the terraces. The displays were vivid but there was something more that Ricky had to know, to complete the picture. He turned back to the doctor, sure now of getting a straight answer. 'What happened after you surrendered for the second time?'

'We had to change sides and drive the Germans out of the country. After the war the uniqueness of Finland's position was recognised in the peace settlement but although we were not occupied, Karelia was lost for good.'

'That's what I've been wondering about. My family's shipping line was based in Viipuri. What do you think would have happened to them?'

'The Russians will have seized any ships or installations they found there as war reparations.'

'So my family would probably have lost everything?'

'We took only what we could carry.'

'But I thought the Saimaa Canal was open for Finnish companies to trade all the way from the lakes to the Gulf of Finland? Couldn't they simply have kept on working through Viipuri?'

'No, those arrangements came later. By the time the peace treaty was signed the Russians had already captured the city and everyone had been evacuated. If your family continued to run a shipping line, they must have built it up from scratch after the war in one of the other Finnish seaports, or on the lakes. Even if they already had branches elsewhere, any of their ships that survived the last months of the war would probably have been seized after the Russians drove the German navy out of the Baltic.'

'What if a company was operating out of Sweden?'

'That would be a different matter. Swedish ships traded quite freely throughout the war. With Germany, with Finland and even with Russia.'

Their conversation had brought them to the end of the last terrace and Ricky opened the back of his camera before reaching into his pocket for a new roll of film. In the process he dropped the used one, which promptly rolled underneath one of the old British tanks. He swore and got down on his hands and knees to look for it. The film had wedged against the tank tracks and as he reached in he saw something that riveted him to the spot.

A brass plate had been fixed to the tank just below the exhaust outlet. Someone had been carefully polishing the vehicles for years and the wording etched into the plate was still legible. It was in English and Ricky knew it at once for what it was.

Finn-Leith Lines
Viipuri, Turku & Leith
Export Licence No 10027
23 November 1939

His mind was flooded by two distinct flashbacks. The first was the picture Elvira had shown him two days before. Grandfather Ernie and his partner had been standing in front of a merchant ship on an unknown dock. Right above their heads, in bold white lettering, had been the name of the shipping line. Finn-Leith Lines. It hadn't struck him then but now it made a simultaneous connection with something else that was buried deep in his memory.

He must have been no more than five or six. He had gone with his grandmother to a dismal, echoing building that smelt of dust and decay. He had no recollection of its location but he guessed it must have been in Leith docks, where the British end of the shipping line had been based.

The office she led him to had grime on the windows and deep shadows in the corners that seemed to reach out for him. He had been so frightened that he sat rigidly on an ancient leather chair under the single light bulb and neither moved nor made a sound the whole time they were there. She had removed some papers and locked the door behind them. He had been learning to read at the time and as they left he had pointed to the words stencilled on the glass of the door and asked his grandmother what they said. Her reply came back to him now, clear as a bell. 'Finn-Leith Lines.'

He straightened up in surprise and banged his head against the hull of the tank. Cursing, he remembered the film and crouched down again to retrieve it. As he rose once more he ran his hand over the warm armour. It had come here on one of his grandfather's ships. They had been importing tanks to Finland at the start of the Winter War.

Ricky knew that he and the tank were also linked in another way: they were among the last survivors of their respective families. He contemplated the vehicle in silence for a moment, standing there on a sun-dappled terrace in the heart of the country that it had helped to protect. If it had been possible to hug a five-ton Vickers tank he would have done it.

The tank proved the truth of at least part of Elvira's story. If everything else she said was true, then perhaps he should be concentrating his enquiries on the Karlsholms rather than the Suomalainens. Everything seemed to point to them. There was the refusal by Bengt to direct him towards at least one Karlsholm who was still living in Tampere. There was the irregularity in the records that he had finally admitted to. There was the mystery of what exactly Katerina Karlsholm had done to his mother and her children. And most of all there was the question of whether or not Satu Savolainen, Katerina Satu Karlsholm and his missing twin sister were all one and the same person.

Yet if they were, why on earth wouldn't she have admitted it? Even if she didn't know the whole story, surely she would have grasped enough of the connections to link herself in some way with his search? He suddenly felt a great sympathy for Pandora. Whatever the cost, he simply had to look inside that box.

By the time they got back to Tampere he had made up his mind. Tomorrow he would go in search of the Karlsholms and when he met Satu again he would have it out with her once and for all. But first what he really needed was to let his hair down. He figured the best thing was to do what most men do when their problems become too complex. He would go out and have a drink with the boys. Several drinks, actually: and then a few more.

CHAPTER 35

Ricky got back to the house in Pispala just as Tim was putting his key in the lock. Before he could turn it the door was thrown open from within and any remnant of melancholy was routed as Ricky saw who was standing there.

'Terrence O'Neal, as I live and breathe.'

'Welcome to you both and come in.'

Tim grunted, looking meaningfully at the door lock.

'It was a thing of little consequence,' declared Terry. 'I have the kettle on but I couldn't find where you hide the coffee. It's a piece of good fortune that you arrived when you did.'

'It's in the jar marked "Coffee",' observed Ricky, instantly sympathetic towards anyone confused by such deviousness.

'Now if there had been an Englishman here earlier, I could have had my feet up and be enjoying it already, instead of looking all over for it like the miser's horde.'

'I suppose this means we're drinking tonight?' said Ricky, looking hopefully from the one to the other.

'Drinking?' exclaimed Terry. 'Would I be just *drinking* on my own birthday? It's *celebrating* we'll be doing, Ricky: and no better people to be doing it with than the Finns. Say what you will about them, they know how to apply themselves to the serious moments in a man's life. Now, would either of you be wanting some coffee, at all?'

'And when they were only half way up...they were neither up nor down!'

The refrain nicely assessed the position of the bar whose merits they were so loudly debating. They had ranged up and down the town for an hour until they hit upon this compromise but it proved a happy choice, for it was perhaps the only establishment in Tampere from which they could have escaped ejection before the night was half done. Terrence O'Neal was not the man to let his birthday pass without due note.

'The O'Neals will have their day,' he stated defiantly. 'Put yerr money on the table and let's be seeing the magnitude of what lies before us.'

All of them, amused English and bemused Finns, threw their wallets down onto the circular table and seated themselves around it while Terry rifled the contents. He presently had a mound of notes and coin with whose magnitude he was pleased to pronounce himself satisfied.

'Right then, here we go,' he enthused, beckoning to the barman while pushing a pile of coins across the table towards Ricky. 'I'd like drinks for all my friends, whatever it is they're wanting and Ricky, would you be so good as to put some money in the jukebox; there's a terrible quiet in here.'

The barman came out and took their orders as if this was everyday practice. As a way of ordering drinks in Finland it was so unprecedented that Pekka and Harri were gobsmacked into silence. Ricky concluded that meek obedience was the order of the day and filled the jukebox with as many coins as it would take, pressing a random selection of buttons and returning to find an overflowing half-litre glass awaiting him.

'Terrence O'Neal!' said Tim, saluting the man of the hour. 'The biggest boozer in Montreux.'

'In Montreux is it?' demanded O'Neal, springing to his feet. 'Terrence O'Neal, the biggest boozer ever to empty his bladder in Lake Leman!'

'Terrence O'Neal!' they shouted, all six.

'Montreux?' queried Ricky, tentatively. 'I could have sworn that last time I visited Montreux it was in Switzerland. In fact it seems a bit odd that you should turn up here at all. I mean, I only have three real friends and two of you are here in Finland. Doesn't that strike you as odd?'

'Nah. I came here because you told me what a terrible place it was and Terry came here because I told him how great it was. It's about as much of a coincidence as Stanley bumping into Doctor Livingstone.'

'Oh.' Ricky thought about it for a while and concluded that Tim was probably the most unromantic bastard he'd ever met in his life. So he raised his glass to the pair of them and poured another beer down his neck.

As each round was consumed a small square chitty appeared on the table, left there by the departing barman, who seemed greatly amused to cast himself in the role of waiter. Terry began to arrange them in a line across the table, declaring his intention of completing the diagonal before the evening was out. 'Not a man of you leaves this table...' and he banged it with his fist for greater emphasis, '... until we've crossed it in bills.'

Ricky groaned inwardly and determined to switch to keski oluts for however many more rounds were still to come.

'Lyttleton O'Rorke!' Terry declared.

'Who?'

'Lyttleton O'Rorke, my old maths teacher. Truly we were a terrible class of brats, so he gave up the teaching and used to play us tunes on a tin whistle he kept in his waistcoat pocket instead.'

True or not it was the sort of tale an Irishman should tell, so they raised their glasses to the man.

'Terry's time in Switzerland is infamous,' Tim announced, with a wink at Ricky. 'Why don't you entertain us all with some of the stories?'

'On my first night there,' Terry responded at once, 'I stayed down by the lake at the biggest hotel in town, The Montreux Palace by name. A grand affair, with uniformed flunkeys to carry your fishing tackle and breakfast served as late as eleven o'clock.'

'Civilisation incarnate.'

'I awoke at an early hour, after a reasonable night's drinking, with an urgent appointment at the nearest convenience. Forgetting where I was and imagining myself to be still in my mother's house in Ireland, I made my way into the corridor, only realising my mistake when I opened the door of the bathroom and found myself in a laundry closet.'

Ricky cast his eyes around the table to judge the reaction of the others. Pekka looked like someone who's just discovered there are whole new worlds of language still to be explored. Harri clearly had no idea what this guy was on about. Tim was unreadable. The sixth member of the group, an English teacher from Runcorn, was practically wetting himself.

'Returning to my room, where I now remembered having seen a well appointed bathroom only the previous evening, I found that I had inadvertently locked myself out.'

'Bummer.'

'Determining to refer the matter at once to a competent authority, I had reached as far as the main staircase when I chanced to look down and notice, as sooner or later on such occasions a man invariably does, that I was bollock-naked.'

Pekka spat beer all over the table, while others among them only just managed to keep to their seats. Then Harri said, 'Please, what is this "bollock-naked"?' and they all just totally lost it. Terry carried on regardless, as if this was the normal state of his audiences.

'After considering various ways of covering my plight, my eyes alighted upon a heavily draped window and a gilt chair. I was in the act of standing upon the one and attempting to remove the curtains from the other when the night porter appeared from down the hall. I am in no doubt that he had been hiding there all along, waiting for just such an opportunity to demonstrate the smallness of mind characteristic of petty officialdom the world over.'

'How did it end?' Ricky pleaded.

'I cut through his officiousness with a knife-like calm and demanded to be directed at once to a place of ablution. I also declined to tip him in a very pointed manner.'

'Weren't you arrested for indecent exposure?'

'I was not.'

'Have you ever gone back?'

'Twice'

'And they let you in?'

'Of course. On both occasions I was fully clad and they affected not to recognise me. I did not, however, seek accommodation.'

'Were you in company?'

'Most definitely.'

'A young lady?'

'Unmistakably.'

'The reason for her not being among those present?'

'This is not a fit occasion for one of her tender sensibilities. Also, she is in Belfast.'

'Has she a special place in your affections?'

'She has.'

'Define it.'

'We have spent a weekend in Paris together in circumstances of unrelieved romance.'

'Give us the flavour of it.'

'We went to a three-rose restaurant overlooking the Seine and ate fresh lobster in a sauce prepared only by special request, consuming two bottles of Dom Pérignon and concluding the evening with the finest brandy and a walk around the Ille de la Cité.'

'How do you keep her remembrance fresh over a distance of a thousand miles?'

'By ways known to all true lovers.'

'What are your principal anniversaries?'

'The occasion just outlined is paramount.'

'How do you honour it?'

'By going alone to the same restaurant and consuming the same meal, in silent remembrance.'

'What, not exactly the same meal?'

'No, I only had one lobster.'

'Why wasn't she there, too?'

'She was slightly injured in a bombing. But she is now completely recovered, thanks be to God.'

'Her name, if we might be privileged to know it?'

'Carmel.'

Ricky stood and raised his glass. 'Carmel!'

'CARMEL!' they roared.

'Heaven smile on her,' breathed Terry in a voice suffused with sadness.

'You're as love-sick as Ricky,' snorted Tim.

Terrence looked over at once, the interest plain on his face. 'Is it true, Ricky? And who might she be, the lucky girl?'

Ricky did his best to appear nonchalant and quickly put his mouth in his beer, where it couldn't get him into trouble.

'She's called Satu,' announced Harri, 'and she's quite a beautiful girl.'

Having almost drowned in his own froth, Ricky looked from one to another of them and was aghast to see the knowledge writ across their faces.

'Ricky,' cried Terrence, 'is it true? Is it...*the Big Smitts?*'

To his chagrin, Ricky blushed. He could feel it going right across his face as they all raised their glasses.

'To Ricky and Satu.'

He could have curled up and died right there: but Terrence was beaming at him and they all seemed to think it a grand thing.

'It's not...' he began. 'I don't... ' He trailed off, five sets of eyes boring into him.

'Say it, man', said Terrence, as if encouraging a new recruit to swear the oath that would initiate him into a secret cult.

Ricky looked at Tim and Tim looked right back, a twist of amusement at the corner of his mouth as he dared him to deny it. And of course he was right. Tim had understood what Ricky himself had only recognised when it was too late. 'She, she's...special.' He blurted it out, his face burning in embarrassment. There was a collective sinking of shoulders at this flunking of the test. Terrence sighed and tried once more.

'Say it, man. If it's true, own it.'

And suddenly Ricky's thoughts were of her, instead of his own confusion. Through the beer-soaked haze he saw her face as clear as if she was standing there before him. He raised his eyes to meet Terry's and they both smiled at the knowing that passed between them. 'To Satu,' he said, lifting his glass as if in a dream. 'The girl I love.'

The cheer, the shouted name and the clash of glasses stopped the bar dead, every head turning towards them. Ricky stood there, grinning sheepishly, then drained his glass and sat down heavily, a beautific expression on his face.

The line of chitties had passed the centre of the table by now and they were all feeling more than a little drunk. Acting on impulse, Terry snatched one up and held it against his thumb, then leant over the table and began counting the number of thumb-lengths remaining before the diagonal would be completed. 'Thirteen!' he cried at last. 'Seven down and six to go. A thirteen gun salute!'

Ricky looked at Tim and Tim looked at Ricky and they both felt suddenly a lot drunker. But before he could protest Ricky was dispatched to shovel more coins into the jukebox and soon there was a rare old sing-song in progress. The manageress came to see what all the noise was about and Ricky saw the barman pointing at the line of chitties, evidently explaining their gruesome intent. At any rate he reckoned he knew horror when he saw it.

He must have misjudged her, however. A little later the barman came over with a tray of drinks and set them down with a smile, saying, 'From the house'. Ricky's initial reaction was almost as charmed as Terry's - but then it occurred to him that they would now have to drink fourteen rounds rather than just thirteen. And Terry had stayed on half litres the whole time!

Ricky must have started to lose track of what was going on somewhere around the tenth or eleventh round, by which time the man from Runcorn had slumped across the table and was giving no outward sign of life. As he came back from the bar, Ricky swayed over him and then burst into loud titters. 'S-S-S'curity man,' was all he could say.

The others looked at him curiously.

'Cap'n Kirk, beam me up Scottie. S'curity man always geshs it.' He was aware that he was slurring his speech but couldn't do anything about it. The others all looked horribly sober, except for the one lying slumped across the table, which just made him titter all the louder. 'Thersh always a s'curtyman who's only innit for togetshot. By aliens. Alwaysh.' Ricky jabbed his finger at the recumbent form and then looked slyly back to the others. 'Never know what his name is. Jush an eshtra. Gets got dead by aliens. Bye bye.'

He had to go suddenly to the toilet at that point and when he came out again the others were dancing by the jukebox. Unfortunately, next day his memory of asking Terrence to dance was quite clear. What an Irish jig was doing on a Finnish jukebox he couldn't imagine but it was a jig of sorts they danced, round and round the table, while those of their friends who were still conscious clapped along in time and proceeded to sing 'Happy Birthday' and 'For He's a Jolly Good Fellow' and then 'The Wild Colonial Boy'.

After that things grew patchy again, until Tim came into the toilet and told him it was time to go. He remembered passing their table and noting with great satisfaction that the diagonal was complete. Then Terrence was on one side of him and Tim was on the other and they were outside on the street, face to face with a brand new sports car. It was long and low and mean-looking and it sat there in the road and stared at them arrogantly with its retractable eyes. They stared back at it, despising its insolent, sneering manner.

'Right then,' said Terry, 'Here we go.'

They stepped off the kerb together and walked right over it. It was built like a set of inclined steps really; just made for mounting. They went up one side and down the other and on up the street without a backward glance.

His next memory was of standing in a large, cobbled square, looking up at a statue portraying classical figures in a jumble of limbs. Terrence was pointing up at a clock tower behind them and saying agitatedly that it was nearly time. Ricky didn't know what time it nearly was or why it was important but Terry's voice must have conveyed a sense of urgency because a moment later they were all hanging onto various bits of Graeco-Roman anatomy and a big clock was striking twelve or thirteen right over their heads. He remembered being surprised at how hard and cold Venus' left thigh was.

At some point after that they were walking up a long, straight road when they came upon something that arrested their progress. It was probably an advertising poster because he had a single vivid memory, like a still from a movie, of a hand holding onto one corner of such a poster, as if in the act of peeling it off the wall. But he had no recollection of who the hand belonged to or of what the poster was about.

All was well and well forgotten after that until they reached Tim's house, where the sudden change to an enclosed space caused him to stumble back out into the street. He thought about the underground toilet and realised he'd never make it, so he had a quick throw in a dark corner instead and felt much better. Then he went back inside, fell over a mattress in the middle of the living room floor and went instantly to sleep.

Sometime late the next morning Ricky awoke to find Tim and Terrence sitting around the table just above his head, washing down buttered toast with strong black coffee. They offered him some and he sat up in bed to accept, eating his breakfast with his head at table level, which made it easier to shovel things into his mouth. After a while he felt obliged to comment, 'I've never drunk so much in my life and yet I feel right as rain. It's uncanny.'

'For sure, that Number Four is a fine drop of beer,' said Terrence.

Ricky shook his head in wonderment and had another cup of coffee. It was then that he noticed the enormous poster of a cow which almost completely covered the floor. It was manifestly an advertisement for milk products. 'What's the cow doing here?'

'You brought it here,' stated Tim, flatly.

'Me?' Ricky said blankly. 'What on earth would I want with a thing like that?'

'You insisted. You tore it off the side of a house, rolled it up like a giant salami and carried it back three miles through the centre of town.'

'Really?' was all he could think of to say. 'How odd.' After eating another slice of toast a ghastly thought struck him. He eyed his companions anxiously but neither appeared concerned with more than the usual cares of life. 'Did we, ah, climb a statue last night?'

'Don't you remember?'

'Not precisely, no.'

'It was in the main square,' said Tim, blithely.

'The main square.'

'At midnight, boy, to celebrate my birthday,' affirmed Terrence.

'Was it a large statue, rather short on clothing?'

'The same.'

'Near a sort of town-hallish looking building?'

'Not just *a* town-hallish building. *The* town hall building.'

'Why weren't we arrested?'

'Luck of the Irish, I suppose. More coffee?'

'Thank you. What happened to the others? There were others, weren't there? I seem to remember one was English and apparently dead.'

'Harri and Pekka took him home. He kept coming round for a few seconds and muttering something about having to catch the last train back to Wigan. We thought it best to keep him away from the railway station.'

'Right.'

'You kept calling up the Starship Enterprise on a cigarette lighter and telling them to beam him back up for medical examination. You said not to send down any more security men until you'd had a full autopsy report from Doctor McCoy on what killed him. You were quite insistent about it.'

Fragments of it came back to him. 'It was alcohol got him, right?'

'Yeah. The alien theory has been generally discredited.'

'Oh well, I guess it must affect some people more than others.' He paused to eat more toast and then looked inquisitively at each of them in turn. 'Anyone got any use for a fifteen foot Friesian?'

CHAPTER 36
Saturday 23rd May, 1981

Ricky spent the rest of the morning mooching about town, suffering the after-effects of the beer in the form of a creeping depression. It was his last full day in Finland but he found himself wishing away the precious hours, for in Satu's absence nothing held his interest.

He extended his routine in the pool by an hour, as if he expected her to suddenly appear. The lanes remained empty but for his forlorn wake, yet he stayed on in the sauna until he was red as a lobster and then dallied long over coffee and pastries, hoping the hopeless.

Around noon he explored the university area, aiming to meet up with Pekka. He eventually bumped into him coming out of a lecture on Finnish-Estonian foreign relations from 1920 to 1939, a subject that reduced the chance of Satu-sightings to absolute zero. Pekka's first piece of news only depressed him further. He had rung round the last of the Suomalainens listed in the Finnish phone books and found that none of them knew either a Satu Suomalainen or a Satu Karlsholm. One woman did know of his family, vaguely, as having gone to live in England a long time ago. She thought they had relatives in America or Canada but she wasn't sure which. It was a dead end.

When Ricky asked if he thought Bengt might now be willing to order a search in the records for the Karlsholms, Pekka looked at him in surprise. 'But I have found them already! That was the other thing I was going to tell you.'

'Found them? Who?'

'The person who Bengt would not tell you about.' He paused before announcing, 'Ricky: it is Katerina Karlsholm – she is in a private nursing home just outside town. I have the address right here.'

'Are you sure? Katerina Karlsholm is still alive?'

'She's the one you think is behind what happened to your mother, isn't she?'

'That's right. According to Elvira she's responsible for just about everything bad that's ever happened to my family.'

'Then I think perhaps you should go and have a talk with her.' Pekka took a piece of paper from his pocket and held it out, only to have Ricky react as if he was being offered the key to the knowledge of good and evil. 'You will not find out by wondering,' Pekka said at last, pressing it into his hand. 'I can show you if you like, the road you have to take is not far from here.'

'Thank you! But how did you find her?'

'It was not so hard. They are one of the richest families in Finland. Getting to see her may be more difficult but I will have to leave that to you: I have another lecture in half an hour.'

'Right. Christ, Pekka; thanks. I really mean it. Are you sure you have time to walk there with me?'

'From the way you are looking, I think I had better.'

Their route took them beside the lake and because he didn't know how to prepare for the coming meeting, he consciously tried to blot it out by looking at the view instead. It didn't really work but it was better than letting his mind race in useless circles.

They stopped for a moment to watch a steamer go by, white and graceful against the dark waters, a handful of people lazing on the sundeck.

'Where do they go?'

'There is a famous route called the Poet's Way that goes north from here: and another one called the Silver Line that goes south, to Hämeenlinna. It's a good way to spend a long, lazy day.'

'Another time, then.'

'You are planning to come back?'

Ricky gazed out across the water, screwing up his eyes against the sun's reflection. 'Oh, I'll be back alright.'

As they strode on over the bridge, Pekka pointed to the long rows of boats tied up along the town jetties. 'That's my boat.'

'Yes? Which one?'

'The blue one. Just there, by the old black hulk that's full of water.'

'How often do you use it?'

'Not at all this year. It needs some work. After the winter you have to do something to it. *Tilkitä*. I don't know the word for it in English.' Pekka frowned at this shortcoming in his own vocabulary, then shrugged and carried on. 'I take it out quite often in the summer for picnics on the lake. Or you can row across to the islands.'

Ricky looked over to the biggest of them and in the haze there was something otherworldly about it, conjuring up childhood fancies. What had Pekka called it? Viikonsaari. Something stirred within him, some instinctive response to the shimmering allure of land across water. But there was no time.

'You have to be careful, though,' Pekka warned. 'At Midsummer we have a festival all across Finland. Everyone makes bonfires and goes out on the lakes with lots of alcohol. The commonest cause of death at Midsummer is drowning. People get really drunk and then they stand up in the boat to piss and they fall overboard. They're too drunk to get back in, so they drown.'

'Some party.'

'Yes but it's like a war; you only hear about it from the ones who come back, so it even sounds quite funny.'

Ricky nodded absently and checked his watch, mentally crossing off the hours before he would see Satu again. He caught Pekka looking at him and gave a self-deprecatory laugh. 'So much to do, so little time.' Then his face grew deadly serious. 'God, I only hope she keeps our date tonight.'

'She will.'

He wished he could be so sure. And even if she did, how could he possibly realise all his hopes in one night? They'd have at best a scant few hours together and the truth was that he wanted it all: the whole fairytale. But first, of course, he had to meet the evil queen.

The nursing home was set well back from the main road, within a landscaped park. The gates were open, so he said goodbye to Pekka, walked up the driveway and went straight on into the lobby.

A middle-aged woman in a nurse's uniform asked him in Finnish what his business was. He wasn't sure that Katerina Karlsholm would see him if she knew who he was but he was averse to lying and didn't want to surrender any kind of moral advantage, so after hesitating for a moment he replied in English that he was her grandson.

Ricky could have sworn the woman smiled to herself but she duly invited him to sign the visitors' book while she rang through to check. She spoke briefly on the phone, looked up at him rather strangely a couple of times and nodded, then asked him to reconfirm his identity.

'She is my grandmother. Her son Thorvald is my father. But we've never met.'

'Yes but she is asking, what is your name?'

He gave her his best smile and prayed. 'Ricky Suomalainen.'

The receptionist repeated it down the phone and then winced at what she heard from the other end. Ricky didn't understand Swedish but the shrill stridency of the tone was clear even from where he was standing. The nurse looked up and shook her head. 'I am sorry. She will not see you.'

Ricky suppressed his natural inclination to say, 'Oh, right, sorry' and instead forced himself to persevere. 'I'm afraid it is absolutely necessary that I see her. I have come a long way and there is something I have to tell her before I go.' He looked the woman right in the eye, pleading empathy. 'It may be the last time, you understand? The last chance for both of us.'

The receptionist gave obvious consideration to turning him down but the look on his face seemed to make her relent. At any rate she picked up the handset, dialled the extension and spoke into the mouthpiece again. There was evidently no response, for she repeated herself and paused to listen before looking at the phone as if it were faulty. Then she turned back to him with a shrug. 'She has put down the telephone.'

Ricky guessed that might be the end of it but he wasn't prepared to give up so easily. While she was still on the phone he had leaned forward far enough to see the light on the PABX in front of her. Each line had both an extension and a room number written against it. Now he glanced around the lobby and saw the direction signs hanging from the ceiling.

He nodded to her as if in resignation, then started walking towards the open doorway leading into the main corridor. 'I'll just use the toilets before I go, if that's OK. This way?' He indicated the sign above his head and she hesitated but he said, 'Thanks' and sauntered through the doorway before she had a chance to object.

At first the ease of it surprised him. As he went into the toilets he noted that they were out of sight of the reception desk, so a moment later he slipped quietly out again, heading in the direction indicated by the helpful signs.

The corridor emerged into a large, well appointed wing with floor-to-ceiling windows on both sides. Outside, water splashed over the sculptured rocks of a landscaped garden. The door with the tell-tale number was right in front of him, across about an acre of marble floor. Whatever ailed his grandmother, it was clearly not lack of cash. He turned the doorknob as he knocked and it swung open in his hand, to reveal a large antechamber: at which point any ideas he had about good luck and poor security were abruptly rebutted.

The shadow that fell upon him was cast by the biggest man he had ever seen. The guy was so big he completely filled the inner doorway, causing Ricky to step backwards as if he had bounced off. The Rock said nothing. He didn't have to. He just held up one huge paw and fixed Ricky with a stare that would have cowed a bear.

A second later the receptionist caught up with him, tugging at his arm and giving him a thorough ticking off, so like a headmistress scolding a naughty schoolboy that the anger in Ricky boiled over. He had come too far and got too close to fail now. The receptionist started to yell in his ear and the gorilla moved threateningly closer - but Ricky told them both to bugger off and stood his ground. Whereupon the Rock smiled, picked him up by the lapels and shook him like a rag doll.

'We will call the police now and you will be in trouble,' declared the receptionist with almost comical satisfaction.

Ricky found himself being carried backwards in mid air and decided that he'd had enough. He spoke just below the level of a shout, making sure that his voice carried through into the room beyond. 'Good. Call the police. I'm sure they'll be interested in what I have to say.'

Even as the gorilla continued to carry him towards the exit, a voice from the inner room cut through the proceedings like a knife. The Rock stopped in his tracks - but unfortunately not before the back of Ricky's head banged against the door lintel. A second later he was left standing there in a daze, rubbing the back of his head in a mixture of pain and disbelief. The receptionist looked as if she was going to object but the voice lashed out and she thought better of it, retreating rapidly out the door instead.

The Rock stood to one side, the retraction of his belly serving as the only invitation for Ricky to enter. As he did so the guy gave a faint smirk and then followed him into the inner sanctum.

The room that Ricky entered was remarkable for its size, affluence and sparseness. The dominant effect was a dazzling whiteness, like a pristine snowfield. The walls and ceiling were smooth concrete but the floor was pure marble. Apart from a set of French doors facing an internal courtyard, all the windows were set high up, so as to shut out any view of the outside world.

The furnishing was unmistakably Nordic. The desk could have been an engineering model, with its sweeping curves of silvered steel, while the chairs were so minimalist as to be more sculptures than seats. Three huge abstract paintings adorned the walls, each more than six feet across and executed in shades of blue and grey.

Katerina Karlsholm sat at the centre of the room in an electric wheelchair. She was dressed in black, save for flashes of black and white jewellery, which more or less reflected the streaks of white in her hair. Ricky thought her face the most elegantly refined picture of malevolence he had ever seen. But then, he was not entirely unbiased.

'You are not even very like him.'

'You mean my father?'

She shook her head in a manner that implied he was slow in the wits for having to ask. 'A fleeting similarity, perhaps, if one were determined to see it. No more than that.' It was as close as she came

Searching for Satu

to the niceties before she got straight to the point. 'Now, what do you have to say that could possibly be of any interest to the police?'

Ricky knew the weakness of his position, so he had little choice but to try and bluff it out. 'I think you know very well.'

'Don't play games with me. You cannot know anything of importance.'

'Then why call me back? We both know the issue: what you really want is to know what proof I have.'

'You bargain with nothing.'

'Alright, let's talk about what I know. After all, I think it's high time you and I had a little chat, eh, granny?'

'And I think it's high time he showed a little respect, eh, Lars?' She gestured to the titan and before Ricky had time to react a giant paw gripped him where his shoulder met the base of his neck, driving him to his knees with unbelievable force. Only when he cried out in agony did the grip relax fractionally, allowing him to look up. She smiled contemptuously. 'Did you really think you could barge in here and threaten me?'

Ricky couldn't keep the rage out of his voice, even though he knew how pathetic he must sound. 'Do you really think you can go on mistreating people and get away with it? What kind of person are you, anyway?'

'The kind that always wins. Now, I will ask you for the last time. What do you know that could be of any interest to the police?'

'I know what you did to my mother. I know you had her illegally committed to a mental hospital and that you had me illegally sent to a children's home. I know how you cheated my grandparents into bankruptcy during the war.'

'Pah! You are wasting my time. I will have Lars throw you into the gutter where you belong.'

'There is proof. The records still exist.'

'They say nothing of any importance.'

'Really? How about the importance of omission?'

'What omission?'

'Oh, I think you know well enough. Missing signatures; reports that were never made to the police; missing records at the children's home. Individually they don't amount to much but taken together they would require a lot of explaining.'

'Old history, of little interest to anyone. None of it linked directly to me.'

'Then let's call the police and see.'

'Perhaps that would be best.'

But if she was willing to call his bluff, then he was equally ready to raise the stakes. 'Inconvenient, though: and just the beginning. I found out that much in a few days; it will be interesting to see what comes to light in a thorough investigation.'

'I know precisely what would come to light: whatever I decide to reveal.'

'Don't bank on it. I think the newspapers would love this story. It has all the right ingredients: one of the country's leading families trying to hide their indiscretions by locking up an innocent woman and her son. It would make a great scandal.'

'You're pathetic. Here people do not have the same puerile English obsession with sex and scandal. The newspapers print news, not silly gossip.'

'Are you willing to risk it?'

She gave him a look that constituted a perfect mix of dislike and disdain. 'So, how much do you want?'

'I don't want your money!'

'Your mother, as I recall, said much the same. But she took it nonetheless.'

'Only what was her due and only because she needed it. I don't.'

'Then what do you want? Why are you here?'

'I came for my sister.'

To his amazement she flinched back in her chair as if he had struck her. Lars' hand instantly tightened into a vice-like grip and Katerina's expression changed to one of naked hate. 'You come here and tell me this? To my face?'

'Of course. What did you expect? Did you seriously imagine anything else?'

'Why? Why now?'

'Because I only found out when my mother was dying. She never told me before.'

'Ah!'

Again it was as if he had slapped her. Ricky was bewildered by the effect his words were having but he did his best to press home the advantage, even as Lars was crushing him into the ground. 'As soon as I found out, I came here to search for her.'

This time Katerina's face went suddenly blank, as if what he had said made no sense. 'To search for her?'

'Of course. I came here to find Satu.'

To his surprise he saw relief and comprehension flood into her face, only to be replaced almost at once by a look of fury. 'So that is your aim after all! You think you can use Katerina Satu to steal from me!'

Ricky dared not show his ignorance of the thing he most wanted to know. He had to press on and hope. 'Naturally.'

'It will not happen.'

'How can you stop it? You're just an old woman and she despises you.'

'It's a lie! She does not!'

'Shit, she won't even use your name. She refuses even to call herself Katerina.'

She practically spat at him. The transformation from elegant matriarch to twisted old crone was extraordinary: and yet the recovery was equally remarkable. After only a few seconds her voice was filled once more with sneering contempt. 'She will not consort with you. She is a Karlsholm. She knows about you Suomalainens, what sort of scum you are.'

'I think you'll find she has a mind of her own.' Ricky wasn't even sure whose mind he was talking about and the pain in his neck and shoulder was becoming unbearable but instinct told him he was on the right track. Yet before he had time to press the point, Katerina seemed to regain her strength.

'Indeed she has - and she will use it. The more you try to get close, the sooner she will see that you are exactly what she had been warned against.'

'And what's that?'

'An ambitious nonentity.'

Ricky sensed that somehow he had lost the initiative and that Katerina was reversing the balance of power between them but he had no idea how this had come about. 'I'm your own flesh and blood. You may not like it any more than I do but you can't escape it. Your son is my father. My family were your business partners. You may have tried to get rid of me when I was a child and you may have cheated them but you can't hide it from her. Not any longer.'

Katerina's eyes spat triumph and her voice was jubilant. 'You little fool! My God, she never told you, did she? She kept up the pretence to the end!'

'What?'

Her eyes jeered at him. 'You've been speaking to that old fool Elvira, of course.'

'My aunt Elvira, yes.'

'Your aunt nothing. She's been insane for forty years. She was weak in the head from childhood. Only a Suomalainen would have been fool enough to marry her.'

'She doesn't speak too highly of you, either.'

'It was her fantasy that inspired your mother.'

'What fantasy?'

'It's all fantasy. No doubt she told you that I cheated your miserable grandfather out of his share of the shipping line. Fools. I didn't have to. When Hitler invaded Denmark and Norway, most of the company's ships were safe in Swedish ports, as my husband and I had arranged. At the start of that day they were flying the Red Ensign, or the blue and white of Finland. By the end of it they were flying the blue and gold of Sweden. By the end of the war we were rich. All the intelligent ones in Sweden grew rich on that war. Your family played heroes and what little tonnage they still possessed ended up at the bottom of the sea. Fortunate for me, unfortunate for them - but all quite legal.'

'And afterwards you refused to reopen the partnership.'

'Of course. With Viipuri gone they had nothing I needed. It was easy enough to replace them with an agent in Newcastle.'

'That can scarcely have been legal.'

'The law is what you make of it. They had few papers, less money

Searching for Satu

and bad lawyers. I had many papers, a lot of money and very good lawyers. Most of all, I had ships. Such is life.'

'It still wouldn't look too good in the newspapers. Collaboration with the Nazis is always good for column inches.'

'It will never be written, not here or in Sweden. There are too many ghosts in too many high-ranking closets.'

'Maybe so - but there are some things you can't sweep under the carpet. Me, for instance.'

'Ah yes, Satu's boy.'

'I'm no fantasy, however much you might wish I was. I'm going to go on searching until I find what I'm looking for. Nothing you can do will stop me.'

'And just what are you searching for?'

'For Satu and the truth.'

'Ha! You will never find your Holy Grail, young man. You will never find it because it does not exist. Like you, it is an illusion.'

'Really. Just watch me.'

'When you first walked in that door, I thought your quest was of a very different sort. And then again, a moment ago... But now I see you are just a young fool, sent on an errand dreamed up by one deranged mind and encouraged by another.'

Katerina looked at him as if noticing his plight for the first time. She arched her eyebrow, then nodded at Lars. He stood back, letting Ricky get up: but it proved to be the final small mercy before she delivered the *coup de grace*. 'You want to know the truth? Very well, I shall tell you, if you have the stomach for it. You say you are here for your sister? You have no sister. In truth, you have no family: no mother, no father - no identity of any kind. You are a walking nonentity.'

Ricky could only glower at her, wondering where this was leading.

'You believe that Satu Suomalainen was your mother and that my son Thorvald was your father, yes?'

'You know that.'

'I know nothing of the kind. Nobody knows who your parents were. You were given to a foundling home as an infant. The foundling home from which your mother stole you before fleeing the country.'

It was so preposterous that Ricky laughed but his eyes didn't laugh with him. They stayed fixed on Katerina's and he saw nothing there to allay the visceral fear forming in his gut. 'That's ridiculous and you know it.'

'Really? Are you so sure? Where, for instance, is your birth certificate? Where are the relatives and friends who can vouch for you? What does the evidence of the record office actually point to?'

'No, you're wrong. The birth certificate is forged, sure - but that's just because nobody knew about my birth at the time. When she fled the country she had to get a false certificate made up.'

'One possible explanation but rather convoluted and unlikely, don't you think?'

'There's a doctor's report that talks about her child...'

'You mean there's a doctor's report recommending that she be admitted to a psychiatric hospital because her behaviour threatened the well-being of her child. But there is no record of your admittance to the children's home, or of your unauthorised departure from it. You see, despite what you think, I am not without compassion. I had no wish to persecute her. She was a very sick young woman: the death of her children quite unhinged her.'

'What do you mean? Which children?'

'The only children she ever had.' Ignoring his disbelieving look, she continued. 'It is true that I was unaware of the birth of her son. That is something I regret even to this day. Had I known of it he might have lived, though that must be doubtful given what happened to the first child. The second twin is always more at risk, you know.'

'What do you mean? What happened to the first?'

Katerina looked at him with something that could almost have been taken for sympathy. 'She also died. Only a few hours after she was born.'

Any pretext of self-control deserted him at those words. 'It's not true! I know she's alive!'

'No, she has been dead these twenty-five years.'

'You're lying! It's just more of your lies. Elvira was right about you.'

'Elvira is a mad old fool who has built her fantasies upon events she never witnessed. Doubtless she told you about the death of her brother-in-law at the battle of Pispala? My husband was, as it happens, an officer with the White army at the time but he played no part in the battle, still less commanded the firing squad. The whole story is the product of a deranged mind.'

'So everyone is mad except you.'

'No, just Elvira and Satu Suomalainen. The one, sadly, sparked off the other. When your mother - I use the word because I recognise that is what she became to you – when she lost both her children, it temporarily drove her quite insane. The first child taken away for fostering and then dying within hours, the second stillborn - any woman would feel for her condition. Over the following days she developed a powerful fantasy that her children had survived and were being held in the children's home endowed by my family.'

'This is all too ridiculous to believe.'

'What is unbelievable is the story that you have come to credit. The facts are simple. Unable to come to terms with the deaths of her children, she stole an infant from the children's home and ran away with him. You were that child. Later, while under psychiatric care here in Tampere, she still retained the fantasy that her daughter was also alive. From what you have said she maintained it to her dying day. It is very sad: but my hands are clean of any guilt in the matter.'

'Then how do you explain the documents? The report that she was abusing her child? What child, if hers had both died?'

'Oh, the child was you, certainly: but the charge was negligence, not abuse. Her kidnapping you from the children's home was the true cause of her incarceration. It could easily have led to a jail sentence but out of consideration for her circumstances I colluded in the pretence that the child was hers and that she was simply an unfit mother, rather than a criminal.'

'This is grotesque. And you accuse her of fantasy!'

Katerina nodded sagely. 'I admit that we used subterfuge to avoid a scandal. After all, it was my son's irresponsibility that originally gave rise to the problem. I have spent a considerable part of my life covering up for his indiscretions but that at least is over. These days he must sort out his own mess.'

'You've cut him off?'

'Years ago. He tries of course but he will get nothing.'

'Then it all goes to Katerina Satu.'

Her eyes flashed - but when she spoke it was with an icy calm.

'Katerina Satu is no business of yours. If you have heard nothing else, hear this. You have no rights, no connection with this family of any kind. You were an orphan, stolen by a madwoman whose only link with the Karlsholm fortune died within minutes of being born.'

'Then why so much effort to conceal it all?'

'Because we could not tolerate her running around making wild accusations. The situation was delicate.'

'You mean it was only ten years after the war and you were still trying to cover up what you'd been doing. Trading with both sides, no doubt.'

'With all four sides, actually. Russia, Finland, Germany and the United States. Plus Sweden, of course. I believe we were the only company to achieve that.'

'You're proud of it?'

Katerina threw it off without even a shrug. 'It's an irrelevance. The delicate situation to which I refer had nothing to do with our war record. It related solely to the things your mother was saying about my son and myself.'

'So you had her illegally imprisoned in a mental hospital.'

'We had her kept under supervision in a psychiatric clinic, to keep her quiet while she was being treated. We did not want publicity and we did not want her prosecuted. Looking back, it might have been better if we had involved the police the first time she took you away from the home. But we felt no real harm had been done.'

'My God, you talk as if you were doing us a favour, when all you were really doing was protecting yourselves from the scandal of your son's actions.'

'You understand. Good. Then you will also understand that I did nothing illegal, save perhaps in failing to report the abduction of a child who was indirectly under my care. Indeed, in that respect my actions were altruistic.'

'Altruistic!'

'Certainly. I protected her from the consequences of her own actions and at the same time ensured that she had the best possible treatment. In the end, unfortunately, it was not enough. A few months later she took you from the home again and fled the country.'

'And you still didn't inform the police. She ran off with a child that wasn't hers and you did nothing?'

'There was nothing I could do, it was a *fait accompli*. In any case, what was the harm? She needed a baby and you needed a mother. As patron of a home for orphaned and destitute children, I considered the outcome not altogether unsatisfactory. Have you come here to tell me that you disagree?'

Ricky didn't know what to say. It was breathtaking and yet it was also horribly plausible. If it was a lie, then it was the most amazing construct he had ever heard - and far too much of it was borne out by what he already knew. *His mother a madwoman.* Every part of him revolted against the idea, yet how could anyone have kept their sanity in those circumstances?

It was horribly plausible but was it true? There was no doubt she had been incarcerated in a psychiatric hospital. She had escaped from the institution - but had she ever escaped from the trauma? Had she sent him here in search of a long-dead child who lived on only in her deluded mind? Or had she deliberately sent him after the Karlsholms to exact vengeance? That would explain Katerina's fear when he said that he'd come for his sister. He stared at his grandmother and knew in his heart that she was lying - but where did fact end and fiction began?

'You are confused. It is natural. You came here for one thing and have discovered something very different. A thing few people ever have to face.'

'I haven't discovered anything, except that Elvira was right about you. I don't believe I'm any nearer the truth than when I arrived.'

'Naturally you will not find it easy to let go of the fantasy that has sustained you all your life: but you will gain nothing by clinging to it. Take my advice on this, if on nothing else. Come to terms with the truth, however unpalatable it may be. The only thing of any importance in life is that you have the strength and willpower to forge your own destiny. The rest is an emotional shackle.'

The effect of Katerina's words was very different to what she intended, for they focused him back onto the real issue. 'You're right: and I know just where to begin.'

She saw it at once. 'I give you fair warning: approach her at your peril.'

'You have no say in it.'

'I doubt that it will be necessary for me to say or do anything. But if it is, I will not hesitate to take whatever action is required.'

He raised his eyebrow in mimicry. Either the impersonation or the implication seemed to infuriate her beyond reason.

'It is a mere dalliance!'

He laughed aloud at her archaic bluster. Whatever his origins, this was his trump card. Provided he had the right Satu. And that was still the great issue, the thing he had to find out while preventing her from seeing that he was still unsure of the answer. Katerina Satu could be his twin, or his half sister, or some kind of cousin, or no relation at all. She might also be the same person as Satu Savolainen, or someone else altogether. He had no option but to brazen it out.

'Thank you, grandmother. I think I shall still call you that? You've removed the last big hurdle that was holding me back. I really thought Satu might be my twin sister. Whatever else you've done, at least you've convinced me that she's not.'

The expressions that went across Katerina's face were too many and too fleeting for him to interpret. He thought he saw surprise, relief and anger but he couldn't be sure. The only thing she allowed to remain was a thin smile and that didn't help him at all. 'I am not your grandmother. And you have no twin. Of that at least you may rest assured.'

'Well, in any case you've helped me to do exactly what you most fear.' He grinned at the expression this put on her face. 'I think I'll be leaving now. I have a date tonight and I don't want to be late. A really hot date, with Satu.'

'She will not be there to meet you.'

'I beg your pardon?'

'She will never see you again.'

'Oh, I think she will.'

'What you think is of no account. The issue has been explained to her and she now understands it fully. She will have nothing more to do with you.'

So they *were* the same! It had to be! He knew she would tell him nothing more unless he could spur her into another unguarded outburst, so he threw caution to the wind. 'You just don't get it, do you? You think just because she listens and smiles sweetly that she's going along with whatever you say. But all the time she despises you. She won't even use your name, let alone do what you tell her. It's her and me, granny and there's nothing you can do about it.'

'You stupid little bastard.'

The whiplash of her tone shocked him into stillness. He wouldn't have believed that anyone could put so much hatred into so few words.

'None of the Suomalainens ever amounted to anything and Katerina Satu knows it as well as I do. You young lout, did you really think you could touch a girl like her? A girl like my granddaughter? A *Karlsholm*?'

The muscles of his face clenched reflexively and he knew she could see it. The tone of her voice merely confirmed her contempt. 'In the end there are only two people who matter in this: I am one and the other, like me, is a Karlsholm to the core. You imagine you've touched her heart, when really she is just playing with you. As soon as she tires of the game, you will discover that she scorns you just as I do.'

He was sick of her lies but he knew they had contaminated him. The anger welled up and he moved towards her but Katerina clicked her fingers and Lars grabbed him from behind in a wrestling lock that nearly tore his arms off.

'Get him out of my sight!'

He found himself being lifted completely clear of the ground and carried bodily towards the door. The strength and power of the guy was irresistible. As he struggled vainly against it, Ricky's foot caught in the telephone wire of the phone on the desk and pulled the jack out of the handset. It was all he could do to speak and he was too enraged to think about how ridiculous he must appear. 'It doesn't end here. You've lied so much I don't know what's true but I know you hurt my mother - and there's going to be a reckoning.' He managed to hook his hands around the doorframe and hold up Lars just long enough to finish what he had to say. Katerina's eyes were fixed on him like a cobra facing a mongoose that was too small to be anything more than an annoyance. 'What happens between Satu and me is none of your business. If you try to interfere then whatever it takes, granny, I will bring you down.'

She said nothing but her eyes blazed hate as Lars hauled him through the doorway and out into the hall. Thirty seconds later he was physically ejected from the building, with Lars giving him a parting cuff on the ear as a deliberate act of ridicule.

Ricky walked quickly down the drive, his face burning with anger and humiliation. Halfway to the road he turned into the cover of the trees and blundered off through the park until he saw the glint of the lake. He went straight down to the water's edge and splashed cold water over his face. Then he sat on a park bench until he stopped shaking.

Maybe he had a sister, maybe not. He didn't even know what to think about the dreadful suggestion that he was not his mother's natural son. And yet he knew the thing that mattered most: Satu was not his twin. It was funny, really. He had come in search of a girl called Satu and he had found one. Not the one he had been looking for, perhaps - but the one he needed to find.

When he felt steady enough, he got to his feet and headed back towards Pispala. He could see it clearly across the water and it looked like home.

Back in the clinic, Katerina Karlsholm clenched her fists on the armrests of the wheelchair until her knuckles turned white. God blast him! And Lars seemed to be taking an age getting rid of him; what was the great useless ox doing out there?

She turned the wheelchair to face the garden, as she always did when stressed. The rocks gave her a sense of calm, of order and predictability. But this time it was no good, she might as well have poured a glass of water on a furnace.

He had come back. Despite everything, he had come back. And now he was going after Katerina Satu! The time for indirect influence was past, they must be prevented from meeting again. She didn't yet know what to do, so she would have to make it up as she went along. An accusation of assault, perhaps, backed up later with some planted evidence of theft. It would get him out of the way until something more permanent could be arranged.

She steered her chair back to the desk and reached for the phone, only to find that the cord was detached. Angered, she pulled herself forward and leaned over to retrieve the jack but the thing was impossible. All at once she felt a great surge of anger and frustration. She wanted to scream with rage. It must be stopped and she was bound to this infernal chair, surrounded by idiots and she couldn't even make the telephone work! The blood pounding in her temples made her feel as if her head was about to burst.

When Lars came back into the room a few seconds later he was on the point of asking Katerina if she wanted anything when he registered what was happening. He gasped as her face contorted in spasm. She started to say something and then, without warning, her head suddenly jerked to one side and she went rigid. As the bodyguard watched, her long, manicured nails started to beat a devil's tattoo on the steel frame of the wheelchair and then her right hand tightened convulsively around the metal tubing. He could see the nails bending under the pressure until finally one of them broke off with a horrid crack. Lars stood rooted to the spot for several seconds, shocked by the effects of the seizure, then he turned and ran for the alarm on the wall.

CHAPTER 37

By the time Ricky joined the others at the pub he had concealed his emotions beneath a veneer of *sang-froid* but it was too thin to resist the slightest pressure. Even the innocent distraction of a game of snooker almost got him into a fight. He partnered Pekka against a couple of tough looking Finns and finding himself with no way to pot the blue, he made a routine safety shot that left the queue ball neatly snookered behind the pink. One of the Finns said something that he took to be a compliment on the shot, so he laughed acknowledgement. The guy said something else that didn't sound at all complimentary and started towards him. Pekka had to jump between them and do some real fast talking to prevent the outbreak of World War Three.

'What's the problem?' asked Ricky, totally bewildered.

'They're really angry,' said Pekka with a tone of censure. 'You did a dirty shot.'

'What do you mean, dirty? I only snookered him, for God's sake.'

'That isn't done here. We never deliberately make it impossible for our opponent to get a shot.'

'But that's half the point of the game.'

'In England, maybe. I've already explained that to him but he's still really angry.'

'Well he can get stuffed.'

'It's like I told you,' said Tim, moving in to help damp things down, 'people here are really straightforward.'

'Really uptight, more like! I only snookered the twat, for God's sake.'

'You're a bit uppity tonight, Ricky,' said Terrence, drawing him away.

Searching for Satu

'She's not here,' stated Tim, flatly.

'What?'

'Satu. You've been getting more jumpy every minute, waiting for her to turn up. If you don't calm down you really are going to start a fight. You've already upset Pekka.'

'What? How? I can't have...'

'Oh, for Christ's sake, just shut up and drink your beer. And stay put until you've got a grip on yourself. What do you think you're doing, mouthing off like that? You can be such a prat sometimes.'

'It really is the big smitts!' declared Terry, delight plain on his face.

'Oh now look...'

'Yeah. He's been chasing after her all week and he's upset because she hasn't turned up for his last night.'

'But that's marvellous! We'll take the town apart until we've found her!'

'No! She's not even due here until eight o'clock.'

'Well stop being such a pain in the arse, then.'

Ricky did his best but by nine o'clock Satu still hadn't showed and he was finding it increasingly difficult to fend off Terry's proposals that they quarter the town's bars until they found her. He kept repeating that she wasn't in town yet, that she was coming on the train from Turku and that she'd said she might be late. But his confidence faded with every passing minute.

'You'll never get any peace until you've found her,' pronounced O'Neal.

'*We'll* never get any peace until he's found her,' corrected Tim.

'No, I've got to wait here. If I leave, I know she'll arrive the minute we walk out the door.'

'Then have another drink; it'll take that sad and sorry look off your face. If she walks in here and sees you looking like that, she'll walk right out again.'

'No, really, I don't want to get drunk. If she walks in here now, the sad and sorry look will take care of itself. I just want to stay here and wait for her.'

'Sweet Mary, it's the Big Smitts alright,' pronounced Terry.

'Yeah,' said Tim, 'I warned you he'd do the mournful bloodhound act.'

'Look, why don't you all go off and enjoy yourselves and leave me here to mope in private? I'm not very good company right now.'

'That's sure enough,' agreed Tim.

'We'll go to the pub across the bridge,' suggested Pekka, returning from the pool table. 'If we go on somewhere else we'll leave word at the bar.'

For the next three-quarters of an hour Ricky sat watching the door and going slowly paranoid, until eventually he couldn't stand it any longer. He knew he risked missing her in passing but he had to do something or go mad.

The station was five minutes down the street and it took only two more to confirm that the last train had come in nearly an hour ago. He walked dejectedly back to the pub, to find fifty people queued up outside. When the town clock struck ten, he decided the whole thing was pointless. She had stood him up, just as Katerina had predicted. There seemed to be nothing for it but to rejoin the others, so he slunk back over the bridge with shoulders slouched, utterly forlorn.

The queue outside the other pub was even longer. It took twenty minutes to reach the front and those twenty minutes saved him. The doorman had just waved him forward and was actually opening the door to let him in when he felt a light tap on the shoulder. He turned his head and there she was.

'Hei, Ricky, where have you been?'

'Satu! We've been up at Salho-thingy-pub. I waited for you but you didn't come, so I went to the station to check on the trains.'

'So, I arrived about nine o'clock but I had to go home first to get changed. I was just on my way to the pub now.'

'God, it's lucky you saw me.'

'Yes, but now here we are!'

'Right. Look, we're holding up the queue. Do you want to go in?'

'No, not really. I was thinking we could go to Viikonsaari, there's a big party happening over there.'

'On the island?'

'Yes. We could go to the boat station and see if we can get tickets.'

'The boat station. Yes. Absolutely. Wonderful!'

She looked at him in amusement. 'So, you like boats?'
'I love boats. I adore boats. Boats are where I want to be.'
'But what about your friends in the pub?'
'Oh, that's OK. It doesn't matter. Let's just go.'

She laughed and took his arm and they set off together into the warm promise of the summer night. Suddenly he felt as if he had giant springs in his legs, as if he was a giant himself. On such a night, with such a girl, he felt that he could leap mountains.

CHAPTER 38
Monday 29th June, 1958

She always felt safe on the island. Ever since they made friends with the ferryboat captain they had been coming here. Ricky loved the boat ride over, often asking her when they were going next. 'Borride' he'd say and 'Ikonsari'. They went every week on Satu's day off.

It had started one day when she had been holding Ricky up so he could stand on the railings and watch people boarding. He had waved to the captain and the captain had waved back and called them over. He had seen them there every Monday and he had children of his own and understood these things.

When TK found her and wanted to meet, it had seemed the natural place. Neutral territory. Familiar, inconspicuous and safe.

Marko had wanted to escort her but she had dissuaded him after a long argument. For all that she loved him dearly, it was her affair and hers alone. Well, hers and Ricky's. She could have left him with Eva but she could not deny him the chance to meet his father. Perhaps even the chance to *have* a father. Any more than she could deny herself the chance to regain the man who, against all reason, she still loved.

It was extraordinary. She told herself a thousand times that he was totally untrustworthy. When Marko and Eva tried to dissuade her, she silenced them by pointing out that there was nothing they could say that she had not already told herself ten times over. It was irrational, perhaps even foolhardy. Yet there was never any doubt in her mind that she would keep the appointment.

And it was really not so rash as it first appeared. The very fact that TK had gone to such trouble to seek her out was evidence that there

Searching for Satu

was some truth in his story. Even more to his credit, he had not gone running to Katerina when his investigation revealed the astonishing existence of his son.

According to his note he had been stricken with remorse, realising he wanted their child as soon as he had lost it. It had driven him mad not being able to find her all these months. Even Eva, who had spoken to him briefly, grudgingly admitted that he seemed contrite. He was a good-looking devil, she had added, with the devil's own charm.

For the moment at least Satu suppressed all the feelings of anger that his note had rekindled. He had come back, sought her out and pleaded for a second chance. He had more reason than she did to fear Katerina's wrath, yet he seemed willing to risk everything for them. As soon as it became known, Katerina would almost certainly cut him off. Having herself risked everything by running away from home to be with him, how could she fail to feel for his position now?

And so they had come to the island. Satu instinctively exercised caution wherever the Karlsholms were concerned and she had always taken care to keep a low profile. Yet she could see no particular reason to fear a trap: and if anything should go wrong, then the ferryboat captain was an ally and nobody could do anything to them without it being seen by a crowd of witnesses.

The meeting had been fixed for Monday. She was back working shifts at the textile mill beneath Pynikki Ridge, which enabled her to make ends meet and repay Eva and Marko for some of their generosity. She worked 12 hours a day so she could take off every Sunday and Monday to be with Ricky. Normally she looked after some of the other women's kids as well, an arrangement in which all the working mothers reciprocated. But on this day there was nothing to distract her from the matter at hand.

It had been agreed that she and Ricky would arrive first and that TK would come over an hour later. They whiled away the time walking the paths through the wood and looking at the boats on the lake. As always, when she thought about TK it made her think about little Satu as well.

She had seen her daughter several times. It happened first purely by chance. They had been down by the boat dock one Sunday afternoon last year and she had paused to rest because she had no pram and Ricky had not yet started to walk. She looked across the dock towards the far side and there, proudly promenading along the waterfront in their Sunday best, were Olli and Hilda Karlsholm. They had been pushing the smartest of new prams.

Satu recognised them at once because after making her compact with Katerina she had been consumed with curiosity about them. Once safely hidden in Pispala, she had used Eva's good graces to find out all she could about the couple who had adopted her little girl as their own. They had been pointed out to her in the main square one spring day when she and Eva were out with the kids. It was important not to draw attention to herself because the whole arrangement with Katerina depended upon her never attempting to contact them.

Yet it hadn't seemed too much of a risk, provided they were sensible. She had already persuaded herself that it was safe to walk openly about town rather than staying in Pispala as she had done at first. There was nothing remarkable about a drably dressed young woman going for a stroll with a toddler.

She took care not to stare, not to approach too closely and not to be seen frequently in the same place. But gradually she got to know their routines. By this means she had contrived to see her daughter eleven times over the past fourteen months, not counting three occasions on which she had observed her pram but been unable to catch a glimpse of its precious occupant.

She had never spoken to them of course, nor seen her daughter close up. Nothing would induce her to put her child's welfare at risk by attempting to do so. Not the pangs that she felt every time she saw her, nor even the yearning to go up and hold her. As long as she kept her part of the deal, she was sure that Katerina would do the same. For what reason had she not to? That was the whole mad beauty of their bargain.

When Katerina had first proposed the method by which she intended to ensure compliance with their agreement, Satu had thought her demented. Yet the more she thought about it, the more sense it made. The simple fact was that for all their wealth and power, the Karlsholms were dying out. Hilda Karlsholm, the wife of Katerina's elder son Olli, had miscarried three times in as many years. The doctors said there was every reason to fear further misadventures. She had conceived again around the same time as Satu but Katerina knew it could well be Hilda's last chance.

Katerina had proposed a radical yet quite simple solution. If Hilda miscarried again, she and her husband would adopt Satu's child as their own. They were due within a month of each other, so the substitution would not be too hard to conceal. The baby would be brought up in the Karlsholm household, under their name and with every prospect of inheriting all of their vast interests. If Hilda's pregnancy was successful, then she might still choose to adopt Satu's baby as well. Otherwise it would be sent to a foster home chosen by Katerina, where she would guarantee that the child would be well looked after.

At first Satu had raised all manner of objections, mostly because the proposal seemed to be riddled with inconsistencies that made her instinctively distrustful. She could still recall, almost verbatim, the conversation with Katerina that had resolved each and every one of them. She had asked the older woman why, if she was so offended by the scandal of an illegitimate child, she was proposing to adopt it into her family. Katerina had looked at her as if she were slow in the head.

'Because if it is adopted into the family as I propose, no-one will ever know that it *is* illegitimate. And after all, it has our blood in its veins.'

'Then why not persuade TK to acknowledge it? He'll do whatever you tell him. You could even persuade him to marry me, if you wanted.'

'I'd sooner have him marry a wog! The only thing you Suomalainens have ever been good for is bearing children. So bear this one and think yourself fortunate that it will have a future you could never give it.'

Satu had grown so used to the offensiveness of Katerina's remarks that it had required only a small effort to bite back her natural response. But it had required every ounce of willpower to ask the obvious next question, for it pained her beyond measure.

'But why do you need it? Olli and Hilda may have trouble producing a family but TK has had other children...' Katerina's contemptuous look cut her to the heart but she had to finish, 'and I suppose he will have more.'

'Doubtless. I've lost track of how many whores he's got up the stick. Of course we could adopt any of them but only by acknowledging them. The bastards would be bad enough: but their mothers... No, this arrangement can only be made now, with you. Hilda may never conceive again. Certainly the timing will never be so good. And for all that you're a Suomalainen you have spunk, girl, I'll give you that. It must be the Scottish blood, there's often good Norse stock among the Scots.'

'Honoured, I'm sure.'

Satu thought then that she understood Katerina's deepest motivation. She both needed an heir and feared it. Most of all she feared an alliance between her wayward son and her old rivals the Suomalainens. If she and TK ever married, their union could produce Katerina's worst nightmare: a rival heir with an unimpeachable claim to inherit the business.

That was the brilliance of Katerina's plan. At one fell swoop she would gain an heir, eliminate a potentially dangerous rival and give Satu herself a vested interest in protecting her child's right to inherit. Satu admired the cleverness of it so much that she was intrigued by every detail.

'But how can you get around the law? There must be requirements to register births and deaths?'

'The Law is a tool of the rich. I own the doctor, the midwife and the local registrar. Besides, there is really very little that needs to be done. One child will be born and one birth will be registered. Only the miscarriage, if it occurs, will be concealed. That is no crime, merely privacy.'

'And if both children live?'

'Then if Olli and Hilda choose to adopt your child as well, the doctor will record that Hilda gave birth to twins. If they do not, your child will simply be delivered anonymously to the children's home, from where its adoption will be arranged in due course. Its birth will go unrecorded but that is of no matter, since everyone will take it for a foundling child.'

'And if I change my mind?'

'Then our agreement will cease. The only one to suffer will be your baby. Besides yourself, of course. You will also be made to suffer.'

Yet in the end it had worked out exactly as Katerina envisaged. Poor Hilda had miscarried again and Satu's little girl had been secretly implanted into the Karlsholm family. Satu felt enormous empathy with Hilda, a woman she had never met, for she too had lost a child and had been kept a virtual prisoner to conceal the truth.

Probably Katerina was the only one who really cared about the avoidance of scandal. As a mother, the thing that mattered to Satu was that both of her children would be well cared for. Her daughter had everything money could buy and she appeared to be genuinely adored by her adoptive parents. Her son might lack for material things but he would never go short on love. The only thing he really needed was a father. And so they had come to the island.

They were standing in front of the restaurant when they heard the whistle of the ferry. Ricky had been starting to kick up a fuss about an ice cream but now he transferred his attention to the boat. 'Erryboat,' he mouthed, 'Dadda come.'

Satu smiled, in pride at her son's precocity as much as in anticipation of the forthcoming meeting. 'Yes darling,' she replied, ruffling his hair, 'Daddy is coming.'

'Go see.'

'Yes, let's. Let's go down to the pier and meet him, shall we?'

CHAPTER 39
Saturday 23rd May, 1981

It was no distance to the boat dock and it only took Satu a couple of minutes to establish that it was a private party and they couldn't get tickets.

'It's funny,' Ricky mused. 'All week I've been looking at that island, wondering what's over there and feeling I ought to go and find out. It seems silly to be defeated now.'

Satu didn't seem to find anything remarkable in this and continued to lean against the railing above the jetties, looking thoughtfully out across the lake. 'Yes, it's not so far, we could row there if we had a boat.'

'You mean gatecrash? Wouldn't they throw us off?'

'They would have to catch us first.'

He thought about this for a while, then made up his mind. 'We do have a boat. I mean, we can get one.'

She turned her head to look at him, her eyes bright with interest. 'How?'

'You see that small blue boat, next to the one that's full of water?'

'Yes.'

'That's Pekka's boat. He showed it to me this morning.'

'Then we can take it!'

'Do you think he'd mind?'

'Oh no, Pekka will not mind. We are borrowing boats from each other all the time. And we will bring it back tomorrow.'

'Shall we do it, then?'

'Yes!' she cried, taking his hand and pulling him after her, then running off down the quay and leaping over the railings with a whoop of delight. She went down the ladder like a sailor on battle stations and danced up the jetties, laughing and calling him on, as if he were a slow but faithful hound. When he got to the boat she already had the mooring rope loose in her hands. 'Shall I row?' she asked, clearly doubting his boating skills.

'Yes, why not? You probably know a lot more about boats than I do.' He demonstrated this by the clumsiness with which he tried to get aboard, an undignified scramble that nearly pitched him sideways into the adjacent hulk. Satu offered him a hand to steady himself, then pushed off and hopped aboard in one deft movement, stepping down with perfect balance and settling herself amidships as the little craft backed out of the line.

She handled the oars with the same easy skill, placing them in the rowlocks and turning the boat with a manoeuvre that Ricky guessed she must have performed a thousand times. He sat back on the stern seat with his hands resting on the gunwales, admiring the lake, the view, her.

Satu began to pull with strong, rhythmic strokes, propelling them across the water so smoothly that they seemed to be gliding. Her face took on a more serious set as she worked the oars, emphasising the high beauty that laughter tended to soften. He took in the movement of her body as she rowed, the taut curves of her legs braced against the rests, the slow ripple of tendons in her arms, the regular swell and fall of her breasts. Then he moved his foot and his shoe splashed through water.

'Satu.'

'Yes?'

'There's water in the bottom of the boat.'

'Yes, that is normal. It has probably been sitting in the water for a long time.'

'Oh.'

'You don't know so much about boats, eh?'

'No. Typical Englishman, me. Even Nelson was seasick, you know?'

'But not on a lake, I think.'

'No. Was there this much water when we got in?'

'I didn't check.'

'I don't think there was. I'm sure I'd have noticed.' He watched the water closely, the quiet broken only by Satu's breathing, the creak of the oarlocks and the soft splashes as the oars cut the surface of the lake. 'It's definitely coming in. I can see it sort of welling up.'

'Oh, are you sure? I should have thought of that. I wonder if Pekka has *tilkitä* his boat yet?'

She said it in Finnish but with a horrible certainty he knew what it meant. It was the same word that Pekka had been unable to translate into English a few hours earlier. Ricky hadn't known it then but he knew it now. *Caulk*. The boat had not been caulked.

'You mean putting tar in between the wood, to make it watertight?'

'Watertight? Yes, I think so. You must do this with a boat after the winter.'

'Or the frost opens up the spaces between the planks and makes it leak, right? Opens up holes between the wood and lets the water in?'

'Yes.'

'Pekka told me this morning he hadn't done that yet.'

'*Perkele!*' It was the first time he'd heard her swear so loud but she sounded concerned rather than alarmed. 'Well, there should be a thing here for putting the water out again.'

'A bucket. A bailing bucket.'

'Yes. Can you see it?'

He looked around. There wasn't far to look. 'No. It's not here. I think I'd better use my hands, it's coming in quite fast. How long do you think it'll take to get there?'

She looked over her shoulder to the island, then at the water now welling up plainly inside and finally back to the jetty, now as distant as their destination. 'I think about fifteen minutes. But it gets harder with more water in the boat.'

'Right. I'll get baling.'

To his surprise it was extremely cold. But then why should that be a surprise? He'd been in this lake before: it was bloody freezing then and it was bloody freezing now. All of a sudden he remembered Pekka's warning about the commonest cause of death in Finland at Midsummer. And it was still only May, the ice only a couple of days off the lake.

His first attempts at scooping out handfuls of water were hopeless.

All he achieved was to splash the front of Satu's blouse. She yelped and then reached down and splashed him back. For a moment they paused in the middle of a freezing lake in a sinking boat and had a water fight like a couple of kids. But then they got back to the serious business of staying alive, he baling like mad and she pulling on the oars with real determination.

He adjusted his position so that he could get his hands right into the bottom and shovel the water over the side before it drained away through his fingers. There was just enough room to do this without hitting Satu's leg: but it wasn't enough. After five minutes his hands were numb with cold and the water was four inches deep. Satu's breathing was becoming laboured as she dragged half a ton of boat and water across the lake.

Now, *in extremis*, her beauty was breathtaking. Even as he baled for dear life Ricky took in the lithe perfection of her body, working the oars like a smoothly running machine while her face was frozen in concentration.

After ten minutes the water was so deep that he had to put his feet up onto the gunwales to keep them clear. Satu kept hers on the rests, submerged to her calves in the icy water. If anything her strokes had increased in both depth and tempo, as if she was working up into her peak rather than fading.

'I'd take over but I can't row like you.'

She nodded, acknowledging the self-evident. This girl was probably born in a boat. He couldn't think of anyone in the world he'd rather sink with.

Sink or swim? 'Can we make it to the shore if it sinks?'

She shook her head with a grimace. 'Too cold. You get cramp...in less than a minute.'

It was going to be close. She was pulling like Hercules but the boat was so heavy it was like hauling a rock through treacle. The bows wavered as she tired, losing the balance between port and starboard oars as her stronger arm started to show. He put his legs back into the water and practically bulldozed it out over the sides but as the boat sank deeper, so more seams opened up below water level. He didn't think they were going to make it.

'Can you see... a bay... with no rocks?'

The croak of her voice shocked him, for she was obviously exhausted. He searched the shore, looking for a clear passage because he realised she was afraid of hitting a submerged rock. There was a small cove just ahead and to his right, with a shingle beach overhung by trees.

'Yes, there! Pull to your left a little, we're almost there.'

Satu suddenly sat upright, ran a hand through her hair and said, 'So, let's arrive properly.' Then she spat on her hands, picked up the oars and began to pull as if she was starting afresh.

Ricky baled like a man possessed. They were both completely soaking by now, her skirt was starting to float as the water reached the seats and he had no sensation left in his hands. They laughed like mad things when the boat grated and crunched over rock and shingle, before settling in open water ten feet from the beach. There were about four inches of freeboard left sticking above the surface, with small waves slapping over the gunwales. They stood up and reached out to hold hands as the boat sank sluggishly beneath them, up to their knees in the freezing water and laughing so much they almost fell overboard.

'We'd better get ashore before we freeze.'

'Yes but we must pull the boat onto the beach.'

'Right. I don't know what we're going to tell Pekka.'

'It will be alright. But we have to get it ashore.'

They jumped over the side and waded to the bows. Freed of their weight, the boat rose just enough for them to heave it up the shallow incline of the beach. But as soon as it hit bottom again the weight of water inside made it too heavy to shift any further. They had to get back in and shovel out more water, then jump over the side and haul it up another couple of feet before Satu felt confident it was secure. She stumbled at the water's edge and he took her arm to help her out until they stood at last on dry ground beneath the trees. As the exertion wore off, the breeze from the lake cut through their wet clothes like a knife. They were both shivering uncontrollably and she looked at him with an expression of urgency. 'We must get dry quickly now.'

Then the intensity of the last few minutes, the narrowness of their escape and the sight of her standing there in front of him, all rose up as one overwhelming force and he reached out to grab her but she escaped his grasp, touching him lightly on the lips to silence his protest.

'No, we have to get dry. It is quite serious. We will go to the party, they are having a barbecue, we can warm ourselves by the fire.'

He had been all ready to advance quite different ideas on how to warm themselves but he was so bloody cold now that he bowed to her pragmatism. She put one hand on his shoulder to steady herself while she removed her shoes and bobbysocks. Then she wrinkled her nose and said, 'So, my knickers are wet, too.' Without more ado she pulled them down from beneath her mini-skirt and let them drop to her ankles, stepping out of them with one foot and kicking them off with the other. It was done so quickly that he hardly had time to gape. 'You are not so lucky. You will have to warm your behind on the fire.'

He hid his confusion by stooping to pull off his shoes and socks before looking up at her again. Her skirt and blouse were soaked and the shock that went through him was electric. He knew she must have noticed but she said, 'So, they will be alright here. Let's go and get warm. I'm frozen and starving.'

They were standing on an earthen path and from the confidence with which she strode off, Ricky could tell that Satu was familiar with the place and quite used to going barefoot. He followed along behind because the path was only wide enough for one, hemmed in between the woods and the rocky shore.

After a couple of minutes they emerged at the edge of a large clearing, on the opposite side of which stood an ornate, three-storey wooden building. One of its long, low wings opened to a verandah with steps leading down to the lawn.

'This is the restaurant of Viikonsaari,' explained Satu. 'But we should go over there, to the barbecue.' She gestured towards a crowd of people off to their right, queuing for food at a row of trestle tables. Closer to the restaurant a band was playing Finnish folk music, while in the middle of the clearing a large bonfire blazed out a welcome.

'Heat. Thank God. Let's get something to eat and then toast ourselves.'

They linked hands and walked through the long grass towards the queue, mingling into its rear echelons and congratulating themselves that no-one seemed to be checking tickets. Soon they were just another couple in the crowd, their bare feet and wet clothes hidden by the half-light and the press of bodies.

Satu did the talking as they worked their way along the tables, stacking up their plates with salads, bread and meat. The last table in line was the bar. There was some conversation between Satu and the guys behind it and she shrugged, gestured at her bag and came away with a couple of bottles.

'Trouble?'

'I don't think so. They wanted to see my ticket but I told them I had it in my bag somewhere and obviously I couldn't get it right then.'

'They're looking at us. Let's go over to the bonfire and disappear.'

Carefully balancing their picnic, they made their way across the uneven turf towards the blaze. Plenty of others were there before them, so it looked natural to move around the far side to get closer to the fire. Safely hidden from suspicious eyes, they turned to face the heat and stuffed themselves with hot food. As he ate Ricky cast sideways glances at her, loving the way her profile was silhouetted against the light of the fire and the darkness beyond. She was still flushed from the exertions of rowing, her expression quite unselfconscious. He wanted her more than ever and he was so absorbed with his thoughts that her words startled him.

'So, shall we dance?'

'Dance?'

'Yes, this is quite a good band.'

'Ah, I'd love to but I don't know how.'

'But I can show you.'

'Are you sure?'

'Of course, it's quite easy. Come.'

With that she led him across the grass and onto the wooden dance floor. The music was like a cross between American Barn Dance and German Um-Pah, with the couples holding each other quite close and going round in ever quickening circles. As soon as they started to dance Ricky lost all reserve, his British inhibition evaporating into the night and before he knew it he was enjoying himself hugely.

Satu was so attuned to the music that even his faltering steps soon found the rhythm. Round and round they went, going faster and faster until they were both laughing and dizzy and then he lost his footing and they fell out of the dance like a slingshot.

They steadied themselves, still laughing, at the edge of the wooden platform and he kissed her on the lips, lightly but seeking invitation. Her eyes sparkled back the promise of maybe and her fingers brushed the side of his face as she slipped from his grasp. 'I am quite thirsty, shall we get another beer?'

'Yes, I'm warm enough now. Even my toes have stopped shivering.'

They both looked down at their bare feet and Satu giggled. 'Do you think they could see my arse when we were dancing?'

It hadn't occurred to him but now that she mentioned it, he thought it quite likely. They were twirling around so fast and her skirt was so short... The thought had such an effect on him that he found it quite hard to walk in a straight line. As a result she was some distance ahead by the time she reached the beer counter and Ricky got a good view of the ensuing altercation. He saw two burly guys close in on her from either side - but before he could shout a warning she grabbed a couple of bottles, darted between them and was off like a hare.

Things moved very fast after that. From where he was positioned Ricky was able to anticipate events and cut off across the grass on an interception course. Fortunately what comes up also goes down and as he ran he got faster, so that he reached the leading pursuer just as Satu was about to be caught. Ricky had grown up playing football in the backstreets of Leith and it barely even broke his stride when he kicked the guy's legs out from under him.

Seconds later they were into the trees and the undergrowth shielded them from view. Ricky heard curses behind him as the slower of their pursuers reached his fallen comrade but Satu was still going, flitting between the saplings and ducking under low branches so fast that he couldn't keep up. Every damn twig and bramble on Viikonsaari seemed to be conspiring to whack him in the face or grab him round the ankle. As a result, when he came upon the hollow where she'd gone to ground, Ricky practically fell on top of her. He grabbed a swaying bough to save himself from going headlong but even so they both went sprawling sideways in a jumble of limbs.

They lay there in a heap, chests heaving from the chase, arms and legs entangled, trying desperately not to give themselves away with their laughter and their gasping. Satu held up the two bottles of beer like trophies and it cracked them up so much that he had to put his hand over her mouth and bite his own lip till it nearly bled.

The sounds of pursuit came closer, then moved away in opposite directions. The branches stilled, their breathing slowed and not even the breeze from the lake reached their hiding place.

The hollow was in the shape of a horseshoe and they disentangled themselves so that they lay facing each other, almost touching. He took one of the bottles from her hand, put it to his lips and drank, watching her mirror his every movement. Then he put his hand on her knee and ran it slowly up her thigh to the hem of her skirt. She stayed motionless, save for her eyes.

He was about to kiss her when she languorously put her arm around his shoulder and pulled him towards her. Gravity brought them together in the bottom of the hollow, her mouth sweet and moist on his, the taste of beer, no promise of passion but a relaxed welcoming to its beginning.

Ever so slowly he glided his hand up the inside of her thigh, making a lazy circle of sensation that drifted gradually upwards. She was just starting to respond when there was a crashing of undergrowth barely thirty yards away and they both froze, hardly daring to breathe.

The crashing came closer, sounding like a bear charging through the woods. They were so sure the bouncer was going to burst upon them that they moved apart, ready for flight - but he went right past, making the branches above them tremble as he bored clumsily through the undergrowth not ten yards from where they lay.

Another crashing came from the other side, the second man coming directly towards them, then altering course at the last moment and passing by as close on one side as his mate had done on the other. The two bouncers met up right in front of them, so near that when they conferred, every word was audible to their quarry.

Risking discovery, Satu raised herself up to look over the rim of the hollow, kneeling in the mossy grass and resting her elbows on the top of the bank as she peered through the screening foliage. Ricky crouched behind her, steadying himself by placing one hand on her waist.

'They've found the boat,' Satu whispered, 'and our things.' There was another babble of guttural Finnish and then some ribald laughter. Ricky could just make out one of them holding something up and then stuffing it into his pocket. Satu went tense beneath him and growled under her breath. 'That bastard's got my knickers. He's going to make a story of it to his friends.'

Ricky looked down at her and his whispered words came as if from a different person. 'Yes - but I've got a better story right here.'

She looked round, not to admonish him but with a distinctly earthy smile. Ricky knew he would never forgive himself if he didn't seize the moment but the bouncers were only yards away and he still didn't know the truth about her. And then Satu's hand entwined with his own and to his amazement led him from her waist to a place that removed any doubt about what she wanted. As he began to explore, she gave a low moan and hung her head between her arms. When he leaned forwards to kiss her neck, she took the weight on her forearms and the position suggested itself so naturally that she looked round with a dirty little giggle and whispered, 'Go on. I dare you.'

'But the bouncers...'

She shot him a disparaging look and wriggled against him: at which point naked desire took over. He had to pull back a little first, before bringing his hands up under her skirt to hold her firmly in place. Then everything happened at once.

The two heavies split up, one of them coming straight towards the hollow. Satu flinched backwards just as Ricky thrust forwards and some salacious spirit of the dell unerringly guided him home. They came to a sudden but exquisitely cushioned stop, Satu giving a little gasp that was echoed by Ricky's grunt as he folded over on top of her. The nearest bouncer looked right at them as they crouched there, stock-still yet quivering, with Ricky nestling in the very gateway to paradise. He buried his face in her hair and she closed her eyes, each praying they would be invisible: and the spirit of the dell smiled on them, for the man looked but could not see.

Drawing on a hundred afternoons spent watching old westerns, Ricky reached out his hand for a stone and flicked it off into the bushes twenty yards to his left. Exceeding all expectations, the guy jumped practically out of his shoes and stormed off after it.

Even before the sounds of pursuit had diminished to the point of safety, Ricky rose up behind her and unleashed a mountainous need. Satu gasped at the abruptness of it but there was no question of holding back now. There was a moment of scrabbling, then his foot found god-sent purchase against a rock and after that neither of them were sensible of anything else. It wasn't long before the ecstasy of it became unbearable and he came with a great, groaning cry as he let go of everything.

Afterwards Ricky lay face down in the moss, unable to summon the energy to move. Satu had rolled over onto her back and was gazing up at the sky. When they finally turned their heads to look, each saw astonishment on the face of the other. Then she laughed, so incautiously that he rolled over and quieted her with kisses until he was sure that she wouldn't give them away.

Presently she disengaged from him and sat up to take a couple of swigs of beer. That done, she got to her feet and quickly shed the rest of her clothes. Perfectly self-assured in her nakedness, she stood in the twilight like a young goddess, calmly surveying her surroundings. He just sat there, stunned and sated.

'So, are you going to join me? I like to make love naked when I do it in the open air.'

'Oh, right! We're going to do it again?'

'But yes, I hope so. Is that a problem?'

'No! Absolutely not. It's no problem at all.'

He nearly tripped over in his hurry to get his trousers off. She helped him with his shirt and they stood together for awhile, watching each other as they touched. Her body was incredible: every curve was perfect, as firm with muscle as it was soft with feminine grace. She ran her fingers lightly over his chest and shoulders, around his hips.

'You have a nice, slim body.'

'*I* have a nice body? *You're* the most stunning girl I've ever seen.'

'I am quite fit. But you have big, powerful shoulders and good legs. When you took me I could really feel your strength. I liked that.'

'You were incredible.'

'So, I am glad you liked me. How shall we do it this time?'

'Absolutely any way you want. Only not just yet: I need time to recover.'

'That's OK, we have plenty of time. Shall we go for a walk first?'

'Now? Like this?'

'Of course.'

'What if we run into those two guys again?'

'Oh, they have gone. I heard them going back to the party. Anyway, we can always run and hide again, just like last time.'

She took his hand and they walked naked through the trees and down to the shore. At the beach where they'd left the boat they found their shoes and socks untouched. The air was rather cool and he slipped his arm around her for warmth. She smiled and led him onto one of the promontories, where they leant up against a tree as they looked out over the lake towards the lights of Tampere.

It was some time before Satu broke the silence and when she did it was as if she had read his thoughts. 'So, it has been a special night for me, too.'

'It has?'

'Yes, of course. It is not every night that I make love with my cousin.'

His eyes went wide and his head jerked round to stare at her. He expected her to laugh it off as a joke but instead he saw that familiar dimple in her cheeks and a knowing smile about her mouth. 'Your cousin?'

She nodded, smiling as one might to a person who has finally woken up to what everyone else has known all along. When he spoke, it was very slowly, as if he was testing thin ice and every word was potentially treacherous. 'You...are...my...cousin? *You're* Satu?'

'But of course I am Satu.'

'But you're *that* Satu! I mean, are you? The one I came here to find?'

'I think so. I am not your sister but I think I am the one that your mother sent you here to search for.'

He looked at her in utter confusion. 'But how can you be? Oh God, I thought you were my sister and it was more than I could bear and then when I thought you weren't...'

'You have been thinking that I was your sister?'

'Yes.'

Her eyes widened and she gave a quite wicked laugh. 'You are even more bad than me!'

'No, I didn't think it just now! Jesus! I thought you were Satu Karlsholm.'

Her eyes blazed and her voice was like a whiplash. 'No!'

'Oh God, look, I'm sorry, this is all too much for me. I don't know who you are. I don't think I even care.' And then at last he looked her straight in the eye and came out with it. 'I only know that I love you. Nothing else matters to me any more.'

She just nodded and to his relief he sensed her relaxing - but when he reached for her, she turned her head away and wouldn't meet his gaze.

'Satu, please tell me what's going on. If you're my cousin, then what sort of cousin - and how long have you *known*? And if you're not my sister, then where is she?'

She turned back to him then, with an expression of sadness in her eyes that he had never seen before. 'Alright Ricky,' she said at last. I will tell you what I know. But I am afraid it is not going to be easy. Not for either of us.'

CHAPTER 40
Monday 29th June 1958

Satu suspected it had been a mistake from the moment he got off the ferry. It wasn't anything he said but the way he looked at Ricky. He seemed to be weighing him up, as if assessing his value. Her hackles began to rise immediately, so that even when he turned on his famous charm she found it false, where once she would have been won over at the first smile. He had obviously decided to endear himself to her by showing affection for their son. That was typical: he could pretend any amount of fatherly feeling without it costing him anything.

'My God, Satu, you look fantastic! And you brought the boy; that's good. Who's a handsome lad, then? That's right, *you are*. Let's talk over here by the trees. My God, he really looks like me. He has your eyes, though. He'll be a right little lady killer when he grows up, won't you, eh?'

It was only fifty yards to the trees but by the time they got there she already hated herself for the weakness that had led her to meet him. But then he gave her that lopsided grin and for a moment there was the familiar aroma of sea salt and tobacco and she felt a deep pang of yearning and regret.

If he had been capable of honesty he might have won her back even then. But that would have required him to be someone else. Instead she saw only a vain, shallow man who cared for nobody but himself. If he was charming, he wanted something.

'I'm so glad we decided to meet here. It's so quiet, so *intimate* - and green always suited you. You've really got your looks back, Satu; it's wonderful to see you looking so well. I've been worried sick about you.'

'Really. That explains all your letters.'

'Oh, don't let's fight. You know how difficult it is on a long voyage and after all, you're the one who hid herself away. You have no idea how difficult it was to find you. I sweated blood. Blood! But here we are at last!'

'Yes, here we are.'

'All three of us together! I can't get over that. I couldn't believe it when I found out about him! A son, my God! It completely knocked me out. And mother still doesn't know about him, that's the most amazing thing.' TK paused to regard this son whose existence supposedly meant so much to him and his brows drew together as if in dissatisfaction. 'He doesn't say much.'

'He's a bit shy, aren't you my pet? Say hello to your daddy.'

Ricky just shook his head and half buried his face in her shoulder, from where he cast occasional sideways glances at this stranger who was his father.

'He looks heavy. Why don't you put him down for awhile?'

'He's alright like this.'

Thorvald hesitated, apparently rather unsettled by his son's refusal to co-operate. Then he must have remembered how he was meant to be the doting father. 'I didn't expect him to be so big!'

'That's really not very surprising, considering that the last time you had anything to do with him he was an egg.'

TK laughed and held up his hands in mock surrender. 'OK, a good hit! But seriously, I feel so proud of you. Both of you.'

'Do you now? Then tell me, pray, why this is the first time he's ever set eyes on you?'

'Satu, I can understand you're being upset. I realise it must have been hard for you but all that's over now.'

'Really.'

'Yes. From now on, everything will be perfect. Just like I said in my letter.'

'Note. Five lines is a note, not a letter.'

'Oh, of course, you were always a big reader. But I was in such a hurry to see you again once I'd found you and the main thing is that we can talk face to face. Some things are better not put down on paper, you know.'

She just looked at him, letting him work for it. It was actually quite amusing to see the difficulty that he was having in getting to the point.

'I want us to be together again, Satu. We should never have split up in the first place. It was a mistake.'

'If you've only just reached that conclusion, I'd say you've left it a wee bit late, wouldn't you?' She shifted Ricky onto her other shoulder, nodding her head towards him as she did so.

'I just couldn't cope with it right then, Satu. I always loved you but it came as such a surprise - and you know what mother was like about it.'

'Oh, I know that alright.'

'Yes. But afterwards, I mean really very soon afterwards, I realised what a terrible mistake I'd made. I should have stayed, I know that now.'

'That's water under the bridge, TK.'

'No, it's never too late. I can make it up to you, Satu, really. It can all be the way it should have been. We can all be together again.'

'We've never all been together, TK. Ricky isn't your son, he's mine. You've had nothing to do with him. You just got me pregnant and then dumped me the moment you found out.'

'Letting mother force me into leaving is something I'll regret as long as I live. But I'm back now - and that's what counts.'

'Christ!'

'What's wrong? You don't believe me? But I can prove it. That's why I wanted to see you: to prove that I mean what I say.'

'TK, you wouldn't know one of your own lies if you met it in the street.'

He blinked, running a hand through his thick black hair. Satu gave a tight smile at his discomfort. He was obviously beginning to realise this would be more difficult than he had anticipated.

'I understand how you must feel. No, really, I do. I know what hardships you've had to suffer but that's all over. You don't have to take my word for it, Satu: I can prove everything I say. I asked you here so I could make amends. I never wanted to leave, you know that: I simply had no choice at the time. But now I do. Now I can make everything right.'

'Oh, TK... '

'I know you don't believe me but just hear me out; that's all I ask. You are the most amazing woman I've ever known, Satu. I know you think that's just the usual TK bullshit but I swear to you it's the truth. None of the others compares to you. I've come to realise that these past few months, especially since I found out about him. Without you and the boy, it's all meaningless.'

It was incredible: not just that he could come out with all that shit but that she once would have fallen for it. So much had changed but he was still exactly the same - and the absurd thing was, he didn't realise it. He thought he could simply walk back into her life and pick up the pieces from where he had dropped them. How could she ever have been so blind?

'Part of it was the boy, of course,' declared TK, nodding solemnly at Ricky. 'A big part of it. I began to understand that soon after we split up. You're wrong to say I had nothing to do with him, Satu. Whatever I may have said or done, he's still my son. And he needs a father: every boy does.' At that point he actually reached out his hand and touched Ricky on the head, like a pope giving his blessing. Then he fixed her with his most serious frown and said, with a wonderful imitation of sincerity, 'Well, his father's back.'

She had to stifle a laugh. 'You can't be serious...'

'I've never been more serious in my life. I still love you, Satu. I always have. I came back here to ask you to marry me. I want us to be together again, my darling. I mean all three of us. I want us to be a family: a proper family.'

Listening to him, Satu suddenly understood her real reason for coming here. She had done it to rid herself of an obsession. She had wanted him finally and irrevocably to disappoint her and bizarrely, by seeking to do the opposite, that was just what he had done. Now that he had asked her to marry him, she knew it to be the last thing in the world she wanted.

'You can't seriously imagine that I'd say yes?'

She could see the anger in his eyes at once, even before he began to answer.

'Satu, I know you're hurt...'

'Hurt? I'm bloody rabid! Did you really think you could make it all better just by waltzing in here and proposing? Christ, you don't actually expect me to be grateful, do you?'

'I'm trying to do the right thing, Satu. The right thing for you both.'

'You missed that chance two years ago! God, even your bloody mother did better by me than you did.'

'It's best to leave her out of this.'

'I didn't have much choice, did I? Shit, you talk about lack of choice, when all you had to do was jump back on your ship and bugger off to bloody Singapore and leave me to pick up the pieces. What could you possibly offer me now that would even begin to make up for what you've put me through?'

'Everything that you and your family have been cheated out of for the past forty years. I can give you everything, Satu. We can have it all.'

'What are you talking about?'

'It's us, don't you see? It's there for the taking and all we have to do is get back together again: you and me and the boy.'

'Ricky. He has a name. Your son's name is Ricky.'

'You see! You do recognise that he's mine, too! And that's the whole point, don't you see?'

'I don't have the faintest idea what you're talking about. And Ricky's getting tired. I should go back soon.'

He flexed his shoulders, casting his eyes skywards. The thin pretence of feeling had been abandoned at the first show of resistance and now he practically snapped at her. 'She's going to leave it all to the little girl.'

Before TK had said another word, Satu understood everything. The rest was just confirmation, fuelling the fury that built in her from that moment on.

'Can you believe that? She's going to leave everything to a babe in arms. Hell, the stupid bitch isn't even giving it to my brother. It's all going to be held in trust for Katerina Satu. Mother thinks she'll live to be a hundred and that she'll be able to bring the girl up as a carbon copy of herself.' He gave a bitter laugh and slapped the nearest tree with his hand. 'God, what a thought. And you know the worst of it? She probably will.'

'You've been drinking.'

'What? What has that got to do with anything?'

'Christ, you couldn't even come here to see your own son without getting half-pissed first.'

'I had a few beers, so what? What's that got to do with anything?'

'Nothing. Everything and nothing.'

'Sometimes I just don't understand you, Satu. You act like you aren't interested and then you bring up something like that. Anyone would think you didn't care about your own future. And what about the boy? If you don't care for yourself, spare a thought for him. His future is at stake too, you know.'

She nearly walked away right then. But grotesque though it sounded coming from him, the appeal on behalf of Ricky's interests was justified.

'That's right, I'm thinking of him here. He's the key to it, don't you see? There's nothing else Katerina is really afraid of.'

'Katerina is afraid of every shadow.'

He looked at her askance. 'You say the weirdest things. Mother isn't afraid of anything or anybody. Except you, actually, in a strange way. But she'll be afraid of him, by God.'

'What do you have in mind, TK?'

'She thinks we'll all just lie down and take it. Well, she's got another think coming. Olli and Hilda may go along with it but not me. He's never had any spine and she's happy with anything that secures her daughter's future.'

'And why shouldn't she be?'

'Alright, I don't hold it against her but fair's fair. All I want is my share. Our share. There's more than enough to go round.'

'TK, will you please get to the point? Ricky's tired and so am I.'

'Alright, I'm getting to it!' He threw out his hands in a gesture that encompassed all three of them. 'It's us, don't you see? Individually we're powerless but together we can beat her. You and Ricky are heir to the whole Suomalainen side of the business. That's why she's afraid of you. Your parents were never able to achieve anything against her because there was nobody on the Karlsholm side willing to help them. But if we're married and working together, she can't afford to fight us. I could corroborate things that would destroy everything she's worked for.'

'You are amazing, TK. Truly amazing.'

'It's pretty neat, isn't it? With a marriage between the Karlsholms and the Suomalainens, coupled with your father's papers, she'll have to come to terms. I'd say thirty per cent of everything for your side and half of the rest for mine - and that's probably conservative.'

Satu didn't even know where to begin, so she started with the one thing that even he would surely have to recognise. 'And you imagine that your mother is going to calmly sit back and let this happen?'

'There's nothing she can do about it. She of all people can't afford to have a court battle within the family: she has far too many skeletons in her closet. You should know that better than anyone.'

'She's been crushing people in the courts for decades.'

'Yes but not within the family. And who's going to side with her? Olli and Hilda will settle for anything that gives them a quiet life.'

'She fights dirty, TK. And you seem to be forgetting the obvious casualty in all of this.'

'Who do you mean?'

'Satu. My daughter. *Our* daughter.'

Something shifty came into his eyes then but he covered it over and cast around him as if appealing for help with this idiot woman. 'Oh, come on, Satu, she'll be OK. She'll still inherit a big slice of it. And don't you see, it means you win out whichever way things go?'

'That's really the way you see it, isn't it, TK? You think everyone else is as greedy and selfish as you are.'

'How can you say that? It's them I'm thinking of...'

'Stop it! Just stop it right now! How dare you pretend that you care anything for them?'

'Oh, come on, Satu...'

'No! Every word you've said proves that you see them just as tools to get what you want. Katerina cut you off, didn't she? That's the only reason you're here. I knew it! Katerina cut you off, so you run back to me because you think you can use us to get your stinking money. Well I won't have it! I won't have anything to do with it!

'Now Satu, don't get upset. It's nothing like that. I'm here for both of you. And the little girl, too. She'll be alright.'

'And that's another thing: leave her alone! Leave her out of this, you hear me? Katerina and I have an agreement and I won't let you screw it up. If you try any of this, I'll go straight to Katerina and tell her everything and by God if it comes to a fight I'll side with her against you.'

'You crazy bitch, what are you talking about?'

'That's right! That's the real TK speaking! So, let me tell you what I'm talking about. You are not going to endanger my daughter's future. If she inherits everything, then I'm glad. Glad for her, glad for Hilda and Olli and glad for myself. My God, if you had one ounce of fatherly feeling you'd be happy for her, too. So leave her alone, TK: or I swear to God I'll help Katerina break you, you son of a bitch.'

'You stupid little fool! Jesus, if you only knew.'

'If I only knew what?'

'Forget it. Just forget the whole thing. Jesus, how can you be this stupid? Anyone would think you were grateful to her. After what she did!'

'I know all too well what she did: but at least she took some care of my children, which is more than their father ever did.'

'Oh, she took care of them alright. But what the hell, let him grow up poor and proud and stupid like the rest of his family. I told you before what you should have done: but now he's here and yet you still won't give him a decent chance in life. Hell, it would have been better if he'd never been born.'

Satu flinched as if he had hit her, then her face flushed and she replied with a ferocious control. 'You unutterable bastard.'

'Oh, don't give me that! You would have got rid of him if Katerina hadn't offered to support you. And don't pretend it never crossed your mind to do what I'm proposing.'

Satu looked at him as if her eyes and ears could no longer be trusted. When she did try to speak, she was talking more to herself than to him. 'You are the most hateful, despicable man I've ever known. How could I ever have imagined that I loved you? And now look what you've done, Ricky's upset. Come on darling, don't worry, we're going. The horrible man made you cry, didn't he? Well you were right not to like him; he's not really your daddy at all.'

'Oh you stupid, *stupid* bitch.'

'Stop it. Just stop it, please. And get out of my way, TK. Let me past!'

'You stupid little cow! You don't just walk out on me like this. He's my son too, you know. I'll fight for custody if I have to - and I'll win! In this country, with your situation and my mother, I'll win. You think about that!'

'Get your hands off me, you bastard. Let go of my arm! Let me go!'

'He's the only little bastard around here. And you're the only one who's stopping him from being anything else.'

As soon as TK grabbed her, Satu had to let Ricky drop to the ground to prevent him from being hurt. She was struggling to release her arm from TK's grasp when Ricky started to wail. The mother in her turned instinctively and the sight of him, combined with TK's final jibe, pushed her over the edge. She clenched her fist and then swung with all her might.

'Oh, you SHIT!'

The blow glanced off TK's mouth, cracking one of his front teeth, taking the skin off her knuckles and nearly breaking his nose. The impact stunned him and left Satu nursing an injured hand, so that for a moment there was a pause between them. Then the shock of it wore off and he struck back at her with the first words that came to him. He was so blinded by rage and pain that he forgot they were the words he must not say.

'Alright, run back to your slum and starve! What's the difference? He should have been drowned at birth like his sister.'

For moment the silence was so intense with realisation that it seared like fire. Then Satu screamed.

CHAPTER 41

He ran to the restaurant, panic surging through him like the blood that soaked his handkerchief. Every jolt sent a searing flash of pain through his nose but the agony of his broken tooth was even worse and as he ran he cursed her to all the devils of hell.

She was a madwoman. An absolute fucking madwoman. She'd fallen on him like a fury, ripping at his face and screaming like a banshee. In the end he'd got an opening through the flailing limbs and knocked her out with a left hook under the jaw. Then the bloody kid started yelling his head off and when he put a hand over his mouth to shut him up the little bastard bit him. In the end he'd just shoved him down on top of his mother and run for the phone in the restaurant.

His luck hadn't deserted him completely, though. Her screams had coincided with the whistle of the ferryboat and nobody saw him run across the clearing because they were all headed in the opposite direction, towards the pier. He guessed that was why nobody had come to investigate. Plus the fact that couples brawling and screaming at each other wasn't really that uncommon.

It was a payphone of course. An old couple sitting on the verandah gave him a funny look. Cretins. Where were the bloody coins? Shit! No, wait, Yes! Thank Christ.

He dialled the number. There was nothing else he could do. She was the only person who could help him now. She had to, she had no choice: but he would have given anything in the world not to have to tell her. It scared him so much he even stopped thinking about the pain. When he heard her voice at the other end he almost shat himself and she nearly hung up because he sounded so weird with the blood and the handkerchief. Then, when she finally understood, there was a terrible silence.

He didn't know how long he waited for her to say something but in the end he couldn't stand it. 'Mother? Are you still there?'

The silence continued a few seconds longer, then she spat out instructions. 'Stay with them. Go back at once and keep them quiet. Nobody must see or speak with them. I am coming with the launch. Speak to no-one!'

She hung up with a crash and he could imagine the look on her face only too well. He badly needed a drink but dared not disobey her by going into the restaurant. He nodded to the old couple as he recrossed the verandah. 'Got hit by the ball.' They just stared. Cretins.

When he got back, Satu was still out for the count and he was relieved to find that the kid's crying couldn't be heard from any great distance. The boy was huddled up on top of his mother, not making so much noise because he was sobbing into her coat and it acted like a muffle. He left them to it and hid behind a nearby tree, where he could keep an eye on them and watch out for Katerina. He was pretty sure now that his nose wasn't broken but the bloody tooth was giving him absolute hell. Who'd have thought the bitch could hit so hard?

The island began to fill again with people from the ferry but it was the last load of the day and there weren't so many as before. They stayed around the restaurant or stuck to the paths by the shore, so provided he kept her and the boy in the shelter of the trees he reckoned they'd escape notice.

Just then Satu began to come round and start moaning, which made the kid start to pull on her coat and call out, 'Mama!' Presently she pushed herself half upright, then she caught sight of him and blanched. At that point the boy began wailing and she drew him close and looked about for help but he wasn't about to let either of them start screaming again. He went over and got her by the throat, speaking to her real quiet and slow to make sure she got the point. 'Keep your fucking mouth shut. One peep and I'll beat the crap out of the brat. Understand?'

Her eyes widened and she tried to draw away but there was nowhere she could go. Then the kid started to yell, so he raised his other hand to let him have it but she cried out and he held off, letting go of her throat so she could pull the little shit into her breast to quiet him.

He really wanted to hit her again, in fact he wanted to beat the living shit out of her but he knew it would only set the kid off again and then he'd have to clobber him, too. He wasn't sure how hard to hit a kid his age so as to shut him up without doing too much damage, so he decided to just let them be and wait for Katerina.

It seemed to take ages. The ferry came back for the last visitors and still she hadn't come. Jesus, what was keeping her? But at least once the trippers were gone he wouldn't have to worry about the noise. He figured it'd be a lot less trouble if he made sure she was co-operative before trying to move them. There might still be people about in the restaurant and he didn't want her going crazy just as they were trying to get her onto the launch.

She was sitting up now, leaning against a tree and holding the kid against her. The boy was snuffling and casting glances but otherwise not much trouble. Not much of anything, really. He wondered if the little sod was even his. He certainly didn't act much like a Karlsholm.

He went over and told her to stand up. She looked scared but he got her by the front of the coat and hauled her to her feet. The kid kept hold of her sleeve, which made it even easier. He hit her on that side first, then enjoyed playing punchbag with her for a minute or so. The kid really started to scream then, so he let him have it round the side of the head and knocked him over. It didn't stop him squalling but it was satisfying and it got him out of the way.

He put his hand around her throat and shook her head from side to side, slapping her around the cheeks. She was still conscious and just about with it, sort of dozy and compliant, just the way he liked. He really wanted to give her one, really hard and up against the tree but Katerina would be there any minute and he wasn't about to risk *that*.

'I see you're exerting your usual charm.'

The voice came from right behind him and he jumped like he'd been stuck up the arse with a pole. 'Jesus, you scared the shit out of me.'

'I said to keep them quiet, not to beat them senseless.' She indicated to where Satu now slumped at the base of the tree trunk. He looked around and cursed. 'Pick her up and follow me. And try not to do any more damage.'

'What about the boy?'

'I will bring the boy. You just keep hold of your whore.' She studied his face and gave an ironic smile. 'Evidently she packs more of a punch than you anticipated.'

'Where are we going?'

'To Dr Jacobson's surgery. I had intended merely to have him sign the papers for her committal but now you will both require medical attention.'

'You're having her committed? To a loony bin? Jesus, that's brilliant! Will it work?'

'Pray for your sake that it does. At this moment I am inclined to think that having *you* committed might be more appropriate.'

'Very funny.' He picked Satu up by the lapels, draped one of her arms over his shoulder and dragged her along beside him. Katerina spoke to the boy and then picked him up with surprising strength, carrying him without apparent effort. The kid looked scared rigid, too frightened even to blub. It wasn't surprising, really.

Katerina's bodyguard and her chauffeur were both in the launch. She obviously wasn't taking any chances, as she shortly demonstrated further.

'Who else knows?'

'Who else knows what?'

'That she's here, you fool. Someone must have seen her arrive and she must be living somewhere, so someone will expect her back.'

'She didn't come with anyone. She's staying with a couple in Pispala.'

'Is that all? Are you sure?'

He started to shrug it off but then he caught her tone and thought harder. 'That's it. I think she may have mentioned something about the ferryboat captain.'

'I am losing what little patience I have left. What exactly did she say?'

'Just that he was a pal. He used to let them ride for free.'

'Then he will have noticed that they did not return on the last ferry. Karl, speak to him when we reach the other side. Tell him that she accepted a lift with friends on their private boat. If he asks who, invent something.'

'What about the ones in Pispala?'

'The committal order will see to that. If they make trouble, we can think of other measures.'

'Jesus, nothing fazes you, does it, mother?'

She turned around and slapped him very hard across the face. It sent screaming knives of agony shooting through his nose and jaw.

'Ah! Jesus!'

'You stupid little fool! This is the last time that you will incommode me. The last time, do you hear? Because of you everything is in peril. Again!'

'Come on, it was just...'

'Oh I can imagine precisely what it was. And from the look of her, she saw through it and had the guts to stand up to you. I almost wish she was my son and you were the Finnish whore.'

'Hey, mother, come on...'

'Don't you mother me! When this is done, you are going away again - but this time for good. I told you that I was going to cut you out of my will but after this little display I've had a change of heart. I've decided to give you exactly what you deserve.'

'Now look...'

'Be quiet!'

He flinched as if she had struck him again. Then he looked down at his boots, dabbing at his injured face and shuffling his feet in sullen silence. The two flunkies pretended not to notice and busied themselves with getting Satu and the child onto the boat. Satisfied, Katerina continued. 'I am going to give you an allowance. A very modest allowance. It will not be quite enough to keep you in booze and whores, so you'll actually have to do some work to make it up. There is of course a condition. You will never see or contact either of them again. If you do, or if I even think you may have done, I will cut you off without a penny. Do I make myself clear?'

He could only look at her in dumb resentment, like a bull that knows it's beaten and lacks the balls to make another charge.

'Go back to Asia. Go and get poxed by some filthy tart and don't come back.'

'I'm your son, for Christ's sake.'

'You are no son of mine. Your father was too soft on you and you've inherited all the worst of him. I have an heir now with a good Karlsholm name and good Karlsholm blood in her veins. Katerina Satu will run this family when I am gone and I tell you this: if there is one thing she will learn from the moment she can understand, it is never to have anything to do with you or any of your bastard offspring.'

The launch cast off and TK could only sulk in the stern and nurse his damaged face, raining silent curses on all of them. The bloody women had won out again. The bitches.

CHAPTER 42
Saturday 23rd May, 1981

Satu's face was more serious than he had ever seen it. 'My parents only told me that we are cousins last night. But I have suspected it ever since you said your mother's boyfriend was a sailor.' She stopped and looked him straight in the eye before adding. 'Ricky: your father is my Uncle Tor.'

'Tor? *Thorvald?* So then you really are a Karlsholm?'

'No!' Her voice was like a whiplash: but it was followed by a shamefaced expression and then a retraction. 'Yes,' she conceded at last, 'I have been Katerina Satu Karlsholm - but now I am just Satu Savolainen. Tor is my uncle and your mother's lover. He is the black goat of the family. Even my father does not speak to him, though they are brothers.'

'But why on earth didn't you tell me this before?'

'I only found out last night. When I told my parents I'd met a boy from England called Ricky Suomalainen, they made such a fuss I knew at once that something was wrong. Then they asked me about you in the way parents do, so I told them I was going with you and they got very angry. So then I guessed you must be one of the people I have been warned against.'

'Warned against? How do you mean?'

'My uncle had many illegitimate children and always I have been told to have nothing to do with them. My father called me home so he could tell me not to see you again. We had such a row! Such screaming! It has been a long time since I have been having such a good row with my parents.'

'I don't know what to say.'

'Yes, it is quite a surprise. You have been the big secret of our family for as long as I can remember.'

'Then you did know about me, after all?'

She turned her head on one side and looked at him quizzically. 'Not exactly - but I knew something was there. Every family has its secrets, things that are not talked about. You never know what they will look like if they come out of the cupboard - but always I have been suspecting something.'

Ricky looked as baffled as he felt. 'But if you didn't know anything, how could you suspect?'

'Because of my name. My mother really hated my grandmother and when they called me Satu I think it was because they wanted to use an old family name to show her that we were Savolainens, not Karlsholms.'

'Satu, you've completely lost me.'

She stroked her fingers through his hair, speaking softly as they stood there naked beside the lake, each acutely aware of their vulnerability. 'A long time ago, Ricky, your family and mine were tied together by business and blood: but my grandfather married a woman who hated both our families and has done everything she can to harm them. She was Katerina Karlsholm, our grandmother.' Satu paused, frowning. 'It's strange. This afternoon we got a phone call to say that she has suffered a stroke. Someone went to see her and she collapsed.'

'A stroke?'

'Yes. Perhaps she will die. I have waited a long time for her to die. Now perhaps I can really be free.'

Ricky didn't know whether to laugh or cry but there were too many questions burning holes in his brain for him to think about it. 'So she's the reason you decided to call yourself Satu Savolainen?'

'Yes. I never stopped being a Savolainen, even when she made me call myself Karlsholm.'

'I can understand that. I never stopped being a Suomalainen, even when my stepfather made us change our name to Carr.'

Satu smiled at him. 'It shows that we are really the same, just as my parents have told me.'

'The same?'

'Yes, we are two branches of the same family. You have a great, great grandmother called Satu Suomalainen, yes?'

'Yes. How did you know that?'

'Because she was the mistress of my great, great grandfather, who was called Juri Savolainen, the same as my grandfather.'

He looked at her blankly, struggling to picture the family tree. 'The records in the Pastor's Office said she was married to a Juri Hämäläinen. They didn't say anything about a Juri Savolainen.'

We think they were never truly married. Juri's real name was Savolainen and he already had a wife and child, so probably they only pretended to be married as a way of disguising an affair.'

'Some affair! They had two children together.'

'Yes - and in the end Juri's real wife found out about it. The scandal was hushed up but Satu had to leave and go to Scotland with her children. It's funny: always our families have been passing down these same names. Most of the girls have been called Satu and most of the men have been called Juri.'

'What happened to his wife?'

'She divorced him and went back to her own family in Sweden. I think that my great, great grandfather must have been quite a rogue. He kept half the business and he even got custody of his son by his first wife. But she remarried and one day, many years later, her granddaughter paid a visit to my grandfather. She was strong willed and he was weak. Within a few months they were married and she was running the family. It was always like that with Katerina.'

'You mean that everything she did to my family was in revenge for my great, great grandmother having an affair with, what was it again… her grandmother's husband?'

'Yes, I think so. My father says Katerina always held the Suomalainens responsible for her family's misfortunes. Of course she hated my family, too. We stole her grandmother's fortune but most of all I think it has been because we stole her son.'

'God, that strikes a horribly familiar chord.'

'I think Katerina learned hatred at her grandmother's knee. Certainly she has done everything she can to hurt our families. I think she wanted to make it as if they had never existed.'

'That explains the missing records. But how did she make your family change their name?'

'Katerina has been clever as well as strong. Always she has been choosing her moment well. There were rumours that my grandfather had been involved in some bad things during the civil war. My father thinks that he wanted to escape the notoriety and Katerina has used this to persuade him.'

'That ties in with what my Aunt Elvira said. She claims he executed her brother-in-law after the fighting in Pispala. But look, I'm sorry Satu but I have to say this: surely you must have known some of this before?'

'Ricky, I never even knew that the Suomalainens were our relatives until last night. Katerina has tried very hard to wipe out all record of the links between our families.'

'But you suspected, didn't you? You said so.'

She looked distinctly guilty at that and traced her finger across his chest, watching its progress as she spoke. 'Always I was brought up to believe that the Suomalainens were our enemies. They have been telling me since as long as I can remember that one of them might turn up and claim to be more than just another of Tor's bastards. Sorry! But they told me it was a lie that someone might use to cheat me.' She looked up at him and wriggled her nose. 'So I knew you might be a cousin in one way, by my uncle: but not in the other way, by my great, great grandfather.'

'God, this is confusing.'

'Not so confusing. It just means we are cousins twice.'

'Yes it does, doesn't it?' They looked at each other then: and both of them blushed. But rueful looks became salacious grins - and when they tried a cautious kiss there was no denying the current that passed between them. Yet there was still one more question that had to be asked: a question that had hung in the air ever since Satu began to reveal what she knew.

'But what about my sister? If she's not you, then where is she?'

Satu's face clouded and she put her arms around his neck and hugged him. When he drew back to look into her eyes, he saw tears forming there.

'Oh Ricky, I am so sorry.'

'Why? Satu, what do you know?'

'This is a very terrible thing I have to tell you. I wish I could tell you anything but this.'

'She's dead, isn't she?'

Satu nodded, biting her lip. 'I think that Katerina killed her.'

'What!?'

'Yes. My parents have lived with it all this time. My poor parents, they had great difficulty having a child. My mother had so many miscarriages. And then Katerina has told them about your mother and suggested that they adopt her baby if they cannot have one of their own. But in the end my mother managed to have a child after all and Katerina told them your mother's baby died at birth.'

'Oh, Jesus. That's what she told me, too.'

'You must understand that nobody knows for sure. My parents have lived with the doubt all these years. They have not wanted to tell me about it but in the end they have done so last night. They think your sister was probably drowned in the lake. It is very terrible but many unwanted babies in this country have been found in the bottom of the lakes.'

'But you said nobody knows for sure?'

'No: but your sister was never seen again and much later they heard about what happened to your mother and the things she was saying.'

'But why would Katerina do it? Surely not just to avenge a century-old grudge?'

'She did it to protect the business. Hate may have killed her conscience but with Katerina the big motive is always to protect the business.'

'From a baby girl? What possible harm could she have done?'

'She was Katerina's biggest nightmare: her own son's child by a Suomalainen.'

'But she was just a baby, for God's sake.'

'Oh but to Katerina she was a threat. Any threat to the business has been like a wasp in her bonnet.'

'There's no proof, though? She could still be alive?'

'Oh, Ricky, I am very sorry but I think there is almost no chance. Truly I have not wanted to tell you this but no-one else would.'

'I'm really glad you did. I'm glad you cared.'

She looked almost offended that he could doubt it; but then her expression saddened. 'I wanted so much to be the one to help you find her. I wanted to make you happy.'

'You did. I am.' And despite the horror of what she had told him, that was the truth. 'I mean it. In my heart I already suspected that I'd never find her alive. It wasn't even her I was searching for any more. It was you.'

'Oh Ricky, I am glad.'

'It's so strange. I came here to find a sister and it feels like I have. Only it turns out she even more. She's everything I want.'

'Is she?' Her eyes were teasing now.

'I think you know how I feel about you.'

'Oh, I'm not so sure.' She grinned at him lasciviously. 'Why don't you show me?'

It was all too much - but he couldn't deny what he was feeling, even if the thought of it did make him gulp. 'Oh well, I guess there's nothing like keeping it in the family.'

'Yes, it was almost like making love with a brother.'

The way she said it, he could tell the idea turned her on. But he was still reeling from the discoveries, scarcely even able to think straight.

'God, it's only just hitting me. *You're* the Satu she sent me to find! I thought I was meant to be looking for my sister when actually it was you she wanted me to meet.'

'You don't mind?'

'Mind? No, of course not, I've always been in favour of incest. My God, Satu: but you knew. Why didn't you tell me?'

'I wanted to give you a nice surprise.'

'Right. Was that the bit about our being cousins or the other bit?'

'It was to discover that you had found what you were looking for.' She smiled and then almost in the same instant was perfectly serious. 'Have you found it, Ricky?'

'Oh yes. I've found it alright.'

'You're not angry with me?'

'Angry? Good grief no; I just can't believe it.'

'Would you have found it more exciting if you had known?'

'It couldn't have been more exciting. Could it? Was it?'

She put her head on one side again while she considered this. 'No, it was... nice. I liked knowing you were my cousin and that I was the one you were searching for. I had already decided to make love with you and I liked being able to give you everything you wanted, all together.'

'You'd already decided to make love with me? When?'

'Mmm, I think it was at the Student House, when I found out you had lost your family and were looking for someone to belong to. But the thing that made it certain was when I took you to bed and asked if we could just be friends and you were so sweet about it.'

'God. I wish I'd known.'

'So, when did you decide you wanted to make love with me?'

'The moment I first set eyes on you.'

'Yes, I thought so.'

'I never realised. I never even dreamed.'

'You were too busy looking for someone else.'

'Yes.'

She nodded and looked slowly around at the lake and the woods. 'Shall we go back?'

'To the dell?'

She smiled agreement and took his hand and led him back. His genie of the lake. His cousin Satu. They stood together in the spot where they had first made love and he ran his hands over her body while they kissed, adoring the satin smoothness of her skin against his fingertips. After a few minutes she drew back and her face was quite grave. 'I want you to know that I am not like her, Ricky. All my life I have felt I was suffocating; that I was being forced to be something I am not. This is why I have refused to let them call me Katerina. But sometimes it felt so hopeless: I was so alone. If you hadn't come along, I don't know what I would have done. I think I was going crazy.'

'You don't have anything to apologise for. You're nothing like her.'

'Really?'

'Of course. I couldn't love you otherwise.'

It was as if he had pulled some hidden trigger: in an instant she was all over him, kissing him frantically and then staring at him as if she needed confirmation that he was real. Whatever she saw must have satisfied her because presently she gave him a salacious grin, then sank to her knees in front of him. She looked up just long enough to lick her lips and say, 'Now I am really going to make it up to you!'

It was like a holy anointment. Satu kept peering up through her fringe to gauge how she was doing, as if the direct evidence wasn't hard enough. And the expression on his face made her grin even with her mouth full.

When he couldn't stand it any longer, he pushed her over onto the moss and she wriggled deliciously as he worked his way down, discovering anew how he loved the scent and taste of her. She giggled at first but then he concentrated his attentions and she started to moan softly, running her fingers through his hair until in the end she threw her hands above her head and surrendered herself to it.

His last girlfriend had taught him how to do this right and he did it now the way she had liked it, as if he was licking powdered chocolate off an ice-cream. He could tell how he was doing from the sounds she was making and after a long and lovely time she gave a series of sharp little cries and her whole body shuddered and then went still, as if she had actually fainted. Yet after only a minute or so she shook off her stupor and gave him the broadest of smiles.

'Ricky! You really know how to give a girl a good time!' And before he could answer she slipped nimbly out of his grasp, reversing their positions as she declared, 'Now I want to be on top, is it alright?'

It came as a sweet surprise to Ricky that despite taking the lead she was the tenderest of lovers, settling herself upon him with a long, deep sigh and resting there a moment with a beautific smile on her face, before leaning forwards to whisper softly that she loved him. And then she began to move, slowly and rhythmically and using muscles that he had thought existed only in myth. She moved in a way that made time seem to stand still, unhurried and yet keeping him on the edge of ecstacy and he only realised how equally she was satisfying herself when he felt another shudder run through her, so that their groans of release fused into each other and she flopped down on top of him just as the last spasms took everything from him, leaving them both in a dead heap.

Afterwards they lay together for a long time, gazing at each other and listening to the breeze rustling the branches overhead. Finally she kissed him very softly, her bruised lips brushing his: and then she moved away a fraction and they were two separate people once more.

'So,' she said with a sweet smile, 'thank you, Cousin Ricky.'

'Thank you, Cousin Satu. That was wonderful.'

'It was, wasn't it?' She laughed that nice, melodious laugh, a completely female sound that expressed joy at the way things are with no desire to change them. Then she looked around. 'But now, where shall we sleep?'

'Sleep? I can't sleep yet! I've got a thousand things I want to ask you. There are so many questions, I can't even think straight.'

'But there will be plenty of time to talk about them in the morning. Now I want to sleep with you.'

She made it all so clear and simple that he saw at once she was right. So he nodded and looked about the little clearing, wondering how best to arrange things. 'Will the party go on all night, do you think?'

'Oh yes, the boat is taking people back in the morning.'

'Then we can get back that way?'

'Yes, I think so. But now we have to make sure we don't get cold. I think they will have some blankets at the restaurant.'

'Alright, you stay here while I go and see what I can find. They haven't had such a good look at me, so hopefully I won't get caught.'

He proved an adept thief and returned with two blankets from a pile he had found on the verandah. They made a groundsheet from one and lay together beneath the other. Ricky fell asleep almost at once, while Satu lay beside him, watching his face as he slept and wondering at the way he had broken through her defences with such unconscious ease. 'I have waited such a long time for you, Ricky,' she said quietly. He moaned in his sleep and she smiled and snuggled up closer. 'You are real, aren't you?'

Ricky licked his lips; and then sealed it between them without ever even knowing. 'Satu,' he murmured, making her go completely still, willing him against all reason to confirm it now, when there could be no lies. At first he merely turned in towards her embrace, so that his face rested against the softness of her breast. Then he spoke again, louder this time, in a strange voice that she didn't recognise. 'If it's true, own it.' She lay there, scarcely daring to breathe: and a second later had all her hopes made real. 'To Satu...' he called out in his sleep, the voice his own now and stronger, 'To Satu... the girl I love.'

CHAPTER 43
Sunday 24th May, 1981

They awoke cold and stiff with whatever the dawn was called when it never got properly dark in the first place. Presently Ricky realised that they had been woken by the whistle of the ferryboat and they dressed quickly and hurried to the landing, in time to see the revellers queuing up to embark. At first they hung back in the trees, wary of the bouncers but it was soon apparent that the need for such precautions was past. As they trooped up the gangplank they, like every other departing couple, were handed a single red rose by one of the organisers.

No sooner were they safely aboard than Ricky remembered why they needed to be there in the first place. 'My God, Pekka's boat!' He jumped to his feet but the ferry was already moving away from the jetty, white water churning as it turned for the distant shore.

Satu pulled him back down and said, simply, 'It's OK. I'll tell Pekka and we can fix it later.'

'You will? I mean, you're sure it'll be alright?'

'Of course. Put your feet up and relax, you need to get your strength back.'

There was no arguing with that mischievous grin, so he put his arm around her and looked out through the rails as the boat chugged steadily across the lake. A wisp of cloud was moving across the sun and his gaze settled on the shadow it cast upon the waters. His features darkened in response and presently he reached out as if to take Satu's hand: but to her surprise he took the rose from between her fingers instead, asking for her permission with his eyes. She nodded, watching in silence as he stood and went to the rail.

He was still for a moment, then cast the bloom far out onto the surging waters. She got up and stood beside him and they watched the tiny spot of red pass far astern until it disappeared in their wake. She kept silence with him, holding his hand, sensing all the different kinds of pain.

'I was wondering,' he said at last, turning his face away from the rail to look at her.

'Yes?'

'I've been trying to decide whether you're a first cousin or a second cousin and how many times removed you are.'

'I am not removed at all. I am right here.'

He laughed and the air seemed to lighten around them. 'No, I mean removed as in distantly related.'

'So, I am your first cousin and also I think your second cousin.'

'Do you think it's legal?'

They both burst out laughing in a spontaneous release of tension. The more they tried to talk about it the more hysterical they became, only pulling themselves together when the boat bumped against the landing stage. Then they filed ashore with the rest and walked arm in arm up the hill, discussing who was related to whom and what exactly each of them had managed to find out.

Their paths separated half way up the ridge, he to take the high road, she the low. Ricky became uncertain, not knowing how to part from such a girl at such a time, while Satu seemed completely at ease. She even teased him, telling him to look her up next time he was going boating. Then he spoke with sudden urgency but she remained infuriatingly casual just when he most needed her to be practical.

'You look so serious.' She pulled a long face in mockery, the one she called her 'Ricky face'.

'Of course I look serious. I love you.'

'I know.'

'I wish you could come to London with me.'

'Only if you ask me.'

'Will you come to London?'

'Of course - but not until the holidays.'

'That's more than a month from now. I don't know if I can wait.'

'But just think how good it will be after we've been apart for so long.'

He didn't know how to answer that, so he raised the next highest issue on his list. 'There's one thing I still don't understand.'

'So. What is that?'

'Why didn't you tell me that you'd changed your name back from Karlsholm to Savolainen?'

'You never asked me.'

He thought about it, then saw the dimple in her cheeks and gave up. 'No, I guess I never did. Not directly.'

'Ricky, I didn't know at first if I could trust you. I was afraid you might be just another shit, like the ones they warned me about.'

'OK: but when *did* you change it back?'

'Last year, as soon as Katerina went into the nursing home. But really I have not been letting anyone call me Karlsholm since I was eighteen. And I never let anyone call me Katerina since as long as I can remember. My parents also wanted to change their name back but they couldn't risk it while she was still alive, or we might have lost everything.'

'She would have disinherited you?'

'Yes. I didn't make anything formal until a few weeks ago: it's in the Turku records but probably it is not yet known here in Tampere.' She gave a dismissive little snort. 'Their systems are not so smart. Also it means I have been able to get a nice cheap rent. My landlord is quite pleased that I do not really exist. I pay him in cash and it saves him from paying some taxes.'

'By Finnish standards, you're quite a major criminal.'

She waggled her nose at him impishly. 'I am following a good Pispala tradition. Those bureaucrats should not be knowing everything about our lives.'

'The funny thing is, I could have found you right at the start, if I'd just read my mother's note properly.'

'She has been writing you a note about me?'

Ricky nodded, pulling it from his jacket pocket where it had been all along. As he unfolded it, he shook his head in disbelief. 'Look, she gave me your name and address. But it was hand-written and she was so ill and in such pain: you see, the writing's almost illegible? When she gave it to me she was rambling and speaking partly in Finnish and she confused me by talking about you and my sister at the same time. I just saw what I expected to see: it never occurred to me that she might have written anything other than Suomalainen. And of course at the time I'd never even heard of the Savolainens.'

'How did she find me, do you think?'

'I'm not sure.'

'Perhaps she has been in touch with our relatives in America. My father says that sometimes they have been a way of contact between our families.'

Ricky sighed and put the letter back in its envelope. It was time for them to part and he couldn't put it off any longer. He looked at her with a mournful expression but she surprised him as usual, taking his hand and shaking it in mockery of his formal English ways. Then she reached up and kissed him as if he was the last man on earth. Finally she put her lips to his ear and whispered, 'I love you, Ricky Finn.' And with that she turned and strolled off down the street, kicking a pebble before her and whistling a tune with the same cheeky insouciance that had captivated him from the first. He watched her out of sight, his heart near to bursting. Then he turned away and walked the slow incline back to Tim's house.

CHAPTER 44
Sunday 24th May, 1981

'Good night?' enquired Tim.

Ricky threw himself down on one of the rickety wooden chairs with a sigh. 'Sank a boat, crashed a party, loved a girl. Slept in a hollow in the ground. Probably the best night of my life. What's for breakfast?'

'Coffee.'

'Terrence here?'

'You just missed him. Left his regards and asked me to pass on his hopes for your future happiness. Who was the girl; Satu?'

'The Lady of the Lake.'

'Got it away with Excalibur, did you?'

'My lips are sealed. But of all the girls, Tim, she is the peach.'

'Uh-huh.'

Tim buried his face back onto his folded arms, while Ricky poured himself some coffee. 'Look, I have to leave in a couple of hours. Do you mind if I take my coffee onto the balcony for a spot of sentimental reflection?'

'Do what you like. I'm going back to bed. That last shot was a mistake.'

'It always is.'

He went and sat on the balcony rail, gazing out over the lake one last time. His eyes followed the course of their sinking boat all the way to Viikonsaari and midway along the island, where there was a small gap in the trees, he thought he could just make out the spot where he'd slept with her. He felt incredibly tired and melancholy and yet deliriously happy.

Satu had said that meeting a stranger from another country gave you the chance to be the person you wanted to be, instead of being shackled to the person everybody knew. But it was more than that. From his first icy plunge to their final act of consummation, every happening on and around that lake had freed him from a little more of his pain and desolation. The past had been dug up, examined and properly laid to rest. He was free of it.

He drained his coffee, bid a silent farewell to the lake and went back into the house. He noticed in passing that Tim was now face down on the bed with one arm sticking out.

'I'm going up the road to Anna's to say goodbye and get a shower.'

'Uhhh.'

'See you in about an hour.' He went through to the living room and negotiated his way between the table and the refrigerator.

'Ricky.' The voice, or croak, came as he was letting himself out the door.

'Yes?'

'See if you can borrow some bog roll, I've run out.'

'And they say romance is dead.'

He found Anna in the kitchen and the first thing she said was, 'Well, did you get your girl?'

He actually blushed. She laughed at his stumbling reply and offered him some coffee. He sat down at the table and drank it gratefully because he needed it and because it enabled him to avoid her enquiring look.

'Well, I am glad.' She said nothing more but just sat across the kitchen table from him, waiting.

He couldn't outlast her contented patience, so he told her what she wanted to know and what he so much wanted to discuss. 'I don't even know for sure when I'll see her again.'

'What arrangement have you been making?'

'None, really. I can't afford to stay any longer and I certainly can't afford to come back anytime soon. And she can't come over until after the university term is finished.'

'Well, that is not so long.'

He fell into a disconsolate silence, as if five or six weeks were an eternity. Anna either ignored his gloom, or else considered it entirely proper. Her voice continued bright with enthusiasm. 'You are really in love, I think.'

'Hook, line and sinker, I'm afraid.'

'Well, that is good.'

'I hardly know her.'

'That is exciting.'

'I don't really know what she feels about me.'

'No? What have you been doing last night?' She ridiculed him with a look that made him grin despite himself - but then a horrible thought flashed into his mind and he gulped at the prospect it brought, drawing Anna's attention immediately. 'What is wrong? You look as if you have seen a ghost.'

'Is Pekka here?'

'No, he has gone to town.'

'Phew. I mean, oh dear.'

'Why, what has happened?'

'I, ah, borrowed his boat last night. We rowed over to the island in it.'

'To Viikonsaari?'

'Yes. We spent the night there.'

'You have been staying all night on Viikonsaari?'

'Yes. We had to.'

'That is quite romantic. But why did you have to stay there?'

'Because the boat sank.'

'Pekka's boat?'

'Yes.'

'You have sinked Pekka's boat?'

'Sunk. We have sunk Pekka's boat.'

'How could this happen?'

'It needed a *tilkitä*. It leaked.'

'Where is it?'

'On the beach at Viikonsaari. We managed to pull it ashore. Satu says it can be fixed but I'm not sure what to do about it.'

'Pekka does not know that you borrowed it?'

'No.'

'You have stolen his boat and sunk it.'

'Yes.'

'It has been quite a night for you, I think.'

'You might say that. Will he be very angry?'

'I think that he will kill you.'

'Ah. I was afraid it might be something like that. Perhaps I should pay him something for the trouble.'

'Satu has said it can be mended?'

'Yes, she said she'd take care of it. It's not actually damaged, just rather wet. On the wrong side.'

Anna thought about this for a moment, then smiled reassurance. 'He won't mind so much.'

'Really? But I thought you said he'll kill me?'

'No. He will be quite angry for maybe fifteen minutes and then he will be alright. Just send him a postcard from London and a bottle of Scottish whisky.'

'I'll do that.'

'You should go before he comes.'

'When is he due back?'

'Not until lunchtime.'

'Can I take a shower first?'

'Of course. If you have seen *Psycho*, you know what to expect.'

'Right. I'll be really quick.'

Ricky was actually stepping out of the shower, still dripping wet, when he heard Pekka come in the front door. He got dressed in a hurry and went downstairs to face the music. He found them drinking coffee in the kitchen. Anna raised her eyebrows just fractionally over the mug as she sipped from it.

'Hei, Ricky! How did you get on last night?'

'Fortunes were mixed.'

'Yes? What happened?'

'I rowed over to the island with Satu.'

'You did? Did you get lucky?'

'Yes and No.'

Pekka looked enquiringly at him, so Ricky sighed and jumped in.

'The boat we were in sank. We were stranded on the island all night. We're in love. Incidentally, her uncle is my father.'

'What!'

'Is it so?' cried Anna.

'Absolutely. She's the one I've been searching for all along. That boat, Pekka, was the greatest romantic aid ever.'

'That's wonderful!'

'Oh yes, Ricky, that is so good!'

'Thank you.'

'She is really your cousin?'

'Yes, twice over in fact. It's very complicated. Her uncle is my father and we also have the same great, great grandfather.'

'Well, Ricky!' said Anna, with a half-serious expression of shock.

'I know. But I think it's allowed.' He laughed. 'It had better be.'

'I am so happy for you. When did you find out, was it just last night?'

'Yes. It's all due to your boat of course, Pekka: it would never have happened without it.'

'My boat?'

'Yes. You were right about it by the way; it really did need a good *tilkitä*. I only found out what that word meant when we were half way across the lake and the water started coming in. They really ought to teach it in language classes, right after 'I think my friend is going to kill me, please call an ambulance'.'

'My boat has sunk?'

'Yes. It's OK, though, we beached it on the island.'

'It is damaged?'

'No. Just wet.'

'Wet.'

'Yes. All except the top two or three inches.'

Pekka began to tap his fingertips on the table, then to drum upon it more and more heavily. Ricky and Anna held their breath, looking at him but he just kept his eyes fixed on the tabletop, which he began to smack with his palms in time to a tempo that was beyond their hearing. Then he stopped and looked up. 'I have been meaning to give the boat a good *tilkitä* for two weeks now. I nearly did it last weekend. Now I'm glad I didn't.'

'You are?' said Ricky.

'Of course. If I had fixed it, then maybe you wouldn't have made it with Satu like you did. This has been the best possible ending. Did you really sink?'

'Yes, absolutely. Glug glug glug: the whole thing. We only just made it to the shore. It could have been really serious. For us, I mean. Obviously it was really serious for the boat. Well, I mean, you know...oh shit.'

This time Pekka and Anna both collapsed in hysterics and Ricky gave up. 'Look, I'm really sorry about this - but I have to go. If I don't I'm going to be late for my bus. Pekka, can I pay you for the boat?'

Pekka had difficulty in keeping a straight face long enough to answer in the negative. Then Anna wanted to ply him with questions about Satu and their plans and he felt a cur for not being able to spare the time to tell her about it, after all the time they had spent helping him. The bus was almost due and if he missed it he'd miss the train to Helsinki and then his flight and he had an APEX ticket and no money to buy a replacement and in the end he had to take his leave and run all the way down the street.

He found Tim drinking coffee at the breakfast table. It seemed to be the universal pastime. There were only seconds to the bus. 'Here's your bog roll. Give us a hand down the hill with the bags?'

Tim tugged his forelock, said 'OK guvnor' and picked up Ricky's wallet. Ricky sighed and hauled his suitcase to the door. They picked their way quickly down the steep slope to the bus stop and stood there together for the brief moments remaining. There was one last thing on Ricky's mind and he couldn't leave without getting it out into the open between them. 'Tim?'

'Yeah?'

'I haven't exactly been around much since the first few days, have I?'

'No. Came to stay with your old mate and buggered off chasing skirt the moment you got the chance. Used me like a third rate hotel.'

'Well it's not exactly the Ritz.'

'It's the principle.'

'Do you really mind?'
'Do you really love her?'
'Yes.'
'Then I don't really mind.'
'Thank you. I mean it, this is really important for me.'
'Anyway, I've seen enough of you. Now bugger off back to Blighty.'

Ricky was still grinning when the transport arrived. Buses in efficient, northern climes are no respecters of leave-taking. There was time for no more than a quick handshake before the automatic door closed behind him. Tim waved a salute as the bus pulled out, his tall figure dwarfed beneath the ridge, his house visible for a moment on the hillside above and then they turned the corner and he was gone.

The Finnair DC-9 headed out over the Baltic, with the islands of the archipelago floating by far below: and as Ricky bid a silent goodbye to the land of his birth, the captain came on the speakers to announce that it was thirteen degrees Celsius in London and raining hard. For some reason Ricky began to laugh. He had no money, no job, it was pissing down with rain and none of it mattered. He felt wonderful. Absolutely wonderful.

EPILOGUE
July, 1982

No-one would ever know exactly what Satu Suomalainen had intended when she scrawled the lines that sent her son off on his misdirected search. Yet almost everyone who spoke at Ricky's wedding described it as being the fulfilment of all her hopes.

On the face of it, the reunification of the long-divided families of Savolainen and Suomalainen did seem reason enough to put a celebratory gloss on things: and it would be a strange person who brought up questions of death, murder and incest at a wedding.

But then, Satu Savolainen was quite a strange person.

She was not the only one. Elvira was the first to raise the spectres of the past, even if only under her breath, in a quip that only those closest to her heard.

'I have waited forty years for this,' she declared in gutteral Finnish, as they sat waiting in the pews.

'For this wedding?' asked Ricky.

Her reply produced a snort of suppressed laughter from Tim. Ricky raised an eyebrow and got a whispered translation that nearly made him choke. 'Not just for this, nephew. For that bitch Katerina to die and a Suomalainen to come back and wipe out everything she stood for.'

Surprisingly it was Olli Savolainen who gave the second hint of what lay below the surface. When he stood up in his capacity as father of the bride, he started by saying that he had written a long speech: but groans turned to cheers when he announced that he had torn it up because nothing better illustrated the points he had wanted to make than the unexpected appearance of Elvira. 'For surely,' he declared, 'this wedding demonstrates how we have buried our families' past differences.'

People clapped at that point and he might have left it there: but he had scripted a humerous ending and in his determination to deliver it, he went on to speak a darker truth.

'You know, when I first heard that Satu was going out with Ricky, I have to admit that Hilda and I were horrified. But once we got to know him, we began to suspect that maybe it wasn't such a total disaster after all. And once we learned the truth about him, we even began to think that maybe Satu really had met her match.

'Ricky, believe me when I say that I am proud to have you for a son-in-law and that I wish you every joy with my daughter. I would also like to wish you a lot of luck. Knowing her, you are going to need it.'

But if Olli's revelations were largely unconscious, his daughter's speech went deliberately to the dark heart of the matter. The audience was relaxing in the expectation of a pleasantly dull list of thanks, heralding the start of the real celebrations. No-one anticipated where her speech would take them.

'Like most of you, I have spent many long hours listening to my father and his friends talking about the war. I mean really long hours. But now I'd like to tell you something that I learned during all those long winter conversations.

'I remember Dad saying that sometimes you have to make peace with your enemy even though it seems disgraceful, because that's the only way you can protect the things you really care about. That's the way it was with Finland and Stalin and that's the way it was with our family and my grandmother, Katerina Karlsholm.

'So you see, Dad, I was actually listening all those times.

'He told me something else, too. He said he learned in the war that you can't tell who the heroes are by the way they seem at first. Some of the bravest men are quiet and unassuming. That's how it was with Ricky. You may find this hard to believe, but when I first met him I didn't immediately think what a gorgeous hunk he was. I thought he was gentle and amusing and sad in a nice way. But before long I found there was real strength there. Of course, later I discovered he has some other qualities that are also quite important to a woman!

'Terry calls Ricky my Prince Charming. Well so he is. I never told him this but my name in English means, "a fairy tale". And God knows he came just when I most needed to be rescued. So now, as with any good fairy tale, the evil witch is dead and everyone is celebrating the triumph of life and love. For this day at least, we can all pretend that the darkness has been banished for ever.' She paused for a moment, letting the import of her words sink in. But she left them in no doubt about what she was referring to.

'Everyone is very happy now about how our families have been reunited. And of course Ricky and I are the happiest of all, since we're the ones who are going to be doing the unifying, a bit later on. But we all know there are some empty places at this feast. Places that would normally be reserved for some very important guests:

'The father and mother of the groom.

'Our grandparents.

'Ricky's twin sister.

'Most of them are dead and the other one we would throw out into the street if he dared to show his face here.

'I'm more glad than I can tell you that our families are reunited. But I have to admit I'm also a little scared. I think that's alright, isn't it, for the bride to be nervous on her wedding day? But it's not my wedding night that I'm anxious about. It's whether I can truly be the fairy tale that Ricky was searching for. Because deep in my heart I'm afraid that the wicked witch put a curse on me and one day I'll wake up and find I'm turning into her.

'Of course, I believe it will never happen. I have all of you to help me make sure there is no more Katerina, only Satu. And most of all I have my handsome prince.

'So here we are, on the last page of the story, where everyone lives happily ever after. And I can assure Prince Charming that his princess is looking forward very much to being swept off her feet and carried away to the castle of her dreams.'

The party went on into the wee, small hours but of course Ricky and Satu slipped away early. They stayed that first night in the bishop's old wooden palace, leaving the windows open so they could enjoy the night air and look out over the still waters. They listened to the silence as they made love and had no need of words to break it.

Ricky awoke first and lay there for a long time, watching as the muted light of early morning played over his wife's lovely body. Presently he noticed the garter lying amid the rumpled bedclothes and he reached across to pick it up, gliding it slowly up her leg. She opened her eyes then and smiled to see him. 'Hello, Cousin Ricky. What are you doing?'

'Hello, Cousin Satu. I wanted you to be wearing this.'

'Oh.' She grinned sleepily. 'You want to be my special cousin again?'

'I thought it might be a nice way to wake you up.'

Satu stretched luxuriously, arching her back and drawing her legs around him. 'Mmm, yes please. Wake me up, Cousin Ricky; I think I must be dreaming.'

He chuckled and settled himself down upon her, loving the smell of her and the soft welcome of her body. Presently the breeze carried the sound of her name across the water, repeated over and over until the final cry was lost in the rhythmic throbbing of the first boat of the day. As the dinghy drew near a flock of lake birds rose in lazy fright, so that for a moment there was a tumult of sound and motion. Then their wing beats receded into the distance with the drone of the outboard, leaving nothing but a ghostly echo to disturb the silence of the lake.

ACKNOWLEDGEMENTS

This book is affectionately dedicated to Nigel Ewington, Tiina Nyrhinen, Eero Mattila, Harri Tuominen and all the others who made those days so wonderful. It was a long time ago but the memories have not faded.

Thanks also to Donna Brunstrom, Melanie Kennaway and the many friends who helped with their comments and criticism. Special thanks to Jessica Bell of Vine Leaves Press for helping to realise the second incarnation of this dream.

ABOUT THE AUTHOR

Alan Brunstrom considers himself English, although he was born in Papua New Guinea, of mixed Scots, English, Swedish and Finnish ancestry. He has lived in Australia and married an Australian but he grew up in Reigate, Surrey and now lives in Oxfordshire. A graduate of Emmanuel College, Cambridge, he has been variously a teacher of the mentally handicapped, an editor of non-fiction books, a computer programmer and a specialist in making the space industry useful in everyday life.

Lightning Source UK Ltd.
Milton Keynes UK
UKHW021817181118
332564UK00005B/333/P

9 780993 387302